Readers give Tracy Bloom five stars

'This is a fabulous fizz of a book!'

'It had everything and I finished it in one night!'

'I am laughing out loud, and actually can't remember the last time I did that – thank you Tracy'

'An absolute must-read'

'As satisfying as a glass of champagne in a bubble bath'

'Had me laughing out loud, not just sniggering, but snorting guffaws'

'Completely addictive'

'It was such a compelling read. I was at the end far too quickly'

'This is a beautiful book that has been exquisitely crafted'

'This book was one of a kind and I LOVED the whole experience'

'A book that I read with tears falling
and roaring laughter'

'I never wanted this book to end'

'I feel as if I've been on a rollercoaster'

'Laugh-out-loud funny, feel-good, and heartwarming'

'I adored the characters'

'It's amusing, emotional, happy,
and poignant all at once'

'This will put your whole life into perspective'

'A book that really makes you think'

'Full of girl power!'

The Wife Who Got a Life

Tracy started writing when her cruel, heartless husband ripped her away from her dream job – shopping for rollercoasters for the UK's leading theme parks – to live in America with a brand new baby and no mates. In a cunning plan to avoid domestic duties and people who didn't understand her Derbyshire accent, she wrote *No One Ever Has Sex on a Tuesday*. It went on to become a No. 1 bestseller and publishing phenomenon. Since then, Tracy has written many more novels and been published successfully around the world. She now lives back home in Derbyshire with her husband and children.

To keep in touch with Tracy, visit her website and follow her on social media.

tracybloom.com
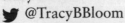 @TracyBBloom
/tracybloomwrites

THE WIFE WHO GOT A LIFE

TRACY BLOOM

HarperCollins*Publishers*

HarperCollins*Publishers* Ltd
The News Building
1 London Bridge Street
London SE1 9GF

www.harpercollins.co.uk

HarperCollins*Publishers*
1st Floor, Watermarque Building, Ringsend Road
Dublin 4, Ireland

A Paperback Original 2021
1

A catalogue record for this book
is available from the British Library

ISBN: 978-0-00-843428-1

This novel is entirely a work of fiction.
The names, characters and incidents portrayed in it are
the work of the author's imagination. Any resemblance to
actual persons, living or dead, events or localities is
entirely coincidental.

Typeset in Sabon LT Std by
Palimpsest Book Production Ltd, Falkirk, Stirlingshire

Printed and bound in Great Britain by
CPI Group (UK) Ltd, Croydon CR0 4YY

This book is produced from independently certified FSC™ paper

For my husband, Bruce, happy 15th anniversary
This counts as a present and a card!

This Diary Belongs to:
Cathy Collins

Age:	~~Late Forties~~ ~~Mid Forties~~ 48 years old
Relationship Status:	Tense with a good deal of resentment occasionally dispersed by the odd moment of joy i.e. married to Mike for nineteen years.
Location:	Bridleton, West Midlands. Famous for its equal ratio of charity shops to pubs.
Family	Son — Freddie, 17 years (unfortunately with the maturity of an 8 year old)
	Daughter — Kirsty, 15 years (unfortunately with the maturity of a 25 year old)
	Mother — Judy, 74 years (great wife, rubbish mother; still incapable of paying me any kind of compliment)
	Father — John, 78 years (great dad, rubbish husband; still incapable of any kind of domestic chore)
	Older sister — Lizzy, 51 years (lives in LA and drives me mad trying to tell me how to live my life)
	Younger sister — Meola, 42 years (lives down the road and drives me mad because she won't let me tell her how to live her life)
	Dog — Barbra Streisand 9 years (named by above-mentioned immature son)

Place of work:	Kitchen table — book-keeper for Ascot Drive Chippy, Fast Eddie's Taxi's and Ralph Flemming, the world's least renowned crime author
Interests:	Are for old people

Motivational Goals

New Year – New You

Set your goals *right now*!

If you can achieve just one goal a month you can transform your life by this time next year.

Keep it simple, keep it smart,
keep it close to your heart.

January	Goals only ever lead to disappointment and misery. I'M not doing it!
February	
March	
April	
May	
June	
July	
August	
September	
October	
November	
December	

January

1 *January*

I wouldn't say I was unhappy. I was just normal.

Neither happy nor unhappy. Somewhere in the middle, just trying to get from day to day without much thinking about how cheerful I was. To be honest, I actually hadn't given it much thought at all until my sister gave me this 'Motivational Diary' for Christmas. A diary! I mean, I hadn't written a diary since I was a teenager and needed to pour out my angst about Paul Backleton and his inability to see beyond my acne, braces and fluorescent Eighties wardrobe.

I was insulted to start with. Why on earth did she think I needed a Motivational Dairy? She lives in California and passes her time mostly up to her neck in yoga poses and kale smoothies and somehow she thought this qualified her to tell me how to run my life. I'd specifically asked her for the sing-along version of *The Greatest Showman* for Christmas, thinking that pretending I was singing and dancing with Hugh Jackman might provide the necessary escape required from another largely dissatisfying family Christmas, but clearly she hadn't listened. On opening the disappointing diary, I immediately sent her a text to express my disgust as I topped up my festive calorific intake with Ferrero Rocher.

A Motivational Diary – WTF?!

Within moments she was FaceTiming me.

You knew it was serious when you sent someone a text and they replied by video-calling you. It meant that serious, maybe even complicated words needed to be said that could not be covered by text-speak or emojis. She was, of course, glowing with health and sunshine whereas I was muted by grey skies, skin puffed out by too many carbohydrates, my up-do frazzled by too much time over a hot stove and an unsightly rash around my neck caused by my 100 per cent acrylic Christmas jumper.

'Before you even start,' she said, 'I know what you're thinking. This diary is some hippy crap that my sister's got into because she lives in LA.'

Funnily enough, that was exactly what I was thinking.

'Well, it's not. My girlfriend Janelle, you know the one who's married to the cousin of the Foo Fighters' drummer; well, she gave me a Motivational Diary for my fiftieth birthday and it's changed my life, honestly Cathy. It's made me put myself first. Made me think about what makes me happy, and that's really hard for people like us.'

'What do you mean, "people like us"?'

'You know: female, a mother, a wife.'

I gave that one a moment's thought.

'If you say so,' I replied eventually, grabbing my eighth Ferrero Rocher of the evening.

She peered at me through the phone and I hoped she couldn't see the gravy that had dripped down the fluffy snowman on my chest.

'All we do is fit around other people's lives,' she continued. 'While we let ourselves go.'

Harsh, I thought.

'We let other people live the way *they* want while we adjust our way round them. Well, it's time to put yourself first, Cathy. Work out what you want to achieve to make yourself happy before it's too late.'

'What makes you think I'm not happy?'

'How was Christmas?' she asked.

'Oh, you know, the usual over-panicking and under-delivering. I've spent weeks in the endless cycle of buying food, then buying even more food in case there's not enough food. Then buying presents followed by buying even more presents in case there are not enough presents. Then hours alone in the spare bedroom wrapping way too many presents before spending hours alone in the kitchen cooking way too much food. Two activities that – as you well know – I hate and am terrible at. It's been great, really it has. An absolute joy, as usual.'

'Might I say you sound a little depressed, Cathy?'

She was making me mad now.

'No, I'm not! I've had a perfectly normal Christmas, Lizzy. That doesn't make me depressed.'

'If that's your Christmas then you *should* be depressed,' she replied. 'Of course it could also be the menopause kicking in. That might be why you are feeling a bit down.'

'Jesus, Lizzy! I was feeling perfectly fine about my typically disappointing Christmas until you put me on the counselling couch and overanalysed it.'

'I'm just saying that at your age you need to be monitoring for symptoms of the menopause. Anxiety and depression can be a part of that.'

'*You* are making me anxious, Lizzy, not my reproductive system!'

'Are you having night sweats yet? Or difficulty sleeping, vaginal dryness, reduced sex drive?'

'Are you reading this from a leaflet or something?'

'No. I have a web page open.'

'Look, I haven't seen any sign of the menopause yet. My periods are all still perfectly normal.'

'You're still having periods!' gasped my sister. She looked truly horrified. As if I'd told her I was an axe murderer.

'Yes! They still keep coming, monthly, like they're supposed to.'

'But why aren't you on the pill, Cathy? I went on the pill straight after I had Alicia. I can't have had a period in eighteen years.'

I paused, flummoxed for an answer to what I realized was a perfectly reasonable question.

'Well, I guess, well, I thought about it but . . . but I never got round to it. I was just kind of distracted by, you know, life.'

'Distracted by other people's needs and not your own, you mean,' said Lizzy. 'You see this is exactly why I have sent you the Motivational Diary. So this kind of self-neglect doesn't happen.'

'I'm not self-neglecting,' I told her. 'I'm perfectly fine.' I reached for my ninth Ferrero Rocher.

'Look, you don't have to put anything difficult in there,' she said. 'Just some simple stuff that will make all the difference.'

'So what have you put in yours then?' I asked her. 'What's your January goal?'

'Well er . . . well, actually I've decided to train for a marathon, but that doesn't mean . . .'

I laughed. Of course I did.

'I'm not doing it,' I said firmly. 'I'll only disappoint myself and then I'll be really unhappy.'

She sighed and leaned back, folding her slim bare arms and revealing the clear blue skies behind her.

'If you say so,' she said. 'But don't come crying to me next year when you're miserable. Just give it a go, sis. Please.'

'I'm not miserable,' I told her. 'Well, I wasn't until I spoke to you.'

My reaction to this phone call was obviously to reach for several more Ferrero Rochers and go into a deep sulk. What did my sister know about my life? I *was* perfectly fine. Plus I knew where that 'Motivational Goals' mumbo-jumbo got you. Self-loathing and disappointment, that's where. Having goals meant increasing your expectations, and that would always lead to dissatisfaction and unhappiness. My approach, I felt, was much more useful, and it didn't require me to sit and scratch my head over a list of things that I was never going to get around to.

It was so much easier to just lower my expectations instead.

I realized some time ago that – so far in my life – creating expectations had only led to disappointment. I could count on the fingers of one hand when my expectations have actually been exceeded.

1. When I was twelve years old and ate my first pizza in a proper Italian restaurant rather than the frozen four-pack kind from the supermarket. I thought my head would explode.
2. How painful childbirth was. I genuinely thought a JCB had entered my uterus.

That was it.

Now if there was a centipede that happened to have

fingers and toes, they would not have enough fingers and toes to count how many times things have not met my expectations and therefore how many times I have experienced the low dull gloom of disappointment.

So that was why I would *not* be writing a list of 'Motivational Goals'. I knew where they led. So no thank you, Lizzy. I was perfectly fine. Life was fine. I didn't need any stupid goals to make me miserable.

5 January

I suppose normal life had to commence sometime post-Christmas, along with the shouting, the swearing, the crying and the utter desperation.

Yes, the first day of term had arrived.

Chill, Mum. My geog teacher has a dentist appointment. No need to be in till later – your loving son xxx

This was the text my son sent me from his pit after twenty minutes of me shouting upstairs for him to get up. My son could not remember what a teacher told him five minutes ago, never mind over two weeks ago, so I was suspicious this was a lie but had no proof. Pretty much my constant state of play with my two children.

I suspect you have been drinking but I cannot be sure.

I suspect you should be doing *a lot* more homework but I cannot be sure.

I suspect you are not constantly watching YouTube or browsing Instagram purely to research future career opportunities, but I cannot be sure.

I suspect you *do* eat meat, you just don't like my casseroles, but I cannot be sure.

Deciding which side to fall on was a constant lottery. Get it right and you would hit the jackpot. Highly perceptive mother who demanded respect. Get it wrong and you lost valuable ground on the trust stakes. A weapon of mass destruction in any argument.

'*You don't trust me!*' had been shouted at me so many times I was starting to feel I should pursue a career in politics.

Of course, I had no such issues getting Kirsty out of bed. Her alarm went off at six this morning and so began the ninety-minute beauty regime until a selfie-ready model appeared out of her bedroom. I cannot believe she sprang from my shabby loins. She had contour brushes for Christmas that cost more than everything in my make-up bag, bathroom cabinet and jewellery box put together. I didn't get it. Why couldn't I do make-up like my 15-year-old? Actually, I knew exactly why. She'd learnt from the experts on YouTube whereas I'd learnt using Crayolas on a Girls' World.

I was about to tell her that I admired her well-defined cheekbones and perfectly applied cat-lick eyeliner when I remembered that I was her mother and, in the interests of the Teenage Resilience Training Programme I'd been desperately trying to deploy, I should bite my tongue and think of something more appropriate to say. Before Christmas I read that the increase in mental health issues in teenagers is partly due to their lack of resilience, having been wrapped in cotton wool by overprotective parents all their lives. Obviously I saw this as the green light to give my kids a tough time, and so I had traded my usual sycophantic confidence-building platitudes for insults.

'Your face looks like you're auditioning for a part as a zebra in *The Lion King*,' I told her.

She stopped in her tracks, turned and studied me, and then drop-kicked an insult back. 'And you look as if you go to the same tanning salon as Donald Trump.'

I gasped. I was hoping no one had spotted my 'subtle' and 'secret' spray tan I'd had in a desperate attempt to do something about my pasty British winter complexion. Still, she had acted in accordance with the Teenage Resilience Training Programme and so I sent her on her way. Not before I told her she was beautiful and that I loved her, of course.

Kirsty left the house in a cloud of designer perfume, in a way I knew I would never achieve, while Freddie was still upstairs. I decided to err on the side of 'LIAR' this morning, as after the enforced family time at Christmas, I had never been keener to get the house to myself. I went upstairs and stood outside his room and turned the specially hidden radio on very loud to Smooth FM and waited. Sure enough he emerged moments later and shouted '*Alexa, switch off*,' at the top of his voice. When this had no effect, I agreed only to switch off the hidden radio if he got up and went to school.

'You are evil,' he breathed at me through his nostrils before he staggered into the bathroom.

'And what are you today?' I shouted at him through the closed door.

'A poor tortured son whose mother doesn't understand him,' he shouted back. 'Who will end up putting the sausage in sausage rolls in a factory in Dumfries.'

'Excellent news,' I replied. 'Finally, a career path.'

*

The minute he was out the door I dashed to my phone and began my daily ritual of comparing myself unfavourably against the rest of the human race. Sure enough, my social media was bombarded with Couch to 5k beginnings, back-to-work pledges, charitable-giving requests and dry-bloody-January promises. Once I had confirmed that I was the least driven, laziest, least charitable human being who ever existed, I remembered the 'Motivational Goals' that Lizzy had tried to trick me into writing. I was tempted to update my status to: Cathy Collins has no interest in setting any stupid goals this year as she knows it will only lead to misery and disappointment but commends everyone who thinks they can and looks forward to an update on your failing to achieve any of them by mid-February.

I was just selecting a coloured background and wondering whether balloons or party streamers would be more appropriate when I realized I would not be able to deal with the inevitable social-media backlash that would encourage and cajole me into thinking that I was the type of person who could achieve great things, so hastily I deleted it. I could of course write the truth. That I was beginning my forty-ninth year on this planet with the usual plethora of menial tasks that needed to be done, none of which I was the slightest bit interested in. I weighed up my options for the morning's activities, such as put the Christmas decs in the loft, find a plumber to fix the tap that has been leaking for approximately five years, do a food shop, call my mother, or look at the computer for work purposes rather than just staring at Rightmove.

I actually really needed to do some work. I say 'work', but somehow it felt rather like homework used to when

I was at school. I did it at home, in my own time, but it existed as a nagging feeling in the back of my mind. I knew it was there but it was something to be endured rather than enjoyed.

I couldn't complain. I mean, it was every parent's dream to work from home, part-time, so they could be around for their kids, right? Especially given that Mike was away a lot with his job. There was no way I could have scaled the corporate ladder as well as him. One of us had to step back. So I'd given up my career in Finance and started taking on freelance accountancy work. And while I didn't miss the relentless pressure of working for a large profit engine, I did miss going to a place of work with people in it, particularly people whose conversations didn't totally revolve around their kids, i.e., young people. People who talked about late-night telly and new bar openings and who fancied who. Water-cooler chat, I guess? I just had a kettle and me. No chat.

I opened my laptop and sighed as I logged onto my email. Frank, the chip-shop owner, had sent a message to say he had a load of receipts in a carrier bag he could do with getting rid of, so could I go and collect them? Maybe I could go over at lunchtime and pick up a saveloy to cheer myself up before I faced delving into a mountain of fat-based expenditure.

Then I opened one from Ralph, my other client, an aspiring author in his seventies. He had no income but liked to tell people he needed an accountant to manage his royalties. He'd been writing his crime thriller based on his career in civil engineering for the past five years. He asked me if I'd had a nice Christmas then wanted to know if I could find out if he could claim his bus pass as a legitimate travelling expense.

16

Before I could delve into the delights of the Inland Revenue website, to my relief the telephone rang. However, it was the landline, so I knew it could only be someone trying to con me into doing something I didn't really want to do.

I was right.

'It's me, your mother,' said my mother.

'Hi, Mum,' I replied. 'How are you?'

'I can't chat as I've got to try and call Geraldine and let her know when Edward's funeral is so she can get her train booked. She's going to come and stop with us for a few days.'

'That'll be nice, Mum.'

'Could you pick up some toilet cleaner when you're out? I'd ask your sister but she does work full time and her children are much younger than yours so she's far too busy.'

'It's fine, Mum. I'll pick some up.'

'And would you come and help me do a bit of a spring clean? You know what Geraldine's like. She spots mildew a mile off and I can see some behind the toilet, only I can't get to it because of my knee. Would you mind just having a go at it next time you come? If Geraldine sees it she'll have a heart attack and we don't need any more funerals this winter.'

'Fine, Mum,' I replied.

'Good, good. I'll ring her back right now and tell her she can stay. See you later on this afternoon then. Bye.'

I sat and wrote a list of jobs for the afternoon. Pick up saveloy for lunch along with chippy receipts. Come home, eat saveloy. Go to shop and buy toilet cleaner and then go to Mum's to clean the toilet.

Mike rang tonight to see if I was all right. As if I'm not used to him not being around. I am *totally* used to it given he spends most week nights out of the home, breaking up some poor company somewhere, in a job that seems to require very little 'consultancy' and much more just telling people they are sacked. Mike's freedom to go off to far-flung places at a moment's notice and have his bed made and eat food off a menu causes no resentment in our marriage. Not one bit. Apparently he is in Liverpool for the next few weeks. A mail-order company needed destroying and children needed putting on the streets.

'Missing you,' he said. 'I got used to being at home over Christmas.'

To be honest, the rest of us had struggled. The three of us had a system whereby we co-existed by shouting at each other, not talking, and then begrudgingly doing what we should have done in the first place. Mike could not cope with the shouting followed by the silence. Mike expected to come home and play happy families and suggest things like, 'After dinner, shall we all sit at the table together and play cards?' At which point Freddie barricaded himself in his room while Kirsty filmed Mike turning the kitchen upside down trying to find the playing cards, saying she was going to put him on her Instagram page, which he foolishly thought was a compliment. Dad Disasters could go viral at any minute.

'I'm getting fed up with working away from home all the time,' he said. 'I feel like I'm really missing out on being with the kids and helping you out. I know they're both going through a tricky stage.'

Helping me out? I'd asked him to have the 'sex talk' with Freddie a while ago and I'd told him to be particularly clear about consent. Apparently Freddie had asked Mike to clarify when you knew you had consent and Mike had told him that basically when you were married it was somewhere between the third and fourth glass of wine but he wasn't sure for other couples.

'I'm thinking of throwing in the towel,' he murmured over the phone.

For a minute I thought he was talking about whether to reuse his super-fluffy hotel bathroom towel in an eco-friendly fashion, or throw it in the bath after one use so it could be unnecessarily washed. He had some tough decisions on a day-to-day basis, did Mike.

'I want to be at home more. In fact, I've been thinking about it over Christmas. I might even go for a career change. It's starting to get to me, all this organizational change bollocks. I think I need something new. I might retrain . . . I think I might like to teach, Cathy. You know, do something good. Contribute positively to society.'

My mouth was on the floor. There were so many issues with this I did not know where to start.

Teach! What could he teach? As a white, middle-class, middle-aged man, how to make sure you always had the most important opinion in the room?

He is fifty-one. You can't be a student at fifty-one. He'd look ridiculous in casual clothes, sneakers and a rucksack.

And how on earth could we pay the mortgage off while he was retraining? How would we pay for the kitchen extension, which *he* had insisted on? Apparently no house could function without an open-plan kitchen/diner these days. He saw one at his colleague's house in Edgbaston and would not rest until we got a room that we could cook and eat in as a family.

We practically never cooked and ate as a family.

'Well, of course you can do anything you want to, honey,' I told him. 'If you think you can stand being in front of an unruly class of smelly fourteen-year-olds, then you go for it.'

'Mmmm,' he said. 'I think I could offer a lot to the teaching world. Only yesterday someone told me that my PowerPoints on organizational culture in the post-mobile workstation era were inspiring.'

This was Mike all over. Absolute confidence that he could turn his hand to anything. No quibbling, no faltering, just utter belief in himself. I thought about how I would feel if Mike became a teacher and I came to a frightening conclusion.

Jealous!

How could that be? I had no interest whatsoever in standing in front of a load of kids and trying to make them learn stuff they'd never really use. None. It sounded like the absolute job from hell to me and yet . . . and yet I was jealous. What of? That he could even think about it? Even think it was a possibility without first thinking of the hundred reasons why he shouldn't do it? Without thinking about the effect it could have on the rest of the family, on the rest of our lives? Was I just jealous of the fact that he was putting himself and his needs before the rest of the family?

'Can we talk about it properly when we get a minute at home?' he asked.

'Sure,' I muttered.

'Great. That would be really good. I really am fed up with hotel life, you know.'

'I know,' I replied. I glanced at the pile of ironing that I'd planned to do while I watched some crap telly. 'What are you going to do tonight?'

'Well, I thought I'd do a few laps in the pool because it was a buffet lunch today and I need to work off a crayfish baguette, and then I'll just grab a steak in the bar later. They've got the match on so I'll perhaps watch that, then get an early night.'

'Never mind eh,' I said. 'Sleep well.'

15 January

Tania came round today. I was in desperate need of some quality Tania time, as I hadn't seen her since before Christmas. Tania lives next door. She is smart, funny, and one of my best friends. She's a bit, older than me at fifty-five, so I guess I look up to her a bit, especially as she does the very awe-inspiring and worthy role of a social worker. And she's in two book groups! The one I'm in, as well as one where they actually read books, including non-fiction!

Within five minutes of me texting her to say, 'Yesterday's dessert?', she was knocking at the door and holding a half-eaten lemon meringue pie. I already had two spoons and two coffees ready at the kitchen table, and so we both dived in before a word was uttered. This was often our Monday ritual. Eating Tania's leftovers from her family Sunday lunch. She was a feeder and I was very happy to be an eater.

'Good Christmas?' I mumbled, trying not to spit pastry at her.

'Oh, the usual Jamaican-British hybrid Christmas,' she

replied. 'You know, jerk turkey, with reggae *and* carols on Spotify.'

I wished I could have spent Christmas at her house instead of mine. Tania would often tell me tales of her Christmases whilst being brought up in the Caribbean. It sounded amazing.

'You?' she asked.

'Oh, the usual English style. No one up until midday, no one really hungry because no one really likes turkey, and I can't keep up with Freddie's "allergies" or Kirsty's diet regime so loads of food went to waste. That's besides the fact that – as you know – I can't cook. Presents were mediocre at best. Mike was his usual thoughtful last-minute self and bought me a dress online that didn't fit. But it was a lovely dress. And funnily enough it fits Freddie, who wore it to a party on New Year's Eve.'

'Fancy dress?' she asked.

'Probably not.'

'How's he doing?'

'Oh, he's Freddie. Still grappling with the astonishing amount of choices he has at his age. University, apprenticeship, work, gap year, which letter he wants to be on the LGBTQ rainbow. I told him he should identify as U.'

'I've not heard of U – what does that stand for?' asked Tania.

'Useless.'

'He's not that bad,' she said with a grin.

'He used my brand-new Ladyshave to give the cat a Mohican on Boxing Day,' I told her. Even now, the thought of it makes tears spring to my eyes.

She put her hand on my shoulder in an attempt to console me.

'Go on then,' I mumbled. 'Tell me what Mabel and

Keresi were doing on Boxing Day,' I asked, bracing myself for the worst.

'They both did a stint at the homeless shelter,' she replied, rubbing my shoulder in sympathy as the tears inexplicably started to flow. I shouldn't be a bit surprised that Tania's daughters are so lovely. After all, they have two mums, and that's an unfair advantage if ever I heard one.

For some reason the tears wouldn't stop. What was wrong with me? I even tried to picture the cat getting her revenge on Freddie by pissing all over his treasured vinyl collection, but even that seemed to have no impact.

'What's wrong, honey?' Tania asked me, attempting to spoon more lemon meringue into my mouth. Like I said, she's a feeder.

'I don't know,' I muttered through tear-stained hands.

'Come on, spit it out,' she said.

I knew she didn't mean the pie and so I was forced to tell her something.

'Mike thinks he wants to quit his job and retrain to become a teacher,' I told her.

'Your Mike?' she asked.

'The very same.'

'But what would he teach?'

'My point exactly.'

'I thought he loved his job?'

I shrugged. 'So did I.'

'And what do you think about it?'

'I think it's a rubbish idea.'

'Why?'

'I don't know.'

'Is it because he's making career plans and decisions and you're feeling left behind. Even jealous maybe?'

'No!' Bloody hell, could she read my mind?

She raised her eyebrows.

'Yes,' I said with my head bowed, feeling slightly ashamed.

'So make your own plans. You know you're not that far away from Freddie and Kirsty leaving home. You really need to think about where you want to be when you stop playing mother twenty-four seven.'

'Oh, shut up,' I replied. 'You're as bad as my sister. She's trying to get me to set myself some goals. Telling me I need to put myself first. Telling me I'm depressed. She even had the audacity to mention the M word.'

'Right.' Tania nodded gravely. She didn't need to be told what the M word was – she's a woman. 'Have you had any symptoms?'

I gulped. Maybe I should share with Tania a few things that were niggling at me and I feared could be symptoms of impending menopause. Nothing major, but enough to unsettle me.

I got up and walked out of the kitchen into the hall, and came back with a navy fleece I'd bought before Christmas.

'Look at it,' I said. 'It's a fleece! It's navy blue! And I love it! It's so warm and toasty and . . . and . . . comfortable! That's not normal, right? Something is happening to my brain.'

'It's a lovely fleece,' she said calmly, a small smile at the edge of her lips.

'And . . . and . . .' I said. 'I've started to be sensible with alcohol.'

That stopped her in her tracks.

'And yesterday I had a hideous experience watching *Mamma Mia*,' I continued.

Tania stared at me. 'You didn't, did you?' she asked in horror.

'I kept rewinding that bit—'

'When Meryl sings "Slipping Through My Fingers" while painting her daughter's toenails?' she asked. I watched tears spring to her eyes. 'I have to fast-forward. I can't bear it,' she added.

We both swallowed.

'I cried so much I had to switch it off,' I said tearfully.

We both embraced over half-eaten lemon meringue pie. Already grieving for the future pain of losing our daughters to the big wide world.

Tania pulled away and stared back at what must have looked close to a blubbering meltdown.

'Things are changing,' she said calmly. 'The kids are growing up, Mike sounds like he needs a change. You're nervous about being left behind, stuck in a rut and you don't know what to do about it. Perhaps your sister is right, perhaps you do need some motivational goals?'

'No!' I said firmly, shaking my head. 'I'm rubbish at them. Hopeless. I'll fail and then I *will* be depressed. Look, I'm fine. It's all fine really. I don't know why I'm getting upset.' I reached for some kitchen roll and blew my nose.

'You keep saying you're fine and yet you're crying all over my lemon meringue,' pointed out Tania.

'Just having a moment,' I said, trying to give her a watery grin.

'Maybe it's a moment you shouldn't ignore. Maybe it's time to be proactive, Cathy. Listen to your sister. Put yourself first. Decide what you want.'

She looked worried. I couldn't bear the worried look from anyone. Someone else worrying about me was all wrong. I didn't deserve anyone else's worrying space. I was healthy (if a little overweight), I had a good husband who provided for the family and I had two healthy, happy (as happy as teenagers ever are) kids. Worrying took time and effort and I couldn't bear the thought of anyone wasting their time and effort worrying about someone as undeserving as me.

'It's just a moment, that's all it is,' I said, shaking my head.

She kept looking at me with that awful worried look on her face, and then her phone pinged and she glanced at the screen.

'Sorry,' she said, getting up and brushing crumbs off her skirt. 'I'm going to have to go. Work summons. Will you be okay?'

'Of course,' I replied. Tania was always being called on to make really difficult decisions on delicate social-work cases. I walked her to the door and we embraced before she left. Harsh, I thought, as I wandered back towards the empty kitchen. Harsh to be reminded of Tania's world of real-life problems while I'm indulging myself in my less tangible ones.

20 January

Mike was due back tonight and had said he wanted to have that talk. I'd decided that I really couldn't deal with him throwing our lives up in the air, and so I had come up with a cunning plan to put him off this whole 'giving up a well-paid job' malarkey and spending more time in the home.

I was going to make sure the home was as unwelcoming as it possibly could be.

So, rather than positioning myself in the kitchen when Freddie and Kirsty were due back from school, which was normally essential to referee fights, protect the contents of the fridge and prevent food carnage on the worktops and the floor, I stood well clear, hiding in my bedroom until I got the signal.

It didn't take long. Within ten minutes the fire alarm was going off and I could hear shouting. I dashed in and, sure enough, there was food scattered everywhere and smoke billowing out of the toaster. There ensued five minutes' pandemonium while I tried to find the sweeping brush to hit the alarm with and Kirsty and Freddie continued their blazing row.

'I only asked her where the tartare sauce was,' Freddie told me once the alarm was a wreck on the floor.

'What do you need tartare sauce for?' I asked.

'Fish-finger sandwich.'

'We don't have any fish fingers.'

'I bought some.'

'How did you cook them?' The smoke alarm was starting to make sense.

'Toasted them.'

'Toasted them?'

'Yep. Toasty toasty.'

'Why didn't you stop him?' I asked Kirsty, turning on her. I thought she would have had more sense.

'I don't know how to cook fish fingers,' she said. 'Don't assume I know how to cook fish fingers. That's just typical, that is. Gender stereotyping or what? Why should I know how to cook fish fingers any more than Freddie?'

'Because you are more intelligent,' I said.

'Being able to cook fish fingers properly proves nothing,' interrupted Freddie.

'You only have to read the bloody instructions,' I yelled. 'Rather than burn the place down! It's not difficult! How are you going to cope when you go to university?'

'I'm not going to university,' he said. 'I'm going to South America.'

My heart skipped a beat. I tried to stay calm. 'Since when?'

'Since I started following an improv group on Instagram. They're touring South America. I'm going to go and join them. They've already acknowledged one of my comments.'

'South America?'

'Yes.'

'Where they shoot people?'

'Very high death rate by gun crime, thankfully,' chipped in Kirsty, staring at her phone. 'According to Wikipedia.'

'Shut up,' both myself and Freddie shouted at her.

I tried to calm my breathing. I wasn't at all prepared for the possibility of Freddie leaving home (if he *ever* got his arse in gear) in eighteen months' time. My only way of coping was to imagine him going to a nice safe little leafy British university, not to possibly the most dangerous continent on the planet. This was some new kind of hell.

I watched as he carefully laid his – burnt on the outside but probably frozen on the inside – fish fingers on the badly cut bread and then slathered them in mayonnaise.

'Decent,' he said, taking a bite. 'By the way, I'm planning on going vegan for Lent. Will you start getting some vegan stuff in from Aldi?'

'You can't, I'm vegan,' shouted Kirsty.

'Since when?' we both said, my head swivelling round.

'Last week,' she mumbled.

'Is that because Caaaaaarl is a vegan?' asked Freddie,

as a blob of mayonnaise fell to the floor and he carefully rubbed it in with his foot.

'No!'

'Who's Carl?' I asked.

'No one,' said Kirsty.

'He's a God-bothering hippy in my year and Kirsty wants to get in his pants,' Freddie informed me.

'No I don't,' she shouted.

'Yes you do. I saw you practically drooling over him in the refectory.'

'Kirsty,' I said, 'I don't think—'

'Don't think anything, Mum. *Please* don't think anything.'

'You really shouldn't . . .' I began.

'It's okay. He doesn't believe in sex before marriage,' said the remarkably informative Freddie.

'Oh my God,' I said, horrified, to Kirsty. 'You're going to join a cult!' I felt very much like screaming.

'Culty Kirsty,' chanted Freddie over and over. 'Culty Kirsty, culty Kirsty, culty Kirsty—'

'Why can't you just keep your mouth shut?' Kirsty screamed at her brother. She picked up a frozen fish finger that had been left strewn on the table and threw it at him. And as if right on cue, in the best piece of luck so far this year, Mike chose that moment to walk in and got frozen fish in the face. My daughter has the most excellent timing and fortunately the most rubbish aim.

To give some credit to everyone involved, the room did go quiet for a few moments. I held my breath to see what would happen next. Given that at no point had I made any contact with the fish finger, I considered that it was not my place to make the first move.

'What's going on here then?' Mike asked eventually as he brushed his forehead free of frozen breadcrumbs.

'Freddie was calling me names,' screamed Kirsty. 'And interfering and telling tales and being horrible like he always is.

'Kirsty is shit at throwing,' announced Freddie simultaneously. 'Honestly, if she can't hit me from there with a fish finger, then I can totally understand why she never made the netball team.'

'I never wanted to be in the netball team,' Kirsty shouted at him.

'You so did,' smirked Freddie. 'When Miss Chantry was the coach. You girls were all queuing up to be her wing attack.'

'That is not true,' said Kirsty, going bright red and looking as though she was about to cry. Freddie had clearly hit a nerve, yet again.

I looked at Mike to settle this battle. Hadn't he said the other night he wanted to be at home more to help with the kids? Well, be my guest, 'Dad of the Century'.

'You'll never guess where I went last night,' he said, taking his jacket off as though the previous altercation had not taken place and he hadn't just been hit in the eye with frozen goods. 'The Cavern Club. You know, where the Beatles got discovered?' He looked at his children for some kind of response, and when he didn't get one he ploughed on. 'Did you know that it started out as a jazz club, and when John Lennon first played a cover of an Elvis track he got told to "cut out the bloody rock and roll".' He laughed to himself as he stepped over the fish finger lying on the floor and hung his jacket on the back of a chair. 'Can you imagine if he'd have listened? We might never have had the Beatles, or probably half the bands you listen to nowadays. You know that Noel Gallagher? He's the lead singer of Oasis, massive Nineties band. Well, he often says how most of their music was inspired by the Beatles . . .'

He looked up and was surprised to see that both his children had somehow evaporated from the room. I was not. Mike's sharing of what he deemed to be 'new news' just because *he'd* only just discovered it was guaranteed to disperse a teenager at lightning speed. I was extremely envious of this ability; however Mike was forever disappointed that Freddie and Kirsty were not inspired by this dissemination of knowledge.

'Where did they go?' he asked me, as though it's my fault he'd bored them out of the room.

'No idea,' I shrugged, resentfully beginning to clear up the mess left by Freddie's foray into creative seafood cookery.

Mike continued to impart other exciting morsels about the rise of the Beatles, gleaned from his trip to the Cavern, but I'd zoned out, angry that Mike had been extremely, if unwittingly, effective at diffusing the argument between his children, and angry that – despite the fact I was nothing to do with the fish-finger missile – I was the one thinking about picking it up from the floor where already all three of them had stepped over it.

21 January

I woke up in the middle of the night to go to the toilet. Not an unusual occurrence. In fact, it was something to be celebrated when I'd 'slept through', as though I was some flipping toddler again. Anyway, I went to the loo in the middle of the night and there it was. My period. Hurrah. Must ring and tell Lizzy!

I went back to bed and allowed my mind to circle round the events of the previous evening, which of course was guaranteed to keep me awake until morning because I couldn't stop thinking about the fact that the blinking fish finger was still on the kitchen floor! I could feel its presence in the house, like someone had planted a land-mine down there. I'd decided to resist tidying up the offending item in an act of defiance, and for the rest of the evening the entire family continued to walk over it and around it, not giving it a second thought while I gently seethed. The assumption that all domestic duties would be carried out by me sat in my brain like a low-level headache. It constantly niggled and occasionally erupted into a full-blown migraine when I got angry and threw things around and shouted at everyone, at which point they'd make empty promises to try harder and do more. That quelled the migraine down to headache level for a while, until I realized they'd all lied – again – and then the migraine would rear its ugly head again. I figured this cycle had been going on for the entirety of my married life.

It was petty, I knew, to be wound up by a discarded piece of frozen fish, but focusing on that was at least stopping me mulling over the rest of the evening's events.

To be fair, we'd actually had a fairly pleasant meal together. We'd all sat down together in the kitchen/diner, which is something to be celebrated. We all ate the same food – again, something of a miracle. The lumpy white sauce and virtually inedible mashed potato were largely ignored, pushed to the side of the plate immediately in a synchronized manner, given my lack of cooking talent was something the family had long been resigned to. Mike and I shared a bottle of wine, deciding to delay our pact not to drink in front of our kids, thereby not reinforcing our reliance on it, until we'd got through dreary January.

The kids bolted the minute their plates were cleared, and so Mike and I were left to tackle the elephant in the room.

'Are you going to pick up that fish finger, or have I got to do it?' I said, trying to be casual.

He looked over at the offending item and said, 'I'll do it,' then didn't move a muscle. I knew then my night was doomed.

'By the way, I'm seeing a life coach,' he said.

'A life coach?'

'Yeah.'

'What's a life coach?'

'I thought you might ask that, so I brought you a leaflet.' He reached into the inside pocket of his jacket and handed me a glossy folded sheet with a serious-looking blonde lady, in maybe her late thirties, staring out at me.

'Hi, I'm Helen,' I said in a faux-Barbie American drawl. 'I'm a government-registered life coach and I help people identify their goals, work out strategies for achieving them, overcome obstacles, and make changes or shifts in their lives.'

'I don't think you are taking this seriously,' he said.

'Hi, I'm Helen,' I repeated, in the same cheesy accent, while waving at him robotically. 'And I'm going to solve all your problems with one swish of my pretty hair.'

'She has a PhD,' said Mike, putting his disapproving face on. The face that always has the effect of making me want to act more stupid. 'She used to work in HR,' he continued, 'and identified that many senior managers became dissatisfied with their work life when they hit their fifties. She's incredibly empathetic.'

'You've already met her?'

'Yes.'

'When?'

'Last night.'

'You never said.'

'She had a cancellation and said she could fit me in for an introductory session.'

Awkward pause while I worked out how to respond.

'You were at book group last night, weren't you?' he added.

'No,' I said. Such a lame attempt at trying to justify why he'd failed to inform me about his secret meeting with a younger woman.

I glanced down. The fish finger was still there.

'So what did she say?' I asked.

'She said I should work out where I want to be in seven years' time.'

'Why seven years?'

'I guess it's far enough away to make you really think that a big change is achievable, but not far enough away to think that—'

'You might be dead,' I interrupted.

'Useful input,' he sighed.

'Does she give useful input?' I asked.

He looked at me in a way a teacher looks at a student who is just not getting it. Was he already practising for his future career?

'I just thought it would be useful to have an outsider's view. Someone who can give me some perspective,' he said.

Someone who didn't have your wife's perspective, I

thought. Someone who didn't have the thousand and one other things to consider, as a life coach decided our fate. Someone who didn't have to consider the impact on my life. Someone who could ignore that and say to you, go on, you do whatever makes you happy.

Ping!

Maybe I needed a life coach? Maybe I needed what he was having. Maybe I needed someone to help me cast aside all selfless thoughts of others and work out what I should be doing with my life. Perhaps she could even help me work out some stupid motivational goals. Lizzy and Tania certainly seemed to think that would be a good idea.

'Can I meet her?' I asked.

'There is really no need to be jealous, Cathy.'

I looked at him. I wasn't jealous, but him telling me not to be immediately had the effect of making me feel I should be. I looked down again at the picture of the blonde, intelligent-looking young lady. Too young, I thought, but Mike had that whole distinguished salt-and-pepper-hair thing going on lately, and what with this career-change idea he suddenly had the air of 'midlife crisis' around him. And we all knew what that meant if it struck the male species. Maybe I *should* be jealous?

'I'm not jealous,' I said firmly. 'I just think I could do with a life coach.'

'What for?'

'Well, because. . .' I picked up the leaflet and rebooted my Barbie impression. 'Perhaps I would also like help to identify my goals, work out strategies for achieving them, overcome obstacles and make changes or shifts in my life.'

35

His jaw dropped and then he said, 'She only deals with executives.'

Jesus! I mean, WTF?

He saw the rage rise immediately. I didn't have to say a word.

'I'm not saying that's right,' he said quickly. 'I'm not saying that just because you are not an executive you can't have a life coach, or that she shouldn't be more inclusive. I'm just saying that her leaflet says that she specializes in . . . yes, that's it, specializes in, so doesn't exclusively deal with executives, so she might see you. I mean, I could ask her – shall I ask her?'

'No!' I said firmly, crossing my arms. 'If she doesn't want to see me, I don't want to see her.' Wow, wild horses wouldn't drag me to that bitch's lair now to hear some elitist advice aimed at 'executives'.

'Okay,' he said, looking slightly relieved. 'So are you . . . I mean, you never said that you wanted to, you know, work out your goals and achieve something.'

I held my breath. Could I let this faux pas drop? I had him on the ropes and I could see he was panicking, but really? I might not be a big fan of goals, but that didn't mean I hadn't achieved anything – like raising our children for the last seventeen years, for instance?

'I mean, I know raising Freddie and Kirsty is the ulti-mate achievement,' he blustered.

How did I explain it to him?

'It's starting to dawn on me that Freddie and Kirsty aren't going to be around for that much longer, so life is changing, I'm changing.'

'What do you mean "changing"?'

'Well,' I said, looking down. 'Apparently I am in the catchment age group for the menopause now.'

'Shit, have you got that?' he said.

'It's not an illness. It just happens. Well, to women. Weirdly men don't seem to have to go through such a process. All you have to worry about is the possibility of erectile dysfunction and, surprise, surprise, they've invented a drug to cure that.'

'I would take it, you know,' he said. 'If it came to that.' He said this as if he had agreed to donate a kidney to me.

'So thoughtful,' I said. 'You just need to be aware that in the not-too-distant future there're going to be three of us in this relationship – you, me, the menopause – and no kids to create a healthy distraction. So well, I guess it's all just making me think, like you, that I need to consider my options, that I need to think about what I want to do with the rest of my life.'

He leant back in his chair, clearly contemplating my input. I'd seen him do this many times before and I was sure it was what had made him so successful at his job. He was very quick and agile at assessing situations, then coming out with a well-crafted solution, as if he'd spent hours deliberating on it.

'Well, I think this is just perfect,' he said, leaning forward and taking my hands. 'Of course you must meet Helen. She'd be brilliant at helping you work out your options and then I'm sure that she'll have plenty of contacts who could also be very useful.'

'Right,' I said, nodding, but feeling a little confused.

'And what perfect timing. I mean it will actually be essential, now that I think about it, that you go back to your career full time. I mean, if I want to retrain to become a teacher, I won't be earning for maybe up to two years, and then of course my salary will be much lower than what I am on as a consultant, so you working full time will make all the difference. Truly it will. This is brilliant news.' He paused and looked deep into my eyes. 'And after all, it is your turn. I mean, you've let me pursue my career all this time and now it's only fair that you get the chance to go back to yours.'

What!

No!

This wasn't what I wanted. I recoiled in horror at the thought of returning to the rat race. Okay, so I missed the chat and the banter and being with interesting people living different lives to me, but did I want the weight of responsibility of a full-time job on my shoulders? I didn't think so. Not any more. Did I want to be the main breadwinner of the family? No – I was more than happy that Mike had taken that role. I knew that sounded terribly sexist, but he chose to be the hunter-gatherer when there were nappies to change and sick to cleared up, so he could blooming well stick to it. I most definitely did not choose to be the hunter-gatherer while he got to do whatever he wanted after the kids have bolted.

'Listen,' I said, getting up. 'I don't think you understand. Kirsty wants to join a cult, Freddie wants to get shot in South America, and if somebody does not clean up that bloody fish finger a murder will be committed in this house tonight. Perhaps you can get "Helen" to sort all that lot out for you while you are discussing your dissatisfaction with your well-paid, interesting career that you have had the good fortune to be able to focus on for the majority of your adult life, while I've done whatever was required to make this family function.'

Book group tonight at Tania's house, so not far to walk. She'd managed, of course, to knock up a cake in between housing homeless kids and training for the Samaritans. When I hosted book group they were lucky if they got some soggy Pringles that had been left in the tube too long.

Four out of six had read the book, which was a pretty good ratio. Sonja and I admitted we'd used 'having to read the book group book' as a means of escape from moments of Christmas family turmoil, whereas Louise said she'd left the 'Booker-nominated' tome on the coffee table all Christmas, in a vain attempt to impress her snooty father-in-law. She'd not touched it, but had thoroughly enjoyed a romcom she'd got in a Secret Santa from a colleague. We all enthusiastically agreed it should go on our list for the coming year.

Fiona tried to explain to us the significance of the lead character, who was apparently a metaphor for the suppression of the donkey in the Nativity story, but we were much more interested in hearing about the antics at Louise's Christmas works do, where some of her colleagues had shagged in the toilets of a Greek restaurant. Louise was quite a bit younger than the rest of us, and somehow juggled small children and working full time in a solicitor's office. In her job she mingled with people born in the Nineties, which to the rest of us was like mingling with people from another planet. We were keen to hear details of the people involved; characters who clearly lived a life whereby they felt the need – and were able – to have sex in a toilet! Where passion overrode all need for comfort or decorum. Where spontaneity reigned supreme. We were all in awe.

'I don't think Ray fancies me any more,' moaned Fiona after Louise had filled us in. 'In fact, I'm sure of it. The only time we have sex is if he's watched Fiona Bruce presenting *Antiques Roadshow*.'

Tania had lit a fire, but had thoughtfully also set up a menopause corner next to an open window for Paula and Sonja, who are deep into hot-flush territory.

I watched them, half terrified, from my new perspective, knowing that this was not far away for me either. They looked normal from the outside; however, clearly stuff was raging inside.

'I'm just exhausted all the time,' admitted Paula. 'I so want to cut down my hours but we need the money. And I've just got promoted so have taken on extra responsibility. I'm fifty-five. What do I want extra responsibility for? I'd like a job where I can take an afternoon nap every day, not one where I'm expected to attend client dinners, in the evening, and be lively and entertaining. I want to be in my pyjamas watching *Love Island*!'

Then Sonja admitted to the heaviest periods of her life. 'It's a proper crimson wave,' she said. 'It's honestly like someone is being murdered in my vagina.'

'I'm so pleased I went on the pill after I had Alice,' chipped in Louise. 'I haven't had a period in at least five years.'

Sonja turned to stare at her. I thought she might actually kill her. I knew exactly how she felt. She looked so distraught that I got up and hugged her as she flapped the bottom of her V-necked jumper in an effort to gain extra ventilation.

'And as if things weren't bad enough, Jack only came home for two days at Christmas,' she bleated with tears in her eyes. 'He's got a new girlfriend who he refuses to let us meet and would sooner spend a whole week with her and her family rather than with us. When will the torture of having children ever end!'

I tried to give her a sympathetic smile but was distracted by the sight of Paula asleep in the corner, drool dribbling down her chin.

These women appeared to be falling apart. They were on the edge. One thing was for sure, they were most certainly not happy.

So, while listening to Paula's exhausted pre-watershed snoring, and watching Sonja fan her armpits and bleat for her son, I made a decision.

I had to do something.

Menopause wasn't looking as easy as I had first thought it would be; my kids were both threatening dangerous choices and my husband . . . well, he was expecting my life to fit around his own particular midlife crisis. It was all making me feel sad and panicky and anxious, and so I needed to do something about it, or else I was going to end up really depressed. Just like Lizzy said I would. I had to take control of my life before it took control of me. My sister was right. I needed to think about what made me happy, however hard it would be for someone like me.

A woman, a mother, a wife.

But I knew I didn't need a list of 'Motivational Goals'. I knew I would not find happiness there. Only the dreaded disappointment. I needed a different kind of list. A practical one, an achievable one, and one that would put right all the things that were causing me distress. I didn't need to go bungee jumping or run a marathon or anything stupid like that. All I needed was just a list of stuff I should do before I got any older, stuff that would improve

41

my life. And I knew exactly the first thing I was going to put on it.

31 January

Motivational Goals

New Year – New You

Set your goals right now.

If you can achieve just one goal
a month you can transform your
life by this time next year.

Keep it simple, keep it smart,
keep it close to your heart

Stuff I Really Need To Do
Before I Get Any Older

January	Write the Above List
February	Ditch Periods
March	Ditch Cooking
April	Get a Life Outside the Family — Preferably with 'Young' People
May	Secure My Son's Future i.e. Put a Rocket up His Arse
June	Secure My Daughter's Future i.e. Teach Her How to Not Get Screwed Over by Relationships
July	Reduce My Carb Footprint (That will be carbohydrate as well as carbon)
August	Agree who will Clean Mum and Dad's Toilet
September	Make the Necessary Announcements about the Menopause
October	Have 'The Chat' (The Really Really Important One)
November	Fall in Love Again
December	Dance with Hugh Jackman

February

Ditch Periods

1 February

I've calculated that I've had 189 periods I didn't need to have.

One hundred and eighty nine!

That's 756 days of unnecessary bleeding out of my vagina.

Not to mention 756 days of needless abdominal pain.

And I can't even think about the totally avoidable monthly stress of *leakage*. Any time, any place, anywhere.

All totally pointless!

What on earth have I been thinking?

Having realized I'd wasted over fifteen years having periods, I was on the phone to the doctor's at eight sharp this morning.

'Can I ask what the problem is?' the receptionist asked me.

'I have endured unnecessary pain and suffering for nearly sixteen years,' I told her.

'Can I ask where?' she pressed.

'Mainly in the West Midlands,' I replied, 'although I have lived in the southeast for some periods of my adult life.'

'I meant where on your body,' she said with a sigh. I

knew what she meant but, hey, who doesn't want to miss the chance to irritate a doctor's receptionist?

'Oh. Stomach mainly,' I replied.

There was a pause while the phone operator considered my medical fate. I felt she needed more facts.

'I would consider that it is the lack of information provided by this practice that is partly to blame for this prolonged illness,' I added. 'I need this situation resolving urgently or . . . or—'

'How does ten thirty sound?' came the reply.

Before he even asked, I told the doctor what I was there for.

'I would like the magic pills that take away the pain and suffering that I have endured for the past sixteen years,' I said.

'I'm not sure there are any such pills,' the doctor said, frowning at me suspiciously.

'Oh, there are,' I replied. 'I heard about them at my book group.'

'Your book group?' he asked. He looked uncomfortable. He wanted rid of me like I was some mad old woman.

'Yes, my book group,' I replied.

'I'm not sure if a book group is where you should be getting medical information.'

'It's a very well-educated book group,' I told him. 'Fiona's mother went to the same school as Judi Dench.'

'How interesting,' he replied. 'Did your book group members happen to mention what these so-called magical pills were?'

'The contraceptive pill. The one which means you don't have to have periods.'

The doctor bit his lip. 'Well, you shouldn't need your book group to tell you that contraceptive pills are readily available.'

'No, I shouldn't,' I agreed. 'You are absolutely right. But . . . but I'd forgotten that they stop periods. Totally and utterly forgotten. But it's really quite brilliant, isn't it? I mean, why don't they shout that from the rooftops *all* the time. They're really, *really* badly promoted.'

'Well I—' began the doctor.

'I mean, it's all about sex, isn't it?' I continued, needing to share my view on the matter. 'All they bleat on about when you take the pill is that you can have sex as much as you like and it will stop you getting pregnant. But it can also *stop your periods*. I mean that's *amazing*. For a woman, that is. I can understand why men don't much care since they are not active beneficiaries of the "not having periods" thing. For them the "not having babies" thing is more applicable; however, I can assure you that the "not having periods" thing is . . . well, bloody amazing.'

'They're not guaranteed to stop periods,' stated the doctor. 'And it's not right for everyone and there are other potential side effects and . . .'

'But there is a pill that *can* stop your periods, am I correct?' I demanded.

'Yes, certain pills can.'

I shook my head in disbelief.

'For the past sixteen years I have known I didn't want any more kids. I've had no need whatsoever to menstruate. I have had 189 periods for no reason due to the very poor communication surrounding the other benefits of the contraceptive pill. Do you have any idea how that makes me feel?'

The doctor was no longer looking at me. Just studying my notes on the screen in front of him.

'How old are you, Mrs Collins?' he asked.

'Forty-eight,' I replied after I had thought for a few moments. I was at the point in life where it took effort and mental calculation to remember my age. I could tell you my mobile phone number more easily than how old I was.

The doctor wrapped a blood-pressure band round my upper arm quicker than a slap band round an overexcited toddler's wrist. As he looked down at the reader he casually mentioned, 'At your age you need to be monitoring for symptoms of the menopause.'

'I know, I know,' I replied. 'I know it's out there. It's partly why I want to go on the pill, so I – not the dreaded menopause – can control when they stop.'

'There are downsides to taking the pill, you know,' he said.

'I know, I know,' I muttered. 'But you had me at "yes, it can stop your periods". I'm definitely too old to have periods though, right? I mean, when did you last see a middle-aged woman in a tampon advert? Tampons are clearly not for us. They are for women in bikinis using rollerskates. I shouldn't be allowed to have periods.'

The doctor took his glasses off and rubbed his forehead. 'Look, I will give you a prescription for a pill which should stop your periods. Happy now?'

I sat there and thought about it for a minute.

Then I broke into a very broad grin.

'Yes,' I nodded. 'Actually I am.'

Slightly frustrated, having read the instructions for starting to take the pill, to find that I can't start straight away. I have to wait until the start of my next period. This feels kind of cruel, given that the only reason I am taking the pill is so I don't live in constant dread of my next period starting. However, I figure this time it will be a period to celebrate because this will hopefully be one of my last.

I read the instructions from cover to cover for some reason. Just in case I'd missed something. Something that was going to tell me: *Sorry, but because you have been, let's face it, a serial sauvignon blanc drinker, this magic pill will not work on you.*

Thankfully I found nothing. What I did discover was that, *There are no indications of any effect of Zetraphol tablets on alertness and concentration*, which was good news, since alertness and concentration were both in pretty short supply. Increasingly I found I was able to remember obscure pop song lyrics from the Eighties more easily than why I had walked into a room. I did however note, in the side effects section, that *Around one in ten women can experience mood changes, depression, decreased sexual drive, headaches, nausea, acne, breast pain, irregular periods or no periods and weight increase.* Since many of those sounded very much like the onset of the menopause, I decided it was a risk I was willing to take.

Grandchildren parade day! Long overdue but needed to be done.

My mother called last week and made the comment that she'd forgotten what Freddie and Kirsty looked like and did they both like their Christmas presents? What she really meant was, *You have totally failed me as a daughter as your children never come and see us. They are also very, very rude as they haven't even had the decency to thank me for their Christmas presents, even though it's now February. You are a very, very bad mother.*

I somehow managed to get Kirsty in the car with the promise of calling in at Boots on the way home. Then I went and tackled Freddie, and to my surprise he said he'd love to go and see Nan and Granddad. Stupidly, my heart rose. Maybe Freddie had turned a corner and was finally feeling some empathy for others. I should have known better. As he walked past me out of the hall he grabbed the car keys off the hook and said, 'As long as I can drive.'

Freddie has had five lessons.

Freddie is rubbish at driving, as he believes driving is a fun game rather than a life-or-death experience.

I'd taken Freddie out twice to practise, and the first time I took him he went down a one-way street the wrong way, insisting that it was allowed if there was nothing coming the other way. The second time he flashed a police car. And by that I mean he lifted his top up right to his nipples and gave them a wink. Why he is not in prison I have no idea.

So Freddie went to get in the driving seat, while Kirsty went to get in the passenger seat, leaving me to get in the back. We all stood at our doors and the standoff commenced.

It took ten minutes to negotiate who was sitting where. Freddie refused to get in the car unless he could drive and Kirsty refused to get in the back of the car if Freddie was driving as she gets car sick at the best of times. I told her that a legal driver has to sit next to a learner, to which her response was that Freddie shouldn't therefore be allowed to drive. And so we continued round this loop for some time until I said, 'This isn't about who will drive, this is about going to see your grandparents, so will you please just get in the car!'

I stood firm, waiting for them to get in, no longer caring which seat. They locked eyes and then Freddie held his fist out. I thought he was going to hit her until she held hers out and they did rock, paper, scissors.

I held my breath. Freddie did scissors, Kirsty did paper, like an idiot, so Freddie clicked open the car door and slid into the driver's seat.

Kirsty got in the back seat and assumed the crash position, for which I had the utmost sympathy; if I hadn't had to keep my eyes on the road, I would have joined her.

We were all doomed.

It was then that I noticed Freddie was wearing a black T shirt with the words 'SUPPORT SEX WORKERS' emblazoned in bright yellow across it. I weighed up the option of asking him to get out of the car and go back inside to change, but decided we would never make it to Mum and Dad's if I did. We would have to deal with Freddie's attire when we got there.

'I need to be home by six,' said Kirsty as we pulled off the drive.

'Why?' I asked.

'Cally's coming round to do biology homework.'

Freddie laughed mockingly.

'Watch that car,' I shouted at him as he veered into the middle of the road. He oversteered, nearly mounting the pavement and narrowly avoiding a woman with a pushchair. Thank goodness Mum and Dad only lived ten minutes away.

'Biology homework, otherwise known as stalking Carl Peters online,' taunted Freddie, looking into the rear-view mirror the whole time rather than through the windscreen.

'The road is that way,' I told him, pointing vigorously forwards.

'I know where he is tonight, actually,' said Freddie as he sailed past the left turn we normally take. I decided to stay quiet. For now he was stable. Best not to rock the boat. 'He's at Kim Wang's, pretending he's helping her research universities when really he wants to have sex with her.'

'Freddie!' Kirsty and I shrieked at the same time.

'Red light!' I cried, bracing myself against the dashboard. 'Red light!'

'Oh yeah,' he said, casually slamming on the brake and promptly stalling the car.

'It's broken,' he said, pressing furiously down on the accelerator. 'It won't go.'

'You stalled it,' I said, trying to stay calm. 'Go into neutral, clutch down, ignition on, into gear and off we go.'

All was quiet until Freddie decided to drag up Carl again.

'Yeah, so Carl has the hots for Kim and wants to shag her, just so you know, Kirst.'

'Freddie,' I said sternly. 'Too much information.'

'What do you mean too much? It's relevant and timely and very succinct. How can it be too much?'

'I don't need to know this stuff.'

'Of course you do. All parents want to know about their kids' sex lives. Think yourself lucky I'm so open about it.'

'Could you just remember occasionally that you are a teenager, Freddie, and you are supposed to want to hide some things from me? That's normal.'

'That's soooo Eighties. We don't do that any more. Oversharing is the new being secretive. Hiding everything only makes the geriatrics suspicious. Overshare and you can sit back, watch them cringe, and then slowly and permanently close their eyes and ears.'

'It's the next left,' I sighed. Freddie is too clever for his own good half the time. Jesus, now I sounded like my mother.

We pulled into the drive outside Mum and Dad's bungalow, which they'd moved into when they retired ten years ago, less than half a mile from the house I grew up in. I still found it a little weird not going 'home' when I went to see them. I craved to get pushed off the tyre swing under the massive oak tree in our garden by one of my sisters one more time, or to hear my Dad ring the doorbell at least ten times whenever he got back from his job driving trucks around the country. Our house in Kimble Lane was packed full of memories, whereas the brand-new bungalow felt devoid of such life. The old battered sideboard that my mum used to make me polish every Saturday as a child sat uncomfortably next to smooth clean walls, and Dad's well-worn reclining chair looked anything but at home in front of the flatscreen

TV. Everything looked temporary, including my parents, and that made me feel sad to the very bone.

I turned to Freddie. 'I thought you said Carl didn't believe in sex before marriage?'

Freddie turned to face me with a pitiful look on his face. 'Mother, Mother, Mother,' he said, putting his hand on my arm. 'When will you get it?'

'Get what?'

'It's all a lie. Saying he doesn't believe in sex before marriage is the biggest turn-on for girls known to man. Suddenly he's a challenge. There are girls gagging to prove him wrong, including your daughter.'

'Freddie!' said Kirsty, landing a punch on his head. I looked round at her. She'd fallen back on the seat, tearful and bright red. He'd hit a nerve yet again. I'd never seen her like this over a boy. All I could think about was this glowing red flag that was just four months away, when her sixteenth birthday would arrive and . . . well, I couldn't think about it. I just wanted to hold her and stop her getting any older. I reached back and clutched her knee to show I knew that Freddie had no right to say those things. I watched helpless as a single tear fell down her face as she gazed out of the window. Suddenly I realized that this situation was far worse than I had at first thought. This was a disaster of epic proportions. This was the worst thing that could be happening. This wasn't just a crush, was it? This could be love. That horrific, vile, heart-rending, angsty love that inflicted itself upon teenage girls.

If I was right, then we were all doomed.

By rights the Teenage Resilience Training Programme needed to kick in immediately. I needed to tell her that teenage love can only lead to pain. A pain that really,

really hurt because your heart was raw and fresh and hadn't had the knocks and bumps to give it some resilience. I needed to tell her that he *would* be a bastard and her heart *would* be broken.

This is her history waiting to happen. This is the truth.

But I knew the truth was no weapon against teenage love. There was absolutely nothing I could say to prevent the horror of what she was about to go through.

I might have to resort to showing care and compassion. Oh God!

'We were just about to have our tea,' was how my mum greeted us at the door.

Translated as . . . You're late.

As usual.

I'm disappointed in you.

As usual.

Her style is the opposite of modern mothering. No ego-boosting platitudes for me. No concern over my mental health or my level of happiness. My mother seemed to have decided that the best way of being maternal was to prevent at all costs me attaining any level of enjoyment out of life that could possibly lead to that vile trait of being 'full of oneself'. She liked an underdog, my mum. She could warm to one of those.

'Hiya, Nan,' said Freddie, bounding into the living room, right as rain. 'Looking fresh as ever.' He stood full frontal with his hands on his hips, displaying his support of sex workers for all to see.

Mum pursed her lips.

'Pretty colours,' she said eventually.

'My Auntie Kitty was a prostitute,' announced Dad.

'John,' hissed Mum. 'Not in front of the children.'

'Alzheimer's,' Freddie mouthed at me, pointing at Dad.

'She was,' he told him. 'Everyone said she was going to choir practice of a Friday evening, but really she was popping down the butcher's to redeem her ration book, if you know what I mean.' He winked at Freddie.

'I'm not sure that's quite the same as prostitution,' I said.

'Of course it is,' declared Freddie. 'The currency was cutlets rather than cash, that's all. Amounts to the same thing.'

'I think she enjoyed it, to be honest,' said Dad.

We let that one hang in the air for a moment.

'Well, she must have done – she ended up marrying him,' he added, booming with laughter.

'So actually she was dating the butcher and he was being kind and dropping her some sausages on the side. Not prostitution, Dad.'

'They were definitely having sex though,' he protested. 'When she should have been at choir practice.'

I made a mental note to tell Freddie never to wear his 'Support Sex Workers' T-shirt in front of Mum and Dad again.

'Shall I put the kettle on?' offered Freddie.

I shook my head in exasperation. Freddie didn't lift a finger at home but became angel child in front of my mum, as though he'd sniffed the whiff of an imminent inheritance or something.

'You really shouldn't let him wear T-shirts like that,' my mum said the minute he'd left the room. 'He's such a lovely boy.'

I used to protest. I used to tell her that I tried my best to tell him what to do but he didn't bloody well listen. He was headstrong, just like his nan.

Speaking of which, I decided to take the bull by the horns. I'd been up to do the cleaning every week since Christmas, and taking Mum shopping whenever she needed to, which I didn't mind at all, but I knew that at some point in the future, as they got older, my sisters and I were going to have to do a lot more to look after them. What I minded was having to do a lot more for them now because Mum was too proud to go to the doctor's to see what they could do to fix her knee. Not to mention the fact that she's obviously in pain and not enjoying life as she should be which is just not right.

'Have you been to see the doctor about your knee yet?' I asked her.

'No, it's been better this week.'

I could feel the anger rising in me instantly. I cast her an evil stare. She could barely walk up the street and she had a collection of painkillers in the kitchen cupboard that would make any drug dealer blush. She was in complete denial that she might be anywhere near old enough to qualify for the classic geriatric operation of having a new knee. Having me run around after her was much less of an indignity.

'Wouldn't hurt to get them to have a look, though, would it?' I told her.

'It's fine. I can still get to the post office. It's fine.'

'Mike's dad is running around like anything since he had a new knee.'

'Mike's dad was much worse than me.'

'How do you know – you've not seen him since Mike's fiftieth birthday.'

'Your Uncle Ted is very poorly, you know,' she said.

'He's back driving and everything,' I countered.

She was wringing her hands together, and looked down at them as she told me: 'Lizzy says I should do some yoga, that would help. And I should take some herbal tablets she's going to send me.'

'When did Lizzy say that?'

'She called us this morning.'

Aaah, of course. The eldest sibling had spoken and the mother shalt listen. Despite being unimpressed by me, my mother was in awe of Lizzy, and her skill in marrying a rich American who funded her every whim. And, just as Lizzy liked to step in from afar and tell me how to live my life with no local insight, she also liked to do the same with Mum and Dad. She had been encouraging Dad to buy a vintage MG so Mum and he could drive it to Paris! Lizzy needed to get her bony, yoga-infused arse over here and see how much weight her mother was putting on because she refused to get her knee sorted, and how many cream doughnuts Dad was knocking back. The thought of getting the two of them into a small sports car was like trying to cram two puffer fish into a sardine tin.

It was so much easier to be the favourite child when you lived in a different continent.

'How's your love life then, young lady?' I heard Dad say to Kirsty, who had so far not engaged, just sat on the stool by the electric fire and stared into her phone.

I wanted to lunge across the room and put myself as a physical barrier between her and Dad. This conversation could prove lethal.

She looked up at him and left the room, tearful.

'Boyfriend trouble?' he asked me.

'She's very sensitive, isn't she,' Mum said. 'You're going to have to watch her. Needs some careful handling.'

Careful handling. What does my mother know about careful handling?

Did she handle me carefully?

No.

I did not call 'not telling me about periods' careful handling. She had handed me sanitary towels in the supermarket when I was eleven, with absolutely no explanation. I had honestly thought they were to pad out my A-cup bra, as I was so embarrassed by my nonexistent chest.

And she hadn't explained sex to me either. I'd had to rely on the tales of Jackie Collins, Jilly Cooper and Shirley Conrad. For a very long time I thought that the only people who had sex owned horses or lived in LA.

And now she was telling me to handle my teenage daughter carefully?

'Could you do me a favour while you are here?' my mother piped up when Freddie brought in the tea. Here we go, I thought. She'd been saving up jobs for me that she couldn't do because of her knee. 'Could you change the beds in the spare room? I'm babysitting your niece and nephew tonight.'

I stared at my mother. She knew I didn't have to speak.

'Nicola needs a social life, you know that,' said Mum. 'She's been very lonely since Ben left her.'

Bullshit. My little sister has been shagging her way around Tinder for the last six months, once she got over the shock of her partner leaving. She has been having the time of her life, out every single weekend. She wasn't at home, scrolling aimlessly through Netflix every night for hours on end before losing the will to live and watching some random cooking programme – when I hate cooking!

'Has she told you he's behind on his maintenance?' she added. 'Why oh why didn't she marry him?'

61

I looked at my mother aghast. 'Because he's a dickhead,' I said.

'If she'd have married him, none of this would have happened.'

My patience was starting to run out.

'If she'd married him, she would have married a dickhead,' I had to point out, but she shook her head in disagreement.

'I'm not getting married,' announced Freddie. 'Not to anyone, dickhead or not. Who knows how someone will turn out and you've shackled yourself to them. What an utterly ridiculous idea.'

We all looked at him. Utter conviction written all over his face.

It did make me wonder if – like most norms in society these days – marriage would be challenged and moulded and reconstructed to suit modern times. Perhaps in the future we would build in a get-out clause after any dependants had flown the nest. Perhaps we would develop a part-time marriage model or a legal marriage rather than an emotional one. Perhaps we would decide to all live in communes and dip in and out – quite literally. Some being mothers, some being lovers, some providers. Do what you do best rather than trying to do everything. Specialization – maybe that was the future of marriage.

That still left us with the fact that Nicola thankfully didn't marry the dickhead that is Ben.

As I huffed and puffed over clean bedding for my sister's children because my mum couldn't do it because of the pain in her knee, I decided desperate measures were called for. I barely ever changed my own kids' bedding, so wasn't clear at all why I was changing other people's. And why couldn't Nicola change the sodding bedding when she got here, anyway, and why couldn't Lizzy offer some useful input from across the pond, rather than her airy-fairy ideas? Mum's knee was going to be fixed if it bloody killed me.

10 February

I have considered my options regarding Mum's knee.

The most obvious thing to do is to call her doctor on her behalf and take her down forcibly and demand that he tell her she must have a new knee. But I know she won't go. She has to decide herself that she needs one. So someone has to convince her, and I know that person isn't me.

I was going to have to ask my sisters for help.

I contemplated ringing Lizzy but I couldn't stand the thought of her potentially asking me about my motivational goals. I'd not been in touch to tell her that I'd pencilled some of my own versions in, because then she would ask what they were and then she would be aghast that I hadn't put learning Japanese in there or some other ridiculous thing. She wouldn't get it because they wouldn't be her kind of goals and then she would make me change them and then I would be back to square one. Disappointed by unachievable goals. Of course I could also pick the phone up to Nicola but I feared that I wouldn't be able to hold back my anger at having to change bed linen for her children while she was out having a good time. So I resorted to what any sensible person does to tackle a tricky issue.

I set up a WhatsApp group and invited both Lizzy and Nicola to join MUM'S KNEE.

63

Me: Hi, both. Hope all is well. Was at Mum's yesterday and her knee's giving her so much pain she's downing painkillers like Smarties! She needs to see a doctor and I suspect she needs a new knee but she won't do anything about it. Any ideas?

It's only 6.30 a.m. on the West Coast but Lizzy is a health freak so I know she'll be up doing something ridiculous like barbecuing quinoa.

Lizzy: I'm sending her some herbal remedies and told her to enrol in a gentle yoga class.

I wanted to write, 'Oh, that's great then, all sorted, I'd never thought of that', but I didn't want to resort to sarcasm so early in the group's career. Message ten or twelve maybe, but not message two.

Me: Lovely, Lizzy – but I think she's beyond crushed cabbage and buying a rubber mat.

Couldn't help it. There was a gap of maybe fifteen minutes as I imagined Lizzy mulling over the problem. I imagined her firing up a NutriBullet and making a healthy shake, whereas I'd be reaching for the large bar of Dairy Milk. I sometimes wondered how we could be sisters at all.

Lizzy: But I thought they were planning on buying a MG and doing it up and driving to Paris?

She was taking the denial route. Living abroad had so many advantages.

Me: *Mum's not driving any more. That's how bad it is.*

Another ten-minute pause. No response from Nicola yet.

Lizzy: *But Dad could still drive it, couldn't he? I've just Googled it and it's only four hours down to Dover and onto the tunnel and thon they are practically there. They could stop halfway for the night. Then it's only a two-hour stint. That sounds doable?*

Me: *I think you are missing the point, Lizzy. Mum's not going anywhere until she's fixed her knee. Forget Paris.*

She'd be sulking now. Suggesting buying a sports car and driving to Paris has kept my sister thinking that she was the daughter of the century for some time. And I'd just poured low-fat yogurt all over her parade.

Lizzy: *I don't know what you expect me to do.*

Me: *I think you need to talk to her. She listens to you. Tell her something that will convince her to go to the doc's.*

Lizzy: *Like what?*

Me: *I don't know!*

Nicola: *Sorry, guys. Only just got in. I had a sleepover at Laurence's.*

She added a winking emoji face. To the MUM'S KNEE chat. Really!

Lizzy: *Oooh – who's Laurence?*

Nicola: *This guy I've been seeing. He's a doctor.*

Lizzy: *Wow – way to go Nic – do spill, have you got a picture?*

Nicola: *No – but he has a hint of the McDreamy's about him.*

Lizzy: *What, him off* Grey's Anatomy*? Double wow!*

She added a hands clapping and champagne bottle emoji. I had to admit I have a bit of a thing for Patrick Dempsey. He was my celebrity crush. I wanted to ask more questions, just out of casual interest, but felt that if I asked now, the purpose of the WhatsApp group was doomed.

Me: *Can we get back to Mum's knee and then Nicola can give us the lowdown on her latest shag.*

Nothing for a good ten minutes.

Nicola: *He's not just my latest shag, Cathy. He could be the one.*

Me: *I really hope so, Nic, and I really look forward to meeting the sexy doctor, as I'm sure Mum will be . . . if she can still walk. So any ideas?*

Nothing for half an hour.

Lizzy: *I feel so helpless all this way away.*

Nicola: *It's not your fault.*

Lizzy: *If I could do something, I would.*

Me: *Will you call her, Lizzy? She likes you. Just try and talk some sense into her.*

Lizzy: *She likes you two too.*

Me: *I know, but you send her presents and stuff. She talks about that all the time.*

Nicola: *It's true, she does. A lot!*

Lizzy: *Okay, then. I'll give it a go. I'll call tomorrow.*

Me: *Thanks, Lizzy.*

Nicola: *Yeah – thanks Lizzy.*

Lizzy: *Got to go. I have a class in ten minutes. Give my best regards to Doctor Dreamy, Nic.*

Nicola: *Will do.*

Me: *Yeah – me too. Looking forward to meeting him.*

I wanted to add 'if it lasts that long', but thought that might not promote sisterly love.

12 February

Mike FaceTimed me from some restaurant in Liverpool tonight. It was just as I was trying to scrape the burnt bits off some sausages. I have no idea how you cook sausages without cremating them and then still find them raw in the middle. Sausages are stupid. Anyway, just as I was cursing the pork, Mike popped up on my phone to show me the dessert he was eating. I mean, it looked nice and all that, but I did not need to see a high-end, restaurant-quality pudding while I was feeding charcoal to my kids. It was incredibly loud and I could barely hear him, so he got up out of his chair and turned his back on the view of his excellently cooked food and raucous company.

'So what have you been up to?' he asked

'Well, the usual. Just the usual. Erm . . . oh, I went to the doc's the other day,' I said.

'What! Shit. Why?' His face distorted in horror. 'It's not . . . is it, you haven't have you . . .?'

'No, no, nothing to worry about,' I said. Christ, was this where we were at? Any mention of the medical profession and it was bound to be because we were at death's door.

'I just asked to go on the pill.'

I have *never, ever* seen him look more confused. He looked over his shoulder and then pushed his face closer to the screen.

'Do . . . do you want to have more sex?' he whispered.

I laughed. It was the only response I could think of.

'No!' I said eventually. He looked crestfallen. 'Why is contraception always about sex? I just want to stop my periods and there is a pill that can do that.'

He drew back. 'Wow,' he said. 'That's good. Why didn't you do that before? I mean, it's not like we were planning any more kids. Think of all the money we could have saved on condoms.'

'And tampons,' I added.

The table behind suddenly roared with laughter, making hearing anything he was saying to me impossible. This was not the right time for a decent conversation. Perhaps that's why he called me while out with his colleagues. So we couldn't have a decent conversation. Since I'd stormed off in a huff and slammed some kitchen cupboard doors, there had been no mention of Helen, or his plans to change both his work and mine. I very strongly suspected, however, that this just meant he was taking his time putting together a strategy of how to get his own way. He would pounce when I least expected it and I needed to be ready.

We agreed this was not the right time to talk, and so I left him to his good food and good company. I put burnt sausages on plates and then stood at the bottom of the stairs and shouted up to Freddie and Kirsty. They came down, grabbed a plate and then disappeared back upstairs without a word.

Faced with another night in front of the TV on my own, I decided I would pop to Tania's and see what they were up to. Last minute I photocopied my list of 'sort of goals', thinking that she would be very impressed with my progress.

I interrupted their dinner. Of course I did.

Tania and Hazel were at the dining-room table, talking to each other, sharing their day. They even had a candle lit. On a weekday! It was a picture of total marital harmony. Tania, of course, invited me to join them. I thought of the burnt sausages that were now in the bin and gratefully took a seat.

'To what do we owe this pleasure?' asked Hazel. If I was honest, Hazel terrified me. She was a lecturer in an 'ology' and she was so frighteningly clever that everything that came out of my mouth in her presence seemed to sound like something an imbecile would say.

'Well, er, I wanted to show Tania this list and ask her if she would, er, keep a copy of this list I've written and help make me stick to it.'

Utter gobbledygook!

'Did you write your Motivational Goals?' asked Tania, placing a bowl of delicious-smelling food in front of me. 'Really? That's wonderful news. I really think that's a good idea, Cathy. Definitely worth a shot.'

'Tania mentioned you were feeling a bit low,' said Hazel kindly.

Jesus, I thought. Tania had told her I was a pathetic mess again.

'It's a bit rough, isn't it, this time of life?' she continued. 'Having something to aim at can really help. When I started the menopause, I decided to undertake a research project in my faculty, investigating feminism and psycho-analytical theory. It really took my mind off it.'

I swallowed. I knew what was coming next.

'Where have you decided to put your talents?' she asked. She smiled at me warmly.

'Er, well, nothing so impressive,' I spluttered. Perhaps I should just go home now, taking my list with me.

'Oh, come on,' said Hazel. 'Let's take a look. I'm sure you can achieve whatever you want to if you put your mind to it.'

I handed it over to her as if I was a student handing in what I knew was a substandard essay.

She read it, her brow furrowing the further down she went. Then she smiled. Smiled at my work. Maybe it wasn't so bad. She then handed it over to Tania, who smiled the whole way through as she read my list of stuff I really needed to do before I got any older.

Then a surprising thing happened. Hazel asked me if she could have my list to include in her study of feminism and psychoanalytical theory.

'Of course,' I beamed.

She got up and hugged me.

'Good luck,' she whispered in my ear.

15 February

Day 26 of Fish-Finger-Gate.

I tried to let it go, I really did. And I sort of did. But not quite.

The fish finger disappeared two days after it had been used as a missile, so I assumed misguidedly that the issue had been dealt with and someone had finally cracked and cleaned it up. Happy days. However, unbeknownst to me, Barbra Streisand, our Boston terrier, had finally tracked it down and gobbled it up. Unfortunately, Barbra had then thrown it up on the utility room floor, along with mangled-up Pedigree Chum and dog slobber. I cleared it up, putting the sticky mess in a poo bag, and informed the rest of the family of the new location of the fish finger and that someone needed to dispose of the poo bag that was sitting on the wall outside the back door.

That had been over three weeks ago.

Today I'd decided that enough was enough so, as I left to take Barbra out for a walk, I tackled Freddie.

'By the way,' I said, 'the fish finger that Barbra threw up is still on the back wall. I want it in the bin by the time I get back.'

He looked at me puzzled for a moment.

'Why *moi*?' he asked.

'You bought the fish fingers and Barbra is your dog.'

'Not guilty on both counts.'

'What!' I exploded.

He thought for a moment. 'I bought the fish fingers out of the five pounds you gave me for food when I went on that psychology field trip, only I didn't need it because Jacko gave me his ham sandwich because his mum had put mustard on it. Therefore you funded the purchase and your constant insistence that Barbra is my dog just because I named her after Madame Streisand is just a convenient false construct to encourage me to be wracked with guilt because I never walk her. Am I correct?'

'Barbra *is* your dog,' I seethed. 'You cried for a week when you were nine because you were so desperate for her. You went on hunger strike for a day. You practically held us to ransom and now . . . now . . .'

'I have no recollection of any of the evidence you are presenting to me,' he said, wide-eyed. 'Like I say, a convenient false construct in order to make me dispose of regurgitated fish finger.' He got up and walked out of the kitchen.

'If it's still there when I get back, I will dry your merino wool boxers in the tumble dryer,' I shouted after him. 'Where they will shrink to nothing!'

'You wouldn't dare,' he challenged, storming back in.

'Try me,' I said, holding his glare.

'I'll wash them myself,' he countered.

'We both know that's a lie,' I said.

He nodded. 'You are holding me to ransom,' he replied, poking his finger at my chest.

'I learnt from the best,' I stated. 'Come on Barbra, I'll take you for a walk, even though your owner is a gobby liar who doesn't take his responsibilities seriously.'

Naturally, I have never admitted to Freddie how much I love walking Barbra Streisand, and what a bonus it has proved to my life having a dog. I figure Barbra has kept at bay at least one roll of fat, as walking her – my one and only form of exercise – has stopped me becoming the couch potato into which I could so easily have morphed. And, most importantly and unexpectedly, I have met some really interesting people and had some very entertaining conversations while our dogs sniffed each other's bums.

And of course, recently, I got to see Toby.

Toby, the owner of a delightful greyhound, whose walk often coincided with my Saturday morning trek through the woods. We were on nodding terms for probably about a year as his unmistakable good looks threw me into teenage trauma and stopped me having my usual dog banter with him. Then one day I found him distressed, having lost Blizzard (his wife's choice, apparently), and so of course I offered to help find him, which I eventually did, with his nose stuck down a foxhole. He was so grateful he offered his name and a smile and a recognition that he could no longer just pass me on the bridge over the stream. Conversation would need to be had.

I looked forward to seeing him, if I was honest. I was not really sure why. It wasn't like I fancied him. I mean, fancying him would have been so utterly pointless. He was perhaps in his early thirties, he wore cool clothes like he was not really trying to be cool; he was well groomed, I was sure he used moisturizer, and he did some trendy job like graphic design or something. Oh, and sometimes he wore a flat cap, which should have looked ridiculous but somehow he carried it off. But no, I didn't fancy him. I appreciated him. He was unmistakably very attractive and seemed like a lovely guy, but I was very aware that fancying him would be like me thinking that one day I might make a soufflé. Just a totally ridiculous aspiration.

Thankfully, I saw Toby out and about today. Not that I'd timed my walk to coincide with his or anything. I mean, I wouldn't do that. That would be juvenile. But the fact that we both liked to watch *Saturday Kitchen* on the TV and then go out for a walk did mean that we often bumped into each other on a Saturday and would have a little review of our week, which was kind of special and not something I would have liked to miss.

'Good week?' he asked as he approached me.

'Pretty crap, actually,' I told him. 'I am currently on a twenty-six-day-long battle with the entire family over who is going to clear up a fish finger. My daughter threw it, my husband touched it last and my son's dog ate it then threw it up. If it's not gone by the time I get back, I'm divorcing the entire family.'

Toby threw his head back and laughed. Proper laughed. He found me funny, I knew he did. And I liked that. It gave me a funny feeling.

'How about you?' I asked.

'Oh, Phoebe went off on one at me again last night. I didn't get home until after nine but I had told her I was going to the beer mixer. I hadn't put it on the calendar so apparently it didn't count that I'd told her.'

'Beer mixer?' I asked.

'Oh, it's a thing they do once a month in the building I work in. All the tenants get together and have a beer and talk and share ideas and stuff. It's good, actually. I've got three clients through those mixers. In fact, someone told me to pop up and see them after last night.'

Fish fingers, I thought. I was falling out with my family over fish fingers and Toby was going to beer mixers to get new clients. I had never felt so old and out of it.

'Where do you work?' I asked.

'The Mustard Factory,' he said. 'Do you know it?'

Of course I knew it. It was an old building on the edge of town that had been recently renovated and converted into luxury apartments and some very cool office space. To me it looked like heaven. If I worked there I'd pretend I was some entrepreneur living in the Meatpacking District of New York, who lunched with clients every day on miso soup and crispy kale. I'd been dying to go and have a nose inside but I wasn't its target market and I was afraid security would throw me out.

'Very nice,' I said. 'I'd love to have a look round there.'

He didn't take the bait. 'Where do you work?' he asked, instead of the 'Oh, come and have a look round' that I had been hoping for.

'Well,' I said, 'I do some freelance accountancy. So

mainly at the IKEA table in our kitchen. We don't have monthly beer mixers in our building, more wine Wednesdays, and Thursdays, and Fridays . . . and Saturdays. Helps with the creative juices when I'm cooking the books for the fish-and-chip shop on Ascot Drive.'

He threw his head back and laughed. As though he thought it was a joke or something.

'Do you have a card,' he said when he'd finally decided to stop laughing heartily. 'You can never know too many accountants.'

Stupid question. Me have a card? I had numerous reward cards cluttering up my wallet that I always failed to make use of. But a card for myself? Really?

'I haven't got any on me at the moment I'm afraid,' I said nonchalantly. 'But you know where I am if you need me. Normally here with my arse in the air, picking up dog shit.'

'Yeah, sure,' he replied. 'Look. Got to go. Phoebe wants to go shopping. Apparently we need a new coffee table.' He raised his eyebrows in a conspiratorial fashion, as if I knew as well as he did that they didn't need a new coffee table, and then he squeezed my arm. Yes, he actually touched me.

I could still feel where his fingers had brushed my skin when I ambled over the stile at the edge of the field. Mike hadn't touched me like that in at least a decade.

With casual affection.

We didn't hold hands, we didn't spontaneously hug, and we didn't even do encouraging rubs of the shoulder. We did distance or sex, nothing in between. What had happened to the in-between? I missed the in-between.

I touched my arm where Toby had gripped it.

Maybe I'll go home and attempt a soufflé, I thought.

I should have smelt a rat before I even went, of course.

Mike had never organized a night away for us. Promised to. Even written it in a few birthday cards, I seemed to recall, but actually booking it himself, no never. And so, to avoid us having a marriage devoid of minibreaks, I had always booked them myself.

So when he called me out of the blue and invited me up to Liverpool for the night, it was a lovely little surprise that I was foolishly excited by. I even let my expectations rise a little. After all, the last time the two of us had gone out together alone was when we had dropped in to the pub on the way home from Freddie's parents' evening over twelve months ago. And that was not to spend time as a couple together, that was to get drunk to obliterate the fact that – according to his teachers – he was very, very bright, but on a road to nowhere as he didn't seem to be willing to apply himself to anything. We drank two bottles of wine and then had a massive row because Mike claimed it was because I wasn't disciplined enough with him at home. I said I would kick his (mostly) absent-parent arse if he ever said anything like that again. I also said he needed to sit Freddie down and have a motivational chat with him. Give him some guidance. Mike ignored Freddie all weekend then left a copy of Barack Obama's autobiography outside his bedroom door.

I went up to Liverpool on the train at lunchtime, fully enjoying a cheese and onion sandwich, a gin and tonic in a can and *HELLO!* magazine. Mike had suggested I should go up early so that I could go to the spa in the hotel, then he would be back around 5.30 p.m. to take me out. But there was no way I would be wasting my time in the hotel spa. I had absolutely no wish to spend my afternoon gazing at some beautiful twenty-something as she tried to ignore the sorry state of my feet and made me green with envy describing the holiday she'd been on to the Caribbean for her birthday, paid for by her adoring boyfriend. I didn't think so. Oh no. Instead I had an afternoon of sitting on the bed in a fluffy dressing gown while drinking tea, eating shortbread biscuits and pitting my wits against the contestants on some quality game shows. That's true relaxation. I did contemplate getting my eyebrows waxed, but really – I wear glasses all the time, so my glasses surely render my eyebrows invisible.

I also spent my time Googling 'best restaurants in Liverpool'. I had seen that there were some pretty swanky ones that had a lavish footballers' wives feel about them. (Again, what was I thinking?!) A couple Mike had mentioned he'd been to already during the course of his placement, so I was hoping he'd scoped out the best and booked us a table. I was ridiculously excited, so excited that I actually gave myself a full forty-five minutes to get ready. I mean, I washed my hair and dried it and everything, and, just in case, I'd packed my sparkly high shoes. We were in Liverpool, after all, where women really dressed up to go out, really put the glam on. A friend of mine, Penny, who'd lived there for a while, had told me that mums dropping off their kids at the school gate on a Friday morning regularly turned up with curlers in their hair, expecting a full day of preparation for a Friday night out. So doubling my usual getting-ready time was the least I could do.

Again I missed the signs when Mike arrived in the room to find me waiting ready to hit the town.

'Oh,' he said.

I waited.

'We're not due there for another hour and I er, I er, well, I thought that we might – you know – take advantage of a hotel room and, er, the fact that you, er, have gone on the pill.'

He gave me that very confused look again. He was clearly failing to understand that I was taking the pill for its other advantages rather than fertilization-free sex.

'If you think I'm taking these Spanx off just so we can have a quick one before we go out, you are wrong,' I pointed out. 'I'll see you in the bar in ten minutes.' Before I shut the door behind me, I informed him I expected him to be wearing his best shirt. I hadn't dressed up like this for nothing.'

I was already a Mojito down by the time he came downstairs. I wanted to have a Cosmopolitan but I was afraid he'd think I was getting all *Sex in the City* and clearly he needed no encouragement.

'So,' he said, rubbing his hands together and sitting down, 'we are going to meet someone before we go and eat.'

'Oh,' I said. 'Who's that?'

'It's a surprise, but don't worry, it's a good one.' He grinned, clearly pleased with himself.

It had to be my friend Penny, I assumed. The one who'd moved here years ago and I'd not seen for ages. How thoughtful. How kind to think that actually I'd like to catch up with her. I'd thought about texting her but didn't think we'd have time, what with the swanky dinner.

'Are they joining us for dinner?' I asked.

'No,' he said with a chuckle. 'But you will have plenty of time to talk when you see them.'

I had a Cosmopolitan next, as I was feeling more amenable to sex now that Mike had been thoughtful enough to hook me up with an old friend. I raised my eyebrows over the rim of the glass as I sipped the sour liquid. I have to say he was looking good. Men get better-looking with age, don't they, whereas a woman's appeal seems to evaporate. I tried to give him an alluring look, the kind that would really get him going when we were dating. He winked at me and I was a skittish young woman again who couldn't believe her luck that she'd finally bagged a successful, good-looking man. Then he smiled and my stomach flipped and I remembered why I'd married him. I tried to grab hold of that feeling and store it up for later on in the evening.

I was, of course, crippled by the time we got to our rendezvous after a walk across town to a converted warehouse not far from the Albert Docks. Perhaps we were meeting at Penny's workplace, I thought, as Mike pressed a buzzer and the door opened and we pushed our way into a small hallway. Mike led me up some stairs. I brushed all warning signals to the side. Why weren't we meeting in a bar or café? How did Mike know where to go? How had Mike got Penny's details? What on earth had given him this idea, which was so out of character?

After three flights of stairs, the two cocktails were making my head swirl unsteadily. Mike pushed through a pair of glass double doors into an empty waiting area. He glanced at his watch and then headed straight for a wooden door at the end of the corridor and knocked, turning to smile at me. A blonde lady opened the door. It wasn't Penny.

'Hi, I'm Helen,' she said, stepping forward and grasping my hand in a vigorous two-handed shake. 'You must be Cathy. I've heard so much about you. Please do come in.'

*

80

What sort of fuckwit invites his wife out for the evening and then takes her along to see his life coach? This was right up there. This was unspeakably bad. I was lost for words as I fell into a low seat and took in the soft furnishings in neutral colours and bookcase lined with self-help books. I should be pretending I'm a footballer's wife right now, not sitting in a stuffy room with over-stuffed cushions, staring at a book titled, *Super Attractor: How to Manifest a Life Beyond Your Wildest Dreams*.

I manifested my best shocked and dismayed face and lasered it over to Mike.

'Isn't it amazing?' he said. 'I rang Helen for you and she said it would be great to talk to you. Not a problem at all. She's only been specializing in executives so far but she wants to branch out. See who else her services might help.'

My face did not change but held its shocked composure. I thought I'd clearly said I did not want to meet Helen and her amazing 'empathy' for overpaid fifty-something executives.

'It's all right,' he said, patting my hand. 'No need to be scared. And she's not even going to charge us for this session. You're her guinea pig, you see. To see if this kind of set-up works.'

I didn't want to be anyone's guinea pig for life coaching. I was only really willing to be a guinea pig if food was involved. I did not want to be here. Two cocktails swilling round my empty stomach and a fancy dinner pushed out of my grasp. We'd better be going to somewhere very fancy after this or . . . or something very, very bad would be happening to my husband.

I took a deep breath. I tried to gather myself. I supposed I ought to at least listen to what she had to say.

'So, I normally start by discussing with my clients what their goals are over the next five to seven years.'

Jesus, I thought, I've been through all this. I didn't do goals!! Not the type of goals Helen was thinking of, anyway.

'To not be dead,' I replied.

She looked up sharply at me and then at my husband, as if to say, 'You said she might be tricky and you're not wrong.'

'Good, good,' she said, writing furiously.

'For my children to be alive,' I added. I did not mention my husband, given that I might well have murdered him by the end of the evening.

'Of course,' she nodded. 'And what about any work-related goals, career aspirations?'

Mike didn't even let me speak. He jumped straight in.

'Cathy was second in command in the finance department at Brontack Construction,' Mike told her. 'They had a turnover of over two million a year. Quite a big concern when she was there.'

'Wow,' said Helen. 'Impressive.'

'She's been doing the accounts for some local enterprises since then,' he added.

What on earth was he talking about? I was sure the chippy and the taxi firm had never been so glamorously labelled. An 'enterprise' operated out of The Mustard Factory where Toby worked, not in a grubby side street where the homeless hung out. Mike was giving Helen a misguided view of my talents.

'Well, that's brilliant news,' she said. I tried to ignore the near-patronizing tone. 'You've kept your hand in. That will really count for something on your CV.'

My eyes flew open. CV? Why are we talking about

CVs? Now this was going too far. The last time I did a CV must have been when I left university, struggling to make being on the college pool team sound like a noteworthy achievement and not just an excuse to spend every night in the bar. Did you still even list interests on a CV? I didn't have any interests. I went to Pilates once last year. Would that count?

'And did you enjoy working for a large company?' Helen asked me as I wondered if the mastery of always buying clothes that didn't need ironing would count as a significant accomplishment on a CV.

I wanted to tell her to mind her own business but I decided to take a different tack.

'Sure, it was all right,' I replied. 'Until he made me redundant.' I pointed at Mike and Helen gasped.

Mike sighed the heavy sigh he always does when I remind him of how we met.

'The consultancy I work for were brought into restructure the company, and unfortunately Cathy's role was one of the casualties.'

He always called it Cathy's role. Not Cathy. Not Cathy being told that an external company had deemed her unnecessary. I guessed you had to be that impersonal if you spent your life putting people out of jobs.

'He pulled me at my leaving do,' I explained to Helen. 'I lost my career but gained a husband.'

'Right,' nodded Helen, looking very uncomfortable. She threw a panicked look at Mike. Clearly this was news to her.

'It was nothing to do with her ability,' he added. 'She knows that. She was really good at her job. She could walk into a medium-sized company tomorrow and be a real asset,' he said.

I noted that he didn't say *large* company.

I blew my cheeks out. I didn't want to be here. This was outrageous. I just wanted to go to a fancy restaurant and pretend – for just one evening – that I was a fancy person who got dressed up and went out for meals, rather than someone who worried about what her son was going to shave next with her new Ladyshave. I also knew I definitely did not want to be talking about qualifications and CVs and planning a route back to the front line.

'A lot of women can be nervous about returning to full-time work if they have been away from it for a long time,' Helen said.

'I do really think it's your turn,' said Mike, leaning over and putting his hand on mine. 'You've sacrificed so much for the family. I want you to know that I really do appreciate everything you've done.'

I swallowed. The last time I'd heard him say that was in the grand argument of 2003. The epic fallout that had ensued when he'd asked me what tie he should wear for a meeting he had the next day in Paris, while I was up to my eyeballs in baby shit. Literally. I nearly threw that nappy at him.

'I only asked you what tie to wear?' he'd said, as I cried wave after wave of tears.

'Is this what my life has become?' I spat at him. 'Choosing your ties for your fancy trips abroad while I stay at home and have my nipples mangled and poo smeared in my hair?'

Now, Mike was smiling at me, although it didn't seem to be having the same effect as it did before in the hotel bar.

'It's your time now,' he said to me. 'Really.'

I could see Helen out of the corner of my eye, grinning at him as though he were the husband of the century.

'I can send you in the direction of some very good courses to help you brush up on your interview skills . . .' said Helen.

I couldn't speak. I was aware my jaw was moving but no sound appeared to be coming out.

'But I'm afraid I have to go now,' said Helen, glancing at her watch and getting up. 'I'm due at an awards ceremony. It's been so lovely to meet you, Cathy. Really it has.'

I stood up and shook her hand in a daze. What the hell just happened?

'And, by the way, Mike,' she said, turning to him. 'I've spoken to the dean at Birmingham University and he says he'd be very happy to meet you and have a chat about their teacher-training programme so you can understand a little more about it. They have quite a high percentage of mature students, if that makes you feel any better.'

I watched as Mike said his goodbyes, as though Helen had just told us that we had the all-clear from a terrible disease and that we could finally move on with our lives. He didn't just shake her hand, he held it between both of his and looked straight into her eyes.

'Thank you so much for everything,' he said, beaming. 'Really, you've made all the difference, hasn't she, love?' he said, turning to me.

'Mmmm,' I grimaced.

'So, we'll get out of your way,' he added, 'and I'll see you the same time next week. Hopefully I will have had time to speak to the guy at Birmingham University by then. Bye, Helen. Thanks again.'

He'd thanked her twice now. I counted that as twice

more than he'd thanked me for all I'd done to improve his sodding life.

As we got to the bottom of the stairs he looked at his watch and gasped. 'Crikey, I had no idea it was that time. We'll have to run or we'll miss our reservation.'

And so I arrived at the swanky dockside restaurant with painful blisters, hair in disarray, sweaty armpits and a complete moron on my arm.

'Shall we order first and then we can talk about Helen?' he said when we were seated.

'Music to my ears,' I said with a grimace, before I hid my face behind the menu.

When the waitress arrived to take our drinks order, I made my first move to show my disapproval of the evening's events.

I ordered red wine.

We always had white because Mike preferred white, whereas I liked both because, well, it's wine. Occasionally I fancied a red but – because Mike preferred white – I always agreed that we would have white.

'But I was thinking of having fish?' he protested, after I'd made a land-grab for the wine list and hastily ordered a Malbec.

'So?' I said.

'White goes better with fish?'

'Says who?'

'Doesn't it?' he asked the entirely uninterested waitress. She blinked back at him and then glanced at me.

'Malbec,' I confirmed, and then closed the menu and handed it to her.

'What was that all about?' he asked when the waitress had gone.

'What?'

'Ordering red? We never have red.'

I swallowed. 'I thought for once that I'd like to make up my own mind.'

'What's that supposed to mean?'

'Like whether or not I wish to waste my time talking to *Helen*.'

'Please don't use the Barbie voice. I thought you'd be pleased. You said you wanted a life coach?'

'I did. But I said I *didn't* want Helen. *You* decided I wanted Helen.'

'But she's good.'

'*You* decided I wanted Helen.'

He blinked back at me. 'Maybe because I thought that if you didn't see Helen, you wouldn't get round to seeing anyone, and then where would we be?'

'We'd be having a lovely meal and lovely couple time and maybe even having sex later, that's where we would be, but that's not going to happen now.'

'But you went on the pill.'

'*Please*, for the love of God, forget I ever told you I went on the pill. Going on the pill has nothing, I repeat nothing, to do with sex.'

He was looking confused again.

'I wouldn't even be here if it wasn't for Helen, would I? You only invited me here to see her, didn't you?' I asked.

He had the decency to look away. 'When she said she could squeeze you in, I thought it was too good an opportunity to miss.'

'But I didn't want to see her. I'd told you that.'

'Do you think this might be the start of the menopause?'

'What might?'

'Forgetting you said you wanted a life coach. I've been

87

reading up on it. Apparently your memory can be quite badly affected.'

Was this how it was going to be now? All my alleged failings would be easily filed away under the letter M for menopause.

'I didn't forget anything,' I hissed. You forgot that I said I didn't want to see Helen. *Your* old age is to blame, not mine.'

'I'm not old and I'm not forgetful!'

'You forgot our anniversary.'

'What! When?'

'Four years ago.'

'Christ, you're right, there's nothing wrong with your memory. I apologized at the time but clearly you still haven't forgotten it,' he hissed.

'Would you like to try the wine?' the waitress asked me as she arrived back at the table.

'No,' I replied. 'Just pour it.'

We stared at each other over the table as the waitress took an agonizingly long time to pour a ridiculously small amount of wine.

'Look, I just thought seeing Helen would be a confidence boost for you,' said Mike when the waitress eventually walked away. 'Make you see you could be a real asset to a company. She's just trying to help, Cathy.'

'But she isn't, is she? She's telling us what is best for you and me without having a clue about who we are. I mean, look at her. She's practically half my age. What right does she have to be telling me what to do with my life?'

'I just thought you might need help,' said Mike.

'I'm perfectly capable of working it out for myself,' I said. 'I don't need a consultant to swerve me in a direction I might not want to go in,' I said. 'I'll find my own way, thank you very much.'

Mike stared at me for a moment and then nodded. 'I'll leave it with you then,' he said eventually.

'You do that,' I replied.

'Shall we talk about something else?' he asked.

'Totally,' I agreed. 'If we are to salvage this rare night away, then I suggest we perhaps discuss less risky subjects, such as Brexit, or whose parents we should spend Christmas with.'

He nodded and took a large gulp of his red wine.

The rest of the evening was pleasant. We did manage to bounce back in the way that long-term couples do if they are to survive the frequency of disagreement. Bland subjects such as last night's TV are a godsend in these situations. Safe and devoid of any reason to fall out. Deep discussions about *Location, Location, Location* have saved many a marriage.

28 February

Book group tonight. I asked Louise in the kitchen how long it took for her periods to stop when she went on the pill. She said it was so long ago that she couldn't remember, but it definitely took at least a few months. This was quite disappointing as I felt the need to be able to cross something off my list to ensure progress was being made, but until they had actually stopped, then I felt as if it would be cheating.

Tania did take me to one side and asked how I was getting on with my list. I gave her an update and she agreed that as I had put everything in motion that I could legitimately tick February off. Mission pretty much accomplished. She looked so proud it nearly broke my heart. She must think I'm such a fuckwit if she was impressed that I merely managed to phone a doctor and get on the pill.

I didn't talk about my period issues in front of the group, though, as the talk of the evening was the absence of Paula. Apparently she'd called Sonja and said she had been signed off sick with stress. She'd sat in a meeting and fallen asleep. Like actually fallen asleep. And she snores when she's asleep. Well, she snored at the last book group, and she did when I shared a room with her at our night away, visiting the Brontë Museum in Yorkshire. I say we visited the museum, but in fact we stopped for a pub lunch on the way up there and forgot the time, so we only got there forty minutes before closing. Still, we could say we'd been – or rather, we could tell other people we'd been – so we sounded like a really fancy book group.

Anyway, Paula got sent to HR who got her to fill out a questionnaire and the questionnaire said she has stress, apparently, which was news to her.

She told her MD that she thought it was just the menopause, at which point he sent her packing, apparently, as though she were contagious, ordering bed rest for two weeks. Sonja said she sounded remarkably cheerful about it. She'd not watched any of *The Crown* yet, so really it was good she'd got two weeks off. And she could really do with some extra sleep. She said she'd be much better after she'd had a rest. Totally back to normal. She said to Sonja she'd definitely be back next month to book group, but Sonja didn't look so sure.

March

Ditch Cooking

1 March

I've cooked at least 3,800 full dinners since Kirsty was born.

Three thousand eight hundred!

And that's a very, very conservative estimate. I can't even take any off for holidays because, to add insult to injury, we often go self-catering!

And I hate cooking. I used to try and get Mum to write me a sick note for domestic science, I was so desperate to get out of it.

At least 2,000 of those meals had been met with revulsion and occasionally straightforward rejection.

I reckoned I'd spent at least twenty-eight solid weeks doing something I hated, quite badly, that no one had appreciated.

If I'd wanted to spend that much time slaving over a hot stove, I would have gone to catering college, wouldn't I? Only I didn't have to. I just needed to get married and have kids and instantly the life of a chef was laid out before me.

'Hello, Pickering Catering College, can I help you?'

'Yes, I seem to have fallen somehow into the catering industry without any training whatsoever.'

93

'I see. Would you like me to send you a prospectus?'

'God, no. I hate cooking. I'd like you to send me one of your students. Preferably a second year. I don't want a complete novice.'

'I'm afraid we don't hire out students to teach people to cook.'

'Nooooo. I don't want them to teach me to cook, I want them to come and cook for me and my family. I'm done with the cooking. It's over. I will cook no more.'

'So you want to hire a private chef for your home?'

'Er nooo, not exactly. That sounds too Victoria Beckham and like they'd cook healthy stuff rather than food that people might actually enjoy eating. No, what I want is for someone to come to my house once a week and cook maybe four or five sets of meals and leave them in the fridge or freezer or whatever. So that I never have to face the disappointing-mash-potato faces of my children ever again.'

'Right, well, that is an unusual request. I'm not quite sure where to direct that one.'

'Unusual? What, you've never had anyone ring up before and ask if your students will cook for them? Have I got through to the right number? This is the Pickering Catering College, isn't it?'

'It is. It's just no one has ever asked for someone to just come and cook their family meals.'

'Well, I think you are missing a trick. There are a lot of women out there who hate cooking, and I'm assuming you have a lot of students who love cooking, are desperate for experience and, more importantly, desperate for cash. Match made in heaven, I'd say. Can't work out why no one has ever thought of it before. We are all idiots doing a chore we hate, day in day out. It's about time we solved it.'

'Well, I'll talk to Chef Watkins and see what he thinks.'

'Good, good. I'll call again next week and you can give me a list of students who might be interested. Goodbye.' I put the phone down, making a note in my diary so I didn't forget to call them back in a week, though I was absolutely sure I wouldn't.

5 March

Maybe the best dog walk of all time. Maybe this is the reason we had Barbra all along, so that I could go on this very dog walk. Today I was so happy we owned a dog that I could nearly forgive Freddie for all the dog shit I'd picked up since he first demanded a pooch nearly ten years ago.

To be honest, I had been semi-stalking Toby ever since he'd asked me for my card and mentioned that it was always handy to know a good accountant. I'd practically lived in the woods, hoping to bump into Toby, and for him to fall at my feet and offer me a wildly lucrative contract doing minimal hours that would show Helen and Mike where to stuff their CVs and interview techniques. But curiously he'd been elusive . . . until today. I saw him coming across the bridge and my heart leapt in a way it hadn't in a long time. Then he gave me the biggest smile when he caught sight of me.

'I was hoping I would see you,' he said as he approached.

Inexplicably my heart started to pound. Why was he hoping to see me, why, why, why, why?

'Did you once tell me you are an accountant by trade?'

My heart sank momentarily. He wanted me for my brain. No, this was good. I wanted him to want me for my brain. Of course I did.

'Yeeeees,' I said.

'Well, I've just had to fire my accountant, long story, but I remember you said that you do people's books for them and well, I wondered if you might consider doing mine.'

Oh my God! My fantasy might actually be coming true. I wracked my brain to try and remember what I'd told Toby about my employment status. Had I been honest and told him that all I did was a bit of book-keeping for a fish and chip shop, a taxi firm and an aspiring novelist, or had I told him the inflated version, which was that I was a much-in-demand master of all things financial with many very important clients?

'I mean, if you are too busy I'd understand. I know you have a lot of very important clients.'

'No . . . no,' I said, realizing I must have oversold my very part-time work at some point. 'I'm sure that I could fit you in.' I stifled a giggle. So childish.

'Only it's coming up to year end and—'

'No, no, honestly, I can look at my schedule and see what I can do.'

'Really?' he said, grasping my arms and giving me the most devastating smile. 'I cannot tell you what a life-saver you are. Honestly, I was awake all last night worrying about it. Look, here's my card,' he said, reaching into his wallet and pulling out a sleek translucent blue card with words so small I could barely read them.

'Toby Myers,' I read out, squinting down at it. 'Freelance Graphic Designer.' I knew it, just knew it. He did have a cool creative job.

'Yeah,' he said. 'I work in The Mustard Factory, did I tell you?'

'You did,' I said, nodding vigorously. 'I could come and

see you there if you like and you could tell me what you need doing.'

'Really, are you sure? That would be so great. I'll book the Connections Room and then we can get some privacy. I share an office with a web designer and a kombucha importer. It can be noisy but hey – we get free kombucha.'

I didn't dare ask what kombucha was. It could be a drug for all I knew.

'So you're definitely interested then?' Toby asked.

Was I interested? Hell, yeah. The chance to work at The Mustard Factory with its table-tennis tables and real coffee on tap and its . . . *beer mixers*! I could go to one of their *beer mixers*. Me, a 48-year-old mother of two, could be there on a Friday night having to apologize to Mike that I was home late because I was at a *beer mixer* meeting potential new clients. That was a world I wanted to live in. That was a world where I could escape the march to menopause. Maybe if this worked out it could even deflect Mike and Helen's evil plan to wrap me up in full-time corporate employment.

'Could be interested in that,' I said, trying to act casual.

'Sure,' he said. 'Do you have a card?'

He asked me that last time. Did he not remember anything he said to me?

'I haven't got any on me at the moment, I'm afraid,' I repeated. 'Why don't I email you some dates when I can come and see you?'

'Great – great. No problem at all. This is brilliant,' he added. 'You have no idea what life-saver you are.' He looked grateful, genuinely grateful.

I didn't tell him that actually he might have just saved my life.

When I opened the door to our prospective new chef this morning, Robbie was not what I had been expecting.

A 19-year-old boy who stood at over six foot with scruffy jeans, bad hair and a plethora of tattoos.

I invited him in and offered him tea as he cased our joint. It did cross my mind that perhaps I had been remiss in inviting a complete stranger into our home, but gave myself a good talking-to that I should not judge a book by its cover and that just because he had a dagger tattoo on his forearm he was not going to murder me.

I put his tea in front of him on the kitchen table and sat down, realizing I had in no way prepared for this conversation. I could hardly just ask if he was a good cook, could I? He could tell me anything. My mind scrambled back to my previous life when I had interviewed many prospective employees and I tried to remember what I used to ask them.

'So,' I said tentatively. 'Where do you get your love of cooking from? Is it your mum? Or your grandmother? Most chefs seem to have been influenced by family members. Sadly my two children haven't got a mother who inspires them about food.'

I was waffling now. I needed to let him speak.

He put his tea down and sighed. 'My mum died when I was thirteen. So I had to learn to cook so I could eat and that.'

Jesus – worst start to an interview ever.

'Right, I see. Well, I'm so sorry to hear that,' I said.

'It's not your fault,' he shrugged.

'No, no, of course. So I imagine you are good at making

something out of nothing. You know, if you had limited ingredients because your mother wasn't there.'

What was I saying? I needed to shut my insulting gob.

'Oh yeah,' he grinned. 'You should see what I can make out of a tin of beans and some custard powder.' He looked down and fiddled with his hands.

'Bean trifle?' I asked.

He looked up and grinned. 'Yeah, something like that.'

'Look, do you want me to tell you what I'm looking for?' I asked.

'You can't cook and you want me to come and do it for you?' he stated.

'Pretty much,' I nodded. 'I was thinking that you could give me a list of ingredients you needed in advance and then come in once a week and cook maybe four or five meals and put them in the fridge or freezer or whatever.'

'Yeah, piece of cake. I can come Mondays from three to five. We finish college early, then I start my shift at the Dog & Parrot at five thirty.'

'You work there too?'

'Yeah, five nights a week. Keeps my brother in jam butties.'

'You have a brother? How old is he?'

'Fifteen.'

'So you live with your dad?'

'No.'

'Right.'

'He kind of lost the plot when Mum died. I moved out as soon as I could and then, as soon as I was old enough, Tommo came to live with me.'

'Right.' I took a breath. What to say next?

I said the only thing I felt I could say. 'When can you start?'

'I know Robbie,' said Tania when I shared the news with her that I'd found a solution to my cunning plan to live the rest of my life cooking-free. 'He was in and out of foster care for a bit after his mum died. He didn't take to his new stepmum and she didn't take to him.'

'He never mentioned a stepmum or being in foster care.'

'Let's just say his dad chose the stepmum over him, so I imagine he's tried to forget her.'

'Well, he's on trial for a month, see if it works.'

'Sounds like an expensive solution,' said Tania.

I shook my head. 'I reckon if I add up what I spend at the supermarket, plus expensive convenience food from the corner shop as well as takeaways, then cut Freddie and Kirsty's food budget at school because they'll be eating better at night, I reckon it should come out even. And *anything* is better than my cooking.'

'Hope so,' muttered Tania, blowing on her tea.

'In any case, I've just found myself a new client,' I continued, 'so I'll be bringing some more money in. That would cover it, apart from the fact Mike still wants to retrain as a teacher. Did I tell you he's seeing a life coach? She's very "encouraging" of his new career plan.'

'Life coaches can be very helpful,' she said. 'An object-ive view can make all the difference.'

I wasn't impressed. Tania was supposed to be my friend. She was supposed to be on my side.

'But how can she give advice when she knows nothing about me or Mike's family or our situation? She's trying to get me to update my CV as well and apply to some big corporate slave-driving machine. I mean, I'm about to go through the menopause. You cannot inflict me on a corporate finance department run by an overpromoted graduate who hasn't got a clue. I might murder them after a night of hot sweats and lack of sleep because Mike thinks I want sex all the time just because I've gone on the pill! It's just not safe, I tell you. I will not be responsible for my actions.'

'You might find a larger corporation is much more clued up than a small company as to how to handle a diverse workforce.'

'Oh, I'll be part of the diversity crowd, will I? Has M been taken yet? Do you identify as LGBTQ at all, I'll be asked. No M actually. M for Menopausal. I wonder what special support I'll get? Cold flannels for the hot sweats and free porn to help with my crashing libido should I need it. Brilliant.'

'Are you menopausal yet then?' asked Tania.

'No,' I snapped.

'Maybe perimenopausal?' she ventured.

'What the hell is that? Some kind of drink made from the afterbirth of menopause?'

'No. It's just a condition leading up to the menopause.'

'And . . .?' I asked urgently. I'd never heard of this 'peri' thing.

'Well, the symptoms are pretty similar, you know: hot flushes, low sex drive, tiredness, mood swings . . .'

'So what is the difference then?'

She sighed before she explained, maybe a little tired of my overreaction.

'You are said to be experiencing perimenopause in the lead-up to menopause. Menopause officially begins when your ovaries stop releasing eggs,' Tania explained.

How come Tania knew everything?

'But the symptoms are exactly the same?' I asked.

'Pretty much.'

I didn't get it. Or rather, I didn't want to get it. I wanted to shove my hands over my ears and shut it all out. It just sounded as if I could have the symptoms of the menopause without being menopausal. None of it made any sense.

'So you've already ticked off number two on your list,' Tania said, probably trying to distract me. 'You are in danger of getting quite good at this. Actually achieving something.'

'Shhhh,' I said. 'Don't jinx it. I've got some biggies coming up. Real biggies. And if Mike carries on thinking like he is then I'm not sure anything on my list is going to get me out of that particular hole. And then I'm doomed.'

12 March

I asked Freddie what I should wear to my meeting with Toby to ensure I didn't show myself up in the uber-cool confines of The Mustard Factory.

'A bag over your head,' replied Freddie.

I asked Kirsty if she would do my make-up, hoping that being in the same room might offer me the opportunity for some casual questioning of the state of play with 'Culty Carl'. She told me she was sorry but she didn't have the time as she left the house to go to school without a scrap of make-up on. I mentally pushed Kirsty's love life up my to-do list. She was already in choppy waters, I could tell. No make-up? This was either to impress the suspicious cult follower or he'd already spurned her and she'd given up and gone into a state of total depression. Either way I really needed to put some more thought into how to get her through this treacherous phase.

I arrived at The Mustard Factory in my usual toned-down Eighties make-up and carrying a bag full of nerves. Why? I had no idea. I had more experience in my little finger than half the people in this building. I was a grown woman, I had given birth twice, and I could see an end to my periods. I had no need to feel nervous whatsoever of a man over fifteen years younger than me who – just because he was really good-looking and did a cool job and worked in a cool place – had no right to make me feel anxious.

I didn't dare sit down in the reception space because the seats were too low and I feared I might have to ask him to pull me out when he came down to collect me. There was exposed brick, obviously, someone with tattoos and a lot of piercings making coffee, obviously, and architectural and design magazines with no hint of celebrity trash, obviously. There was a collection of vintage toys in the corner to play with. Roller-skates with four wheels, a pogo stick, a Chopper bike, and a space hopper. '*Oh, how quaint these old toys are,*' I could hear the hipsters saying as they passed through reception. What would be left of your generational toys, I thought. Nokia 610s and a bunch of NanoPods. At least we had real toys.

And there were dogs! Dogs wandering in on leads and gulping from designer water bowls at the end of the reception desk. Clearly they were the young workers' must-have accessory. BlackBerries were no more. Welcome to the pooch. If I'd have known, I'd have brought Barbra.

It would have been nice to have someone closer to my age to talk to. However, she would probably have barfed up the cow muck she ate this morning all over Toby's designer shoes, which perhaps wouldn't have been a good start.

He bounced down the stairs having kept me waiting ten minutes, full of apologies about a difficult client on the phone.

'I'm not good at telling them that the changes they are asking for at the eleventh hour will take me six hours to complete and so I will have to charge them more. I'm too soft and just let it slip by.'

'Well, my first advice as your accountant is to knock that on the head straight away,' I said, raising my eyebrows at him. 'You're not a registered charity, are you?'

'No,' he said. 'Close, if I don't start chasing some invoices up and getting some money in.'

'Right,' I said, my chest swelling. I knew how to play this game. 'You'd better show me exactly how much shit you are in.'

It took two hours for him to take me through the mess he'd let himself get into. I told him it was pointless us sitting in the 'Connections Room'; he might as well show me the worst and sit me where he kept all his paperwork. So we retired to his desk and he brought me a chipped mug of tea while he took me through his nonexistent system and tried to find where on earth all his invoices and receipts were.

'So is that it?' I said when I thought he'd finished.

He looked at me and thought for a minute. He fluttered his eyelashes. 'I'm just a boy, looking for a girl to organize his life,' he whimpered.

104

Jesus Christ, I thought. What was that? Was he so used to using his looks that he had totally forgotten who his audience was, or did he see me as some desperate house-wife willing to do anything for a few flattering words?

I took a deep breath and presented him with how I could help.

'You don't just need an accountant, you need a finan-cial and office manager. Now, I can do these things for you, and then perhaps you will still be in business by this time next year. So I propose that I do fifteen hours a week leading up to year-end to get the groundwork in, and then we will review.'

He threw his arms around me and thanked me profusely. 'I knew you were the right person for the job,' he said in my ear. 'That day you leant me wet wipes because I'd got dog shit on my hands, I knew that you were going to be my work mother. This is going to be great.'

Work mother! Work mother! What the hell was a work mother?

'I have tell you, though,' he said as I tried to work out how I felt about this label, and also the spontaneous hugging, 'that – as you can see – I'm not quite running at a profit yet, so I can only afford to pay you a minimal rate. However, as soon as you sort me out and get me out of the red then I'll be more than happy to make up for it.'

All I could think about was what Mike would say when I told him I'd taken a job working for a hipster start-up. '*What the hell have you done that for? All crea-tive ideas and absolutely no idea about how to make any money.*' Which would be a fair description.

I looked around. I wanted this. I wanted to be here. I

105

liked it here. So it might not pay the mortgage, but it would be more fun to be here than at some money-churning corporate entity.

Before I left he introduced me to Jimmy, a web designer with whom he shared an office, who looked really impressed when I said I was a real living, breathing accountant and asked if he could have a chat after he'd paid off his debts. And Veronique (a very nice South African girl) offered me some kombucha to try. Turned out not to be a drug but some kind of fermented tea.

'It tastes like I imagine a compost heap to taste,' I told her.

'I know that,' she laughed. 'But the coffee shops of Shoreditch think it tastes like heaven! I love this country.'

Toby and I shook hands at the door. He was really grateful. I just hoped it worked out long enough for me to make it to a beer mixer.

16 March

There was silence at the dinner table and I knew it had all been worthwhile.

By now there would usually be a bottom lip thrust out somewhere and the sad, sad scrape of cutlery pushing inedible food around a plate. Instead there was a beautiful silence as they all tucked into an absolutely delicious turkey lasagne. Kirsty was currently off red meat but had decided she could not survive without poultry. Freddie's threats to turn vegan had so far not materialized.

I wondered who would crack first. Of course it was Freddie.

'There is no way on this planet you have made *that*

plate of food. Where are the packets, Mum?' he asked. 'You been putting ready-meals into your own dishes again.'

'I did that *once* when you had a playdate,' I said. 'I was trying to show I was a good mum.'

'It was out of date and you gave us both food poisoning.'

I sighed.

'That's one of the best lasagnes I have ever tasted,' said Mike, licking his lips. 'What type of cheese is on the top? It's not Cheddar, is it?'

'No idea,' I said. 'Robbie made it.'

'Who's Robbie?' asked Mike, looking up.

'Robbie,' I said, 'is a student from the catering college who has agreed to come and cook us some meals once a week so you don't have to eat my appalling food any more.'

'Is that why the fridge is all tidy?' asked Kirsty. 'I took a picture of it and put it on my Instagram page. It looks so . . . so wholesome.'

I nodded. The first thing Robbie had done when he'd arrived on Monday at 3 p.m. sharp was ban me from the kitchen. He had then organized the fridge properly so it looked like one of those fridges on MTV Cribs. I was not sure I had ever been so happy.

'He tidied our fridge?' said Mike in astonishment.

I nodded. 'And he can cook, and he washed up after himself and Barbra Streisand absolutely loves him. He spent a good half-hour stroking her. She honestly thought it was Christmas.'

'But she loves me more,' stated Mike.

'I doubt it,' I gasped. 'When was the last time you looked at her, never mind gave her any attention? Robbie said next time he comes he'll bring her some treats.'

'Barbra is not that easily bribed,' pointed out Mike. 'She knows who she can rely on. You never said you were going to get someone in to cook,' he added. 'When did you decide all this?'

'Probably around the time you decided you needed a life coach to help you work out how to improve your wellbeing. I think you'll agree Robbie has already had a much bigger impact on the happiness of this family than Helen has.'

'We so need to keep this dude coming,' said Freddie, helping himself to more lasagne. 'Whoever he is. What I'd do for a man who cooks like this.'

'Me too,' said Kirsty.

'Me too,' I added.

Mike opened his mouth to say something but clearly thought better of it. I wondered how much he was paying Helen for her services, knowing it would be way more than what I'd agreed to pay Robbie. I was confident that Robbie was going to prove to be a lot more valuable to my sanity.

19 March

I knew I shouldn't have ignored it but I refused to be a slave to my phone. It was not a pager, I told myself, when it was fizzing and buzzing on the side while I was trying to pretend I was not watching reruns of *First Dates*. I was the master, not it. I would not go running the minute it started calling me. My phone would wait for me and not the other way round.

Massive mistake today.

Huge error.

Sometimes a conversation takes on a will of its own without you to guide it, without you adding the words of wisdom necessary to keep a chat on course that would ensure it delivered your objectives and yours alone. I'd had this happen to me before when an ignored WhatsApp thread had led to the other members reaching the conclusion without me that we would *drive* to a Christmas party. I mean, what kind of crazy-assed decision was that?

The escalation of this particular chat had massive ramifications. Like huge. Like enormous. This unwatched pot had boiled over in a way that led me to think that I should never ever leave my phone unattended ever again.

MUM'S KNEE

Lizzy: I have good news and good news. Mum went to the doctor's last week and has been referred to the hospital. She called this morning to say she's got an appointment for next week.

Nicola: Wow, Lizzy. Well done. What on earth did you say to her?

Lizzy: Well, that's the other bit of good news. I rang up and invited them to come over for a visit in the summer but said that she had to get her knee fixed first or else they may not let her fly.

Nicola: Wow, she swallowed that? I mean they would let her fly, wouldn't they?

Lizzy: Probably, but I thought a little incentive might work. Really good news, eh Cathy?

There was an hour's gap in the conversation here where my input could have made all the difference; however unfortunately I was busy ignoring my phone because someone else was bullying me via text to try and get me to volunteer to run a coffee morning for the PTA.

Lizzy: Can I tell you what the other good news is?

Nicola: Oh yes – do spill. Have you bought Dad an MG? Oh, how I wish I'd married a pilot. How is Patrick, by the way? You are a lucky cow, Lizzy. Still, if I marry this doctor . . .

Lizzy: Patrick is fine and no, we haven't bought Dad an MG. Mum said she and Dad were too old to fly here on their own so I said not to worry, everyone can come!! Patrick can get flights for everyone. It's about time we all got together. And it's Mum's 75th birthday so we can have a party here. You will come, won't you? I was thinking maybe ten days in August. Not sure Mum will get her knee done if you can't get her here?

Nicola: WTF! Are you serious? All of us. Even the kids?

Lizzy: Yes of course. Now Patrick's boss of all the pilots he gets loads of flights so should be all good.

Nicola: Wow, Lizzy, that's amazing. If I'm still with Laurence can he come?

Lizzy: I guess so. It's still going well, is it?

110

Nicola: Totally. Going like a dream. Oh my God I am so excited. The kids are going to explode when I tell them. You were right. Utterly brilliant news.

No, it was *not* brilliant news. My mouth slowly started to run dry as I scrolled down the chat. I could feel my heart starting to pound. What had I done? How had I let this happen? This was an extremely generous offer and I should be so grateful but the negatives were popping up in my mind at an alarming rate. Taking my mum and dad on a long-haul plane trip . . . torture. Mother could not complain quietly. Last time I had been on a plane with her she had asked the stewardess if she could move seats because the man beside her had bad breath. While the man was sitting beside her! Ten days of having my sister's gloriously wonderful lifestyle shoved down my throat. Ten days of kale ice cream! Ten days of Nicola and the doctor giggling and shagging at every possible moment while I tried to explain to her kids why Mummy had disappeared upstairs with 'Uncle Laurence' to look for his passport again. The scenarios flipped through my brain like rapid fire as I tried to summon up how on earth I could get out of it.

Me: Brilliant news about Mum's knee, Lizzy. You are a star. Perhaps we should wait until she has a date for her operation before we make any concrete plans? She might be stuck on a waiting list for a while and then she'll need to recover which could take us past when the kids need to go back to school.

Lizzy: Sorry – forgot to mention that we've paid for her to go private. She should be in by the end of the month and then will have three months' recovery so will be up and running marathons before August.

Damn it!

Me: How brilliant. That's so kind of you and Patrick.

Lizzy: Well, it's no good sitting in the bank, is it! So you will come then, won't you? Now we know Mum's knee is going to get sorted?

Fuck! How could I say no when I'd asked her to help and she had? How mean would I sound!

Me: I'll have to talk to Mike and the kids but all being well, yes. That would be fantastic. Something to really look forward to. Got to go now. Speak soon. X

Lizzy: By the way, Mum needs a lift to the hospital next week. Can either of you take her?

Nicola: Sorry, I'm at work.

I saw a plethora of hospital appointments swimming before my eyes.

Me: Yes of course. I'll go.

Book group is at my house this evening. The ladies were somewhat confused as there were fresh Pringles, a brand-new tube and . . . a homemade dip. Robbie had whipped one up out of leftovers, just like that. I'd just happened to mention I had friends coming round and he said he'd been trying to work out what to do with some spare tomatoes he'd not used. I sat and stared at the coffee table for a good ten minutes before everyone arrived. It looked so lovely with the dip in a pretty bowl Robbie had found at the back of the cupboard, full of glistening chopped-up tomatoes and onion and some kind of herb and some other things that made it delicious. It made me happy to look at it. Dips are such a happy food. Everyone dived in and there were appreciative oohs and aahs. I told everyone that Robbie, my new kitchen assistant, had made it. Fiona thought 'a Robbie' must be some kind of newfangled appliance that she hadn't heard of and immediately asked where she could buy one. I told her that 'a Robbie' was unique and special and there was no way she was getting her hands on him but she might like to try phoning Pickering Catering College to see if they could help her like they had helped me.

They all looked a bit shocked at my radical plan for feeding my family decent food rather than ash and vomit-inducing congealed messes, but when I talked them through my logic, they got it. Admired it, even.

Then Louise piped up, saying that it was exactly what a man would do in the same situation. If he couldn't cook, he'd find a way round it. But then, as Tania said, no one would assume a man could cook anyway. Being able to cook would be a bonus in a man but was somehow mandatory in a woman.

We all agreed while we made the most of Robbie's dip. Unfortunately Paula was still not back with us. Sonja reported that she had been to visit her. Well, she had tried to, but Paula's husband wouldn't let her in. We all agreed that was very strange while we pumped Sonja for details on what Paula's husband was like. Somehow we'd never met him as he worked shifts or something so was never around when it was book group at her house. She said he was good-looking but surly. I admitted that I was never really sure what surly meant and after much debate we decided that Russell Crowe was perhaps the best example of this trait. Sonja concurred that his manner was similar to Russell Crowe in his latter years but certainly not reflective of his heart-wrenching and brave performance in *Gladiator*. She also confirmed that Paula's husband's physique was more fat Russell Crowe than Gladiator Crowe. The general consensus at the end of the meeting, after several bottles of prosecco, was that – based on Sonja's brief experience – we didn't like or trust Paula's husband. I agreed that I would go with Sonja the next time she went to visit and we would demand to be let in to see how she really was. The rest of the group would be available on the phone as back-up should we need them.

Unfortunately there was no time to discuss the book so we agreed that we'd try again next month.

April

Get a Life Outside the Family – Preferably with 'Young' People

1 April

Well, it had to be April Fool's Day. My desire to spend more time with young people had come true already, but what I hadn't been expecting or wanting was to be holed up on a Friday night with an 11-year-old and an 8-year-old.

Somehow I had been dragged in to babysit for Nicola's two kids. Apparently Mum already had plans. She was going to the bingo with her friend Sheila. Of course Dad couldn't be trusted with minors. He'd probably end up feeding them beer and thinking it was okay to watch *Killing Eve*. They'd have a wonderful time but could possibly be scarred for life. So Nicola had called me and begged.

'It's a big deal or I wouldn't ask, Cathy, honestly. Laurence has invited me to go to a quiz night at his golf club. This is a big step for us.'

'But you hate quizzes,' I said to her.

'I know, but I don't think you understand what this means, Cathy. I'll be meeting his friends. That's major in today's dating world. Like virtually proposal level.'

I sighed. I didn't want to spend my Friday night with children who ran riot until well after their bedtime and

117

then would demand I read them a story. What a major step back that would be. I still had nightmares about the agony of the bedtime story, a child-free lounge and a glass of wine so near and yet so far. They should make teenagers read bedtime stories to young kids. Best contraceptive ever. However, I did want to see my sister happy. Of course I did. And I would also get to meet the McDreamy lookalike which was an opportunity too good to miss if only to lord it over Lizzy.

My sister had pulled out all the stops when I arrived. She looked beautiful. Of course she did. After all, she was the pretty one. Effortlessly slim (whereas being slim for me took every ounce of willpower I had for at least six months), with a classically pretty face and long dark hair, she should have been the type of woman who could attract anyone she wanted. Sadly she only seemed to attract the good-looking tossers. Or perhaps all attractive men were tossers, whereas the rest were at least grateful.

'How do I look?' she asked, looking uncharacteristically nervous.

I wanted to tell her she was trying too hard. I wanted to tell her that it looked as if she was perhaps wearing what she thought Laurence would want her to wear and not what *she* wanted to wear.

She was wearing a cardigan! I'd last seen my sister wear a cardigan as part of her school uniform. It was a lovely cerise colour, but nonetheless . . . My sister normally dressed downwind of her 42 years, in plunging necklines and short skirts, which she totally got away with as she was so pretty. What had Laurence done to her? Or maybe I'd just forgotten the laws of attraction, as I'd been married for so long. When you dress to suit other people rather than yourself.

The minute I opened the door to Laurence, I realized why she was wearing the cardigan. He was old! Very good-looking but nonetheless . . . old. Older than me! Maybe mid-fifties, I reckoned. He smiled a crinkly smile and stepped forward to embrace my sister and kiss her on the lips. I looked away. He turned and shook my hand with both hands like an elder statesman then produced a massive bar of chocolate for the kids.

Great, I thought. Kids hyped up to the eyeballs on sugar on a Friday night.

'I'll have that, shall I,' I said, taking it off him before the kids could see it. 'It's lovely to meet you at last, Laurence. Heard so much about you.'

'Oh, really?' he said. 'All good, I hope.'

'Of course,' said Nicola, reaching for her coat off the peg in the hall. 'Although I haven't told her the really good bits.' She giggled.

I thought I might throw up.

'So, off to the golf club quiz then,' I said, trying to make conversation.

'Yes. Meeting my good friends Richard and Sarah and Charles and Linda. We usually win, actually. Sarah has a near-photographic memory and Charles studied history at Cambridge.'

I glanced over at Nicola. She'd gone a bit pale. My sister's idea normally of a good night out was two-for-one at Angeline's Cocktail Bar on Friar Gate. Not scratching her head over who succeeded Edward III to the throne.

'Well, have fun,' I said as they left. Nicola looked back and raised her eyebrows. I actually felt sorry for her.

I didn't get the chance to ask her how it went when they rolled back in at 11 p.m., surprisingly tipsy for a golf club quiz night. What I did learn was that apparently they had come second. (I wondered if Laurence's ex-wife was their art expert and Nicola hadn't filled that gap.) I sat awkwardly on the couch as he settled himself in, clearly waiting for me to depart so they could have a good neck on the sofa or perhaps more . . .

I drove home in a daze. I wasn't sure that Nicola was right, that he was the one. My assessment was that Laurence couldn't believe his luck post his divorce that a beautiful 42-year-old was willing to be his plaything. Because my suspicion was that a plaything was what my sister was. Someone to be paraded at the golf club in a nudge-nudge, wink-wink fashion that would be entertaining for a while but at some point the novelty would wear off. I suspected that what Laurence really wanted ultimately was someone who could also help him win the golf club quiz. Not my amazing, bubbly, fun-loving but kind of crazy little sister.

I hoped I was wrong. I really hoped I was wrong.

I went home and sneaked into bed behind Mike who was snoring at full throttle. Put my arms around him and kissed his shoulder. Life wasn't always easy with Mike, but it was a damn sight better than being out there in the dating wilderness.

3 April

I was due for an important meeting with Toby at The Mustard Factory, but when I looked in the mirror as I was about to leave, all I could see was 'work mum'. We needed to go through his accounts and I had some tough things to say, so I needed to look the part. I needed confidence clothes! I had meant to go shopping but somehow I hadn't had the time so I was left with only one course of action. I dashed upstairs to Freddie and Kirsty's rooms to see if they had anything I could pair with my supermarket jeans.

One step into Kirsty's bedroom and I realized my error. The pile of man-made fabrics littering the floor told me I had about as much chance of finding something suitable as finding the French-book in there that she hadn't seen since the start of the year.

I tiptoed into Freddie's room – quite why, I have no idea, as there was not a soul in the house – and tried to avoid looking at anything that might offend me.

Too late. I glanced into a corner and thought a dead, shrivelled-up Dolly Parton was sitting there. On closer inspection I realized it was just a mask of her face on which Freddie had drawn wrinkles and then attached over the head of his large childhood teddy bear. The image was unsettling, to say the least. Really, what *was* I going to do about Freddie?

I found the dress that Mike had given me for Christmas in the bottom of the wardrobe. It had probably lain there since Freddie wore it at New Year's Eve. But I knew it still wouldn't fit and so decided to leave it where it was.

This was hopeless. I was destined to walk into the coolest building in the town and sit in front of Toby in a beige cardigan and elasticated trousers while he called me his 'work mum'. I actually felt like crying.

But then I caught something out of the corner of my eye. Something black with a splash of yellow. Something I recognized. Something that would definitely fit, and might just ramp me up the cool chart in a Mustard Factory kind of way.

*

Toby's eyes did actually light up when he saw me as I waited for him in reception. Like really lit up. Maybe even lit up on stalks level.

'Like the T-shirt,' he said.

'Thanks,' I replied.

'So were you in some way involved in the industry?' he then asked, looking puzzled.

'What! The sex industry?' I said, horrified, looking down at the 'SUPPORT SEX WORKERS' slogan emblazoned across my chest. When I'd looked in the mirror at home I had been slightly concerned that putting that message across an ample pair of mature bosoms sent out quite a different message to when it was draped across my son's front. I was worried that the words, SUPPORT SEX WORKERS, could be misconstrued, by their very positioning, and that people might assume I was in desperate need of a new bra. I dismissed this thought, though, deciding that surely the inhabitants of the Mustard Factory would get that this was a fashion thing and not a cry for help.

'No! I just – well – thought it was a cool T-shirt,' I said feebly.

Toby gave me that very confused look that I seemed to be getting a lot recently. Whenever I tried to do something a bit nonstandard. As though I'm no longer allowed to go off-piste. As if it was now my job to conform. Was conformity the only option to those in middle age? Was that why so many middle-aged women disappeared into the background? Just faded away. Was a woman in her middle years not allowed to stand out?

I realized I should have brought my beige cardigan; then at least I could have covered up my plea for new underwear. I followed Toby dejectedly up the stairs as I prepared to inhabit the role of 'work mum'.

Since I'd last seen Toby and taken a load of his paperwork home with me, I'd worked out that he was, as I had suspected, a total fuck-up when it came to running a business. Okay, so he was great at drawing pretty pictures. Very good, in fact. I'd found myself spending far too long gazing at his website in awe of his talent; however, when it came to running a business, he hadn't a clue.

'Do you want the good news or the bad news?' I asked him in the Connections Room. While he was out making me a coffee, I'd tried to fold the T-shirt in such a way that you could only see the word 'SUPPORT', but I figured this looked even worse, especially I was wearing one of my oldest bras and so I was looking more unsupported than usual. I tried again so the words 'SEX WORKERS' were the only ones visible, but I could only position the phrase directly over my two breasts, which looked as appalling as you can imagine. I contemplated tucking a discarded napkin in my collar to hide the slogan altogether, but I figured that was quite an odd look to brazen out at a meeting between an accountant and a client.

'Good news, of course,' said Toby, grinning.

'You are owed a total of four thousand nine hundred and forty-two pounds.'

'Brilliant!' exclaimed Toby. 'Wow, you are amazing. I had no idea.'

'The bad news is that, because you haven't got any of your clients to sign contracts, then it could be quite diffi cult to recoup these payments.'

Toby shook his head. 'They're all kind of people I know. You know, mates really. I didn't think I needed contracts.'

I thumped my fist on the table in what I hoped was an Alan Sugar-type fashion.

'Mates, schmates,' I said. 'This is business, not the pub. You need proper contracts and business terms and penalties for not paying.'

Toby's eyes flared wide. 'You're scaring me now,' he said.

'I mean, take this,' I said, holding up a printout. 'The brewing company you did all the logo design for six months ago. Do you realize they have not paid you a bean? Not a bean.'

'Oh, that's Will's company. He's on the next floor up. We were mates but then I think he's been avoiding me, to be honest. I did see him on the stairs a couple of weeks ago and reminded him and he said he'd totally forgotten but he'd do it by the end of the week.'

'And he hasn't, has he?'

'No,' Toby replied. 'No, he hasn't.'

'He's upstairs, you say. Which room?'

'Straight opposite the lift. They've recently taken more space so I guess it must be going well.'

'Right, let's go and see him then,' I said, getting up.

'What, now?'

'Yeah, now.'

'But . . . but . . .'

'But nothing. He owes you money. So let's go and get it.'

I had of course forgotten I was wearing a potentially offensive T-shirt until we arrived in the reception of Binkie's Brewery. That's how successful they were. They had a receptionist-cum-secretary-cum-possibly an intern, whereas Toby had two chipped mugs and a desk tidy.

The receptionist's eyes were on stalks staring at my chest, as I demanded to see Will Plainer.

'Is he expecting you?' he asked.

'He should be, yes,' I announced. 'We are here to collect some overdue payments.'

The receptionist scuttled off and soon arrived back with a bemused-looking Will, who didn't even look at my face but just went straight for the chest.

'Hi, Will,' said Toby. 'So sorry to disturb you but . . . er . . .'

'Hello,' I said, sticking my hand out to shake Will's hand. 'I'm Toby's accountant and we have just been going through outstanding payments and we see that you owe him two thousand, three hundred pounds from last November and we wanted to see if you would like to settle that debt now before we add late payment penalty clauses. Toby insisted on giving you the option, seeing as you are a mate and everything, which is very generous, don't you think?'

'Oh,' said Will, glancing from Toby to me. 'I er . . . well yes, of course. I'll get Steve onto it today. It must have slipped his mind or something.'

'For six months? He's in today, is he?' I asked. 'Only I will have to add late payment penalty costs after today.'

'Er, yes, I think he is,' replied Will.

'Great. Let's go find him now, shall we? I have a copy of the bill here so I can put it in his hands and make sure he doesn't forget again.'

'You forgot to pay Toby's bill,' Will said to Steve when we found him. 'Can we get it paid today?'

'But you said—' began Steve.

'This is Toby and his accountant,' Will interrupted, as

my T-shirt distracted Steve. 'They have agreed to waive any late payment costs if we pay it today.'

Steve was looking at me through those wide eyes I was getting used to. I decided to press my advantage. 'Why don't you do it now?' I suggested. 'Just in case you forget again.'

Steve looked to Will who nodded his head. And we waited while Steve tapped some keys on his computer. 'All done,' he replied, shooting daggers at Will.

'Wow,' said Toby when we got back to the Connections Room. 'You were amazing.'

'I know,' I admitted.

To be honest I was pretty proud of myself. It wasn't like me to be so confrontational. But something had come over me when presented with the situation. I felt different. I'm not quite sure what it was but I think it was something to do with – 'I will not be put down by the bullshitter.' I'd experienced plenty of people like Will in my life. Who thought they could tread on everyone else in order to get what they wanted. I didn't care for them. More importantly, I didn't care what this man thought of me, which was my usual default. All my behaviour typically stems from needing to be liked by anyone and everyone. But I realized the minute I clapped eyes on Will that I had no care for his feelings about me whatsoever.

'I think it was the T-shirt,' I told Toby. 'It blindsided him, confused him. He didn't know how to handle me, so while he was working me out it left the door wide open to get your money.'

'So did you wear the T-shirt on purpose then?' he asked me. 'Is it your debt-collecting T-shirt?'

'It is now,' I grinned.

'Whatever can I do to thank you?' he said, looking into my eyes.

I felt a bolt. A serious bolt. I guess I just wasn't used to a younger, extremely good-looking man looking at me like that. It was bound to mess with me. He looked *'grateful'* again. Like *extremely grateful*. I couldn't remember the last time someone had looked at me in that way. My kids certainly didn't. They viewed me with disdain, or exasperation and often utter contempt. As for Mike. Not sure he ever looked at me. Like *really* looked at me. I was like a comfy sofa in the corner of the room. He knew I was there and that I provided a service, but to be honest, never really took much notice.

But here was Toby gazing into my eyes, looking totally and utterly grateful and asking me what he could do to thank me. I had no idea what to do in this situation. It was confusing, to say the least. I could feel the wheels of attraction slowly clunking themselves into action having remained unused for many years. No, no, I didn't need this. This was a business relationship, end of. I didn't want to feel attracted to anyone apart from my husband. It was just a shame that my husband didn't look at me . . . gratefully.

7 April

I had been trying to work out how to tell Mike about my extra work at The Mustard Factory. I know, I know; I should have told him before now, but it somehow felt like a big deal. It wouldn't be what he was expecting when I'd said I wanted to look for my own work rather than have Helen telling me what I should be doing. Working for Toby at The Mustard Factory wasn't something that required a CV or training in interview techniques. And it certainly wasn't going to fill the gaping hole that Mike was intending to create if and when he left his consultancy role, but somehow it was filling a gaping hole in me and that was what mattered. It was what I needed. I'd somehow found a life outside of the family. Complete with 'young people'. But I was not sure Mike would get it.

So I decided to just drop it into conversation one night on the phone. As though it wasn't a big deal, see if that worked.

'So I've got some extra work coming in,' I told him after we'd been through the normal chitchat about kids and bills and family invitations.

'Great,' he replied. 'That's really great, Cathy. What kind of work?'

'It's for a graphic designer called Toby. He's based at The Mustard Factory.'

There was a moment's silence. I knew exactly what was coming.

'So a hipster start-up then,' he said. 'All creative ideas and no idea of how to actually make any money.'

My God, we had been married way too long.

'It's a fair summary,' I admitted. 'But I'm going to help him. Get him into the black.'

'He's in the red?'

'Yes. But not for long. I'd say his prospects are good that he will be turning a profit in a couple of months. We just need to get a few debts collected in.'

'You're debt collecting?'

'Yeah.'

'You are so much better than that, Cathy. What are you doing?'

I thought about how much I'd enjoyed the satisfaction of getting Toby's money from slimy Will.

'Actually really enjoying myself.'

He went quiet for a minute again. I knew what was coming . . . again.

'How many hours are you doing?'

'Fifteen a week until the end of the month, then we will review.'

'What rate?'

'Minimum wage just until he's in the black.'

'Minimum wage!' said Mike. 'Why the hell are you doing a skilled job for minimum wage?'

Because it was fun. Because I felt as if I was achieving something. Because I was meeting people I would never ever have crossed paths with normally and having conversations I would never usually have. I was having conversations not based around kids or schools or after-school activities or exams or work experience or university applications. A few days ago I'd gone into work and tackled a brewery owner about his debt.

And I'd won.

How fucking cool was *that*?

And I knew that meant I wasn't earning all that much, but what I was realizing was that it was more important to me to do something I enjoyed rather than to earn the maximum amount of money that I could. Much the same as Mike was thinking. Well, I think he was thinking. I suspected that it wasn't that he wasn't enjoying his job, he'd just stopped enjoying the lifestyle, and somehow Helen had wormed into his head that the only answer to that was to do something dramatic. I couldn't really believe he wanted to be a teacher. Not in reality. He probably liked the idea of being a teacher but, seriously, Mike was not a teacher.

'Like I said,' I said to Mike, 'we'll review when we get into the black, and besides, there could be other opportunities in The Mustard Factory. I'd no idea how many businesses there were in there.'

'All making a loss, no doubt,' mumbled Mike.

'Let me give it a chance, Mike. It could lead to a lot more, really it could. I just need a bit of time.'

'All right,' he said with a sigh. 'We've got time. I wouldn't be starting teacher training until January probably, anyway, so plenty of time to get ourselves organized . . . and for this Toby bloke to go out of business.'

He wouldn't be going out of business I thought. Not if my T-shirt had anything to do with it.

10 April

I'd taken to wearing the SUPPORT SEX WORKERS T-shirt to The Mustard Factory every time I went to see Toby. Word of my reputation had spread like wildfire. Apparently the intern on reception at Binkie's Brewery had told everyone at the Floor Four table-tennis tournament on Friday night about the scary woman with the sex T-shirt coming to collect debts from his employer. Now, whenever I was in the building, there seemed to be a steady stream of curious onlookers wanting to meet me and shake my hand and ask me if I would perhaps consider doing some consultancy for them, otherwise known as 'chase their debts'. I told them that was possible, of course, if they were prepared to pay for my services. So I kept wearing the T-shirt to remind them all of my debt-collecting talents.

However, I did sometimes forget what was written

across my chest, which could lead to some awkward encounters, such as today. I arrived home to find Freddie sitting waiting for me on the kitchen table, swinging his legs, with a massive grin on his face. Robbie was also there doing his weekly conjuring.

'Kirsty has a man in her room,' Freddie announced.

'What!' I shrieked. 'What sort of man?'

'Carl, of course.'

'Culty Carl?'

'Yes, Culty Carl.'

'The one who pretends to not believe in sex before marriage just so girls want to have sex with him, before marriage?'

'The very same. Although to be perfectly honest with you, he *might* believe in not having sex before marriage. I'm just assuming that it's all a con. I mean, it's just such a ridiculous idea it has to be a con, right?'

'I don't know,' I shrieked. 'I'm relying on you for this information. Does he believe in no sex before marriage or not?'

'He says he does but—'

'He's a seventeen-year-old boy,' Robbie interrupted, turning round from the hob.

'My thoughts exactly,' agreed Freddie. 'And Robbie doesn't like him, do you.'

'Don't you?' I asked.

He shrugged. 'I offered to make him a cup of tea. Just being polite, you know. He ignored me. Like I wasn't even here.'

'Robbie says he's a little shit,' added Freddie. 'He's nailed him and he's only met him for five minutes.'

He shrugged again. 'I've known a lot of Carls,' he said, then turned back to stir something on the hob.

Honestly, the more time Robbie spent here, the better it got.

I looked up at the ceiling, as though I'd be able to see what they were doing. 'What do I do?' I asked Freddie.

'You need to hook him out of there, of course.'

'Do you think?'

'He's a seventeen-year-old boy who might believe in sex before marriage.'

And he was up there alone with my daughter.

I dashed upstairs, hotly pursued by Freddie. On the landing I paused, listening.

'Are you listening to see if they are having sex?' whispered Freddie.

'Not helping,' I hissed back.

A high-pitched giggle from Kirsty came from the other side of the door.

My heart was pounding. What should I do? I was tempted to burst in and grab this boy by the scruff of the neck and drag him out on to the street and kick seven bells out of him, but what if it was just totally innocent? What if she had brought him home to play cards or something? What if I burst in and embarrassed her and she never forgave me and actually I'd ruined the relationship she was about to start with the only boy in the school who didn't believe in sex before marriage. Jesus, this was a dilemma. I needed back-up.

I ran back downstairs, still hotly pursued by Freddie, who clearly loved the drama that his sister had brought to the house.

'What are you doing?' he gasped, back in the kitchen.

'Ringing your father,' I said, grabbing my mobile out of my bag.

I called. He didn't pick up but responded with a text saying:

In a meeting, will call you in half an hour.

I typed back – *It's an emergency!*

'What's wrong?' he gasped, twenty seconds later.

'Kirsty is in her bedroom with a seventeen-year-old boy who may or may not believe in sex before marriage. What do I do?'

'For Christ's sake get him out of there.'

'Do you think?'

'Yes. Of course. Why did you let her take him into her bedroom in the first place?'

'I wasn't here. I was with Toby.'

'Who's Toby?'

'The guy I'm working for at The Mustard Factory. I told you about him.'

'Did you?'

'Yes, I did.'

'Okay. Well, anyway. Just go up there and tell him to leave.'

'But what if they aren't doing anything?'

'I don't care. She's fifteen, Cathy. Just get him out.'

I told Freddie to go into his room while I performed the deed. I didn't need an audience for this particular parenting nightmare. But of course he refused. He stood on the landing grinning while I tentatively knocked on the door.

'Can I come in, darling?' I asked. Freddie put his fingers in his mouth, gesturing how sickly I was, then he pretended to load a shotgun and shoot it in the air.

I knocked louder and said, 'I'm coming in.'

I took a deep breath and braced myself. They were lying on her bed . . . eating chocolate Magnums.

I was appalled.

'For goodness' sake, Kirsty, how many times have I told you not to eat ice cream in bed. It gets everywhere.'

'Muuuuuum,' she cried, leaping up and going bright red.

The boy stumbled his way off my daughter's bed and stood up. He was staring at my chest. Actually staring at my chest. Jesus – who was this guy?

Shit, I'd forgotten I was wearing the SUPPORT SEX WORKERS.

'Muuuum,' cried Kirsty again, also staring mortified at my chest.

'I'm, er Carl,' said the boy, now thankfully looking at my face.

'I know exactly who you are,' I replied in a totally unnecessarily accusatory tone.

'Muuum,' came the cry from Kirsty for the third time.

'Well, er, I can see everything is in order in here,' I said, backing out of the room quickly. 'Just wanted to say hello. That's all. I'll – er – leave you to it, shall I? Yes. Bye. Okay then, bye.'

I pulled the door shut behind me.

Freddie shook his head and mouthed WTF at me.

About half an hour later I heard the front door open and shut and then Kirsty walked into the kitchen.

'I have never been so mortified,' she said. 'Why on earth did you do that?'

'Your dad told me to,' I said.

'He's not even here.'

'He rang and told me I should get the boy out of your room.'

'How did he know there was a boy in my room?'

134

'Because I rang to tell him.'

'You did what!'

'We're just worried about you. We didn't want anything to happen to you and I'm not sure it's appropriate for you to have an older boy in your room.'

'Why not?'

'You know why not.'

She stared at me, breathing heavily.

'We're just friends,' she said.

Really, I thought. I really needed to sit her down and make her watch *When Harry Met Sally*. Friends? A 17-year-old boy wants to be *friends* with my 15-year-old daughter. Friends!

'Is that what he's told you?' I asked. 'That he just wants to be friends?'

'We agreed,' she replied. 'Just friends, so you've nothing to worry about, okay? Are you happy now?' She stared at me, tears brewing in her eyes.

Oh my God, could this be any more complicated? He just wanted to be friends, supposedly, but that was unlikely since he was a boy and so would be thinking about sex . . . maybe, but maybe not, as it was possible that he didn't believe in sex before marriage so maybe he genuinely just wanted to be friends; however my daughter was in love so didn't want to be just friends, she wanted to be a whole lot more. She wanted to be his girlfriend. She wanted his friendship and his love and his affection and his kisses, but I was hoping to God she wasn't interested in the sex part because, quite frankly, why would you be interested in that bit at her age? Who in their right minds would want to have sex with a teenage boy? They were rubbish at it. And she was only *15*!

None of this was making any sense. She wanted Carl

to be her boyfriend or the idea of what she thought was a boyfriend in her head and he wanted . . . well, we didn't know, really. But for now they were just friends which inevitably would make Kirsty miserable because she didn't want a friend, she wanted a boyfriend.

So what advice should you give to a girl in this situation?

'Fuck him,' said Freddie.

'Freddie!' I shouted.

'No, no, I meant you know, stuff him, not literally fuck him. I didn't mean that. I meant I don't trust him. Pulling the old "let's just be friends" trick? Well, he's messing with you, in my opinion. Steer clear.'

'Well said,' I nodded. Sometimes my son was a genius.

'You just don't want me to be happy,' Kirsty shouted at both of us before she stormed out of the room.

'He's bad news,' said Robbie, carrying a dirty frying pan over to the sink. 'You need to watch out for him. Hey, dude – you going to wash this pan up for me?' he said to Freddie.

'Sure,' said Freddie, rolling his sleeves up and heading for the sink.

Unbelievable!

15 April

OMG (am I too old to use that phrase?)! I had been invited to the beer mixer! I didn't think I had ever been invited to anything so exciting in my life. And Toby had just invited me casually, as if it was no big deal. He'd just said, 'You free on the last Friday of the month? You really should come to the beer mixer if you are.' And then he'd walked off. He hadn't even waited for me to answer. Lucky, really, as I was doing little squealy up-and-down jumps.

Of course, ten minutes later I was in a pit of despair. What the hell was I going to wear? I suspected that I had only been invited due to my notoriety while wearing the SUPPORT SEX WORKERS T-shirt, but I could hardly wear that again. That was my work uniform. And yet I needed something that lived up to my newfound edgy debt-collector reputation. I knew I had nothing. Like absolutely nothing. I could put it off no longer. I was going to have to think very hard about my appearance, which, to be honest, I don't think I had done since Kirsty was born.

In my twenties I had a fabulous work wardrobe, because hey – you might just be meeting the man of your dreams in the workplace so it was worth making the effort, right? I was even still trying when I was pregnant with Freddie. I was all Mamas and Papas and flowing apparel with strategic accessories and make-up. I mean, I still wore make-up, for goodness' sake! I wanted to be that glowing pregnant lady who still tried to be present-able for her husband and for all those who might judge if she so much as let a bra strap slip or – heaven forbid – a 'flat shoe' appear on the end of her swollen ankles. Then, for some reason, even after Freddie was born, I carried on the back-breaking façade by throwing myself into the 'yummy mummy' look of brightly coloured cardigans over plain white Ts and knee-length skirts – and still make-up! I mean, really?

I didn't do too badly at keeping this up. I mean, I was in a very competitive NCT group, which helped. The sort of group who sent each other pictures of what they'd managed to make out of butternut squash that week and smug-looking shots of the whole family out on autumnal walks, looking as though they had stepped out of a fucking catalogue.

I was the first to get pregnant again. Freddie was only eleven months old. Despite me claiming it was all planned, the NCT group dumped me for failing to meet with their high standards of organization and so my maintenance went into decline. I no longer had anyone to impress. I had my man, he was stuck with me now, what with one toddler and a child on the way. I could have let myself go completely, looking like something out of the *Star Wars* Cantina, and still he would have been vilified for leaving the wreckage of me with two kids. I wasn't going out to work so there was no reason to be tidy, or even clean on a daily basis any more. And I had fallen in with a group of mums away from my NCT group who thankfully seemed to share my view on self-grooming. What was the point when someone was going to poo or vomit on you at any point?

I did smarten myself up a bit, I guess, for the school gates. Nothing major. I was at least clean. Mostly. Though my coffee moustache would often be pointed out by the harshest of my critics.

And in recent times, well, I would go from one extreme to the other. Mostly homeless hobo but a rare night out would have me putting on the glitz in a major fashion, as if that would make up for my scruffiness the rest of the time.

Looking at my wardrobe, trying to find something for the beer mixer, I realized it was a desperate situation. I needed new clothes, or else at some point someone would give me a sandwich and a hot drink if I loitered outside of Subway for too long.

And it was not because of the whole Toby thing, either. I mean, him calling me his 'work mother' hadn't niggled at me in the slightest. I'd not found myself looking in the mirror at my elasticated-waist trousers, V-necked sweater and Skechers trainers thinking, why on earth would anyone call me their 'work mother'?

So on my way home I found myself in a shop that was aimed at women at least two decades younger than me and wondering why the shop assistants weren't asking me if I needed any assistance. I mean, was I invisible or something? Of course I was. I was a woman over forty. I was probably a stereotype on one of their head office customer insight boards, labelled 'Older Lady – do not approach. Will only ask you why you don't stock any items over a size twelve and will then buy a size twelve plain T-shirt and return it a week later because well . . . she worked out she's not as young as she thought she was.'

I wandered round, bewildered. The shop appeared to only stock scraps of material not capable of covering up one of my boobs, never mind both of them. I eventually found a tea dress in a nostalgic pattern that I thought, if I ran at it, might just fit. The lady at the changing rooms gave me a token and looked at me suspiciously, as if I was asking to enter a strip club, not the women's changing room of a well-known fashion chain.

I just about managed to get the garment over my head and squeezed it past my chest. The tan and orange print made me look as if I should be about to have a sepia photograph taken, not attending a super-cool beer mixer with an average age under 30. When I turned around I noticed it was backless. I mean, backless! Who could get away with not wearing a bra? I just did not understand.

If I didn't wear a bra it would look as if I'd left two odd-shaped balloons up my front since Christmas three years ago.

I then tried to get the dress back over my head. I was still trying ten minutes later. I was red in the face and out of breath and had nearly dislocated my shoulder. I contemplated shouting for the snotty assistant, but I couldn't bear her condescension, her pity, and the look in her eye that would tell me that I'd be the talk of the staff room the next day. 'The old lady who got stuck in the tea dress. Yes, the one that Jessy from *Love Island* wore to the opening of a new app. I mean, what was she thinking? She had such saggy tits it was disgusting.'

I gave one last tug and I heard the sound that no one wants to hear in a store fitting room. A loud rip. Right up the side of a zip that I had failed to find because it was so crappily made. My heart started to beat very fast. I threw it on the floor and put my clothes on, still panting. I was in a fog. Nothing like this had happened to me before. What on earth should I do?

I took the only possible course of action.

I poked my head out of the fitting room, saw that the assistant had left her post . . . and ran. I ran until I was safely in a coffee shop on the lower floor. Then it dawned on me that they probably had CCTV. My quest for cheap tarty clothing had led me to be a criminal on the run for damage to property.

I could no longer be seen in an indoor shopping centre. I needed to escape. I half expected security guards to swoop at any minute. I made a run for the lift, paid a fortune in parking for just thirty-five minutes and took myself to an out-of-town shopping centre with free parking and bland middle-aged clothes for bland middle-aged people. After a fruitless twenty minutes trying to find a garment that made me look more late thirties rather than late forties, I gave up and went to the pet superstore, had a cuddle with a rabbit and bought Barbra Streisand a plastic rat to destroy.

18 April

It was early. My period was early! Really! What was going on with these stupid pills? I had a good mind to take them back to the doctor's and demand a refund. There should have been some indication that the end was nigh by now, shouldn't there? Some little scrap of hope that soon I would be sailing past the feminine hygiene aisle with a spring in my step and a reason to be thankful for my age.

I was so devastated that I resorted to my usual self-medication at this time of the month, which seemed to help negate the slight nausea in the belly and the down-ward mood swing.

Large bars of Cadbury's Dairy Milk.

I reckoned I had got through at least two of these for every period I'd ever had. So that must be at least 378 chocolate bars. I reckoned periods were to chocolate sales what Christmas was to toy sales. Maybe Cadbury were the ones stopping the message getting out there that there was a pill that could stop your periods. Perhaps the pill was on their yearly strategy document when they identified opportunities and threats. Major threat being that women might discover they didn't have to have periods and therefore the sales of chocolate would plummet.

It was a fair assumption that if I hadn't had those 189

periods I wouldn't have eaten 378 chocolate bars and therefore I wouldn't have constantly been at least a stone overweight.

That made me sad. Really sad, as I broke off my second strip of the good stuff. I felt genuine grief for all the clothes I could have worn if it hadn't been for my 189 periods and 378 chocolate bars.

I would have loved, for once in my life, to have worn a strapless dress – just once. But what with the back fat and boob fat it was never an option.

And sleeveless. Sleeveless would have been totally my thing, had it not been for the dimpling of skin of the upper arm and the two huge pink marshmallows standing guard to my body whenever I put my arms by my sides.

Suddenly I realized exactly what I wanted to wear to the beer mixer. Having failed on my shopping trip to find any clothes that were the perfect mix of cool and sexy, while also being age appropriate, I suddenly realized I had the perfect outfit sitting in my wardrobe upstairs. The only outfit I had ever owned and worn that made me feel like a million dollars.

I dashed upstairs and there it was.

My dream outfit.

Once in my life I'd been successful in losing weight. A man had been involved. It was a revenge diet, which works particularly well as diets go, I find. I was invited to a wedding in my late twenties, to which my horrible snake of an ex was also invited. I had months to make sure when he saw me that he would regret the way he had two-timed me. Nightly excursions to the gym resulted in my dream outfit being purchased, of a Chinese-style dress with high splits up the sides, opaque tights and knee-high boots.

Even if I do say so myself, I looked great. The best I had, possibly ever.

The hideous ex was suitably impressed, I could tell. I enjoyed his sideways glances across the church aisle at my fabulous attire. I even allowed him to walk me home at the end of the night and kiss me at my hotel room door. He was sorry he'd let this sultry woman go and he said so. He said he couldn't believe he'd gone off with the slapper he worked with and it had been the biggest regret of his life. He said this as though I'd already agreed we were back on.

The next day he made it clear he would like to attempt a rekindling, now I had 'refreshed my look'. I calmly declined. Mission accomplished. I made him want me and this time I got to reject him. It felt really good. So, so good.

I still had that dress and every year I tried to diet in the hope that I would be able to wear it for Mike's work Christmas party, because genuinely it was the best I had ever felt in an outfit. But every year the diet failed because of the periods and the chocolate bars and the lack of motivation to wreak revenge on my nasty ex-boyfriend.

I took it off the hanger and tried it on, and of course it didn't fit. I hung it back up and looked at it longingly. It represented success, achievement, power – so many things.

But then it struck me that perhaps mostly it represented that rarely do you attract the right kind of guy in a tight dress with thigh-high splits and knee-high boots. Those are the guys you turn away.

I took the dress off the hangar again and added it to the pile of stuff in the spare room waiting to go to the charity shop.

'I'll be home late on Friday night because I'm going to the beer mixer,' I told Mike when he called from Liverpool.

I didn't think I had said anything quite so brilliant in a very long time.

'What's that?' he asked me.

'Remember I told you,' I said, exasperated. 'Toby invited me. They have one every month in The Mustard Factory for everyone who works there. It's a chance for everyone to mingle and share ideas and stuff.'

'But you don't like beer?'

'You don't have to drink beer. I'm sure there will be other drinks.'

'So you can go even if you're not an actual tenant?' he asked.

'I'm Toby's plus one. All the tenants can take a key supplier if they want. It's great for networking.'

'Mmmm,' said Mike, clearly distracted by whatever he was watching on television in his hotel room while he ate room service.

'Did you get an email from Helen? She's dug out a list of recruitment consultancies for you that specialize in accountancy.'

'I've been too busy doing Toby's books,' I told him quickly. Mike was still dismissing my work at The Mustard Factory as a little hobby until I found a real job. Unfortunately I wasn't getting paid enough to categorize it as anything else as yet, and so the threat of a return to full-time corporate life was still very much present.

I could hear him munching crisps as he conjured up his next move.

'Is it okay if I invite Phil and Olivia round on Friday night? Phil's got a new company car. All electric, and he wants to come and show it to me.'

'I just told you that I'm out on Friday at the beer mixer.'

'Oh, right yeah. What about Saturday then?'

'We agreed we were not going to have anyone round at the moment, don't you remember?'

'No. Why on earth did we agree that?'

'Because we are on exam lockdown! Remember your daughter is revising for her GCSEs and your son has exams too. We discussed it and agreed that having your mates round for boozy late nights was not conducive to revision conditions.'

'Right, yeah okay,' said Mike. 'Of course. I forgot. I might go out for a beer with Phil on Friday then. If that's okay? Or why don't we all go out for a meal? We could book Angelo's? Don't they have a two-for-one on Fridays?'

'I'm going to the beer mixer on Friday.'

'Oh yes, right. This Friday?'

'Yes, this Friday.'

'Do you get paid to go?'

'No.'

'Right. So can't you go next Friday, then we could all go to Angelo's?'

'No! They only do them once a month and Toby invited me and I said I'm going so you can do what the hell you like on Friday. I won't be here. I will be at the beer mixer!'

There was silence at the end of the phone.

'Has Robbie been this week? Will there be any food in the house?' he asked.

'Yes,' I said.

'Turkey lasagne?'

145

'I'll make sure I leave you some of Robbie's turkey lasagne,' I told him.

'Well, that's all right then. See you Friday.'

25 April

So the beer mixer was interesting!

I was kind of nervous so I asked Toby to meet me outside.

He whistled as I approached. In desperation to find new attire I'd resorted to watching daytime TV and their couch-potato-friendly fashion segments. This particular dress was modelled by a dinner lady from Bradford who was at least two sizes bigger than me and looked amazing. The super-skinny and young presenter said it was 'flattering for all body types and was very age-appropriate', as if she'd know what that meant if it hit her in the face. But still I ordered the dress from some obscure mail-order company and I was now desperately trying to work out how to unsubscribe from their hourly email messages.

'Well hello, Mrs Collins,' said Toby as he kissed me on both cheeks. 'Or should I say Mrs Robinson?'

I giggled. Of course I giggled.

Toby was an absolute gent. For a while he didn't leave my side. He introduced me to countless more people who worked in the building. Admittedly he introduced me as the lady who collected his debts in the SUPPORT SEX WORKERS T-shirt, but still it was a hell of an ice breaker and soon I found that I had given out countless business cards and shaken countless hands and had heard countless people tell me that Toby couldn't stop raving about me and how much I had done to help him turn his business around.

I was glowing. From the wave of compliments and the beer because, despite the fact I'd assumed there would be a choice of drinks (who just serves beer at a beer mixer?), there was only beer, oh and kombucha, and quite frankly I'd rather drink my own urine than that hideous concoction.

I did, of course, have to be careful about what I said and I did come close to screwing it up a number of times. I was talking to a group who worked for an architect's practice and in my wisdom I quoted the line, 'If you build it, he will come.' Everyone looked at me blankly. 'You know, from *Field of Dreams*?' I said. 'Kevin Costner?'

Still blank looks.

'Kevin builds a baseball diamond in a cornfield and dead people come and play on it.'

Still more blank looks.

'When was that released?' one of them asked me.

'I don't know,' I replied. 'Maybe early Nineties?'

'Oh, right. No wonder. I was born in 1992.'

Jesus, talk about an aggressive answer. So showy.

'It's a classic,' I said. 'You really should watch it.'

'Yeah, I love a sports movie with dead people in it,' he replied, in what I think was an unkind manner.

I also happened to mention to an intern who was doing work experience with a search optimization company that when I'd first started working, web pages hadn't existed; in fact, I hadn't even had my own computer on my desk. I had to book time in a room to use one.

'Yeah, whatever,' she said. 'My dad told me about that. He also said that you all used to finish at five p.m. and go home *and* you'd have a proper lunch hour. And apparently, in the olden days, if you did work experience you actually got paid. Not like doing an internships now which is just a glorified term for forced labour.'

I steered clear of her for the rest of the night.

Every so often I caught sight of Toby across the room and he'd look over and give me a quick thumbs-up to see if I was all right. I'd nod and grin then carry on my conversation.

Boy, was I giddy by the end of the night.

I was out, out.

I was having adult conversation.

I was with young people who mostly were interested in my opinion when I wasn't screwing it up by referencing popular culture from pre the millennium! This was exactly what I'd wanted. A life outside of the family with 'young' people. Nailed it!

Then suddenly it was nine o'clock and the packed reception area had all but dwindled to a handful of people. Toby came over and said the stragglers were going to the Swan but he was starving so did I fancy a cheeky curry?

Oh my God. I wasn't sure if I could do it. I couldn't sit and look at him over a candlelit table. I couldn't go out for a meal with another man. What would people say? Look at that. Look at the mum taking her son out for a meal. Perhaps he's a student here? I couldn't share a poppadum with someone other than my husband, could I? Sharing poppadums at my age was practically the same as having an affair. In fact, preferable to having an affair. What would you rather? A curry or sex? Now there was a tricky one. No, it was far too intimate. I couldn't do it.

'Come on, my shout,' he said.

'Go on then,' I giggled. Jesus, I had to stop this incessant giggling.

'Where did you go last night' Mike asked me the next morning at the breakfast table.

'The beer mixer. I told you at least a dozen times,' I replied.

'Oh yeah. With Tony?'

'Toby! We went for a curry after.'

'Who did?'

'Me and Toby.'

'Right. Which one?'

'The Raj.'

'Oh. That would have cost you.'

'He paid.'

'Right.' He looked thoughtful and then he said, 'That's fine. You know I go out for meals with female colleagues all the time, so that's fine. It's fine.'

I nodded and got up and went back to bed.

But it wasn't really fine.

I'd had a really great time.

He'd looked me in the eye and asked me questions. Questions about my life, and then he'd listened as though he was actually interested. I could bring out my A-game stories because he'd never heard them before, like the one about the time when I was a student and we took a cardboard cut-out of Mariah Carey out on a pub crawl and she had a fine old time until she got pissed and ended up in the canal. And then of course there was the epic story of when a bunch of us drove to Italy in our twenties and we went to Venice but missed the train home so we sat drinking vodka in St Mark's Square with all the musicians until four in the morning. And of course I had to share the tales of the epic party house in Coventry where I had my first graduate job and how we had an *It's a Knockout* party with real Custard pies and gallons of water and costumes and everything.

'It was just like the real *It's a Knockout*,' I told him.

'What was *It's a Knockout*?' he asked. 'I don't remember that show.'

When would I learn *not* to reference popular culture from over thirty years ago, I told myself for the hundredth time?

He listened to these stories as though he was genuinely interested. Not like Mike, who rolled his eyes whenever I mentioned my youth and could practically roll out the punch line to each anecdote as if he had been there himself.

It made me a little bit sad.

I realized my funny stories were all from before I was married and had kids. My life – my activities – no longer seemed to have the potential to evolve into funny anecdotes to entertain and amuse my acquaintances. These days my conversations, I reckoned, were 60 per cent logistics. Who is doing what, where, when and how. Thirty per cent kids. Seven per cent what I watched on telly last night and 3 per cent stuff personal to me, possibly, if something had actually happened to me that week. How did my life become consumed by everything else apart from me?

But then Toby started laughing.

I asked him why he was laughing.

He said he'd just had an image flash through his mind of me squaring up to Will Plainer in a SUPPORT SEX WORKERS T-shirt.

So I started laughing. Really laughing. Until we were both crying. Crying with laughter.

And I realized we were talking about a funny story about me. About *recent* me. Not student me, not independent traveller me, not pre-family me.

Just me. Me now, and my SUPPORT SEX WORKERS debt-collecting T-shirt.

'You are a damn good debt collector,' he said.

'I know,' I replied. 'It's my hidden talent.'

28 April

Book group tonight. I'd actually read the book so I was somewhat excited to go. In a show of hands, however, it transpired that only two of us had. Sonja had assumed that much of the evening would be taken up with me and her updating everyone on our visit to see Paula a couple of days ago. Fiona and Louise had assumed that we would be discussing last month's book as we hadn't talked about it at the last group, and so reading the new book would be unnecessary. So that left just me and Tania to confirm that this month's book was really very good and everyone should read it, so we decided not to discuss it until everyone else had read it to avoid any spoilers.

This then, of course, meant we could spend the rest of the night discussing mine and Sonja's visit to see Paula, which everyone was very keen to hear about. I confirmed that Paula's husband, Richard, reminded me of a fat Russell Crowe and initially refused us entry. However, Sonja and I had anticipated this and our strategy was that Sonja would make a cake and take it in a tin and we would persuade him to let us in saying we needed her tin back.

Everyone agreed that was a genius move.

151

We then went on to explain that while Richard was in the kitchen extracting the cake from said tin, we'd gained entry to the lounge and found Paula on the sofa under the blanket. We confirmed that she was indeed still alive and would welcome any TV recommendations as she had finished *The Crown* and had been giving *Game of Thrones* a good stab but couldn't get into it. We sat and chatted to her for about half an hour until she announced she was really very tired. She looked exhausted, to be honest, even though she hadn't been doing anything. When she spoke she often got distracted halfway through a sentence, as if she didn't have the concentration span to make to the end of a thought. Eventually, after Sonja and I had exchanged increasingly concerned looks, Sonja suggested that she should perhaps be going to see her GP, just for chat and a check-up. I enthusiastically agreed, saying I would take her, drive her, book her the appointment, whatever she needed, just to get her in front of a professional.

'You did the right thing,' said Tania, nodding at us both. 'She does sound like she needs professional help. Did she say she would go?'

'She said she'd think about it,' Sonja told everyone.

There was a heavy silence.

'Then Sonja popped out to see if she could locate Richard and her tin. See if she could have a word with him,' I explained. 'I didn't know what to do so I went over to her to give her a hug and sat and held her hand. She didn't say anything, just held my hand really tight.'

'I found Richard,' said Sonja. 'He was eating beans out of a tin in the kitchen. I told him he had to help her. I made him promise to try and get his wife checked out.'

'Do you think he will?' Tania asked.

'I think so,' she replied.

'Is there anything we can do?' asked Fiona. 'Should we all go and visit now?'

'Why don't we see what happens after she's been to the GP?' said Tania. 'I'm afraid it does sound like possible depression.'

No one said anything for a moment.

'If only they could put your head in a scanner and see what was wrong,' said Louise. 'You know, something like a mammogram.'

'Oh, I've just had a letter asking me to go for one of those,' I said. 'Must be my age, is it?'

'Hazel's just been,' said Tania. 'That's her second though, I think. It's probably every five years from your late forties. I've had at least two.'

'Do they really crush your boobs between two iron slabs?' I asked.

'Pretty much,' replied Tania. 'Small price to pay though. You must go. It's really good that they can detect cancer through these tests. As Louise says, it's a shame you can't do the same with mental illness.'

A very weird thought entered my head and I really didn't know why I'd said it, but we were in quite a deep mood and it just sort of fell out of my mouth before I could stop it.

'What would you rather,' I said. 'Depression or cancer?'

Everyone went quiet and sipped more prosecco. No one had expected to head down this conversational route. Perhaps we should have discussed the book.

'Obviously both are terrible,' I hastened to add. 'Wouldn't wish either on anyone.'

'Depends on whether the cancer is going to kill you,' said Fiona, squinting her eyes in concentration. 'If I knew I was going to survive, I think I'd rather have cancer.'

153

'I think I agree,' said Louise. 'You know what you're fighting with cancer. Whereas depression, well, fighting anything that's in your head, that's the hardest thing we ever have to face.'

'Shall we talk about something different,' I offered.

'Absolutely,' said Sonja, nodding vigorously. 'Please tell us about work, Louise. Has anyone shagged in any toilets recently?'

May

Secure My Son's Future –
i.e. Put a Rocket Up His Arse

2 May

I can't really believe it myself but at midnight I was outside some kind of drinking establishment, feeling very bleary-eyed. If only I had been drunk.

Well, I assumed it was a drinking establishment. It was one of those places that apparently felt the need to pretend it was not a bar. Instead it looked like a shop that sold boilers when, in actual fact, hidden behind the scruffy door at the back of the counter was a den of iniquity akin to a proper bar.

That was cool, apparently, these days. To pretend a bar was something other than a bar.

I mean why do that? Why hide a bar? Why was that cool? Why was it hilarious to tell your mates that you'd meet them outside the scruffy shop that sold boilers? Did this generation really think that our generation would be fooled by this? That just because the entrance looked nothing like my teenage haunt, The Paradise Club, with its neon Eighties palm trees, that there would be no way I'd trespass into this conclave of youth, for fear I might actually end up in the back room of a boiler shop.

This was, of course, my fear, as I sat outside waiting for Freddie to come out of a party at 12.15 a.m., furious that he had kept me waiting for fifteen minutes but too scared to walk into the apparently empty boiler shop and make a complete ass of myself when the police arrived to arrest me for breaking and entering.

I decided to leave it five more minutes, but I knew if I didn't do something soon I would fall asleep and then I'd have a policeman knocking on my window and arresting me for loitering outside a bar with young people in. I decided to call Lizzy as it would be afternoon with her and we were due a catch-up.

'Hiya,' she said after a couple of rings. 'What are you doing up at this time?'

'I'm sitting outside a bar – well, I think it's a bar, waiting to pick Freddie up. It's dark and it's raining and I wish I was in bed. What are you up to?'

'I'm about to meet a girlfriend for a power walk along the sea front.'

I sighed and watched the rain drip down the pitch-black windscreen.

'Is everything all right?' she asked.

'Oh yeah, great,' I replied. 'Just fine, just wondering how we could be living in such parallel universes.'

'Well, it rained on Sunday, if that helps. First time in three weeks. I've been meaning to ring you actually, and ask if Mum is all set for the op next week,' she said.

'God, she's so excited,' I told her. 'It's like she's going on holiday, not going to have her knee fixed. She's telling absolutely everyone about how she's going private at your insistence.'

'I'm just pleased she's getting it done.'

'Yeah, I know. It really is very generous of you, Lizzy. Thank you.'

'Don't thank me. You were the one who made us all

take notice. I would have had no idea if you hadn't said anything. You know what Mum's like.'

'Yeah, stubborn,' I said. 'Listen, have you heard from Nicola recently?'

'She's sent me a few texts about the hot doc.'

'I met him,' I told her.

'Really! Why didn't you say. And?'

'Well,' I sighed. 'He's hot but in an old kind of way.'

'Old? How old?'

'I don't know. Mid- to late fifties maybe.'

'That's not that old.'

'I know but it is for Nicola . . . and she went to a quiz at the golf club with him . . . in a cardigan.'

'He was wearing a cardigan?'

'No, she was.'

'Wow! That doesn't sound like Nicola.'

'Exactly. I didn't get a good feeling about him, Lizzy. I got the impression that he was out for a bit of fun, to be honest. I just hope I've read it wrong.'

'Christ, I hope so, Cathy. She sounds pretty convinced when she texts that he's practically going to propose any minute, which seems ludicrously quick, but I was praying it might just be one of those "love at first sight" things. That she was going to live happily ever after.'

'I think she's so desperate to live happily ever after that just a live one will do. I daren't say anything to her because she'll just say what she always says.'

'It's all right for you, you're married,' Lizzy and I both chimed together, then laughed.

'Exactly,' I replied. 'If only she knew,' I added.

'If only,' said Lizzy. 'Look, I have to go or I'll be late for my power walk.'

'Have fun,' I said.

159

'Hope Freddie appears soon,' she replied.

I hung up and watched a couple of people I recognized from Freddie's year leave the boiler shop. I checked my watch and called Freddie for the fifth time. Still no answer.

I had no choice. I had to do that thing Freddie made me promise I would never do. It was his own fault: he'd kept me waiting for twenty minutes after midnight.

I was going to have to go in and turf him out.

I went into the boiler shop and then through the scruffy door behind the counter that I'd seen Freddie's schoolmates come through. I expected to be immmediately embroiled in music and noise and the stale smell of alcohol, perhaps mingled with teenage vomit. But no. I was indeed in a back room. An empty back room with no visible means of exit apart from the door I had just come through. My heart started to pound in fear, though why I had no idea. This made no sense – he had to be in there somewhere. I'd seen people come out. I went back in and squinted round the poorly lit room. This was ridiculous. I didn't want to be in an episode of *The Crystal Maze*, I just wanted to pick up my son from a bar.

I started tapping walls. Actually tapping walls. Like I was some Russian spy, not just some angry mother looking for her son in the middle of the night.

I was too old for all this cloak-and-dagger business. Give me an enormous neon sign any day that said ALCOHOL SERVED TO PEOPLE WITH FAKE IDS in large letters that I didn't need my reading glasses to read. This was stupid.

For some reason I suddenly thought there might be a tunnel. Maybe that was how you got into a bar these days. I looked for signs of a trap door, but could see

160

nothing in the gloom, so I peered under shelves desperately looking for signs of life. There was a sink in the corner with a mirror over it. Maybe it was a two-way mirror so everyone could see the idiot who had no idea how to get into the cool bar that was pretending not to be a bar. Or worse, there was a camera in there filming me scrabbling around in this dingy room and I was being beamed on to a big screen and currently everyone at the party was laughing at me hysterically. I looked up into the corners of the ceiling, as though I was in some weird *Big Brother* scenario. I thought I could see a camera, right above the mirror over the sink. I started to wave and shout 'Where's Freddie?', hoping someone would come to my aid. But nothing – clearly no one was watching.

I spotted a chink of light underneath the sink. Just a small strip. I lay down on the floor to try and squint through this chink to see what was behind it.

It was as I was lying full-length on the ground that I suddenly became aware that the sink was moving. Yes moving. Moving towards me at rapid speed, as though I was in some awful nightmare.

'What are you doing on the floor, Mrs Collins?' someone said.

I scrambled up to see that the sink and mirror hid a false door behind which resided the music and the noise and the alcohol and the sick stench.

'Lost an earring,' I said, squinting at a girl I remember Freddie bringing home in Year Ten. 'Do you know where Freddie is?'

'He was, er . . . dancing, I think,' she said, stifling a giggle.

'Right, I'll go get him.' Then I said the unforgivable: 'Is your mother coming to get you? Do you need a lift home?'

161

'Er no,' she said, looping her arm into her male companion's. 'We're good, thanks.'

They walked off laughing.

I battled through sweaty teenage bodies with my eyes half-closed, desperate not to see anything I shouldn't. I just wanted to go home and go to sleep, despite the fact I'd already had two hours' sleep on the sofa between the hours of nine and eleven.

He'd been drinking, of course he had. I expected that. He'd proudly shown me his fake ID before he left. Everyone has one, apparently. 'Although *you* don't need one, of course,' he added. 'I mean that face!' he laughed. I noticed he was wearing eyeliner for the first time in a half-Goth, half-drag fashion. It looked pretty good, actually. I let out a depressed sigh that my 17-year-old son already showed more competence than me regarding the wonders of Maybelline.

He stared at me as if he had seen a ghost as I waded towards him through the crowds. This would teach him, I thought. He would never be late again when I picked him up.

He squealed in exaggerated horror. Pointing not at my face but at my feet, covering his eyes like the heroine of a silent film.

'Slippers, Mother!' he cried. 'For the love of God, you've come out in your slippers. Again! Why oh why? I keep telling you slippers are for indoors. Not outdoors.' He walked towards me and took me by the shoulders, turning me around and propelling me back towards the shop façade.

'Nothing to see,' he said to passers-by, waving them away. 'It's just my mother. Touch of early-onset Alzheimer's, that's all. Absolutely nothing to worry about. I'd better get her home, though. Can't have her wandering the streets in her slippers, can we? Not in this weather. Bye all! Have fun! It's been an absolute blast.'

'Where *were* you?' I demanded the minute we got in the car. 'You kept me waiting for over twenty minutes out here.'

'Lost track of time,' he mumbled, as he struggled to get the seat belt into the buckle. I waited while he continued to miss it, then grabbed the belt and snapped it in as if he was a toddler again.

'I'm not used to being up this late,' I grumbled as we pulled away. 'I'd normally have been in bed for at least two hours. Have you any idea how tired I am and how lucky you are that I've come to pick you up?'

'It's because you love me and don't want me to get murdered,' he said, nodding thoughtfully.

'I've been counting the minutes until I could come and get you and then you keep me waiting. It's just not on, Freddie. I won't do it again.'

'You should have just left me,' he said. 'Punished me for being late by leaving me there at the party. That's what you should have done.'

'Then how would you have got home?'

'Walked.'

'It's four miles and you might have got murdered.'

'Why didn't you send Dad?' he asked eventually.

'He's in Liverpool. You know that. At a team builder, which apparently involves bowling and brainstorming.'

'Is that a thing?' he asked.

'No idea. Whatever, he's working.'

'On a Friday night! I'd hate his job. It's just bullshit, bullshit, bullshit all day long, isn't it? Bullshit and bowling. Who wants to do that?'

163

'Well, not your dad for much longer.'

'Is he retiring?' He did a large belch that stank of vodka and orange.

'No. Actually, he wants to retrain.'

'At his age? What as? A bus conductor?' Freddie collapsed into peals of laughter, as though it had been the funniest thing he had ever heard.

'I don't think they have bus conductors any more,' I said.

'Oh my God, you're right,' he said, turning and gripping my arm very tightly. 'I may never, ever in my life meet a bus conductor.'

'I bet they still have them in developing countries,' I added.

'Yes! They will have them in South America. I will go to South America and seek out a bus conductor so I can tick that off my bucket list.'

Bugger, he was still thinking of going to South America and now I'd given him another reason to go. I really needed to keep my mouth shut.

'So what does Dad want to do?' asked Freddie.

I sighed a big sigh. 'He's thinking of going back to university to train to be a teacher,' I said.

There was silence. I glanced over at my son.

'Un-fucking believable,' he muttered under his breath. 'What the hell does he think he's playing at?'

'I don't know,' I said, 'but he's going to meet the dean at Birmingham University next week to talk to them about a post-grad.'

'What!' squealed Freddie, nearly leaping out of his seat. 'Birmingham! But *I* want to go to Birmingham.'

This was news to me. This was *great* news to me. This was utterly brilliant news to me. He wanted to do something at a further educational establishment. I nearly stopped the car to hug him for showing signs of motivation towards something . . . anything.

'You never said anything about Birmingham?'

'Well, Cally and Jack mentioned they might apply for biomedicine there and, well, apparently there's a pretty good psychology course, so you know it was at the back of my mind and well, it's fucking typical, isn't it? The minute I decide I want to do something, Dad tries to steal my thunder. Who on earth on this planet wants to go to uni with his *dad*? It's just like the time he decided he was going to coach the under-nine's football team. It was a disaster, do you remember? He . . . he . . . had me on the subs bench the whole time and then put me in goal . . . until I scored an own goal and he put me back on the subs bench. Is it any wonder I turned out like this? An eyeliner-wearing, football-hating, avocado-loving, *Rocky*-movie-adoring total mix-up. If Dad hadn't taken over being the coach of that football team, I could have been Mark Owen. Just a straightforward footballing hero.'

'Michael Owen,' I pointed out. 'Mark Owen was in Take That.'

'Whatever!' He slammed the dashboard in frustration. 'We need a drive-through,' he demanded. 'Don't we, Mum? This is a crisis and only deep-fried crap can fix it.'

I hastily agreed and twenty minutes later we were sitting in a cold, rainy car park, grease dripping down our chins and feeling a whole lot better about life.

'Can you imagine what it might be like,' Freddie mumbled eventually. 'I'll be hanging somewhere and Dad will pop up and try and be my mate. Try and pretend he's a dude, and it will be so cringe, so *utterly* cringe.'

'I can understand why you wouldn't want to go to the same university as your Dad,' I said.

'*At the same time!*' he added.

'It's your time,' I told him.

'Exactly,' he mumbled, stuffing his face full of fries. 'I have an absolute right to my student years and Dad is just trying to steal them from me.'

'Mmmm,' I nodded, in what I hoped was an encouraging and yet not at all traitorous way to my husband. This conversation was going well. This could be a turning point in our lives. This was not what I'd expected to be talking about, but I liked it, I liked it a lot. It was the first time that Freddie had talked so positively about university. Before now he'd been slightly vague, with no real plan as to what he was going to do after sixth form, apart from follow some drama group around South America. Who would have thought that all it took to whip him into action was a whiff of his father doing it instead? All his competitive juices had come to the fore and going to university had become a matter of principle, a birthright, something he had to fight for and protect. Halle – fucking – lulah. Perhaps some good could come out of Mike's career wobble after all, if it got Freddie motivated.

And if it got Mike to back off from this retraining malarkey, all the better. Everyone would be happy. I would be very happy!

'Tell your Dad how you feel,' I encouraged Freddie. 'Don't bottle it up. Tell him you're not comfortable with him studying as well as you.'

'Too right I will,' said Freddie. 'I'm not having him showing up at the Student Union in his 4x4 wanted to join me in a protest against environmental pollution caused by factory farming.'

'More chicken?' I asked.
'Absolutely,' he replied.

5 May

MUM'S KNEE

Lizzy: I've just spoken to Mum and she says she should cancel the papers while she's in hospital. Is there any chance someone could go to the newsagent's for her?

I leave it a good hour but of course Nicola doesn't respond.

Me: I'll do it on my way to pick Mum up.

Lizzy: Can you do it before as they need 48-hours' notice she said.

Me: OK.

Lizzy: Mum also says she needs a new dressing gown because she's worried hers is too shabby. Can anyone take her into town to get her one?

I knew where this was coming from. This was because she was going to a private clinic and she was worrying that her barely worn beige towelling number that I bought her for Christmas last year wasn't good enough. But she wouldn't dare tell me that. Not after she'd asked me to drive her to the private clinic that happened to be eighty miles away, rather than the NHS hospital on our doorstep.

I'd reorganized my week so I could take her and stay overnight in a Premier Inn with my dad. Not that Dad was bothered. He was totally overexcited about the prospect of a buffet breakfast rather than worrying about his wife's major surgery. He'd actually rung me – on the phone – to make sure I'd booked us in. He last rang me on the phone over twenty years ago on the first day of the new millennium to wish me Happy New Year.

> **Me:** *I'm struggling, as I've had to move all my work to today and tomorrow so I can take her to the clinic. Can you go at all, Nicola?*

6 May

> **Nicola**: *Sorry, guys, I missed this. I've been and cancelled the papers so can you take Mum to get a dressing gown, Cathy? It's late-night shopping tonight. I can't because of the kids. Sorry. x*

Well, it was something to look forward to I guess. Going round the shops looking for a dressing gown that my mum didn't need, while she bent my ear about how marvellous Lizzy and Patrick were for paying for her to go private, and how she couldn't believe how lucky she was and how supportive Lizzy had been, even though she lives in California, and how she had been ringing her every other day just to check how she is, even though she's really busy with her yoga company, and the time difference is a nightmare for her because she has to call so early in the morning, and really she's just an incredible daughter. And when we get home would I get her suitcase down from the loft and give it a dust because it hasn't been used it in ages because they never go anywhere, do they? But of course Lizzy has been kind enough invite us all over in August, so she'd get to use it then, so could I give it an extra good wipe? Thanks, love.

7 May

I got home from my shopping jaunt with Mum to find Tania sitting at the kitchen table with Robbie. He got up as soon as I entered, looking a little flustered, as though I'd caught him doing something he shouldn't.

'Oh, for goodness' sake sit down, Robbie,' I said, slapping shopping bags on the table. 'Can I make everyone a cup of tea?'

'I'll do it,' said Robbie.

'No,' I said, putting a hand on his shoulder. 'Sit down. Thank you for keeping my friend company.'

'We've been catching up,' said Tania.

It looked as if they'd been having a deep discussion. Robbie was looking thoughtful. I hoped that Tania had managed to get more out of him about his home life than I had. He'd offered me the odd snippet, but nothing major, and never asked for sympathy, despite the fact it must have been so hard for him to be the main carer for his brother. I'd wracked my brains to try and work out how I could help him more, but I'd decided that giving him extra employment while he trained was probably the best I could be doing.

The three of us sat and chatted for a good hour. Well, Tania and I chatted. Robbie mostly listened for a bit, then pulled his chopping board onto the kitchen table and chopped as we chatted. Adding the odd comment. Asking the odd question. We talked about Paula and both agreed we would give her a call to see if she had made it to the GP. We talked about the kids. I told Tania about Culty Carl and Robbie gave his opinion. 'He's a tosser.' Tania gave me her opinion, 'She'll grow out of him.' I told her about Freddie's revelation that he actually wanted to go to university now that he'd found out that his father might be stealing his thunder. Robbie gave his opinion. 'Freddie will get it right in the end.' Tania gave me her opinion. 'Freddie will find his way.' I told Tania that I was driving my mum down to have a knee op the following day and she'd been driving me mad because she wanted a million and one jobs doing before she left the house and insisted on the bathroom being spotless as well as the kitchen and she'd 'inspected', yes 'inspected' my cleaning after I had finished and called me out on a smear on the shower cubicle door.' Robbie gave me his opinion. 'I really miss my mum.' Tania gave me her opinion. 'Me too.'

That shut me up.

8 May

So it's midnight and I'm hammered, trying to get to sleep on the sofa bed in my dad's room at the Premier Inn, Milton Keynes West. Not how I imagined this day ending!

We were on the road by six at my mother's insistence, even though we didn't have to be at the clinic until ten a.m. She was worried about traffic; their neighbour's friend's uncle had driven south two years ago and they'd had a terrible journey, apparently, so she'd felt it was better to be safe than sorry.

My parents had of course been outside on the pavement checking their watches by the time I pulled up at 6.02 a.m. precisely. Mum had looked a little nervous but Dad seemed excited, to say the least, and asked immediately if we would be stopping for a McDonald's breakfast en route. I was just about to say that we would be going to one straight away away as I hadn't even had a coffee yet and a trip has not started as far as I'm concerned until you have had a Sausage McMuffin, when Mum stepped in and said they'd already had muesli and a cup of tea and wouldn't need to stop until we were halfway down the motorway ahead of rush hour.

We got to the clinic two hours early. Two hours! I was about to suggest we go and find a café but Mum was already out of the car and shouting at Dad to get her case while oohing and aahing over the landscaping of the grounds and the stunning hanging baskets, as though she'd just arrived for a weekend at a spa, not to have her leg cut open.

'I'm Mrs Judy Green,' she told the lady behind the reception desk as we walked in. 'However, my booking might be under my daughter's name, Mrs Elizabeth Ryan. She lives in California, you see, so she can't be here today, but she and her husband have been kind enough to pay for my operation because she really wants us to go and visit in the summer, so I really had no choice but to accept her generosity, even though I'm not sure I totally agree with private health care, given that me and my husband have paid taxes all our lives, but when someone else offers to pay, then what do you do? I need to get my knee fixed so I can visit my daughter in California.'

'Of course you do, Mrs Green,' said the receptionist. 'And we are delighted you are here. Now you are in luck that your room is ready, so I can take you down there and you can get yourself settled in and wait for the consultant to come and see you.'

Mum turned and raised her eyebrows at me. 'My room is ready,' she said. 'Isn't it a good job we set off early?'

I had never been so bored in all my life. It felt as if we had waited for weeks for the consultant to come, while Mum dithered over whether to change into her nightie or not and Dad sat glazed, watching some programme on the wall-mounted TV about door-to-door salesmen.

Eventually Mr Cartwright swept in, wearing a dark suit and with an entourage trailing behind him. He spoke to Mum in a perfunctory fashion, shouted at a nurse and then left.

We were none the wiser.

No instructions had been uttered as far as we could tell, just very long words. Fortunately, a senior nurse came in moments later and fully explained everything that would happen, leaving us feeling much more reassured.

'Perhaps he just speaks "consultant",' I said after the nurse had left.

'He seemed lovely,' my mother said. 'Have you texted your sisters to say he's been. I'm sure they'll be worried.'

MUM'S KNEE

Me: *Consultant's been. She should go in for the op in two hours. We've already been here two hours. About to slit my wrists!*

172

Lizzy: Has Mum taken those herbal tablets I sent her? They're very good for healing.

Me: I've no idea. But she enjoyed the Sausage McMuffin we had on the M1 at 7.30 this morning.

Lizzy: Have you any idea of the toxins in that?

Me: Of course! But there wasn't a kale McMuffin In sight.

Lizzy: Mum really should be eating healthier food than that. Processed food won't do her any good at all.

'What's she saying,' Mum asked as I tapped away.

'Nothing much,' I replied. 'Just wishing you all the best.'

'And Nicola?'

'Must be busy with the kids. She's not replied.'

'She brought her boyfriend to see us last week when she dropped the kids off,' Mum added.

'And what did you think of him?' I asked.

'Arrogant tosser,' my dad muttered.

'No he wasn't,' interrupted my mum. 'He's just clever.'

'Doesn't mean you have to be arrogant,' I said.

Mum looked at me. 'Just be happy for her,' she said. 'You were lucky with Mike.'

She looked away. Subject closed.

What was that supposed to mean? That I had punched above my weight? That Mike must have had a major relapse when he asked me to marry him? That I didn't deserve him? What *did* that mean? Jesus. How could I be breaking my back to be a good daughter, getting up at the crack of dawn, taking her for a McDonald's breakfast, for Christ's sake, and yet I still felt like an utter failure. What was this special skill she had to make me feel like this? I absolutely had to ensure I did not make my daughter feel like this. When it came to my daughter, I would not be my mother.

It's midnight and Dad's snoring really loudly.

We'd had a top night, actually. We went to find some lunch when Mum eventually went into surgery and then came back a few hours later. She'd been very groggy and hardly made any sense, and the nice nurse told us that we would be better off coming back the next day. She was in safe hands and we should both go and get some sleep, as we looked shattered. I was just thinking what a fine idea that sounded, when Dad whispered in my ear that there was a Harvester attached to the Premier Inn we were staying at and we should treat ourselves to a slap-up meal given the stressful day we'd had.

We were the first ones there at 6 p.m. and the last ones to leave at 10 p.m. Dad seemed to treat it like the Last Supper or something. We shared three starters because he couldn't decide between Brie wedges or nachos or calamari. Then he had a mixed grill. I mean, I haven't seen a mixed grill since 1979. I expected him to sprout horns and a tail he ate so much meat. He was on beer and I worked out it was cheaper to order a bottle of wine than buy two glasses, stating firmly to Dad that I'd ask to keep the screw top so I could take what was left home.

I didn't need the screw top.

It was great. Really great. We talked about all sorts of stuff, rubbish mainly, and it made me sad, so very, very sad that I hadn't done this more often. Sat down and got drunk with my parents. Why hadn't I done this before? Why did we find it so hard to ask our parents the questions we really wanted to ask them. How did you meet? Was it love at first sight? Where did you go on dates? Where was your first kiss? How was your first kiss? Do you still kiss? Are you still happy? Did you make the right choice? Do you have any regrets? What can you teach me now? What should I know about life? Please tell me what I should know?

Dad did get quite deep at one point. It was after we'd shared a sticky toffee pudding and a tiramisu and I was in full-on drunken waffle mode, telling him about my work at The Mustard Factory. He wasn't really listening. He didn't give a toss about the hipsters and their start-up moneymaking ideas and their Friday night beer mixers.

'All I ever wanted to do was make enough money to put food on the table for your mum and you three and have two weeks in Spain every year,' he said. 'Nailed it,' he laughed, raising his glass to congratulate himself.

He laughed good and hard. The laugh of a contented, happy man. The laugh of a man with few regrets. Maybe he *had* nailed it. Maybe the secret to contentment was to set your sights low then nail it. Strive for less so that you overachieve. Don't follow your dreams. That plan works for the fortunate few. But, for the rest of us, it could totally ruin your life.

'Is there stuff you wished you'd done?' I asked him as I shook the bottle of wine upside down over my glass, hoping it would emit a gush that had been hiding somewhere inside the transparent bottle.

He paused for a moment, tiramisu-laden spoon hovering beneath his mouth.

'I'd have liked to have gone to a live wrestling match. Just to see what it was like. But your mother didn't approve, so I took her to the pictures instead.'

'Right,' I nodded.

'Your Uncle Gerald used to go all the time with your Auntie Janet, but she had a thing about men in leotards if you know what I mean.' He winked at me.

I thought about my Auntie Janet, now an octogenarian who walked with a stick and wore polyester dresses with gravy stains down her front. Hard to imagine her leering at men scantily clad in Lycra.

'There have been times when I wished I was a woman,' he then said, waving his spoon at me.

I nearly spat my tiramisu at him. Seemed so unlikely. My father was so obviously of the generation that believed in stereotypical roles, which in my eyes left him with a cushy number. Waited on hand and foot by his wife and shielded from the vast majority of child-rearing trauma.

'No way, Dad,' I said. 'Why on earth would you want to be a woman?'

'Because they get to spend more time with their kids.'

He dug his spoon back into his pudding then carried on eating.

'Not that I really felt like that at the time,' he said. 'I mean, some mornings I left early to go to work just to avoid the screaming match that for a while was breakfast with you all. It's just now I look back, I realize that I missed so much. I can't remember your first words or your first steps, but your mum can. I can't remember any of your first days at school or sports days or school prize-giving or Nativity plays.'

'I never won a school prize,' I pointed out.

'I know, love, but Lizzy did.'

'Of course she did.'

'Every year she won the form prize,' he continued, 'and I never ever went to see her get it because I was at work doing something not nearly so memorable. Your mum went every time. Brought me back the programme to read with her name in but it wasn't the same.'

'You came to my graduation,' I said. 'I remember that.'

He nodded. 'A great day. One of the best.' He smiled. 'Many, many great days but I wish . . . I just wish I'd seen more of you. Been more like your mother. Been involved more. Witnessed more. Had more memories to scroll through now, rather than knowing what the best stops are on the M25 and remembering that time I had the best bacon butty ever in a lay-by just outside Reading.'

'Oooh, where was that?' I asked. Always good to know where you can get a decent bacon butty.'

'It was in 1978,' he replied. 'I reckon Barry's Café is long gone.'

'You do realize that being a mum isn't all prize-giving and school assemblies, don't you?'

'I know, Cathy,' he said, wiping his face with his napkin. 'But I think in hindsight I'd rather have been a mum than a lorry driver.'

Dad asked me in the hotel corridor if I would sleep in his room as he hadn't slept in a room on his own since the day he got married. How lovely is that? I thought about the fact that probably Mike and I were the opposite. Spent more nights apart than we had together, somehow.

I said I'd go and fetch my stuff, but needed to give Mike a quick call so I'd be about twenty minutes.

'Hello, what's wrong?' Mike said when he picked up.

'Nothing. Just wanted to hear your voice.'

'I was asleep. I've been up since five getting ready for a big powwow with the CEO.'

'Oh, sorry. Just wanted to let you know Mum's op went okay.'

'Right, yeah, of course. I'm sorry, I totally forgot. Is she all right?'

'Off her head on drugs but yeah, she's going to be fine.'

'You're not still at the hospital, are you?'

'No. Me and Dad have just finished having dinner at the hotel. I'm just getting my stuff then I'm sleeping on the sofa bed in Dad's room.'

'That's a bit weird.'

'He says he's never slept on his own since he got married.'

'That's really weird.'

'Do you miss me when you're away?'

'Of course I do. I really am sick of hotel life, you know.'

'I know.'

'Oh, by the way, I spoke to the dean of Birmingham University on Monday. He says I'm just the type of person they are looking for. That I'd definitely get accepted. I think it helped that Helen did her PhD there. She knows him and so I wouldn't be surprised if she put a good word in. When I rang to tell her that it had gone well, she wasn't a bit surprised.'

I felt a tear spring to my eye. I was tired and emotional and wasn't happy that he'd spoken to Helen before he'd spoken to me, however hostile he thought I might be.

'Cathy, are you still there?' he asked.

'Yeah,' I said. 'I'm really tired. I'll call you tomorrow, okay?'

'Yeah, sure. Give your mum my love.'

'Will do.'

Dad was fast asleep by the time I let myself into his room. I hunkered down on the sofa bed at the end of his bed, listening to his contented snoring and thinking about my dissatisfied husband.

MUM'S KNEE

Me: Mum still groggy this afternoon but the consultant said it went very well. Will go back to see her in the morning. Dad sleeping soundly though snoring a lot.

Lizzy: Good to hear. Are you sharing a room?

Me: He didn't want to sleep on his own!

Lizzy: Bless him.

Me: Thanks for Mum's new knee, Lizzy. Xx

Lizzy: Don't mention it. Thanks for being there. Sleep well xx

21 May

Mike was due home tonight and I knew Freddie had plans. He'd not mentioned anything directly to Mike about university since our chat, but he had quietly seethed and plotted. I could see him thinking it all through, working out the best way to tackle his father, while I

179

had been beside myself with delight that Freddie was suddenly so motivated. Whatever Freddie had planned, it was going to be good. I was expecting nothing less than a spectacular piece of drama to play out before my eyes.

We had already opened a bottle of red and Mike had informed me he'd spoken again to the dean at Birmingham University and he was looking forward to telling me all about it. I told him we should wait until after dinner and thankfully he seemed happy with that.

I heard the door and in walked Freddie.

I was in awe. For this scenario he'd chosen his best preppy outfit. He looked like Zac Efron in *High School Musical* with his baseball jacket, plain white T and beige chinos. He even had a raft of books under his arm. And he smelt amazing! He sat down at the table and asked if he could talk to us about his future.

Mike and I exchanged looks. I, of course, pretended to have no idea what was going on and gave Mike a small shrug.

We sat across the table from our son as though we were about to start an interview process. He cleared his throat and I noticed that Freddie was wearing foundation. It was expertly done. Again I bemoaned the fact that both my children were better at make-up than me.

'I have been giving my future education some serious thought,' he began. 'I have been looking through prospectuses for several universities.' He fanned the glossy literature out in front of us. I thought Mike was going to burst with pride.

'Brilliant news, Freddie,' he said, glowing. 'So good to hear that you have been thinking about your future.'

'Well, I have made a decision,' he said seriously.

'Good, good, that's really good,' said Mike. I nod enthusiastically.

'The thing I really, really want to do is go to Birmingham University to study psychology.'

'Right, right,' said Mike without missing a beat. 'And what is it about that course that appeals in particular?'

Freddie looked momentarily blindsided.

He swallowed.

'They do a week's residential in Berlin and I have always wanted to go to Berlin because the clubbing scene is supposed to be epic.'

Mike's jaw dropped.

'Don't worry. It's free. It's all part of the tuition fees. You might need to pay for food, I guess, and of course they won't pay for your entry to get into the clubs and that, but I'm sure I'll find the money for that from somewhere.'

He trailed off, perhaps realizing he had gone down the wrong track.

'Why Birmingham University in particular?' I asked him. I looked at him pleadingly.

'Because it's a cosmopolitan city with a very diverse culture and I think I would benefit from being immersed in that. Oh, and everyone says their pastoral care is second to none.'

I made a mental note to look up what exactly pastoral care means. I'd heard the term so often in relation to education, but I was not exactly sure of its definition. I thought it meant that they '*really* care', but didn't want anyone to quote me on that. I knew it was a good thing, anyway, whatever it meant. They certainly didn't have it while I was at university. You were lucky to get a flushing toilet somewhere on your floor, never mind anything as fancy as 'pastoral care'.

'Well, it sounds like you have really thought it through, Freddie. Well done. So what do you have to do next?' asked Mike.

'Well, there are open days, which I would like to go to, and obviously I have to complete the application process,' he replied.

'And get the grades,' added Mike.

'I will get the grades,' replied Freddie.

Mike glances at me.

'I know you will,' I said to Freddie, reaching across the table to squeeze his arm. 'I know when you have made your mind up to do something, then you do it.'

'Well, I think this is just great,' said Mike, leaning back in his chair and grinning. 'I wasn't going to say anything just yet but, seeing as you seem so keen on Birmingham, I might as well tell you, I could be joining you, son. Actually, I spoke to the dean of Birmingham this week. I'm thinking of retraining and becoming a teacher and the PGSE course is excellent and I can commute from home. After all, it's only twenty-five minutes on the train.' He leaned forward and squeezed Freddie's other arm. 'How about it? We could be fellow students. What a thing that could be.'

Freddie glanced at me and then glared at his dad. Here it comes, I thought.

'That is the worst idea I have ever heard of,' Freddie declared, standing up and shaking off our hands. 'This is *my* time, *my* dream,' he said. 'All my life I have wanted to go and study psychology at Birmingham University and you come along and want to be there alongside me. Are you insane? If you set one foot inside that campus, all this,' he says, indicating his preppy, studenty look, 'all this is up in smoke.'

He's good. He's really good.

182

Mike left to go back up to Liverpool at 5 this evening. It's unusual for him to leave on a Sunday. Normally he gets up really early on a Monday and gets the train, thus avoiding 'ruining a family Sunday'. But since he and Freddie were not speaking to each other, then there was no family Sunday to ruin.

After Freddie had thrown his toys out of the pram on Friday night and stalked out, Mike threw his hands in the air in exasperation.

'That's just typical, isn't it?' he said.

'What is?'

'That he's being such a drama queen over me wanting to study at Birmingham.'

'Please don't call him a drama queen. I'm sure you're not allowed to call people that any more. Particularly men. Well, actually women as well. Either way I'm sure it's offensive . . . to everyone these days.'

'Would you call that little display . . . undramatic?' he asked.

I thought back to the *High School Musical* tribute act that may have just passed through our kitchen.

'Possibly, a little,' I admitted.

'And you know what's going to happen now, don't you?'

'What?'

'He's going to apply to Birmingham, demanding that I don't, then he's going to fail his exams and not get in, and then where will that leave me?'

'Still with a job that pays really well and that you have always loved up until you got to fifty and someone perhaps pointed out that the grass might be greener in a secondary school where no one will be the slightest bit interested in your middle-class mutterings and half the class will be playing truant so that they can keep up with their porn addiction.'

His jaw dropped. I felt that perhaps I'd gone too far.

'And tell me, Cathy, how is work going for you? Still earning minimum wage from a bunch of no-hopers?'

Ouch, that hurt.

'Look at it this way,' I said. 'You've made your son really want to go to university. It's exactly the rocket up his backside he needed to get him motivated. Helen might not have set you on a sensible career path, but she might have inadvertently pushed our son in the right direction. Perhaps she was worth talking to after all.'

I think the other reason he might have left early to go back to Liverpool was because he wasn't speaking to me either!

29 May

Finally a decent book discussion tonight. Everyone present had read it and most had enjoyed it. Fiona was a bit unsure. I knew she loved it really, but she liked to present a façade of not being really keen on 'genre fiction', as if it was some badge of honour to put it down. But I watched her eyes well up when we discussed the sad ending. It had got to her – which in my book is a bloody good book!

We were two men down, though. No Paula *or* Tania. I wasn't sure where Tania had got to, as she was typically the most reliable person in the room. Come to think of it, I had not seen her in days and in particular had not partaken of her fine desserts.

Sonja and I could update everyone on Paula, however, as we'd both been in touch over the last couple of weeks. She'd gone to her GP who'd agreed she was indeed suffering from depression. Thankfully she'd signed up for counselling as her preferred route to dealing with it and was awaiting an appointment. Paula said she wasn't really up for seeing everyone but felt a little better for knowing what was wrong with her and that there was a plan. She knew it could be a long, tricky path but at least she was heading in the right direction.

I'd asked after Richard, thinking that this would be hard on him as well. Paula had told me he didn't really understand, or perhaps he didn't want to understand because he didn't know what to do.

'He's escaping down the pub most nights,' she'd said. 'Which is fine by me because I haven't got the energy to talk to him anyway. I can't worry about him as well. He'll have to sort himself out.' She rang off, giving an excuse that she had something in the oven, but I suspected that was a lie. I suspected it had taken all of her energy just to pick up the phone and she had had enough.

We discussed what we could do to help Paula but struggled to come up with anything useful. Louise said if it was bastard cancer we'd all be round there trying to cheer her up, whereas it was hard to know how to cheer up someone with depression since that was the problem in the first place.

We couldn't think of anything other than to let her know we were here and we cared. So as we were at Louise's, and she has primary-school-aged children, we decided we would make a card with all her kids' craft stuff. The cacophony of glitter and glue and tissue paper that we pushed through Paula's door the next day might

185

not work to cheer her up, but it had certainly put a smile on all our faces.

I nearly called in on Tania on the way home, but it was late and all their lights were off. It wasn't like her to just not turn up. Maybe she'd had a crisis at work. That must have been it. She had fully intended to come but a family needed help somewhere and she'd rushed to their aid. Typical Tania. Always there for everyone else.

June

Secure My Daughter's Future: i.e. Teach Her How to Not Get Screwed Over by Relationships

1 June

Kirsty walked into the kitchen and asked if she could have a word with us both. Mike and I looked at each other. Relations were still somewhat strained following the last chat we'd had with one of our children, so it was no wonder that we both sat down a little nervously.

But she was smiling. Which was good.

Her demeanour recently had mostly consisted of shrugged shoulders and downcast eyes, which could have been exam strain or her still struggling with her 'friendship' with Carl. Either way I'd decided not to ask about Carl until after the exams had finished and then she and I would tackle the issue together. I planned to work out a way of giving her some essential lessons in how to tackle the tricky issue of love. I just didn't know how yet.

However, today she looked brighter, lighter, and I felt mightily relieved to see it.

'So, you know it's my birthday in the middle of GCSEs,' she said, 'and so I'm in danger of not getting to celebrate my sixteenth at all?'

'We said we'd take you out for a meal after your exams have finished,' said Mike. 'Angelo's? It's two-for-one on

189

a Friday. But that's just the set menu so we'd need to agree to choose off that.'

'I'm sure, as it's her birthday, she can have whatever she wants,' I pointed out.

'Oh yeah, sure, sure. I'll get it booked and you have whatever you want, Kirst, and me and your mum can do two-for-one.'

'I don't want to go for a meal,' she said.

'We don't have to go to Angelo's,' I said, thinking that actually I didn't want to be restrained by the set menu either. 'We could go to Noki's if you like. You like it there.'

'Do they do a two-for-one?' asked Mike.

'No!' I replied. 'It doesn't matter. It's our daughter's sixteenth birthday. We don't need a deal.'

'I don't want to go anywhere for a meal. I want a party.'

The colour drained from both our faces.

'At the Methodist Hall?' I asked, hopefully.

'No way.'

'What's wrong with it? You had your seventh birthday party there.'

'Exactly. And I still have nightmares about that magician pulling a rabbit out of the bottom of his trousers. No, I mean a party here.'

I looked forlornly around at my lovely house.

'Great idea,' said Mike. 'Why not? You're only sixteen once, after all.'

I put my head in my hands.

One of the side effects of Mike being away a lot with work is that it means he is out of the local loop and not privy to the horror stories of teenage house parties. 'Clueless' would adequately describe him. He's never been part of the regular hushed conversations outside the post office, hearing of the devastation and havoc the latest party had wreaked on someone's home. If he had, there would be no way he would have come out with his ridiculous response.

'No way,' I said.

'Oh Muuuuuum! Dad said yes,' leapt in Kirsty.

'Why not?' he asked.

'I like my house just the way it is,' I said. 'Not ransacked for spirits and pebble-dashed in vomit.'

'It won't be like that,' pleaded Kirsty. 'Only a few friends, I promise. And just people I know. And only people in my year . . . apart from Carl, of course, but you've met him and he's a friend so he can come, right?'

Wow, it all makes sense. This is a Carl Capturing party. A party purely laid on to leapfrog Carl from friend zone to boyfriend zone.

'Please, Mum, please,' she gasped.

'Oh go on, let her,' said Mike, giving my arm a squeeze. 'It'll cost less than a meal out at Noki's. Some Coke and some crisps and maybe a few cans of beer?'

'Oh Dad, you are the best,' she said, leaping on him. He looked happy and a little bit smug, grateful to be in the good books of at least one of his children.

You have no idea, I thought. This was going to cost a whole lot more than you could possibly imagine.

3 June

I went to see Tania today. My texts had gone ignored and no explanation had appeared for her lack of presence at last month's book group. Tania was solid and reliable

191

in a way I wished I could be. This was so out of character. So I'd made scones (completely out of character) – with no help from Robbie, I might add – and put them in Tupperware and taken them round.

'Oh, hiya,' she said, opening the door, looking just how she always did apart from perhaps a little tired. She looked at her watch. 'I need to get out soon, I'm afraid. A meeting at the council is imminent.'

'I brought scones,' I said, holding up the plastic box and putting my foot inside the door. 'Come on, you've got five minutes for a quick cuppa and to enjoy my culinary delights. It doesn't happen every day, does it?'

'Well, I suppose,' she said, looking at her watch again and closing the door behind me. 'Go on through.'

I sat at the kitchen table as she went through the motions of making a cup of tea. She whistled quietly as she went.

Eventually she sat down in front of me and handed me a steaming cup of tea.

'So what's occurring then?' I asked. 'You been busy or something.'

'Always,' she replied. 'You know, usual stuff. Work is mental at the moment, but no change there, and Mabel is on work experience this week so I have to drive her to Birmingham every day. Keresi just finished her A levels so she's sleeping actually, mostly.'

'Hazel okay?' I asked, blowing on my tea.

The pause was a nanosecond too long.

'She's at work today.'

She looked up at me and sighed.

'Actually, we're waiting for some scan results. Yeah, they found a shadow on her breast so she had to go for some extra tests and now we are waiting for the results, which I'm sure will be fine because, you know, she's fit and healthy and showing no other symptoms, so it's just procedure, isn't it? They won't find anything wrong. And if they do, well, they'll be able to do surgery because they will have caught it soon enough and then it will just be a bit of chemo to be sure and we will all be back to normal. But it won't come to that because we'll get the tests back and they won't find anything. It will be them being overcautious. So we are really relaxed about it. I mean, you have to be for the kids, don't you? We haven't even mentioned it to Keresi and Mabel yet because what's the point in worrying them when it's more than likely to be nothing, and of course Keresi has been doing her exams so it would be a disaster to have worried her for no reason, so we decided not to tell anyone about it because really, what is the point if it comes to nothing, and what if something got back to the girls and we hadn't told them? So we've told no one because it's really nothing to worry about. It's all going to be fine, isn't it?'

'Yeah,' I whispered, reaching over the table to grab her hand and squeeze it really tight. 'Of course it is.' I couldn't stop my eyes filling with tears. Tania looked at me and her eyes instantly did the same.

She sobbed for half an hour.

We ate all the scones.

We hugged and went on with our day, trying to avoid any thoughts of impending potential catastrophe.

4 June

The kids were both out tonight. Mike was away, of course, and I felt incredibly alone. I'd been thinking about Tania

193

and Hazel all day, little shivers running up and down my body whenever I dared stray into thoughts that led to an unhappy ending. I rang Mike, wanting to share my worry with him, or maybe I just wanted to hear his voice.

As soon as he asked how things were, I told him it had been rubbish and I told him why. That the C word was looming over next door and I was worried sick about them.

'So they've found a shadow and they are doing more tests?' he asked.

'That's what I understood, yes,' I replied.

'So it might not be, you know, cancer?' he asked.

'No,' I said, 'it might not.'

'Well, all we can do is hope then,' he said quietly.

'Yes, that's right. I rang Lizzy, actually, because she's pretty hot on these things, and she said that breast cancer is one of the best ones because they have got so much better at treating it than they used to. She said a mum from Alicia's school had it last year and had chemo and everything and now she is totally over it.'

'Good, good to hear,' replied Mike. 'Greg at work too. His wife had it a few years ago. He had a bunch of time off. It really cut him up at the time. But this summer they are driving across America together. She's totally clear. Got her hair back and everything. Funnily enough he showed me a picture of her the other day. She looked really well.'

'Great, good,' I said, feeling slightly better.

'I'm sure it's going to be fine, Cathy,' he said.

'I hope so,' I replied. 'Tania looked terrible, Mike. I mean, those two are the most loved-up pair I have ever met. I don't know what she'll do if it's bad news. You know she makes Hazel her packed lunch every day and every day she puts a Post-it note in with a message, and every day Hazel brings the note back and sticks it on a cork board in their dining room. There must be hundreds of them.'

'What on earth does she write every day?' asked Mike.

'All sorts from "I love that you took the bin out yesterday when I didn't feel well" or, "You look really hot in purple." I mean, they manage to treat each other like they've just met, like they've just fallen in love. I have no idea how they do that. It's just so sad.'

'You can't think like that, Cathy. You have to stay positive, for Tania.'

'I know,' I replied.

We didn't talk for much longer. Everything else seemed a little trivial in comparison.

When we said goodbye, though, I said, '*Take care,*' which I don't normally do. And he said it back.

Our equivalent, maybe, of hundreds of Post-it notes.

10 June

Hazel needs surgery.

She has cancer.

That's all I know.

Well, Tania did tell me more than that but my brain literally went to jelly when faced with such conversations. There was no way I could have been a doctor, a mortgage advisor or a taxi driver. If anyone started talking to me about anything medical, financial, or gave me directions, my brain went into sleep mode for some reason, as if it had already decided it had absolutely no capacity for such information.

In this situation, of course, this is a nightmare, because people like facts, don't they, when someone's been taken ill. They like to know exactly what type of cancer, what stage it's at, exactly what the treatment is and for how long it might go on for and what the prognosis is. The facts are necessary for people to be able to have accurate discussions about something so serious. But as Tania was telling me the facts when I went over again a few days later, the minute she said 'cancer', my brain just went to immediate emotional overload of what the implications would be of this diagnosis, and so I stopped listening, too worried for my friend and her family to be able to decipher details.

But really there is only one fact you want to know. All the other facts are bluster and buffers to the only essential question, which is – will they live? The one question which was somehow impossible to ask for fear of getting the wrong answer and then having to deal with the fact you had made someone tell you that their loved one was about to die.

I didn't ask. I couldn't ask. But I could see by the lines on Tania's forehead and occasional cracking of her tone that whether Hazel would recover was a grey area. Tania's message was not about a process that needed to be got through and then all would be well. She only talked about the process and did not confirm the end result which, I could only assume, meant that they didn't know.

I was at a loss as to what to do.

I confided in Robbie what was happening. He visibly paled under his tattoos, and then I felt bad. It must have brought back memories of what had happened to his mother.

'Can I cook them something?' he asked. 'It's the only thing I can do and I would like to do something.'

'Yes!' I gasped. 'Of course. Can I . . . would it be okay if I helped? I mean, you don't have to let me, I'm rubbish, but I need to do something and I don't know what to do.'

'Sure,' he said. 'Grab a chopping board. You can be my sous chef.'

So for the next hour we chopped and he talked. He told me about his mum and how it happened. About how his dad reacted. About moving out. He told me all about losing his mother, his father and his home, all in the space of two years. He said everything quietly and steadily and matter-of-factly without any request for pity or even sympathy. It happened. He dealt with it. The scars clearly buried deep.

Then we both went round and knocked on Tania's door.

My heart was pounding, as it was the first time I would have seen her since the news.

Hazel opened the door.

Of course she did.

I froze.

Robbie said, 'We brought you a turkey lasagne.'

Hazel threw back her head and laughed.

So I laughed.

And Robbie laughed.

'It's all going to be fine,' she said to us. 'It's all going to be fine but I am so happy you brought me turkey lasagne. So, so happy. Thank you. Tania isn't here but she is going to love this. It's so very kind.'

'Good,' I replied. 'Any time. Just, you know, say the word. Whatever you need.'

'Of course,' said Hazel, suddenly looking a little grave. 'If you'll excuse me, just have something . . . you know . . .'

'Sure,' I replied, backing away. 'We'll see you soon.'
'You will,' she nodded.

20 June

Out of nowhere, and in amongst all the turmoil going on next door, party day arrived.

To say I had been dreading it was an understatement.

I think I would rather have had my toenails extracted one by one by a known terrorist than this.

Anything was better than the thought of thirty-five 16-year-olds having a party in your home at the end of exams when they all felt duty bound to go a bit crazy and to think they are all grown-up when they are not.

I was aware that some of Kirsty's friends' parents were avoiding me for fear I would rope them in for some kind of assistance, while others would approach me on the street with a mocking look on their face and say things like, 'I hear you're letting Kirsty have a party – good luck with that. I hope you have good house insurance.'

I'd post-rationalized that I'd only agreed to the party because she was so down about bastard Carl wanting to be 'just friends' that I was worried her misery could affect her exams. Anything to stop her mooning round like a dressed sloth. Anything to make her look forward to something in life. Anything to see a smile on her face again.

What the hell was I thinking? She was a teenager, for Christ's sake. She was not supposed to have a smile on her face.

A few days before the party, I'd gone into damage-limitation mode. I sat her down and told her that under no circumstances were there to be any social media before or during the event. A kindly friend had rung me up and told me that they'd had a party that their son had invited people to via Facebook and two hundred people had turned up. They'd had to call the police to dispel the crowd. It's a very small cul-de-sac that they live on.

I was tempted to tell Kirsty that no mobile phones would be allowed either, as I was worried that the minute they started posting pictures online then word would get round and we'd need riot police, but it was all starting to feel a bit *HELLO!* magazine at a celebrity wedding, and it was only a sixteenth birthday party after all! Wasn't it?

That didn't stop me making the house look like something from a crime scene before everyone arrived. In fact, I was surprised my face hadn't been put on some sort of 'highly suspicious person' list after I had walked out of the DIY shop with copious amounts of plastic sheeting, rope, lots of plastic buckets, bleach and masking tape.

All carpets were covered in plastic mats; a barricade of a borrowed child's gate and copious amounts of masking tape blocked off access to upstairs. All personal items of any value had been locked in the garage. Photographs, paintings, trophies, you name it. The house resembled a very poorly furnished Airbnb by the time we had finished.

At 7.55 p.m. I lined the back patio with buckets in the hope that if anyone was sick they would be kind enough to use a bucket rather than me finding it all over my rose bushes.

After much negotiation with Kirsty, we had got her to agree that we would be present outside the front door on duty to check for gatecrashers. Under no circumstances were we allowed in, unless she came to fetch us. Mike and I took up our posts on camping chairs outside the front door at 8 p.m.

'Good luck,' I said.

'See you on the other side,' he replied. After he'd over-ridden my advice that we should not allow the party, I had filled him in with some horror stories, so now we were on the same page as to how scary the night could be.

21 June

I wasn't sure how I felt about last night. In some ways it had been a lot better than expected and in other ways a hell of a lot worse.

They had all arrived calmly enough. The girls came in their barely-there dresses, which I frowned upon at first until I realized that this prevented them smuggling in copious amount of alcohol. The boys, of course, were a different matter, and when Mike insisted on searching a rucksack thrown casually over one youth's shoulders, he quite easily gave up the bottle of vodka he'd wrapped up in a waterproof jacket. I expected a standoff as Mike demanded he leave it at the door, my finger poised over the emergency number on my mobile phone, but he just shrugged and strolled in. (Freddie did tell me later that said boy had stashed another bottle of vodka down his pants, which is why he'd given up the bottle to Mike so easily. Apparently it's a well-known trick to have water in a vodka bottle to give to the parents to put them off the scent. Little prick!)

Freddie was, of course, hopeless. He'd promised to

200

be stationed outside with his dad and me so he could check that all the arrivals had actually been invited. However, the minute a couple of particularly attractive friends of Kirsty's arrived, he claimed he needed a drink of water.

We didn't see him for an hour.

Sometime around 9 p.m. five slightly older-looking lads arrived who didn't look at all familiar. Mike, buoyed up, no doubt, by the confiscation of two further bottles of water masquerading as vodka, barred their way and asked them if they had been invited to the party.

'Yes,' they said gruffly.

'By who?' asked Mike.

'The lad whose party it is.'

'It's my daughter's party and you're not coming in.'

'But I know your daughter.'

'What's her name?'

'My mate knows her, actually. He said to meet him here.'

'You're not coming in,' said Mike.

'Shall I go and get Freddie?' I said.

'Who's Freddie,' someone asked. 'Your Rottweiler?' The entire crowd burst into jeering laughter.

I could feel tears prickle at the corner of my eyes. I was back at school again. They were horrible boys and I didn't want them anywhere near my house, my daughter or me.

'Look, just leave,' said Mike, pulling down his V-neck sweater in an authoritative manner. It had got a bit chilly.

This was it, I thought. This was the moment I would have to call the police. My hand edged over the phone in my pocket.

'Oi, what do you think you're doing?' came a shout

from a tall lanky lad coming up the path, with an abundance of tattoos and a cap pulled over his face.

'I'm just telling this lot to sling their hook,' said Mike, going a little pale at the sight of the new arrival.

'Yeah, right,' jeered the crowd, laughing.

'You lot, scram,' the lad continued, approaching the boys. 'If you don't get out of here, Shelton, I'll be telling your dad I caught you skipping school, and you know that's not going to be pretty if he finds out.'

I watched as one boy, presumably Shelton, cast his eyes down and kicked the grass verge.

'Shit party anyway,' he said. 'Come on, lads. Let's go and find some real action.'

Muttering, they all turned and sauntered down the path.

'Thank God you were here,' I gasped.

'Who the hell do you think you are?' said Mike, turning on our inked hero. 'I was handling that. Now kindly get off my property and go away.'

'Mike,' I said, 'this is Robbie.'

'Who's Robbie?'

'Turkey lasagne Robbie.'

Mike looked poor Robbie up and down. 'But you never said . . .' began Mike.

'That I've got tattoos and I'm six foot three?' queried Robbie, holding his hand out to shake Mike's.

'No, actually,' said Mike. 'No, she didn't.'

'But what are you doing here?' I asked. 'I mean, thank goodness you were here and all that—'

'I was handling it,' interrupted Mike.

'Yeah, whatever. So were you just passing, Robbie?'

'Freddie invited me.'

'Really!'

'Yeah, he said I could be useful.'

'Well, you have been.'

'I said I'd pop in for half an hour. You know. Just to see how it was going and to say happy birthday. I won't stay long. I'll go in, shall I?'

'Yeah, sure,' I said. 'And thanks again. For your help.'

'Anytime,' he said, giving me a quick salute.

'*I* was handling it,' insisted Mike yet again, as he screwed the top off one of the confiscated bottles, took a swig, then spat it out as he realized it was water.

'Well, it was handled,' I said. 'Doesn't matter by who. Hopefully the rest of the night should be fairly event free.'

But the worst was yet to come.

The absolute worst thing happened. The worst thing of all.

At 10.35 p.m. Carl sauntered up the path. Kirsty had been on high excitement mode all day, clearly thinking this could be the night they moved their relationship on from 'just friends'. The endless time spent thinking about him would all be worthwhile when he came to her party and . . . their love story began.

She had been absolutely over the moon when he said he was coming. Like, beside herself. He'd even asked to bring a friend. Which meant he was definitely coming, right? He was committed.

However, when he said he was bringing a friend I didn't suspect that Kirsty had thought for one minute that it would be Kim Wang, who he was currently escorting up the path while he slobbered all over her left ear.

'We're totally and utterly screwed,' I muttered to Mike as Carl rapidly approached us. 'This is so going to end in tears, and for once in my life I actually mean: this is so going to end in tears.'

'Hi, Mrs C,' Carl said cheerily, offering his hand out to shake. I couldn't see his other hand but it wouldn't surprise me if it was feeling Kim Wang's arse. 'And this must be Mr C,' he added, turning to Mike with a full-blown charm offensive. 'I have heard so much about you from your daughter,' he said. 'Sounds like you have a very interesting job. Wouldn't mind going into consultancy myself one day.'

I watched as Mike's chest positively swelled and he brought himself up to his full height. God, what a sucker!

'Well, it is a very interesting job, very challenging, but if you ever wanted the inside track then come and have a chat and I can tell you what route you should follow should you want to pursue a career in management consultancy, son.'

Son! Son! What the hell was Mike doing? This 'son' was about to break his daughter's heart and he was five minutes away from adopting him.

'Well, that's incredibly generous of you,' replied Carl. 'I'll be in touch. So good to meet you.'

I watched Mike gaze after him admiringly.

'Now there's an example of a decent, well-brought-up lad,' said Mike. 'He'll go places, will that one. Not like those other losers we've just chased off the property.'

'He's a manipulative psychopath,' I told him.

Mike stared at me.

'You're right,' I continued. 'Sadly, he will go places, because he's smart, but he uses it to manipulate people and within half an hour you will wish he had never set foot in this house. He will do far more damage than those knuckleheads could ever dream of.'

'What are you talking about, woman? He looks like a really nice boy.'

'He is the devil,' I replied. I looked nervously at the door. Should I go in? Should I go in and stop this boy breaking my daughter's heart and ruining her party? I should have stopped him at the door. Why did I let him go in? I should have said that actually the house was full and we were now turning people away. Anything to stop what was about to happen. I sat back on my camping chair, chewing my fingernails and trying to imagine what was happening inside. Trying to talk myself into going in to see if Kirsty was okay.

'Mrs Collins!' I suddenly heard someone shout. 'Mrs Collins.'

I looked up. It was Ella, one of Kirsty's closest friends. The slightly loopy one who had no common sense but nonetheless was your favourite because she made you laugh and she stopped your daughter taking life too seriously. Her lipstick was smeared all round her mouth and her mascara had run. She looked a right state, if I'm honest.

'Is there a key to the bathroom upstairs?' she asked. 'Or do you have one of those metal poles the police use to get into locked rooms?'

'Does she mean a crowbar?' my husband asked me, looking horrified.

'Yes,' she said. 'Yes, that's it, a crowbar.'

'Why do you need a crowbar?' I asked Ella.

'Because Kirsty's locked herself in the bathroom and won't come out. But we need to be quick because she could suffocate, couldn't she?'

'Is this because of Carl?' I asked her, casting a glance at Mike.

'Yes!' gasped Ella again. 'Evil bastard.'

I tossed Mike a look.

'So where's your crowbar?' Ella asked Mike.

'No need for a crowbar, Ella,' I said, putting my hand on her arm. 'I'm going in,' I told Mike. 'You cover me outside.' He nodded gravely then said, 'Be careful in there.'

'Thanks,' I said, a nervous lump already forming in my throat.

I decided as I approached the back door that I should do my best not to look at anything that was going on. Just focus on Kirsty and getting her straight and then leave. Information on the state of my abode at this stage of the night was dangerous, and not something that I could probably deal with alongside my daughter's emotional turmoil.

However, as I entered the kitchen, intending to make an invisible dash for upstairs, I could not help but notice that Freddie was peering into the grill at a line of fish fingers and had bread all over the worktop. Robbie was standing behind him with his arms folded.

'What are you doing?' I said before I could stop myself. He wasn't even supposed to be at this party, he was supposed to be outside defending our property.

'Robbie's showing me how to grill,' he said cheerfully. He turned to a crowd of four girls who were watching him adoringly from the breakfast bar while drinking something, probably vodka, out of my best Denby mugs. I'd provided perfectly good paper cups. Why had they got my mugs out?

'Last time I made fish-finger sandwiches,' he told them, 'I put them in the toaster, frozen, can you imagine? Then Barbra, my dog, ate them and threw them up and they were a nightmare to clean up, weren't they Mum?'

I shook my head at him in disbelief.

'Oh, and by the way, someone's thrown up in the log

basket,' he added over his shoulder as he attempted to turn over the fish fingers.

'The wicker log basket?' I asked, immediately visualizing vomit oozing through the weaving.

'The very same,' he replied. 'She never liked it,' he told his adoring crowd. 'Good job really.'

I walked away. I had to walk away.

I made my way to the stairs to find that our barricade had been totally broken down. There were children sitting all over the steps and I had to pick my way through them. I noticed at least two girls crying – sobbing, in fact. Weren't parties supposed to be fun? We would be being advised to invite a statutory counsellor to all teenage parties next. I eventually reached the bathroom door. Ella was kneeling in front of it, trying to shout through a nonexistent keyhole.

'Your mum's here now,' she shouted, getting up. 'You need to come out or else she'll shut the party down.' She winked at me. Yes, actually winked.

The door immediately flew open and I was confronted by Kirsty's tear-stained face and bedraggled attire. She looked nothing like the photoshoot-ready model I had seen parading up and down the hall in anticipation earlier in the evening.

'Quick, get in,' said Ella, pushing me and herself through the door and slamming it behind her.

'They're in the lounge talking to Archie Sanders and Chloe Fitzpatrick,' Ella declared. 'Carl keeps touching her arse and Kim is wearing that dress you wanted from Topshop but your tits were too big for it. It's only because she has no tits that it fits her, so I wouldn't be jealous if I were you, apart from the fact of course that she has just walked into your party tonguing your boyfriend.'

'He's not my boyfriend, is he?' said Kirsty. 'Never was. We were just friends and so he can tongue whoever he wants. I shouldn't be upset.'

'But he led you on,' I interjected. 'He might have just said friends but he came over all the time and ate all our Magnums and I think it's fair to say he encouraged you to believe it might go further. I think you are entitled to be upset.'

'And he did say that he never goes out with under-sixteens and that after you turned sixteen then he'd consider you as a potential girlfriend,' added Ella.

'He said *what*?' I roared.

Kirsty blinked at me. 'He promised he'd kiss me when I turned sixteen,' she said, 'to see if we had any chemistry, and if we did then he'd think about being my boyfriend.'

'Manipulative bastard!' I cried. 'I'm throwing him out.'

'Go Mrs C,' said Ella, clapping her hands excitedly.

'No!' cried Kirsty. 'You can't.'

'She's right,' agreed Ella. 'A mum kicking a Year Twelve out of a Year Eleven party. Very uncool.'

'What is that?' I shrieked, catching sight of my lovely cream towels which had brown streaks all over them, as though someone had used them to wipe their arse. Jesus, was there no end to the crimes on display tonight?

'Oh, I think that was me,' said Ella.

'You wiped your backside on my towels?' I said, totally incredulous.

'No! Course not. It's fake tan. I just noticed I had a few streaks that needed sorting. Sorry, Mrs Collins.'

I shook my head in dismay.

'You need to go out there and enjoy your party,' I told Kirsty.

'I can't if he's there.'

'So you tell him to leave then.'

'I can't,' she cried, burying her head in her hands.

'Well, you can't stay in here for the rest of the night,' I tell her. 'Not an option.'

I had no idea what to do next. We were at a teenage-party impasse with nowhere to go. My husband was outside, willing to let any sweet-talking bastard in. My son was downstairs making fish-finger sandwiches and my daughter had locked herself in the bathroom. What on earth was my next move?

There came a massive bang on the door.

'Sis!' Freddie shouted. 'Sis! Me and Robbie have kicked that fucker Carl out. What a sleazeball. I told you, didn't I?'

Kirsty lunged for the door.

'You did what?' she shrieked, before her face fell. There, outside the bathroom door, was Freddie, with his arm draped around Kim Wang.

'It's all right,' grinned Freddie. 'I told Kim that Carl had been sniffing round here for weeks, stringing you along.'

'I had no idea,' said Kim. 'He told me he'd joined a band and was going to band practice.'

'So Robbie's just making Kim a fish-finger sandwich because he knows how to put lettuce and tomato in,' said Freddie. 'That foxed me, I can tell you, and then I'll walk her home. Is that all right, Mum?'

'Come on,' Ella said to Kirsty. 'Let's sort your face out and then do some shots. You need to drown your sorrows.'

'No shots!' I shouted as they walked towards her bedroom.

'Thanks, Freddie,' Kirsty said, as she brushed past her

brother and he squeezed her shoulder in a moment of sibling camaraderie.

'Yeah, thanks Freddie,' I said.

'You're welcome,' he grinned. 'By the way, Dad's asleep on the grass outside. I think he necked a bottle of vodka. I told Robbie to make him a fish-finger sandwich too. Good job he's here.'

25 *June*

It took me a long time to work out what to do with Kirsty after the party. Inevitably she *did* do shots, and so at midnight, after we had kicked everyone out, I spent a good hour with her heaving over the toilet being sick and crying. It was pretty harrowing, I have to say.

I should perhaps have grounded her for getting so drunk, but I didn't have the heart. She was miserable enough.

After five days of her not speaking and Billie Eilish on a loop making me want to slit my own wrists, I knew drastic measures needed to be taken. I needed something radical.

I went up to her room and knocked before I entered. I gasped as I peered my head around the doorframe. My daughter's room had clearly been ransacked by the most ruthless of burglars. Though I thought it was strange they hadn't entered the rest of the house.

I looked over at her, slumped on the bed, staring out the window.

'When did we get burgled?' I asked her.

She looked at me wanly but didn't speak.

'Your room?' I indicated.

She shrugged and turned over to face the wall. Was that . . . was that my grandmother's best Royal Doulton serving plate with a half-eaten piece of mouldy toast on it? That had been missing for weeks. Had the burglars broken into Kirsty's room, nipped downstairs, made themselves some toast, taken it back up to her room on my grandmother's plate, tucked in then ransacked her room before making a hasty getaway?

'Don't shout at me about the mess,' she mumbled. 'I just haven't got round to tidying it today.'

Today! Today! So no burglary, just my daughter would like to live in a tip. I was about to launch into a tirade when I remembered why I was there. The tirade would have to wait until later. It was talky time.

'Get your coat,' I told her. 'We're going out.'

'Where?' she asked.

'You'll see.'

'But I don't want to go out,' she said, looking mournfully at her phone. 'I want to stay right here.'

'Where we are going there will be a phone signal,' I said to her with a sigh. 'So if anyone needs to call you they can. Okay?'

'Okay,' she agreed eventually, pulling herself up. 'But where are we going?'

'The pub,' I told her. 'Well *a* pub.' That woke her up. She wasn't expecting that.

'But it's four in the afternoon?'

'I know. Chop chop. We'll just go for one. We'll be back within the hour.'

'I'm not going in there,' she said when we drew up outside The Hope Arms, a dodgy-looking pub on the wrong side of town. 'Looks rough. Benjamin Foulk's mum goes in

211

there and she got stabbed in the arm with a fork because she looked at a woman in the toilets wrong.'

'Well, we'll not go in the toilets then,' I told her, getting out.

The pub was fairly empty, apart from the expected dropouts and stragglers you might get in a suburban pub at 4 p.m. on a Saturday afternoon; people who had been there since noon and wouldn't go home until midnight.

'Cath!' came the bellow I was hoping for. 'Is that you? Cath! Bugger me. It's been way too long.'

The burly man came out from behind the bar. Or rather his massive belly came out first, followed by the rest of his scruffy body encased in a large apron covered in grease and grime, no doubt courtesy of a deep-fat fryer somewhere in the back kitchen. He smelt of chips and grease and nicotine as he engulfed me in a bear hug.

'You,' he said grinning, 'just get better with age. Really you do.'

'And you look well, Phill,' I said, unable to somehow avoid nodding at his belly.

'Fuck off,' he laughed. 'I've got fucking gangrene in one leg and I've only just got past having my gallstones out. Fucking falling apart, I am. Fucking be glad when I'm fifty and have a fucking excuse to sit down more.'

'This is my daughter,' I said, indicating Kirsty, who was virtually hiding behind me.

'I thought so,' he bellowed. 'Chip off the fucking block I reckon,' he said, managing to eye her breasts and mine at the same time. Perhaps this had not been such a good idea. I pushed Kirsty back behind me. 'Can we have two small glasses of dry white wine?' I asked.

'You can have two glasses of wine,' he replied. 'Fucked if I know what type they are.' He went back behind the bar and reached down to take a bottle out of the fridge, revealing many inches of arse crack as he did so. He sloshed an undetermined amount into two mismatched glasses and handed them over, never once asking whether Kirsty was underage. I paid, and when he gave me the change he clasped my hand in both of his and looked meaningfully into my eyes. I withdrew my hand sharply the minute he loosened his grip.

'Well, I'll let you get on,' I said. 'Good to see you. I'll say bye before we leave.'

I dragged Kirsty over to the furthest corner and sat down hastily, taking a gulp of the very acidic wine. Kirsty eyed her wine and me suspiciously. She looked thoroughly confused.

'Who's that then?' she asked after she'd taken a cautionary sip. She pretended to enjoy it by giving an appreciative 'mmmm'. The wine was absolutely rank.

'He's my Carl,' I informed her.

'What?' she replied, snapping her head up and going bright red. The most colour her face had seen in days. She really needed to start using blusher again. Pale didn't suit her at all.

'He's my Carl.'

'What do you mean?' she asked, staring back over at the lump of a man who was now sitting with his back to us on a stool next to one of the regulars. He was leaning forward on the bar and so his bum crack was a fixture of the view for the foreseeable future.

I took a large gulp of wine.

'He was my first love,' I told her.

'Seriously?' she said. I thought she might gag.

'I was fifteen,' I began. 'So was he. He was much slimmer then, of course. I know it's hard to believe but he was fit! I mean *really* fit!' She looked back at the large lump at the end of the bar. It *was* really hard to believe. But actually, I could still see it. It was his face; his smile that somehow appealed to me, and it still did if I was being honest. Even when we'd walked in today, I couldn't deny that my heart had skipped a tiny beat when his face lit up. It was still there. That feeling. That first-love feeling, over thirty years later.

'I fancied him for ages,' I told her. 'But from afar. We didn't go to the same school but we both went to the same youth disco, so I'd only see him twice a month, but I spent the whole of my time thinking about him. Like *all* of my time. Like every waking hour. Like if I thought about him all the time then somehow he'd be drawn to me, notice me, fall in love with me.'

Kirsty was studying something on the floor. Not looking at me but I knew she was listening.

'I would go to jelly when I was even near him. It was the best and the worst feeling.' I thought for a moment. 'It was heaven and it was hell.'

She looked up at me. 'What happened?' she asked quietly.

'Back in those days at discos we had slow dances at the end of the night. It was a great system really. Like an early Tinder, I suppose. Girls would loiter at the edge of the dance floor pretending they didn't care and then a boy might come and drag you onto the dance floor. He didn't ask you or anything. Just *swiped* you and then you'd press your bodies together for all you were worth while the slow music was on. They used to call it "the erection section", for obvious reasons,' I told her.

'Mum!!' she whined, before grabbing her wine. She

214

took a gulp then screwed her face up like she had just drunk pure lemon juice, which wasn't far off the truth.

'One day he swiped me,' I continued. 'Phill swiped me, pressed me close. I thought I had won the lottery. It was Whitney Houston playing. "Saving All My Love For You". Do you know that song? Possibly the most romantic moment of my life.' I went into my own little reverie for a moment. That song makes me so nostalgic for a time when all that mattered was love. When love was absolutely everything. It almost made me want to go back to the pleasure and the pain of it. To the sheer romance of it.

'What happened then?' asked Kirsty.

'Oh, let's see,' I said, breaking out of my haze. 'Well, we danced, and then he took me outside the back of the community centre and put his hand up my top.'

'Mum!' Kirsty cried again. She put her hands over her ears. 'Please no!'

I pulled her hands away. 'You need to hear this. This is important information. I went out with him for a while,' I continued. 'We were boyfriend and girlfriend, although really all that consisted of was meeting for a walk, finding a quiet spot in the park, him putting his hand up my top and then going home, so not a deep relationship or anything, but I was on top of the world. And then he dumped me. He rang me and told me that the previous night, at a party I hadn't been invited to, that Debbie Ratcliffe had sat on his knee all night and he'd liked it and that was that. I cried for a week. A whole week, Kirsty. It felt like the end of the world, like my entire future was over. That the man I was destined to spend the rest of my life with had been savagely ripped away from me. I thought the world had ended because I wasn't going to spend the rest of my life with the man sitting

215

over there, on that bar stool, scratching his arse crack with a pencil.'

She visibly winced as she looked over and saw that indeed he was.

'Why are you telling me this?' she asked.

'I'm telling you this because although you may think I'm old and an idiot, I was your age once and I can remember how it felt. And while I can't stop you feeling the way you do, what I can do is tell you that at some point in your life you will get past this and be able to look back and wonder: why on earth was I ever in love with that arsehole Carl?'

I was oddly unsettled when I got home. I think confronting your past can do that to you. You see where you were then and where you are now. It makes you think long and hard about the choices you've made. All those sliding-door moments you must have passed through largely unknowingly in your life. Phill had dumped me. What if he hadn't? What if he had been as smitten with me as I had been with him? What if we had lasted the distance from childhood sweethearts to husband and wife, to mother and father? Where would I be now? Where would he be now? Would I be in the kitchen of The Hope Arms slaving over a chip-fat fryer, or together would we have ended up somewhere entirely different? Would I have shaped his life or would he have shaped mine? It made me shiver, that kind of thinking. Made me think about the responsibility of the choices we make. The magnitude of it. The sheer utter randomness of it. What if Phill had fallen in love with me? Where would I be now? I dreaded to think.

Kirsty came down to say goodnight to me at about 10 p.m.

She never normally does that.

'Thank you,' she said.

Then she was gone.

I made a good choice today. I went through the right sliding door.

28 June

Two women down again at book group. Tania sent her apologies but Hazel was going into hospital the next day so they were having a family dinner. Of course everyone was asking me the details, full of concern for Tania's wife. I did my best to be specific until finally I apologized for my vagueness and inability to listen to medical information and said all I really knew was that Tania hadn't yet said it was going to be all right which was deeply, deeply worrying. We sat and shared stories of other people we knew who'd had cancer and had pulled through, as though if we could think of enough examples then that would mean that Hazel was going to be fine. No one mentioned the cases they knew where it had ended badly. Not the time or the place.

On a positive note, apparently Paula liked our home-made cards and she'd put them up on her mantelpiece. She'd now seen a counsellor for one session so far and Sonja said that it was early days but it wasn't as bad as she had thought it was going to be. She'd been signed off work for another three months but she was no longer spending every day on the sofa and was thinking of taking up Nordic walking, which seemed like a glimmer of positive thinking.

What with everything going on, only Fiona and Louise

had read this month's thriller and so they gave us a brief summary of the plot. Fiona again claimed to have not enjoyed it but gave us a very detailed account of the main characters before Louise let it slip that the orthopaedic surgeon did it, which meant that it was pointless the rest of us reading it now. Never mind.

July

Reduce My Carb Footprint
(That will be carbohydrate
as well as carbon)

1 July

I figure I have been on at least twenty-five, mostly unsuccessful diets.

I have got on the scales optimistically at least two and half thousand times. I had been disappointed with the reading at least two and a half thousand times.

I have attended two different slimming clubs on five separate occasions, spending a not-inconsiderable amount of money.

I have purchased every type of substitute diet food launched onto the market.

None of the above have had any impact on my weight whatsoever.

Apparently, as I approach menopause I will start to struggle to lose weight. I find this hysterical, as if any woman in the history of the universe has ever found it easy to lose weight.

And I have to admit that over the past five years the pounds have crept up in number a bit. I'm totally kidding myself that it's the washing machine that has shrunk my jeans, and not in fact my expanding waistline that has made them feel as if I am trying to stuff jumbo marshmallows into a shot glass.

I felt as if I had hit a weight management 'fork in the road'. Did I go sod it, I'm nearly 50, who gives a toss about how much I weigh any more, and just let it all go? Indulge in every guilty pleasure I've tried to deny myself for my entire adult life. Have white toast for breakfast with lashings of real butter, order cake at the coffee shop as well as a full-fat latte, go large at McDonald's, order a pudding as well as a starter when out for a meal, give myself the largest portion of lasagne when doling it out around the family dining table, buy biscuits – lots and lots of biscuits . . . That sounded like so much fun, that sounded so free, that sounded how I would like to enjoy food. But I knew where it would lead. Those custard creams would land on my thighs quicker than Mike leaves a room when there's washing-up to be done. That portion of apple pie with cream would convert to an increased dimpling on my upper arms faster than Barbra Streisand takes to throw up fish fingers. The extra fries with barbecue sauce that would complement my Big Mac would clog up my arteries and make me feel as though I had sold my soul to the devil. And I couldn't even begin to contemplate the shame of anyone I knew seeing me sitting alone in a McDonald's restaurant, having 'gone large'.

No, I was not sure the deliciousness was worth it. I knew that the moments of sheer satisfaction when I downed my fourth Hobnob of the morning would soon disappear to be replaced by woe as I realized that I had indeed quite literally 'gone large'.

To help me veer down the right fork in this critical path, I took myself to a woefully depleted high street in town with its pound shops, vaping emporiums, fast-food joints and yes . . . fat people. It was harsh, I know, perhaps cruel, probably extremely discriminatory, but overall it was very, very effective. Five minutes spent on a neglected British high street and you would see an abundance of women over 50 who had weight issues. I wondered if they had reached the fork in the road at my age and decided to go down an indulgent route, or had they been on that road all their lives. Either way, they didn't look happy. They didn't look pleased as punch that they had 'gone large'. They looked sad and miserable and awkward and lost. I didn't want to get lost.

So I would stay on the path of denial in the vain hope of at least keeping my weight and my health in some sort of check. But rather than going to the so-called experts and throwing money at them, getting them to tell me what I couldn't eat, I decided to devise my own mantra. That I should keep it simple. So as well as reducing my carbon footprint, which everyone is now absolutely duty bound to do, I should also attempt to reduce my carbohydrate footprint.

Bread is dead!

Hasta la vista, pasta!

Spuds are duds!

I wouldn't totally cut out carbs, of course. I'd decided grains would be my sustenance as I was not keen on rice or couscous or quinoa, so my portion control was excellent where those were concerned. I would, however, be experimenting with cauliflower steaks and purchasing the dreaded spiralizer.

Might work, might not. The key would be to avoid increasing my intake of fat and sugar to compensate.

But at least I had an incentive. California next month and the thought of standing next to my twig of a sister was enough to put anyone off jacket potatoes!

I have never ever, ever been so hungry in my entire life. All I've had is fruit and yoghurt for the last seven days for breakfast, and now I am literally ready to eat my own hand. How can anyone survive without carbs in the morning?

I'm nervous today. It's a big day, and what do I normally do to calm my nerves? Stuff my face full of carbs, of course! Nothing like biscuits to settle the butterflies. I considered cracking open the wine to avoid caving on reducing my carbohydrate footprint, but decided that I couldn't give up just yet.

What was making it worse was that Mike was hovering in a suit and a tie for no reason whatsoever.

'Whose funeral?' Freddie demanded when he came downstairs and took one look at his dad.

I turned to see my son dressed in jeans and a T-shirt that ironically had a picture of a tie printed on it.

'Couldn't you at least wear an actual tie?' pleaded Mike.

'No. Not to a university open day,' replied Freddie. 'Only geeks wear ties, period.'

'Then why are you wearing a T-shirt with a tie printed on it?' asked Mike.

'Because that's different,' said Freddie. 'I'm going nowhere with you while you are wearing a tie.'

Mike looked at me. I nodded. He took his tie off, rolled it around his hand and put it in his pocket.

Freddie stuck his hand out.

Mike looked at me. I nodded. He put his hand back in his pocket, took out the tie and handed it over to Freddie.

Then of course Freddie, being Freddie, unrolled the tie and tied it around his own neck without breaking eye contact with his father. Now he was wearing a T-shirt with a tie printed on it and a real tie over the top.

'Are you seriously going like that?' asked Mike.

'Oh yes,' nodded Freddie. 'I am loving this statement.' He indicated his attire.

'And what is your statement exactly?'

'Anti-establishment,' replied Freddie.

'You are attending a century-old British university, to which you wish to gain admittance, wearing an outfit that you hope communicates the statement "anti-establishment"?'

'Exactly,' said Freddie, slapping his dad on the shoulder. 'We students have to play hard-to-get these days. I don't expect you to understand this, as you got your studies courtesy of the taxpayer; however, since your generation voted to abolish free tuition fees, then all the "establishments" just want our moolah. So you see I *have* to play a little hard-to-get. Hence the highly intelligent, anti-establishment uniform. Now, shall I drive?'

No one said much on the way. I had been relegated to the back of the car like some aged auntie just short of a blanket to cover her knees. I stared out of the window, contemplating the fact that we were on our way to see the place for which my son might flee the nest in just over a year's time. Nothing so far had been said about Mike's previous interest in also attending said university. Overconfident Freddie had assumed his over-the-top production would ensure that Mike would not dare be a student within fifty miles of his son, but I wasn't so sure that he had sealed Mike out completely. Mike was a management consultant, after all. Supremely trained in the art of people manipulation. It was possible that Mike was hovering over his decision to attend Birmingham University in order to keep Freddie absolutely focused on stealing that dream from him. If that was Mike's game, then it was indeed a masterstroke for which I could only commend him. Equally I knew very well that Mike possessed a tunnel vision when it came to getting something he wanted, so it was quite possible that all of Freddie's pleading had gone totally over his head and Mike was as intent on retraining to become a teacher as he had always been.

I had been looking forward to touring the establishment with my son and discussing the various pros and cons of courses and accommodation and student life, but of course it didn't happen like that.

We parked. Freddie checked his phone and announced that he'd call us later when he was ready to go home. He was off to meet Kim Wang and her parents outside the vice chancellor's introductory talk. Then he was going to see the psychology department and Kim's parents were taking them for lunch before they looked at the accommodation options.

I had no idea what order to address this in. No idea whatsoever. So I just said what I deemed to be the most important.

'You are going to lunch with Kim's parents? Is it serious then? Are you girlfriend and boyfriend?'

Freddie gave me a quizzical look.

'Sort of. I guess. Not really thought about it. It's just that they know a great Chinese restaurant that apparently does the best chow mein in the country.'

'Wow, can we come?' I asked before I even thought about it.

'Not good for your carbohydrate footprint, Mum,' said Freddie, shaking his head. 'And I wouldn't subject Kim to you two today.'

'Now hang on a minute,' interjected Mike. 'So it's all right for you to spend all day with your girlfriend's parents but not all right for us just to say hello?'

'She's not my girlfriend,' Freddie replied firmly.

'If you are eating chow mein with her parents then that's girlfriend and boyfriend status if you ask me, and we have a right to meet them at the very least,' I said.

'You don't care if you meet them,' replied Freddie. 'You just want to eat the best chow mein in the country.'

My stomach rumbled at just the thought of it. But he was wrong. I was also desperate to meet what could be Freddie's future in-laws. Or perhaps I was getting ahead of myself.

'Look, Freddie,' said Mike, pulling himself up to his full height. 'Don't you forget that you will be coming to us for handouts for food and accommodation and all that other stuff, apart from your fees, so I think the least you can do is involve us in what you are doing today. We have a right to be involved.'

'Okay,' said Freddie sulkily. 'You can come for chow mein.'

I was about to cheer when Mike interrupted with a firm no. 'I don't care about chow mein,' he said.

I do! I thought. I wanted to try the best chow mein in the UK and hang my carbohydrate footprint.

'We will meet you outside the psychology department after the vice chancellor's introductory talk. Is Kim looking at psychology too?' asked Mike.

'No – she's thinking of anthropology.'

I don't think I have ever been more proud. My son had a sort of girlfriend who was smart enough to do an 'ology' that I didn't totally understand at university. How incredible was that? Freddie had come such a long way. And Kim's parents knew where to get the best chow mein in the UK. This was a match made in heaven. This *had* to work.

So the vice chancellor's introductory talk was fun. *Not!* She seemed like a lovely woman. Hugely positive and proud of her university and all the students who went there. I wasn't sure there were supposed to be questions at the end. In fact, in a lecture room full of maybe 500 people, I was sure that there was no intention to field questions, but as the vice chancellor made her closing remarks my husband stood up. Yes, stood up in an expectant fashion, as though he expected to be invited to take the floor. I glanced over at Freddie who thankfully was sitting as far away from us as possible with the Wangs. He was shaking his head in a resigned fashion as the vice chancellor asked if she could help Mike at all with his issue.

'I notice from your financial statement last year that your income has risen dramatically since the introduction of tuition fees. What examples of investment in student resources can you show that has made the most of that increase in income, and what are your plans for investment over the next five years?'

Jesus. I sank down in my seat and squirmed. The vice chancellor had clearly met this kind of beast before, however. The overachieving father with a desire to show control and command in a situation where he had no real right to show any control and command at all.

'We have increased our capital expenditure by 28 per cent in the last five years, 95 per cent of which has been invested in student infrastructure. Any more questions? No . . . good. I have another group waiting to come in, so might I suggest that you go and familiarize yourselves with all that Birmingham University has to offer and I sincerely hope that I will be seeing some of you again in just over a year's time.'

'Quite a brusque answer I thought,' said Mike, as everyone got up to leave.

'Quite an inappropriate question at an inappropriate time,' I replied. 'I doubt very much that the Wangs will be inviting us for chow mein after that little display. I think Freddie was about to die with embarrassment.'

'What is with your obsession about eating chow mein? I never even knew you liked chow mein,' said Mike.

'When you have barely eaten carbs for three weeks then you would be obsessed with chow mein,' I told him feeling like I was going to faint with hunger if I wasn't fed soon.

'Mr and Mrs Wang,' said Mike looking over my shoulder. 'How very nice to meet you. We have heard so much about you.'

'And the chow mein,' I blurted before I could stop myself.

Mr and Mrs Wang looked at me quizzically.

'I . . . I'm reducing my carb footprint at the moment,' I continued in a rush. 'And so the mention of anything that contains any carbs at all sends me into some kind of automatic spasm that makes me obsessed with eating it at that very second.' I didn't think I was explaining it very well.

Mr and Mrs Wang remained silent and confused.

'Mrs Collins is trying to reduce her carbohydrate footprint as well as her carbon footprint,' Kim offered by way of explanation. She nodded and smiled at me. She is such a lovely girl.

'No flying? No driving?' asked Mr Chow.

I nodded. 'As well as no bread, no potatoes, no pasta. Just for health reasons. But I do of course care for the environment too. I recycle practically every day.' I looked at Freddie in desperation. This was not going to plan.

Mrs Wang took a step forwards and took my hands. 'You must join us for lunch,' she said slowly, as if talking to a child. 'At our friend's restaurant. It really is excellent.'

'Yes,' I gasped, thrilled to have secured an invite. 'Of course. That would be lovely.'

'Right,' said Freddie. 'Glad we got all the awkward introductions out of the way. Shall we meet back here at twelve? Good. See you later, guys.'

'There are so many exciting things to try, aren't there?' Mike said after we had toured the Grand Hall where all the societies and sports teams had displays. He'd been Mister Sociable, chatting to all the scruffy, semi-homeless-looking students who clearly had been told to make sure they engaged with the prospective parents. He'd asked them all thoughtful questions about their societies and their teams and then gone on to ask them about their courses and how they thought it was going. He'd even secured the phone number of a female first-year psychology student who would be happy to talk to Freddie about the course structure. She also happened to be the secretary of the Baking Society. I was tempted to ask her what the secretary of the Baking Society did. How did someone come to university and end up being the Baking Soc secretary?

Seeing all these displays made me feel a bit sad, reflecting on all the opportunities I must have had at college that I just didn't appreciate.

Total number of societies joined at university – 0.

I just hadn't thought any of them were me. The thought of trying something new had been terrifying. I did remember that I went to one trampolining club session because my neighbour in halls was desperate to go but wouldn't go on her own. It was supposed to be for beginners but loads of people had clearly done it before. I didn't belong.

'Yeah, Baking Society, I reckon, and there's a mature students' football team,' I heard Mike say.

I turned to stare at him. 'You haven't played football in over ten years.'

'So?'

'You're over fifty. You'll break something or rip something. Football becomes an extreme sport when you are over fifty. You should do walking football.'

'What kind of sport is that?'

I looked at Mike and sighed. 'When are you going to tell Freddie that you are still thinking of applying?'

'After he's applied,' Mike replied. 'Keep it quiet until then. We don't want this run of ambition from him scuppered, do we? He'll be so pumped about coming by then that he will have forgotten about me being around. Especially if he's still seeing Kim and she's coming. I'll promise to stay out of his way. I reckon our paths will barely cross.'

My heart sank. I was very dubious. Freddie was so fickle; the slightest thing could turn him off. And any hint of his father being a student at the same university would be more than enough for him to throw his toys out of the cot. Mike was right about Kim, though. Freddie's continued interest in going to university was being massively helped by the presence of Kim in his life. We had to nurture this one. We needed to do everything we could to keep that relationship going until at least after A levels. Maybe I needed to start thinking of ways to make Freddie more attractive to Kim. Tell him to shower more often? Teach him how to cook something half-decent? Ditch most of his weird wardrobe?

'You never know, I could stand for student president,' I half heard Mike as I mused about what Freddie might look like if he dressed normally for a change.

'What are you talking about?'

'If I come back to uni I could stand for student president. I always fancied it at Loughborough but I got offered the graduate training job with the consultancy and couldn't turn it down really. Nothing to stop me now, though. Imagine how effective I would be as a student president. All that experience and knowledge I've gained over the years. I'd give the vice chancellor a run for her money, I can tell you.'

'I thought you wanted to come back to college to give something back to the community. To learn how to teach. Not to run a management consultancy project on the entire university?'

'That *is* what I want to do. I'm just saying that my experience would make me an excellent candidate for student president.'

I looked at my husband. I had a gnawing feeling in the pit of my stomach. His itch to do something different was not going to go away but his solutions to this urge were all over the shop, taking him places that were completely and utterly ludicrous. Student president at over 50! Potentially at his son's university. The Baking Society! A football team! Teaching! Jesus, it might just be easier if he had an affair. That would seem like a much more straightforward solution to a midlife crisis at this point in time. And still all at my expense. He was clearly still assuming that all this would be made possible by me finding a job that paid much more than what I earned at The Mustard Factory. I'd taken on a bit more work from Jimmy and Veronique who shared an office with Toby, but I was still earning nowhere near enough to compensate for losing Mike's salary.

The terrible gnawing feeling in my stomach was growing and I knew there was only one solution to that. Total carb overload. And I mean carb overload. It was time for lunch.

9 July

The guilt was about killing me but I became a different person yesterday on a full belly of chow mein. My carbohydrate footprint had sadly expanded, however my contentment factor was back on track.

In the interests of fully encouraging Freddie and Kim's relationship I invited Kim over for a meal with us last night. When she arrived I saw that she'd brought her overnight bag, too, the assumption being that she would be staying over in Freddie's room. They hadn't asked. Of course they hadn't asked. I hustled Mike into the utility room when it became clear that this was the intention so we could have a conference on the issue at hand.

'Freddie's thinking that Kim is going to stay in his room tonight,' I hissed.

'Really?'

'Yes. What do we do?'

'Say that they can't, don't we? Are we ready for that under our own roof?'

'Well, I'm not ready, but what if that causes them to split up and then Freddie doesn't go to university?'

Mike looked at me, confused.

'As discussed earlier,' I spelt out, 'Kim is a key component in Freddie's desire to go to university, and so we need to keep this relationship going. If we don't allow her to sleep in his room, we may jeopardize it.'

'Are you saying that if we don't allow them to have sex in our house that Freddie might not go to university.'

I thought about this. 'Yes,' I replied.

'I'm not sure you have eaten enough carbs yet,' he replied. 'You're being stupid. Freddie's sex life has nothing to do with whether or not he goes to university.'

I knew there was logic to my thoughts that they were directly linked, but clearly Mike didn't agree. Perhaps I did need more carbs.

'Do you want Kim to sleep in Freddie's bed tonight?' Mike asked.

'I'd prefer it if they didn't.'

'Right, then.' He opened the door to the utility room and strode out. Freddie and Kim were looking at something on an iPad at the kitchen table.

'Just so you know,' he announced, 'your mother is just going upstairs to make up the spare bed for Kim to stay in tonight.'

'Thank you, Mrs Collins,' Kim said to me, smiling.

MUM'S KNEE

Lizzy: In total countdown mode now. Cannot wait to see you all. Have managed to get you guest memberships at our pool club so don't forget your bikinis! Will have to work a few days but you'd be welcome to join me and do my class. I won't charge you!

Nicola: Beyond excited. How many bikinis should I bring?

Me: Beyond excited. Haven't owned a bikini since I was 20!

Lizzy: How are you all getting to the airport?

I knew exactly what was coming.

Nicola: I've no idea – what are you doing, Cathy?

I needed to choose my words carefully or else I would be organizing everyone's transport to the airport.

Me: Haven't thought about it yet.

Nicola: When you do, will you include us four?

Dammit. How is this happening?

Me: Four?

Nicola: *If you are thinking of booking someone to drive us all down in a minibus you need to count for four of us.*

Bloody hell.

Me: *I wasn't thinking of booking a minibus.*

Nicola: *But how else are you going to get all of us to the airport?*

Me: *Can't Laurence drive you to the airport?*

Nicola: *Then he'll have to leave his car there and pay parking for ten days.*

Lizzy: *I'm sure you'll work it out. Just don't forget Mum and Dad!!!*

Me: *Tell u what, Nic. I'll worry about Mum and Dad and you sort out your family.*

Me (internally): *But you can't get six in Mike's car so you might as well book a minibus for all of us?*

But I didn't want to because I'd have to spend loads of time on the internet researching minibuses and then I'd have to call them for quotes and half of them would be unavailable because we would have left it too late or they'd be disapproving of where I wanted to go and how many people I wanted to take and how much luggage we would have and how many locations they would have to attend to pick people up and then I'd get it all sorted

236

and tell everyone what time it was coming and how much it cost and someone would complain about how expensive it was and couldn't I have found a cheaper one, and actually the times I had agreed were far too early or late so wouldn't it be better if we did it in a different order to make it easier for everyone and could I check if they had booster seats for the young ones because they didn't want to take the booster seats with them but obviously they couldn't go in a minibus without booster seats and could I ask which route the driver is thinking of taking because the last time a friend's neighbour's half-sister went to Heathrow they got stuck for forty minutes on the M40 so we really should check if they were going to take the M1 because that would be the better route at that time of day. Then after all that someone would say, do you know what, we are not going to come with you in the minibus after all. My college friend lives five miles from Heathrow so we are going to drive down and leave a car there and she'll give us a lift to the airport the next day so we'll meet you there!

Me: *I'm not booking a minibus.*

Nicola: *But you said you were thinking about it.*

Me: *I didn't but I just have and I'm not booking a minibus.*

Nicola: *Are you still reducing your carb footprint? You don't seem yourself.*

Me: *How do you know about that?*

Nicola: *Mum told me. She said you are grumpy and out of sorts and the sooner you start eating chips again the better.*

Lizzy: *I found giving up carbs hugely liberating. Well done, Cathy.*

Me: *Fuck off, Lizzy*

16 July

Couldn't tell you how much I had been looking forward to going on holiday and not having to think about periods. I thought I'd nailed it. It had been six weeks since my last period. Six weeks. I thought I'd finally shed the dreaded curse. But no. It's back! Now I would have to pack tampons and towels and worry about leaking in a strange bed.

I needed a cure for periods.

I needed chocolate!

I needed carbs!

19 July

I had put on a new top I was saving for my holidays today. I didn't know why. Actually I did know why. It was a size 12. The reduction in my carbohydrate footprint appeared to have had some effect and my boobs had shrunk which was awesome and almost made the nightly dreams of carbs worthwhile. And it was my last visit to The Mustard Factory until after we came back from California. So for some reason I'd thought I'd dress up for the occasion and, to be honest, I couldn't possibly go out in a size 14 top now that I knew I was officially a size 12. That would just be depressing and unnecessary. Plus the fact that the 'work mum' title seemed to have resurfaced, with Toby occasionally throwing me the odd email entitled 'Work mum, I need you!' and Jimmy having designed an avatar for me with me wearing an apron that made me look like some browbeaten 1950s housewife! I was not happy.

So I made my way up to the office that my three office children shared and there was Toby at the door waiting. Unusual.

'Hi, Cathy, hello, Barbra,' he said, bending to give the dog a pat.

'What are you doing out here?'

'Little surprise in here,' he said, giving me a wink. Yes, a wink. He popped his head around the door behind me and asked if the occupants were all ready and then he pushed the door open in front of him so I could step in.

There in the darkest corner was a desk and chair, with a mug on it and a dog bowl beside it and fairy lights dancing above it.

'I'm confused,' I said. 'Is there somebody else moving in?'

'It's for you,' said Toby. 'To be honest, someone upstairs was chucking the desk and chair out, and well, we all wondered if you'd like to be able to bring your laptop here sometimes and work from here so that if we need you then, you know, you are here, right here, and I can come and harass you about what I should charge and contracts and tell you who's not paid their bills and all that. But you know, only if you want to. You don't have to, we all just thought that you might like the option to do all our shit here sometimes rather than at home.'

I looked around at the three of them grinning at me.

'Look,' said Jimmy, 'we got you a mug too.' He grabbed the mug and held it up to me. It was black with SUPPORT SEX WORKERS written in bold yellow letters on it. I seized it and laughed, and laughed, fingering the letters.

'And we got Barbra a dog bowl,' said Veronique, 'so she can come too. We could get her a jar of dog biscuits as well, couldn't we, guys?' she continued. They all nodded their heads vigorously.

'You do like it, don't you?' said Toby. 'I mean, you don't have to say you do. You don't have to use it, we just thought it might make life easier for you and, well, for us too really.'

I laughed.

I looked back over at the corner. My work corner. I had a desk and chair and a mug with the word sex on it. And . . . and I had fairy lights. I had never seen a more beautiful work environment in my life.

'I love it,' I said, struggling to keep my emotions in check. 'I absolutely love it and yes, I understand you have installed this piece of tat that was about to be thrown away purely so you can have me on tap more than I currently am but, that said, I love it, and I will be very happy to occasionally spend my time at that desk sorting your shit out.'

'Hooray,' shouted Veronique. 'I think this calls for a celebration, don't you? Anyone for some kombucha? I've got a new variety in.'

'Fuck off,' said everyone in unison. Then we all laughed together. My new roommates. My new young roommates who bought me a mug with sex on it and some fairy lights.

Life at that moment felt very good.

'By the way, loving the top,' said Toby. 'You've lost weight, haven't you?'

Life at that moment felt extremely good.

There was no better feeling in the world than someone noticing you had lost weight when you had truly suffered in order to achieve it.

'Thank you,' I grinned. 'It's new, and I have lost weight.'

'Well, it really suits you,' he said, flashing me a mouth-watering smile. 'And well done for losing weight. So hard.'

'Thank you,' I said again. My mind flashed back briefly to this morning when I had walked into the kitchen to be confronted with Freddie eating cold chow mein out of the fridge while he told me I looked as if I was going for an interview at a department store. I asked him why and he said that I looked tidy and smart and dull.

'Those Californian men are not going to know what hit them,' commented Toby, picking up my sex mug. 'Coffee?'

20 July

MUM'S KNEE

Nicola: Just so you know, there's only three of us for the minibus now.

Me: I haven't booked a minibus! I said I wasn't! I'm not booking a minibus!

241

Nicola: *But how are me and the kids going to get to the airport?*

Me: *I've no idea. You and your doc boyfriend need to sort yourselves out.*

I slammed my phone down at that point, totally frustrated. Half an hour later I picked it up again to call Kirsty and noticed my sister's latest message.

Nicola: *You are a heartless bitch.*

Christ – way harsh.

Me: *Wow, Nicola – just because I haven't booked the minibus?*

Nicola: *No! Because you clearly have no sympathy for the fact that I've just been dumped.*

What was she talking about? I scrolled back up to see that I had missed some key messages that she'd sent half an hour earlier.

Nicola: *He's no longer my boyfriend. He's not coming to California.*

Nicola: *I can only assume from your silence that you don't care that my boyfriend has ghosted me for the past week then turned up last night and said he'd started seeing a nurse in paediatrics and he was going to Corfu with her rather than California with me!*

Nicola: *Why are you never there for me?*

After that message she accused me of being a heartless bitch . . .

Me: *I'm so sorry, Nic! That really is shitty.*

No response.

Me: *Are you OK? I really am sorry. I know you really liked him.*

No response.

Me: *What can I do to help?*

Nicola: *I just don't know what to do with myself. I really thought he was the one, Cathy.*

Me: *I know. I'm so, so sorry. There is someone out there better for you, I know there is.*

Nothing for half an hour.

Me: *Look, if it helps I'll book us all a minibus to the airport. Give you one less thing to think about, OK?*

Nicola: *That would be great – thank you. I'm in no fit state to organize anything at the moment. Got to go. Speak soon. Bye xx*

I *knew* I would end up booking a damn minibus to the airport. I spent an hour online and on the phone trying to get one organized and then I picked a bottle of prosecco off the shelf and went to see my little sister.

When I arrived she was stirring tinned spaghetti on the hob, tears streaming down her face. I extracted the spoon from her hand, sat her down on a chair and attempted not to screw up cooking spaghetti on toast for her kids.

Two hours later I left. Tilly and Jude seemed to be delighted with being allowed to sit and eat tea in front of the telly in the lounge while their mother balled her eyes out in the kitchen and hovered between shouting 'what an utter bastard' and whimpering 'but I thought he was the one'.

I decided not to share with her that I'd had my concerns when I'd met him. That he reeked of older man looking for a bit of fun. I also decided not to share with her that Dad had labelled him arrogant. No good ever comes of post-break-up analysis. The amount of times I'd told people that I had never liked their ex-boyfriend anyway, only to see them get back together and have to backtrack my way back into their good books. So, in the interests of sisterly love, I poured her prosecco and passed her tissues and kept my mouth shut.

22 July

Tissues and prosecco came into play again this evening. Tania popped round, eyes rimmed red. She'd left her house to give Hazel some time with her parents who had come to provide 'moral support'. Tania found their visits quite harrowing at the best of times, as Hazel's dad still couldn't find it in his heart to love his daughter's wife like she deserved to be loved. This was despite Tania being the dream spouse who loved his daughter with her very bones and lavished care and affection and respect on her in a way I find very rare in any marriage. Particularly Hazel's parents' marriage, which seemed to consist of Hazel's dad treating her mum like a doormat while her mum seethed and simmered, moaning about him whenever he was out of earshot.

It was very clear that Hazel's dad could not forgive Tania her gender and took against her for merely being a woman. I suspect, given the choice, he'd rather have seen his daughter grow up and spend her life unhappily married to a man she didn't love. Much the same path I suspect his wife had trodden.

Tania sat at the kitchen table and said that Hazel's dad couldn't even bring himself to look at her. Didn't even acknowledge her existence.

'It was as if he genuinely blames me,' she said, a look of horror on her face. 'That this is happening because she is a lesbian and I made her love me and it's all my fault.'

She looked distraught and exhausted. She didn't look anything like my friend Tania. My steady, reliable, down-to-earth, wonderful friend. Hazel's illness was changing her too and it broke my heart.

'I can understand his distress,' she said. 'It's his daughter. But she's my wife. We both feel this way because we love her so much. That should unite us, not separate us. Why can't he see that?'

'Perhaps he's jealous,' I said. 'You have a happy marriage and he doesn't. He doesn't know how to deal with that. You are two women and you have a better marriage than his, a man and a woman. That does not compute in his world.'

'We need to . . . we have to work out how to connect over this though,' sniffed Tania. 'I can't be falling out with him now. That won't help Hazel. I can't leave Hazel to deal with his prejudice. I need to handle it for her.'

'You'll find a way,' I told her. 'You always do.'

She sighed.

'It's why she loves you so much,' I add. 'You'll handle it. You will so handle it.'

'I know,' she nodded. 'I just wish I didn't have to.'

Then she looked at me for a moment too long and I had this overwhelming feeling that I didn't want to hear what was coming next. She drew breath and I braced myself.

'We saw the consultant yesterday,' she said. 'The surgery she had went well but . . .'

My brain went fuzzy at the word 'but'. I tried so hard to take in exactly what she was saying. To listen to the relevant details, but all I heard were the massive red flags. Words such as 'spread' and 'multiple organs' and 'intensive chemotherapy' and perhaps the worst of all, 'we need to be positive'.

I wanted to put my hands over my ears and stop hearing what she was saying.

I didn't, of course. I held Tania's hands and tried to say the right words, which of course were the wrong words because there are no right words. Just rubbish, stupid pathetic words that come nowhere close to trying to help your friend whose heart is breaking before your eyes.

She went back home some time later. Exhausted.

246

Red-eyed. I went to bed and lay there trying to work out how life could be so utterly shitbag awful.

30 July

Book group was at Sonja's tonight.

Paula was there when we all arrived. This was a lovely surprise, although she wasn't looking great. She looked smaller than when I'd last seen her. She looked less. Pale, shrunken, definitely not her usual self. We were all overjoyed to see her but did our best not to overwhelm her; she seemed to sink further into the large chair every time anyone addressed her, as though she was actually trying to disappear.

This did present us with a somewhat awkward situation, though, as Tania had also decided to come. Hazel had been very stern with her, apparently, and told her she needed to carry on doing normal things. This was no time to stay at home moping, she had said.

But what should we discuss? Where should we start? Tania? Paula? The book?

Clearly the book wasn't going to get a look-in tonight, but we all contemplated each other nervously as we wondered who was going to ask who how they were. Fortunately it was Paula whose voice broke the ice and decided for us.

'How's Hazel?' she asked Tania as soon as she sat down.

A hush fell over the room instantly. I looked nervously at Tania. This had to be one of the hardest things. The constant supply of information required.

She sighed. 'Not great, to be honest, Paula,' she said.

'It's spread so she's on for a course of chemo that's going to knock her sideways, but we're trying to be positive.'

She nodded. The room went quiet again.

Paula heaved herself up out of her chair and walked towards Tania and gave her the cancer hug. The heartfelt embrace, mingled with tears, that you see women of a certain age give each other in these circumstances. The hug that tells you that cancer looms darkly somewhere in their lives.

We murmured round the subject for quite some time, doing our level best to console Tania. Until it was clear that Tania no longer wanted to be in the spotlight. Her answers to our questions became short and terse. She'd come out for a level of distraction and we weren't providing it.

It was then a tricky segue from cancer-stricken wife to depression. Paula flushed deeply when Louise finally said that it was really good to see her back. She glanced at Sonja, as if wanting her to explain things for her. They exchanged a nod and then Paula spoke.

'I wanted to see Tania,' she said. 'See how she was. That's why I'm here. You don't need to hear about me. What I am going through is nothing compared to Tania.'

'Bullshit,' said Tania, suddenly animated again. 'Depression is an awful thing. Don't diminish what you're suffering. How is the counselling? Is it helping? *Please* tell me some good news.'

Paula nodded, tears brimming in her eyes. 'I'm making progress,' she whispered. 'But can we not talk about it? Please. I didn't want to come here and talk about it,' she said, shaking her head. Sonja reached over and grasped her hand.

There was an awkward pause.

'Bollocks,' I muttered. 'Does that mean we have to talk about the book then?'

Everyone laughed and then we did our best to be normal as we gossiped and drank and tried hard to give Paula and Tania some escape from their own private hells.

I decided to share my exercise with Kirsty, to tell them all about taking her to visit Phill at the pub so she could see 'what could have been', had my first love worked out.

'Do you think it worked?' asked Fiona in awe.

'Put it this way,' I replied, 'she's not mentioned Carl since, and I actually heard her singing in the shower the other day.'

'Impressive,' said Tania, giving me a proud look. 'Seriously impressive. Well done.'

'Thanks,' I replied, glowing slightly. 'You should all try it.'

'My first boyfriend was the son of a baron and now lives on his family's estate in Wiltshire,' said Fiona.

'Bloody hell,' I replied. 'What did you ditch him for? We could have been coming for book group in your own library or something.'

She thought for a minute.

'He slept with my sister,' she replied.

'Of course he did,' I laughed.

We spent the rest of the evening discussing our first loves. I can highly recommend it. Turned out Sonja's became a vicar, which we all found hilarious for some reason. Louise's still lived in Manchester where she grew up, and her parents still talked about him whenever she went to visit.

'He's a barrister apparently,' she said. 'A barrister with zero sense of humour who probably still has bad breath,' she added. 'But apparently being a barrister cancels all that out in my parents' eyes.'

Then Tania admitted she'd had a holiday romance with a boy when she was 15. His name was Callum and he had acne on his back.

'I thought I should at least give "not being gay" a go,' she said. 'But I knew the minute I kissed him by the swimming pool and ran my hands over his back that I was definitely a lesbian.'

'Good call,' we all agreed.

'Richard was my first boyfriend,' said Paula.

There was a pause.

'Wow,' I said. 'How amazing. Good to hear first loves do sometimes work out.'

She nodded but said no more.

There would be no book group next month as it was school holidays.

As we all left we hugged a little harder than normal. The cancer hug.

August

Agree Who Will Clean Mum and Dad's Toilet

1 August

Well, I was never going to get that day back, was I?

I knew it would be hell from start to finish and I wasn't wrong.

I didn't think it was my natural role in life to be a chief; I was more of a foot soldier. But for today it was deemed that I would be a chief. Chief of a tribe that consisted of my parents, my children, my husband, my sister, my niece and my nephew. And I had to somehow transport them from the heart of the West Midlands to California in an orderly fashion.

It all started before the minibus even picked us up.

MUM'S KNEE

Nicola: *Where are you?*

Me: *At home?*

Nicola: *I thought you were picking us up at 6?*

Me: *No – I said 7.*

253

Nicola: But we're all ready?

Me: What do you expect me to do?

Nicola: The kids have been up for three hours!

Me: Have some coffee

Nicola: On my third! I am bouncing off the walls.

Me: Call Mum – she'll be up.

Nicola: Good idea. See you in a bit. Oh, have you bought Lizzy a gift for having us?

Me: No! Have you?

Nicola: No! Mum mentioned it last night. She said we should be taking her something local to remind her of home.

Me: Like what?

Nicola: Cheese?

Me: Let's get her something at Heathrow.

Nicola: A Heathrow umbrella – perfect. See you later.

Lizzy: No cheese and no umbrella please! You don't need to bring anything, just yourselves.

We picked Mum and Dad up last. They were waiting on the side of the road, of course. Mum in her travelling gilet that she had bought at Marks & Spencer twenty-five years ago and never travels anywhere without. It was padded, fur-lined with a hood, and was waterproof. Perfect for the climate in LA! Dad was in his sandals and socks and was wearing his straw trilby. His own personal travelling outfit to absolutely anywhere.

'Most excellent hat, Grandpa,' said Freddie, grabbing it off him and trying it on for size.

'I bought that in Majorca in 1985,' he told him. 'Last time I went on holiday with your mother, I reckon.'

'He made me do karaoke,' I informed Freddie. 'I have never, ever forgiven him and vowed never to go on holiday with him ever again.'

Dad climbed into the back of the minibus and immediately produced four chocolate bars to give to each of his grandchildren. It was 7.30 in the morning. Freddie, Tilly and Jude screamed with delight and immediately dug in. Kirsty thanked her grandfather and stashed it away in her bag for later.

'So now we are all on the bus,' said Mike, standing at the front, 'have you all got your passports? Shall we all get them out so they can be seen? No use once we've set off saying you've left it at home. Come on, let's see them all?'

I didn't really want to be chief tour guide for this particular trip but, having said that, I didn't want Mike to assume the role either. He'd done bugger-all on the organizational front. He'd barely even packed his clothes; had just thrown some in a heap and expected me to decipher what he wanted to take with him. No, he'd very much played a passive role in the lead-up to departure but, in typical Mike form, given any group activity, he'd immediately taken a leadership role once we were with the others. And that pissed me off. I'd booked the minibus, for goodness' sake. I'd organized the pick-up times, then subsequently spoken to the driver at least three times as people changed their minds. I'd even got the cash out of the bank to pay him at the other end, and still I wasn't in charge. Oh no. Apparently Mike was designated chief of this little shindig. And it wasn't even like it was his family he was taking leadership of. Mike had decided he was the leader in my family group with no prior qualification whatsoever.

And the annoying thing was, everyone listened! Everyone got out their passports and dutifully showed them to Mike, immediately recognizing his leadership qualities. If I'd have asked them they would have laughed in my face and told me to stop being such a worrywart.

'Have *you* got your passport, Mike?' I asked him.

He looked at me blankly. 'Well, I'm assuming you packed it,' he said.

'I didn't pack it,' I replied.

The colour drained momentarily from his face.

'Seriously?' he said.

'Where's your passport, Uncle Mike?' asked Tilly.

'You seriously didn't pack it?' he said, looking at me. 'But you always pack all our passports.'

I reached into my bag and made a show of peering into it. Then pulled out four passports. 'Oh, it's here, look,' I said. 'Lucky for you I did pack it, or else you would have looked very silly having asked everyone if they had their passport and then had forgotten yours.'

'You have packed my passport, haven't you?' I heard my dad whisper to my mum.

'Shall we go now, Derek?' I asked the driver. 'Oxford Services is the first stop, if you remember, as my mother rates them as the best toilets on the M40.'

Arrival at the airport was carnage. Dad and Freddie disappeared faster than a toddler hearing the tinkle of an ice-cream van. One minute they were there and the next minute they were gone.

'Where's Dad?' I said to Mum the minute the minibus had left us on the pavement outside our terminal.

She shrugged. 'He'll be about somewhere,' she said.

'I'm not sitting next to Freddie on the plane,' Kirsty shouted in my ear. 'Anyone but Freddie. He smells and he'll lean all over me.'

'Sit next to me!' shouted Tilly, bouncing up and down while clutching Nicola's hand.

Kirsty went pale.

'I'm sure Kirsty would love to sit next to you,' said Nicola, grinning. She mouthed thank you to Kirsty who responded with a dazed smile. She'd be begging to sit next to Freddie within half an hour of takeoff.

'Where's Freddie?' asked Mike.

I spun round. Freddie and my dad were nowhere in sight. Both AWOL.

When I thought about it, Dad and Freddie on holiday together could be a recipe for disaster. I often said Freddie took after him. Said the first thing that came into his head, had a total lack of filter and didn't really worry about what other people thought of him. Dad's socks and sandals were like Freddie wearing my dress to a New Year's Eve party. He just didn't give a damn.

'We'll just have to wait here until they come back,' I said with a sigh. 'They'll have to come back at some point, won't they?'

'Jude needs the toilet,' said Nicola. 'Would you take him, Mike? He doesn't like coming into the ladies' any more and I hate to send him into the men's on his own.'

'Sure,' he said, holding his hand out to Jude. 'Let's go, buddy.'

We watched them walk away together.

'Useful having a husband, isn't it?' said Mum.

'Occasionally,' I replied.

'Must be,' sighed Nicola.

We were still waiting on the pavement ten minutes later for all the men of our party to return. I looked to Mum for some guidance on what to do, but now I was around she had absolved any responsibility for anything so was not the slightest bit worried by the absence of four members of our family within moments of arriving at the airport.

In the end I called Mike on his mobile.

'Where are you?' I gasped when he picked up.

'In the newsagent's.'

'Why?'

'We saw your dad in the toilet and he suggested we all go and get sweets for the plane so we're just getting a pick 'n' mix.'

'Do you have Freddie and Jude with you?'

'Yes.'

'Do you think you should all come back so we can check in before we worry about sweets on the plane?'

'Well, I did suggest that, but your dad reckons the sweets are cheaper this side of check-in so I didn't want to argue. Hang on a minute. Freddie wants a word.'

'Hi, Mum,' he boomed. 'Can me and Grandpa sit together on the plane? I'm hoping they'll be showing

Deadpool 2 and we're going to watch it together because I think Grandpa is going to love it but I might have to explain some stuff to him. He also said he'd slip me his alcohol because he doesn't like to drink on the plane. Being on holiday with Grandpa is the best. Hang on a minute, he's asking what pick 'n' mix you want?'

The phrase 'herding cats' was, of course, invented to describe trying to get nine family members with an age range of 8 to 78 through an airport to take an international flight. There were many low points and no highs.

Freddie insisting on trying to negotiate with the check-in lady that we should all get an upgrade was mortifying. He'd clearly had a chat with Dad and so out came the story that it was his dying wish to travel business class with his entire family. Poor Deborah looked horrified before she painted on a false smile.

'I'm really so sorry to hear that you are not well, sir; however, we just don't have any space in business class on this flight, I'm afraid.'

'Oh, I'm not unwell,' replied my Dad. 'Fit as a fiddle in fact. For my age.'

'You can have a dying wish and not be dying,' pointed out Freddie. 'How about complimentary champagne instead?'

I was convinced that it was this comment that meant Deborah assigned us seats right at the back of the plane, next to the toilets, and therefore next to the near constant queue of people and intermittent wafting smell of urine.

It kept Dad happy, though. He sat next to the aisle as he reckoned he had the longest legs and proceeded to chat to pretty much everyone who went to the toilet on that ten-hour flight. There were people avoiding that cubicle by the end, as they didn't want to get involved in another discussion with the old man at the back of the plane. I think he went through every spectrum of conversation from British politics to American politics to his preferred brand of ketchup. He had a particularly long conversation with one American lady about the difference between UK baked beans and American baked beans. She never used that toilet again.

In the meantime he kept asking the flight attendants for cans of beer in his own very charming way, so that by the time we landed at LA airport, Freddie was pretty sozzled.

Everything was going like a dream.

Everyone was in a right old grumpy state at the sight of the very long queue at immigration. Getting everyone to behave and stand where they were supposed to was a nightmare. And it was impossible to convince Dad that he was likely to get arrested if he tried to engage the security guards in the great 'British baked bean versus American baked bean' debate.

Lizzy and Patrick were waiting in the arrivals hall looking as fresh as daisies, while the nine of us looked as if we had arrived from hell. Much hugging and hand-shaking ensued. Mum lifted her skirt to proudly show Lizzy and Patrick her new knee, courtesy of their gener-osity. Lizzy cried and kept saying how happy she was that we were all there. Patrick looked worried at the sheer abundance of his wife's relatives; something that living on a different continent meant he didn't have to deal with very often, I guess. His façade was congenial host, but behind his eyes you could see the sheer panic at the prospect of a bunch of unruly Brits disrupting his carefully organized life. I watched as Mike approached him and thanked him for his generosity in inviting 'the clan' over.

I also heard him say he was a brave man and did he have any idea what he had let himself in for?

Patrick looked at him and said, 'It's going to be amazing. Wonderful for Lizzy to have you all here. I'm only upset that unfortunately I couldn't take any time off work so won't be able to spend as much time with you as I would have liked.'

'I understand,' said Mike. 'Totally understand.'

3 August

Today was a disaster. I think it has quite possibly ruined me. I mean, is there really anything worse than having it shoved in your face that someone with exactly the same genes as you has nailed life?

'Oh my God this is a fucking mansion,' were my son's exact words as he walked into my sister's house somewhere outside LA. Meanwhile I was trying to act really cool about the utter beauty of her abode by droning on about how awful the food was on the airplane when really all I wanted to do was gather my mouth up off the floor and look around.

'Mum, I need a quiet word,' Freddie said later when he came to find me in the kitchen where my sister was making us all coffee on her fancy, shiny machine. I was perched on a particularly high bar stool. I'd only just made it up there so I told him to whisper in my ear for fear of never being able to get back up there ever again.

He cupped his hand around my ear. 'They have an *infinity* pool,' he whispered. 'A real one.' I looked at him in shock. He had to be kidding. My sister had said this

261

was an upgrade to their last house, where we had visited them over six years ago, but an infinity pool? I did not think there was anything in our genetic make-up that might suggest anyone in our family could possibly live in a house with an infinity pool.

'I just have to go find something for Freddie,' I said, falling off the high stool and nearly breaking my ankle. I had to go and see for myself. Freddie could just be winding me up.

But there it was. Not enormous, but still . . . It was an infinity pool and no mistake. And to top it all, an ocean view.

'How are we related to people who can live somewhere like this?' asked Freddie. 'I cannot really understand how this is happening.'

I knew what he was saying. Standing there in my elasticated-waist Marks & Spencer travelling trousers, with my sweaty armpits and my canvas unbranded slip-on shoes that screamed middle-/old-aged more than the queue outside the post office at opening time, I had never felt so out of place. I felt like some hillbilly who'd won a luxury holiday competition, only to find they had no idea how to act in these here parts.

'Is Uncle Patrick a complete knob-end?' asked Freddie, who was still standing next to me.

'A bit,' I replied truthfully. 'Why do you ask?'

'Need a reason to not hate them for living here,' he sighed, turning his back. He took a few steps back up towards the house then turned and ran full kilter in his travelling clothes and screamed as he flung himself into the air and into the infinity pool. I watched as his T-shirt billowed up and then his head appeared, grinning.

'Oh Freddie,' shouted my sister, running up behind me.

'Would you mind not jumping in the pool with your clothes on? Uncle Patrick banned it last spring break when he found one of Alicia's friend's tops blocking the filter. He insists that everyone wears a one-piece or shorts, and that they shower before they jump in or else it messes with the PH levels. He's very concerned about the pool's PH levels.'

'He *is* a knob-end!' rejoiced Freddie, cheerfully raising his fist in triumph.

I was going to celebrate with him too at the discovery of why we weren't going to be turned inside out with jealousy this holiday, but Lizzy looked mightily dismayed that Freddie was still in the pool.

'Get out, Freddie,' I chastised. 'Please don't aggravate Uncle Patrick's PH levels.' I turned to Lizzy. 'He's just very excited to be here,' I added. 'He'll calm down soon.' Lizzy only had a daughter Alicia, who was 19. She didn't understand normal boys, never mind Freddie.

'Patrick suggested taking him on a bike ride,' said Lizzy. Her brow furrowed. 'Thought he might like a decent hike through the mountains. Mike too.'

I knew that wasn't going to happen. Freddie on a bike? Outdoors? Freddie and any kind of sport were not friends. He lacked any kind of need to show off any sort of masculine prowess. And as for Mike? He was too smart to pit himself against Patrick in a race he couldn't win. He'd make up some minor ailment that rendered cycling impossible, thus thwarting Patrick's status-setting exercise.

'Let's see, shall we,' I said. 'Now where's that coffee?'

'I was just coming out to ask if you want dccaf?'

'No!' I said. 'Full caf, please. Always.'

'I'll have a beer if you've got one, Auntie Lizzy?' asked Freddie as he hauled himself out of the pool like something out of the deep lagoon. His cheap denim jacket was dripping dye back into the perfectly balanced PH-level water.

'He's not far off eighteen,' I told her. 'He has the odd one at home.'

'We don't actually keep any alcohol in the house,' said Lizzy. 'Patrick's father was an alcoholic so he's quite wary of alcohol, and certainly won't let Alicia drink until she's legal at twenty-one.'

'She's at uni, right?' asked Freddie, loping over and putting a wet arm around me.

'Yes, Princeton. She sends her apologies but she's attending summer school and can't get away.'

'And she doesn't drink?'

'No. She promised her dad.'

'Right,' said Freddie. 'Right. Good for her. I'll have a latte then. Two sugars.'

'We don't have any refined sugar in the house.'

'Was Uncle Patrick's second cousin a diabetic?' replied Freddie so quickly I had to suppress a giggle.

Lizzy gave me a disappointed look then turned and headed back towards the house. I raised my eyebrows at Freddie. There clearly was unlikely to be any uncle/nephew bonding over this holiday.

'Wow,' breathed Freddie when she'd disappeared. 'Clearly Uncle Patrick doesn't follow Alicia on Instagram.'

'Why do you say that?' I replied.

'Well, it looks like she is having a great time at Princeton.'

'What, like drinking and partying and stuff?'

'Oh yes. A lot of that, I reckon.'

'Is she really at summer school?' I asked.

'Not unless it's on a boat off the coast of Hawaii.'

'Perhaps best not to mention that to Uncle Patrick or Auntie Lizzy.'

'My lips are sealed.'

4 August

MUM'S KNEE

Nicola: You never said you had a pool boy, Lizzy! I am so happy sitting by the pool watching how he handles his net!

Lizzy: That's Anton. He's majoring in medicine at Starbucks.

Me: Starbucks?

Lizzy: Damn predictive text. I mean Stanford. Patrick hired him for the summer because he gets the whole PH levels thing. You know, being a scientist.

Nicola: Well he's certainly doing something for my PH levels!

Lizzy: He's like 20!

Nicola: So! I can at least look, can't I? Oh, he's playing with the kids now. Wow, he doesn't even mind Tilly pulling his hair. He's coming over! Bear with. Just sucking my belly in.

Me: What's he saying – what's happening?

Nicola: I have never held my breath for so long. He came to ask permission to get in the pool with the kids and play volleyball with them. He is to die for. I'd be in there with them but I can't keep my belly in for long enough. He just took his top off. OMG I think I am going to faint.

Lizzy: He does work out a lot. And he plays football for his college.

Nicola: Come and take a look, Cathy. I guarantee you will not be disappointed. Where are you anyway?

Me: I'm just getting dressed. Will be down in a minute.

Lizzy: Be nice to him. I mean, don't intimidate him. Stanford-educated pool boys are hard to find.

Me: You really need to listen to yourself sometimes.

5 August

I have to say that this lifestyle was so suiting me. Waking up to the sun and the sound of the ocean. Long lie-ins perfectly timed so Patrick has already left for work by the time I sauntered downstairs for a leisurely breakfast. Admittedly the breakfasts in this joint were somewhat lacking, what with the abundance of fruit and yogurt and

NutriBullet concoctions and the decided lack of anything that had even touched a carbohydrate, but it was doing wonders for my energy levels, I had to admit, and for my carb footprint. Then Lizzy had got us all into doing a touch of poolside yoga after breakfast, which was initially met with much giggling and sideways glances, but actually I had to admit I had felt the most chilled-out I had felt in a very long time. Then there was lounging by the pool to be done. I'd even read books. I'd read all the books that I should have read for the book group, which was really quite remarkable.

Mornings were bliss. Utter bliss. Until this morning.

'Kirsty is kissing Anton in the pool house!' Tilly came into the kitchen screaming as Nicola and I were taking our turn to prepare lunch.

Nicola and I looked at each other in horror. Nicola had launched a thinly veiled campaign to pursue Anton, always being down at the pool first and showing an abnormal interest in PH levels that could only have been fuelled by severe lust. Lizzy had been continually warning her off, but Nicola's ego was so fragile that it had been clear she needed the attention of a young, attractive lad to pick her back up off the floor where Laurence had left her. At least the pursuit had stopped her moping around, and Anton had looked as if he was quite enjoying the attention of an older attractive woman, so Lizzy and I had agreed that it was better to just let her get on with it. Nothing was going to stop her, anyway.

So far Kirsty had only taken a passing interest in Anton. Thankfully she seemed unaffected by his good looks and charm, which was why it was such a surprise to hear Tilly's announcement.

'Are you sure, Tilly?' I asked her.

'Absolutely,' she said, nodding vigorously. 'They've been in there on their own for ages.'

I wasn't sure if it was Nicola or I who got to the door of the pool house first. But we both grabbed at the handle and then proceeded to virtually fall into the glorified storeroom.

'Get your hands off her, she's sixteen!' I heard Nicola cry.

I was speechless. My sister had taken the words out of my mouth, albeit I was pretty sure her motivations were very different.

I looked over at the secretive couple. They were nowhere near each other. Kirsty was standing holding a couple of chairs and Anton was trying to get some inflatables down from a shelf. Clearly nothing untoward had been happening at all.

'What are you talking about, Auntie Nic?' asked Kirsty.

'Yeah!' I cried. 'What the hell are you talking about, Nicola?' I gave her my best astonished look and threw my arms in the air. She mouthed the word 'bitch' at me. Charming, I thought.

'I'm so sorry,' she said blushing. 'But Tilly came in saying you were kissing in the pool house and me and your mother were justifiably concerned.'

Thanks a lot, I thought.

'We were just getting some equipment out,' said Kirsty, incredulous.

'I can see that now,' said Nicola. 'I just wanted to make sure that you weren't getting yourselves into trouble, that's all, what with Kirsty being so young and all that.'

'Auntie Nic!' exclaimed Kirsty.

'I want you to know, Mrs Collins, Ms Nicola,' said Anton, 'that I would never do anything to compromise your daughter and niece. Never. But . . . but I have to admit that I have been wanting to ask you if you would give permission for me to take Kirsty to see a volleyball game down at the beach. She said she's never seen one and I would be very honoured to take her, if you would allow it.'

The funny thing was that he looked at both Nicola and me for our permission.

'Oh wow,' said Kirsty. 'Please, Mum. I would love that.'

I looked at Nicola. 'What do you think, sis?' I asked her.

She pulled a face and walked off without saying a word. I felt sorry for her ego but realized that perhaps my daughter needed this ego boost too.

'Sounds fun,' I said. 'Of course you can.'

7 August

I asked Lizzy today if there was anything I could do to help with the preparations for Mum's seventy-fifth birthday party tomorrow.

At which point she told me that it was all totally in hand.

The cleaners were due at nine in the morning while we all went out for brunch at Patrick's country club.

The florist would be arriving at noon with a few small displays, nothing major. Mum didn't really want a fuss, so she'd told the florist just three arrangements.

The caterers would arrive at two and start preparing the celebration dinner. Now she had not used these caterers before, because the one she usually had for Thanksgiving actually hadn't done a great job last time, so she was going on a recommendation. But her friend Jenny up the road used them all the time and she was like the fussiest eater she had ever met, and so she thought they should be great.

Then the servers would arrive at 6.30 p.m. and they would be ready to serve champagne on the patio by the pool from 7 p.m. Dinner would be served at 8 p.m. then a photographer would be arriving at 9.30 p.m. to take some family shots of us all.

Actually, one job I could do is to make sure everyone knew there was a photographer coming, so to dress up smart.

As she was telling me all this, I thought back to Mum's birthday last year when I picked up fish and chips for us all on the way to their house and we sat round the kitchen table scoffing them with a bottle of wine. I did actually make a cake. I didn't decorate it or anything. Just stuck a candle in it, but I was kind of pleased with myself that I'd made it myself and not just bought a Battenberg from the Co-op.

'Shall I make a cake?' I offered.

'Oh no. I'm picking that up from the bakery on the way back from brunch. It's fatless. Tastes incredible.'

Lizzy had certainly pulled all the stops out for Mum's birthday celebrations. In quite an obscene, over-the-top, decadent fashion.

In a 'please make me your favourite daughter' type of fashion.

8 August

So I tried, right? I tried to be civil all day. Tried to enjoy my mother's seventy-fifth birthday. The first time in probably a couple of decades when I wasn't the one making sure it didn't go unmarked. It should have been great, really it should, what with the champagne and the caterers and the flowers and the sunshine and everyone together.

I didn't mean to push Lizzy into the pool.

And how was I to know that her white shift dress with a weird train thing would go completely see-through and that because she was so blooming scrawny she didn't have to wear a bra, so that when she crawled out of the pool, steam coming out of her ears, she literally looked like a drowned rat.

Rumours had gone round the house earlier in the day that there was champagne in the kitchen and – even more exciting – actual bread. Better than that, French bread. Kirsty came to tell me that she had sighted carbs in the kitchen and we both heaved a sigh of relief. This was major news. Living with my sister had reduced my carb footprint even more, and for the first time in twenty years I suspected I might just have fitted into that Chinese dress, had I not ceremoniously thrown it away. Why did that always happen? Decluttering *always* led to regret. ALWAYS! Screw you, Marie Kondo. I'd waited twenty years for my moment in that bloody dress!

Both Freddie and Kirsty came to our room at 6.30 p.m. and asked if they would be allowed a couple of glasses of champagne, to which I said yes as Patrick's no-alcohol regime was wearing mighty thin.

We decided – in order to secure the success of the night – we should arrive before Patrick and Lizzy and down as much alcohol and bread as we could. When they surfaced onto the patio at 6.55 p.m. sharp, we had already downed three glasses of champagne each and eaten a whole loaf of French bread.

'Great champagne,' giggled Mike, holding his glass up.

'It's not from France, so not actual champagne,' pointed out Patrick. 'It's from right here in California, but I reckon we give those French guys a run for their money, don't you?'

'Oh yes,' we all agreed chirpily. Buoyed up by champagne and full bellies.

'Is the bread from France?' asked Freddie.

'A French boulangerie actually, isn't it, Lizzy?' replied Patrick. 'No additives, no preservatives, made exactly how they do it in their Parisian sister shop, I believe, somewhere off the Champs-Élysées.'

'What's a boulangerie?' asked Freddie, his eyes wide and innocent looking.

'You don't know what a boulangerie is?' asked Patrick. He looked at me in astonishment. Freddie knew perfectly well what a boulangerie was.

Then we all went in to sit down for a wonderful family dinner to celebrate my mother's seventy-fifth birthday!

The waiters came out and laid our main course in front of us. It was some kind of protein, maybe a white fish on layers of something sitting in a small puddle of something.

'But where are the potatoes?' asked Mum. 'Haven't they done potatoes? Your dad will need some potatoes. Have they forgotten them?'

'There's a layer of potato under the fish, Mum,' replied Lizzy, smiling and tucking in.

Mum looked suspiciously down at her plate. She poked it with her fork then dejectedly picked up her knife and began to eat. The whole room went quiet.

'It's great love, really,' said Dad. 'Delicious. I know I'll want seconds.'

He'll be lucky, I thought.

'There are seconds, aren't there?' he asked, looking slightly panicked.

'It's so good to eat healthy, locally sourced food, don't you think?' bellowed Patrick down the table. 'Makes you feel good inside and out.'

We all nodded, thinking we could eat a lot *more* of the healthy, locally sourced food.

Then Nicola got drunk. And I mean *really* drunk.

She sat at the end of the acre-long table next to where the servers came in from the kitchen. I noticed that she nodded at her glass any time anyone came within spitting distance of it with a bottle of wine.

'Do you remember this time last year we had fish and chips at your house, Mum?' she piped up when she'd cleared her plate. 'Bit different that was to this, eh? Still, me and Cathy do see you every year, I suppose.'

Lizzy and I glanced at each other then looked away quickly.

'I mean, it's not about how much money you spend, is it? It's about how much you care. And being there and all that,' continued Nicola. 'You know, when they need to be taken somewhere or have their shopping done. That's what matters, not throwing money at them or anything.'

I stared at Lizzy while desperately trying to remember the last time that Nicola had taken Mum shopping – or anywhere, in fact.

'Have you any idea what I'd give to be able to see them more often?' said Lizzy defensively. 'To help out more? I agree, Nicola. That's what matters, but when I do get to see them, the least I can do is to make sure they have a good time.'

'We're having a lovely time, love,' said Dad, putting his knife and fork down on his plate and reaching forward to swipe the last bit of bread.

Nicola turned to look at her father. 'But it's not fair, is it, Dad? She gets to live like this. And me . . . and me . . . I get to make ten packed lunches a week and stay up late watching television on my own every single night with half a bottle of Lambrini. Why didn't I get this life, Dad? And I'm the pretty one! *This* should have happened to me!'

There was an audible gasp around the table.

Wow, she must be really drunk.

'I have to disagree with that,' piped up Mike. 'I think you'll find that Cathy is the pretty one.'

Wow, *he* must be really drunk!

I looked at Mike in astonishment. It was possibly the nicest thing he had ever said about me. It was a lie, of course. I was firmly bottom of the ladder in the pretty sisters' stakes. Nicola was factually pretty, always had been, which was probably why she found it so easy to attract the wankers. Lizzy's Californian lifestyle meant she had made the absolute most of what she had. She had a body to die for and, shall we say, an interesting face, if not conventionally pretty. On the other hand, I was in permanent 'before makeover' territory. Frizzy hair that no product could tame, amateurish make-up at best, typically a stone overweight and an unintentionally Nineties retro wardrobe. Post a makeover I might have been in Lizzy's league, but in my current state I was nowhere near.

'Thanks, Mike,' I beamed. It didn't matter that he was lying, at least he'd said it.

'I have to say Lizzy is bearing up really well too,' said Patrick. 'That Botox made all the difference.'

'You had Botox?' my mother, my sister and I all said in unison.

'Just a little,' she replied. 'Hardly anything at all really.' She glared at her husband.

'It's just not fair,' said Nicola. '*And* she gets Botox! I'd *love* some Botox.'

'We can get you Botox,' said Patrick. 'Our guy is great. If you want some while you are here we can arrange that. Maybe for those bags under your eyes or perhaps a little on your neck?'

Nicola started to cry. Properly cry. Mascara ran rivers down her face.

'Let's go outside,' I said to her, getting up and grabbing her arm as well as a bottle of wine.

'I'm going too,' said Lizzy, following us out of the dining room.

'Look,' said Lizzy when she caught up with us on the patio. 'I really do wish I was around more to help with Mum and Dad. Really I do.'

I stared at her. Was that really why she thought Nicola was crying?

'Why couldn't I have married a Patrick?' wailed Nicola.

I stared at Nicola. Was she serious?

Lizzy turned to me. 'If I was in England I'd be at Mum and Dad's as much as you two, doing whatever they needed doing. Just like you do,' she stated.

'No, you wouldn't,' I said. 'I mean, what have you done today? Organized other people to do everything. You've not actually done anything yourself, have you? Come the time they can't do it themselves, you won't be cleaning their toilets, just as Nicola won't be. It's going to be me left cleaning the toilets, isn't it? Like it always has been.'

Lizzy looked at me, dazed. 'Look, we'll pay for a cleaner if it comes to that. It's no big deal, Cathy. I'm perfectly willing to contribute to whatever needs doing. You know I will.'

'That's a great idea,' added in Nicola, who had paused her crying over not marrying Patrick and was now listening to our crisis talk. 'Just pay for a sodding cleaner.'

I felt that somehow everyone was missing the point.

'But it won't be just toilet cleaning, will it? It'll be taking Mum shopping and to the doctors and to see Auntie Mabel. I'm going to be the one left doing all that, aren't I?'

'Set them up with an Uber account,' said Nicola. 'Easy. Don't you think, Lizzy?'

'Great idea,' agreed Lizzy. 'Patrick has some kind of connection to the founder of Uber, actually.'

'And who's going to pay for that? There is no way Mum is going to pay to take taxis everywhere.'

'We'll pay,' said Lizzy. 'Take it as my contribution as I won't be around as much as you two.'

'You mean Patrick will pay,' I said without thinking. There was a short silence.

'That's a really mean thing to say,' replied Lizzy.

'I know,' I said. 'I'm sorry.'

'Just because Patrick earns a lot more money than Mike, there's no need to be mean.'

'That has absolutely nothing to do with it,' I exclaimed. 'Who cares whose husband earns more? Mike is worth ten of Patrick, if you ask me. I wouldn't have Patrick if the world were on fire and he was the only man left with a hose.'

'If Mike were the only man left with a hose and the world was on fire, he'd set up a consultation to make sure everyone had a say on whether they used the hose, and in the meantime the world would burn down.'

We were getting diverted. This wasn't supposed to be a comparison of our respective husband choices. This was supposed to be me making sure I didn't get stuck with all the toilet-cleaning duties.

'If he'd just applied himself like Patrick has,' Lizzy continued fatally, 'then maybe you would be offering to pay for Mum's knee and a cleaner rather than getting your knickers in a twist over who's going to clean their toilet.'

I didn't know why I pushed her. Really I didn't. I think it was because she was my sister and, as far as I can remember, the only people I have ever pushed in my life have been my sisters. So I pushed her. And she fell in the pool. And her white shift dress with the curious train and her lack of bra genuinely made her look exactly like a drowned rat.

9 August

Tonight Mum and Dad read us their will.

Everything divided exactly three ways.

Everything.

Exactly three ways.

Apparently they had been planning to share it with us this holiday. Wanted to make sure that any disagreements were sorted out while they were around. So they could be there for any arguments. Smart, aren't they?

All three of us cried at the magnitude of it. Of

confronting the knowledge that one day it would be just the three of us, without the anchor we had always had.

I hugged Lizzy and told her I was sorry. She said sorry back.

Mum asked us what we had fallen out about.

'Who's going to clean your toilets when you can't clean them yourselves,' said Nicola.

'Oh,' said Mum.

'Lizzy's going to pay for a cleaner,' she added.

'Oh,' said Mum, furrowing her brow. 'I'm not sure about that.'

'No, she's not,' I said. 'I'll clean them, Mum. You've cleaned enough of my crap up in the past. It's my turn.'

'Are you sure,' asked Lizzy. 'I'll spring-clean every time I come and visit. All your houses.'

I nodded.

'I'll do them as well,' added Nicola. 'When I can. I'll take my turn.'

'No you won't,' we all said in unison. Even Mum.

10 August

Lizzy and I went for a stroll tonight along the beach, as it was our last night. We'd had a few glasses of wine over dinner so we were loose enough to talk. Properly talk.

'I wish you weren't going,' she said. 'It's been good having you here.'

'Go on,' I told her. 'I bet you can't wait to get your house back to yourselves. Get some sanity back.'

'I think I'll miss the chaos, actually,' she admitted. 'I didn't realize how much I missed seeing you all the time until this last week. It's hard knowing I'm missing out on all that family time.'

'Oh yeah,' I replied, looking out to the ocean, feeling the sand between my toes. 'You've got it really hard, I can see that.'

She sighed. 'I know it looks like the dream lifestyle. I know I'm incredibly privileged. I get to live here and do pretty much whatever I want . . . but seriously, I wish that I just got to spend more time with you all. I'm so pleased that Mum's knee getting fixed got you all out here. I can't tell you how happy that has made me.'

She looked a bit teary so I gave her a hug.

'You remember that diary you sent me?' I told her. 'Well, I have been using it and I did set some sort of goals . . . eventually.'

'Really?' she cried. 'Did you? You never said.'

'Well, I knew you'd be all over it and I didn't need the pressure,' I admitted.

'So? What have you done?' she asked.

I thought for a moment. Wondering which of my list of stuff to share with her.

'Nothing like your aspirations but I did manage to go on the pill, finally.'

'Wow, Cathy, that's wonderful,' she replied, as though I had actually run a marathon.

'And this month my goal was to agree who's going clean Mum and Dad's toilet when they get too old to do it.'

'Oh. So that's what the other night was all about?'

'Yeah. So epic fail there, eh? It's going to be me cleaning the toilet. But do you know what? I don't mind. Because we talked about it and agreed it, I'm not resenting it any more. So actually I have achieved something, so that's good.'

Lizzy nodded.

'Cleaning toilets. Never thought that would be up there as a motivational goal.'

'Says it all, sis, I reckon. The difference between you and me.'

12 August

Home again, back to a puddle on the patio rather than an infinity pool, and a view of next door's garage rather than the Pacific Ocean. But I couldn't complain. The holiday had been, on the whole, a success. So many good things had eventually come out of it. I could follow Lizzy on Facebook again as I now fully understood the sacrifices she was making in order to enjoy the trappings of her husband's success. And Mike publicly declaring me the prettiest of the three sisters had done a lot for my own ego and had brought up some much-needed positive thoughts towards my husband. That, along with the comparison to Patrick, had raised his stock somewhat, and I came home committed to make this warm glow that was currently surrounding us last.

And I'd also watched Kirsty blossom in her relationship with Anton. Anton the medic studying at Stanford. This was so good for her. She was starting to look herself again, albeit a California-tinged version. Healthier, sun-kissed, more full of fruit.

And as I watched Freddie FaceTime Kim every night, I pinched myself, thinking that things were finally looking up on the whole Collins family relationship front. Maybe we weren't all as bad at them as I'd thought.

I was well over halfway through my list now, but I was aware that I had the biggies still to come. The ones that I was convinced were really going to make a difference to my happiness. And I still hadn't solved what I was going to do about Mike and his midlife plans yet. There were some big challenges to come and time was quickly running out.

Oh, and my periods *still* hadn't stopped.

16 August

Exam results day! Kirsty wouldn't let me go to school with her to pick them up. I told her that several mothers I knew were accompanying their children and she firmly told me that she would refuse to go at all if I went with her. So I was forced to sit at home and await her return, ready with tea and cake to either celebrate or commiserate, depending on what she had achieved. I had no idea, to be honest. I mean, she had taken them when she was going through that awful time with Carl, so she could have screwed it all up, which would lead me to blame myself for not intervening sooner.

An hour after she left she sauntered into the kitchen and I fought the urge to shout, '*Where have you been!*' I searched her face for signs of what had happened in the last hour but she just looked me blankly in the face and threw a piece of paper at me. I tried to decipher it but my brain was all over the place. It was just numbers. They looked like good numbers but they changed the system so often I had no idea.

'What does it mean?' I said desperately.

'That your daughter's a genius,' she said with a grin.

'Really?' I gasped.

At that point Freddie walked in and picked up the sheet and gave it a quick scan.

'Bitch beat me on everything but psychology,' he muttered.

'Really?' I squealed. I knew this was good news. Freddie had actually done all right in his GCSEs, so if Kirsty had beaten him this was very good news indeed. I squealed and lunged at my daughter, giving her a big hug.

'That's brilliant,' I said. 'Well done you. I'm so proud.'

'Cheers, Mum,' said Freddie. 'I can see who's the favourite in this house.'

'I'm officially cleverer than you,' said Kirsty smugly. 'There's no denying it now.'

'Just because you can do exams it doesn't mean you're cleverer than me,' he hit back.

'Yes it does,' said Kirsty. 'And you know it. You're the family dunce.'

'No I'm not. You got lucky, that's all. Everyone knows our year's exams were rock hard.'

'Bullshit! Tell him Mum,' shouted Kirsty. 'I'm cleverer than him. Make him, say it. He has to say it. I did better than him so I'm the cleverest. Mum, tell him.'

'Look,' I shouted back. 'Can we just celebrate the fact that you have done really well? Ignore Freddie. I'm really, really proud of you. Why don't you FaceTime Anton. I'm sure he'd want to know.'

'Why?'

'Well, I'm sure he'd be interested, wouldn't he? I mean, you did get close in California . . . didn't you?'

'Yeah but, you know, it was just a holiday romance,' she shrugged. 'Great while it lasted but not worth dragging it out. Besides which, I'm not up for a boyfriend for a while. I don't really need one.'

I didn't think I had ever been more proud.

'I did say I'd text Robbie though,' she said, picking up her phone. 'He said he wanted to know I'd done okay.'

'Robbie did?' I asked.

'Yeah. He said he'd make me a red velvet cake if I got higher than my mocks.'

'Did he?'

'Yeah.'

'That reminds me,' said Freddie. 'He said he'd come over when we got back from holiday and teach me how to make turkey lasagne. As a surprise for Kim.'

'Did he?'

'Yeah. Will you remind him, Kirsty?'

'Sure. As long as I can learn too.'

'If you must.'

'Right, well, good for Robbie,' I said. 'Why don't you invite him over? We could cook for him for a change?'

'What!' cried Kirsty.

'Are you insane?' asked Freddie. 'Just tell him to come over and teach us how to cook turkey lasagne. We don't all want food poisoning.'

September

Make the Necessary Announcements about the Menopause

1 September

I had decided that forewarned was forearmed, so this month I was going to do the grown-up thing and talk my family through the menopause in an instructive and informed way. I did Google to see if there were any books on the market that put it all in simple terms for kids to understand. A bit like those picture books you can get to explain to them about the birds and the bees, but it seems that no one has written one of those yet about the menopause. In fact *I* would have found a simple picture book helpful, to be honest, but there seemed to be only massively long tomes written by women with tidy hair and perfect make-up.

So I did my best to explain the menopause to my family in the hope that it would allay any fears or trepidation they might have about the life-changing process I was about to go through.

'So pretty much you are going to go through puberty again,' Freddie said, when I'd finished my brief presentation. Kim sat next to him, looking awkward. When I'd asked if everyone could be present on Friday night for dinner because I needed to talk to them about something, I hadn't expected him to bring Kim along. When I explained it was a family matter, Freddie had said that anything that needed to be said to him could be said in front of Kim. Apparently they were officially boyfriend and girlfriend as of last week. What that meant, I had no idea. Perhaps it just meant she could gatecrash our family meetings whenever she liked. Oh, and she'd also been wearing the SUPPORT SEX WORKERS T-shirt, which I'd been finding highly disturbing.

'I mean it's the same, isn't it?' Freddie confirmed. 'Raging hormones, grumpiness, anxiety, depression, discombobulation, forgetfulness, that sort of thing.'

'Nice use of the word discombobulation,' said Mike in admiration.

'Teenagers aren't forgetful, though,' said Kirsty.

'They are!' both Mike and I said at the same time. 'What about the time I said I'd pick you up outside school after your hockey coaching and you totally forgot and went home with Justine?' he added.

'I don't think it's forgetfulness actually,' I said. 'Just teenage selfishness,' I pointed out. 'A complete and utter inability to think of others. That's really very different to masturbation.'

'What!' said Freddie, cupping his hands over Kim's ears. 'What did you just say?'

'That teenagers are selfish, whereas masturbating women are just forgetful.'

'Mum!' shrieked Kirsty, cupping her own ears.

'What?' I asked.

'You keep saying masturbating rather than meno-pausal,' said Mike, putting an arm over my shoulder.

'No way?' I said, clasping my hand to my mouth. 'Sorry, Kim,' I said, turning to her. 'See, already forgetful. Can't even remember the word for . . . for . . . menopausal.'

Actually, comparing it to puberty seemed to help everyone understand it better. Made it normal. Made it a thing that happens and we should just be open about it.

'I think what your mother is trying to say is that we may see changes in her,' said Mike, 'and everyone needs to be sympathetic because it's beyond her control.'

'Like when I say I can't get out of bed because I'm a teenager and so tired and you say get out of bed now or else you will slice my testicles off?' said Freddie.

I looked at Kim, whose eyes were suddenly as wide as saucers.

'I don't really say that,' I said to her.

'You do,' said Kirsty.

'Oi, whose side are you on?'

'The side of truth,' she said. 'And the side of you having more sympathy for me the last time I asked if I could stay at home because I was having a bad period and you told me to go to school and sit near a radiator.'

I sensed my Teenage Resilience Training Programme was backfiring on me.

'Look, all I'm asking for is for you to be, erm . . .' I realized that I could no longer use the word 'sympathetic' as I was clearly not demonstrating much sympathy to my own children's situation in life.

'I'm just asking for you to be aware,' I said eventually. 'That I might be going through stuff. And if I'm acting strangely, you will know why.'

They nodded. Kim looked from me to Freddie in bewilderment. She opened her mouth to speak, then closed it again. Clearly deciding she was better off staying out of this one.

'So, any coming-of-age stuff you'd like to share with

us, Dad, while this lovely chat is occurring?' asked Freddie.

Mike looked at him.

'My knees hurt a bit,' he said eventually.

'Good for you,' said Freddie. 'Well, much as we have enjoyed this discourse, I think Kim and I might go and take Barbra Streisand for a walk so that Kim can ask me what the hell just happened.'

'You are taking Barbra for a walk?' I asked, shocked and incredulous.

'It's a hormones thing,' he told me. 'Suddenly I have the urge to walk the dog.'

'Well, that's just great, Freddie,' I said. 'Finally, after all these years.'

'They're going for a neck in the woods,' said Kirsty getting up. 'Keep up, Mum.'

4 September

Mike called from Manchester. He's there pulling the innards from a local newspaper group. I was delighted when he stopped going to Liverpool, as I thought it meant that he wouldn't be seeing Helen any more and so his continued thoughts of becoming a teacher would go unsupported. But I was wrong.

'Have you seen the email I've forwarded from Helen?' he said.

'Helen who?' I asked.

'Life-coach Helen.'

'I thought you were in Manchester now?'

'I do video-conferencing with Helen. We are working on my personal statement for my application.'

I could write him a personal statement, I thought. 'My name is Mike Collins and I'd like to screw up a perfectly good career please by becoming an adequate teacher. Thank you.'

'An ex-colleague of hers asked her if she knew anyone who would be interested in a job in their finance department. It's Cringolds, Cathy. Sounds right up your street.'

Cringolds is a producer of luxury knitwear. I occasionally go to their factory sales and vomit money at them in exchange for the most gorgeous jumpers you have ever felt. Mike was probably thinking this was a double whammy. If I worked there I'd get staff discount, and so would be vomiting less money at them while they also paid me a salary.

I thought of my scruffy desk in the corner of The Mustard Factory with its fairy lights and SUPPORT SEX WORKERS mug. I wasn't sure any amount of cashmere jumpers could rival the set-up I had going there. Not sure at all.

'I'm really enjoying it at The Mustard Factory,' I said.

'But this is full time, Cathy. Pension, holidays, private health care, sick pay. It's the real deal. It's a great opportunity to get you back in the game, you know before . . . before . . .'

'I'm past it?'

'You know what I mean. I know what it's like, Cathy. There won't be many opportunities out there for people wanting to return to the workforce in their late forties. However, the guy at Cringolds said he was sick of young graduates coming and getting their training and then buggering off. He wants someone with experience, but more importantly, some loyalty. He wants someone he knows is going to stick with it for a few years.'

It felt something like being condemned, if I'm honest.

'I think you should at least give it a try. Wouldn't hurt, would it, to just go and have a chat?'

I supposed not. Maybe it would be a way of getting Mike off my back. I could use it as an excuse to pop into the factory shop while I was there. I also wondered when was the last time they reviewed who does their graphic design and their web design. I could do a bit of digging. Maybe drum up some work for Toby and Jimmy.

'Okay,' I said with a sigh. 'But I'm not doing it if I have to write a CV. I'm too old for all that, Mike. Honestly.'

'I thought you'd say that so I've already done one for you. If I send it over to you now you can send it to Helen's contact and tell him she recommended you. Job done. How does that sound?'

A bit like I'm being stitched up here, I thought. Still, if I didn't have to write a CV, what did I have to lose? It would be very interesting to see what kind of picture my husband had painted of me.'

I told him to send it over.

12 September

I think my husband could make Donald Trump sound like a Nobel Peace Prize candidate. I read his CV for me in awe. He made the trampolining class I once did at university sound as if I was training to be at the Olympics. He made my role at the construction firm that *he* made redundant sound like the lynchpin of the entire company. He also made it sound as though I was finance director of the entire Mustard Factory. If I didn't know Mike, I would find this ability to bend the truth most disturbing.

Hence, due to his brilliant CV, I was sitting in a chair opposite the finance director of Cringolds within the week.

He wasn't what I had been expecting. Which was a fat old man in a suit and tie who wanted a glorified PA to do all his donkey work. No, Giles was far from fat or old. He was perhaps in his late thirties. He wore a suit. But no tie. He wore glasses. Nondescript glasses that made no statement about whether he was trying to be cool or not, which actually was refreshing compared to the extreme effort that went into glasses-wearing at The Mustard Factory. And he looked knackered – like, seriously stressed. Things perhaps weren't going too well at Cringolds. Oh, and he had sick over his left shoulder that clearly no one had pointed out to him. Though how he couldn't smell it, I have no idea. I toyed with the idea of telling him but decided that humiliating him by pointing out the sick on his jacket was not the right way to start the interview.

Everything began well. He asked me about my training and my time at the construction company. I tried to recollect pertinent facts, but it had been nearly twenty years ago so I had to admit that my memories were somewhat faded. Then he asked me to explain my role at The Mustard Factory. I started off trying to make it sound as grand as Mike had made out, but then Giles yawned. Like a proper yawn as he propped his head on his hand and tried to keep his eyes open.

'Toby's graphics company had a terrible history with debtors,' I told him. 'Seventy per cent of his invoices were unpaid when I arrived. All debts have now been cleared and we have introduced new payment terms which have ensured that all debtors are now paying on time.'

'Impressive,' he nodded, his eyes closing sleepily. 'How did you go about collecting the debts?'

'Intimidation,' I replied. His eyes flew open.

'Intimidation? You mean you sent the heavies in?'

'Yes.' I did not glance at my breasts. I swear. 'I personally visited his debtors and persuaded them to pay up.'

'Did you threaten them?' he asked.

'In my own way,' I replied.

He looked at me thoughtfully.

'How would you describe your management style?' he asked.

'No bullshit,' I replied.

I was bored now with this interview game. It was all just lies really, wasn't it? You went into a company and told them exactly what they wanted to hear, which was usually a pack of lies. You spoke in their language, not your own. Then they recruited you and wondered why it didn't last.

'I just say it how it is,' I explained. 'No bullshit. If someone isn't pulling their weight, I tell them. I think you can fancy up management as much as you like, really, but actually what works is just being honest. No bullshit seems to be the best management style.' Christ, if Mike could hear me now he'd have a hernia.

Giles's mobile phone jangled urgently on his desk. He cast a glance over to it then looked at me apologetically. 'Would you mind if I just take this?' he asked. 'I shouldn't be a moment.'

I knew it was his wife. I could tell by the resigned look on his face. I tried to find something interesting on the wall while he reassured her that baby Robin was probably just full, that was why he was refusing to suck.

'How old?' I asked, nodding at his phone as he put it down.

He looked at it curiously. 'Not sure. It's a work one.

Maybe had it a couple of years. You'd get a new one if you joined the company, of course.'

'I meant the baby,' I said.

'Oh, right, yes, of course. Three weeks.'

'Wow, tiny. No sleep then, I guess.'

'Not much.'

'It gets better. You need to enjoy this stage. You want to see sleepless nights when you've got two teenagers out and about and you're waiting for them to come home.'

He grinned. 'Yeah. I can imagine. It's just . . . it's just that my wife, well, it's her first week home alone with him and she's . . . well, she's struggling.'

'What are you doing here then?'

'Well, I've had all my paternity leave.'

'So! Take a day. Surprise her. Go home and give Robert a cuddle.'

'Robin.'

'Sorry, Robin. Go home to bed. Go get some sleep. You look like shit and you've got sick all over your back.'

'Have I?'

'Yes.'

He tried to strain round to see. He put his hand over his shoulder and rubbed it before sticking it under his nose. He recoiled in disgust.

'I . . . I'm sorry. I'm not at my best. This isn't how I'd normally conduct an interview.'

'Go figure. Look, stick an out-of-office on. Then go and find your second-in-command and tell them that they are in charge but they are to call you if anything urgent comes up. You're not going to achieve anything here today, are you? So go home. Get it together. Come back tomorrow without those bags under your eyes and sick on your shoulder.'

'But I have two more people coming in for interview.'

'Get your number two to do it. Great experience for them. I'm all for delegation, and if you are going to get through being a decent dad and home on time and at the school concerts and all that other stuff you should be doing, then you'll need to start delegating or else you are screwed. In any case, if either of them are any good you can ask to see them again.'

Giles was looking at me open-mouthed by now.

'I won't want to see them again,' he said.

'Why not?'

'Because I'm going to offer you the job.'

'Why? Because I told you that you stink of sick and you need to skip work?'

'Precisely that. I need someone to . . . do what you just did. Cut the bullshit and get on with it. The last person I had in the position – well, I was in the HR office with him more often than I go to the toilet. Forever moaning about conditions or other colleagues or his mobile bloody phone coverage. You may not be up to date on some of the systems and you may be a bit rusty on some of the latest financial regulations but we can teach you that. What we can't seem to teach is that—'

'Attitude?' I ask.

He nodded.

'Comes with being a mother and wrangling the trickiest team on the planet, otherwise known as a family. No time for bullshit, you see.'

'Well then, I think we need a lot more mothers working here then. So will you take it? It's full time, it's twenty-one days' holiday a year, and we have a pension fund of sorts. Helen said it was just the type of thing you were looking for.'

Helen said! Helen said! How does she know what I'm looking for? She might have a point, though. Giles seemed like a decent kind of a boss; it was local, it was full time, so undoubtedly I'd be getting paid a lot more than at The Mustard Factory, and of course all those lovely cheap jumpers. I couldn't believe it but I was tempted.

'Could I just go and meet some of the finance team?' I asked. 'And I know this must sound really weird. But I'd like to just see the office, if that's OK?'

'Of course,' he said. 'Bear with me while I put my out-of-office on.'

I couldn't resist calling in at the factory shop before I went home, of course. I could have spilt some serious cash, but really who needs an identical wool cardigan in three different colours?

Then I spotted it. The perfect thing to buy. So perfect it brought a tear to my eyes. It wasn't cheap, even with the factory shop discount, but it was so worth it.

I didn't bother to take it home and wrap it or anything. Instead I took it straight round to Tania's. I knocked on the front door, praying they would both be in. They were. They'd just got back from a chemo session at the hospital.

'Is it a good time?' I asked. 'I can come back later.'

'No, please come in,' Tania said. 'We were just having a cup of tea. Hazel's in the front room.'

I poked my head round the door, worried she might be asleep or something. I had no idea what one did after chemo.

She was sitting up in a chair, eyes fixed on the TV.

'Am I disturbing you?' I asked.

'God no,' she replied. 'I was just watching *Countdown*.

I'm trying to keep my brain lively even if my body is dragging me down.'

She was pale, undoubtedly pale. And thinner, I think. Certainly not her usual robust self. She had a scarf on her head. It had a skull and crossbones on it.

I told her I'd bought her a present because Tania had mentioned that she really wanted something for over her shoulders while she sat having chemo.

She looked at me and took the brown paper bag. She muted the TV, then drew out the pure wool shawl that seemed to include all the colours of the rainbow.

She looked at it in awe. Then she cried. Then Tania walked in and said, 'You made her cry!'

'I didn't mean to,' I said, panicking. 'Honestly I didn't.'

'I love it,' Hazel said, peering at me through watery eyes. She draped it over her shoulders and pumped her shoulders out. 'A perfect chemo cloak.'

'It's beautiful – where did you get that?' asked Tania. 'And why didn't you get me one?'

So I sat down and drank tea and we talked as though everything was perfectly normal when nothing was normal at all. I told them my story of going to Cringolds for the interview and getting offered a job.

Hazel sat and listened really intently. I felt as if she was watching me. I felt as though I was being observed. She was listening really hard. Taking it all in.

When I finished, she leaned back in her chair, resplendent in her chemo cloak and said, 'You know that list you wrote? The sort of happy list you brought round months ago?'

'Yes,' I replied.

'Was it on there that you wanted to go and be a full-time financial person in a cardigan factory?'

298

'No.'

'So don't do it then.'

'But it wouldn't be so bad, would it?' I said. 'It means Mike could comfortably give up his job. I mean, I could do it. Doesn't necessarily mean I want to do it, but I could do it.'

'Will it make you happy?' asked Hazel.

I couldn't lie to her.

'I doubt it,' I admitted.

'Then don't do it; promise me you won't do it. Why on earth would you start anything that doesn't make you happy at your age?'

I looked at Tania. She shrugged. 'You have to do as she says,' she said. 'She had chemo this morning.'

'Yep, I'm pulling the chemo card,' said Hazel. 'No one is allowed to disagree with me when I pull the chemo card.' She grinned.

'How is the chemo?' I asked.

'Utter shit,' said Hazel. 'So do me a favour. I have no choice, but you do. Don't do it, Cathy. Don't spend the majority of the rest of your working life doing something you don't enjoy.'

Then she said it. The words I didn't want her to say but she did.

'Life's too short, Cathy. Life's too short.'

14 September

I agonized for two days then I called Giles and afterwards I called Mike.

'What do you mean you said no?' Mike raged at me. 'I don't understand. Make me understand.'

'Well, they do what they call "agile working".'

'Yes, yes. Most large companies do these days. And . . .?'

'So there was nowhere to put fairy lights,' I told him.

I could hear his sharp intake of breath. Perhaps understandably, I admit.

'And there was a big sign in the kitchen that said no mugs with offensive slogans.'

'Forgive me for thinking that these are all minor considerations when considering your place of work?'

'No,' I said. 'No. I thought really hard about it, Mike. I really did. I wanted to like it. But . . . but I just couldn't see myself enjoying it. There was absolutely zero personality there. It was so . . . so faceless. They were like robots operating in a void. And I don't want to spend the next dozen or so years like that. I don't want to go to work every day and be told what I can have written on my mug. Or that I can't even have a desk to call my own. I don't want to spend the majority of my waking hours in a characterless box.'

'I bet it wasn't characterless. I bet there were graphics on the walls and plants dotted around. Companies realize they need to create a clear vision in their environment. And anyway, agile working leads to increased communication. You would meet and converse with loads more people, and that makes a team a whole lot more cohesive.'

'Bullshit,' I said. 'Agile working costs less. And that's the bottom line.'

'You've just been out of the workplace for too long, you're just not used to being in an office. You'll soon get used to it.'

'I've got my own desk now at The Mustard Factory.

And some fairy lights and a mug with SUPPORT SEX WORKERS on it. Oh, and Barbra has her own bowl.'

'Well then, if you are choosing your employers based on whether they supply a dog bowl, then I'm sure you can call Cringolds and ask if they'll be happy to add dog refreshments to your package.'

'I sense sarcasm.'

'I sense stupidity. You must know that 90 per cent of those companies in that building will be out of business within eighteen months. And you'd rather stick with them than work for a business that's existed for over a hundred years. Are you serious?'

'I'm not taking the job,' I told him firmly. To be honest, the thought of facing Hazel and telling her I'd taken the job was the only thing that was stopping me from caving in to Mike.

He sighed deeply. 'What am I going to tell Helen? She really went out on a limb to recommend you.'

'I didn't ask her to. Helen can stick her recommendation and file it alongside her nose, which she needs to stick out of our business. I'm sick of Helen deciding what I should be doing with my life. And what you should be doing, to be perfectly honest.'

'And what is that supposed to mean?'

'You've let a consultant downsize you.'

'I have no idea what you are talking about.'

'You have let her review your business, put an idea in your head, and encourage you to go down a path without really thinking whether it's the right one for you. And she's pushing it because she knows that you will be the most excellent case study on her website. Consultant turned schoolteacher. What a turnaround. Might be for a while, until you are crying every night over unmarked books.'

'But I want to give back, Cathy. I want to do something positive.'

'So go and volunteer in your spare time. Visit old people. Be an advisor for a charity. But teaching? Have you any idea how difficult it is?'

'My current job is difficult.'

'Have you actually spoken to anyone who teaches? You have only spoken to people in whose interests it is for you to make this change. Helen, the dean at Birmingham University . . . But what about somebody on the ground, somebody who knows what it's really like? What about them? Have you asked a teacher what it's like to teach?'

He sighed again, clearly frustrated with me. 'This isn't about me; this is about you turning down a great opportunity just so you can play pretend commerce with a bunch of kids. It's all going to end in tears.'

I could not believe my ears.

I slammed down the phone, stormed out of the room and grabbed the dog lead.

My safety net in times of crisis.

I left the house, slamming doors in my wake. People needed to know I was angry. The neighbours needed to know I was angry. The street needed to know I was angry. Who else needed to know I was angry? I knew exactly who.

Somehow Barbra took me to one of her favourite places. The place with her own dog bowl and snack. The place where she got more fuss than at home. Within twenty minutes we were at The Mustard Factory. I nodded at the receptionist and cruised up the stairs. I was home. How peculiar was that? Despite my age I felt at home in this wildly funky, youthful, creative building, and I knew that this was where I belonged, not in the regimented rows of robots at Cringolds.

Only Toby was in the office. He looked up as I walked in and was instantly out of his seat and grabbing my shoulders.

'What's wrong ?' he asked. 'You looked terrible.'

'Me and Mike have had a big row,' I sniffed.

'Jesus,' he said. 'Right, sit down and let's get out the commiseration pale ale.'

'Is that the new brew from upstairs?' I asked, taking my coat off.

'It is. And it's not terrible,' he replied, handing me a bottle. I took a full swig, narrowly avoiding spitting it out.'

'So what happened?'

I explained about Mike wanting me to leave to go and work for the dark side and that I'd had an offer but I'd turned it down.

'He just doesn't understand why I like it here,' I said.

'Do you want me to have a word with him?'

'No!' That was a terrible idea but I admired the sentiment. I actually loved the idea that Toby was willing to go to my husband and defend me.

'I'm so glad you turned the job down,' he continued. 'Cathy, I don't know what we would do without you now. Seriously. You hold us all together. I would be out of business if it wasn't for you. You came in and sorted me out. You . . . you . . . complete me.'

God, he was cheesy sometimes, but I sort of liked it. Bit of an ego boost, to be honest. I mean it was a ridiculous idea that I might complete Toby. The most unlikely combination in the history of double acts. The cool dude hipster graphic designer and his work mum.

'In fact,' he continued, 'if the circumstances were different then . . . well, I would . . . is all I can say.'

He smiled at me and had a twinkle in his eye.

What did he just say? Did he mean what I think he meant?

'What do you mean?' I asked.

'Well,' he said, 'I mean if you weren't . . . you know . . .'

'Married,' I offered.

'Well, I was actually more thinking if you weren't quite so old . . .'

He left that statement hanging out there to consider.

Right, so marriage wasn't a barrier but age was! Rude!

'Well, thank you, Toby,' I said, getting up. 'But you're really not my type. You and me? No, never would have happened.'

I looked down at him and he looked slightly shocked, I have to say. I wondered if he had ever been rejected before, even in this weird theoretical realm we had momentarily entered. I suspected not.

I felt a surge of power. Something unusual had just happened. I think I just sort of turned down a man. I'd never turned a man down. Never. All my boyfriends were a result of me identifying a potential future partner, stalking them for a while and then manufacturing a situation where they would have to get off with me. To be fair I was reasonable with my expectations. I knew what I was capable of. I knew that if David Beckham had gone to my school that I would not even have thought of the stalking stage – there would have been no point. I was more on a Paul Scholes level or, at a *real* stretch, Gary Lineker pre-TV-presenter makeover. I would never have put myself in with the professional Premier League players, I was more amateur Sunday League level. Players not fit enough to get away!

But I'd heard of women who did get to knock men back. Apparently some women inspire men to be pro-active and bold and approach women and tell them of their undying love. I wasn't in that category. Even when I got off with Mike (funny that, isn't it – thinking that way back in the past you 'got off' with your husband; had your first clandestine snog, normally in a dark and crowded room, blind drunk, while everyone else leered at you), I had sort of stalked him for a few weeks. He was so confident and smart and clever and had a knack for making everyone feel at ease. And when he said my name and smiled at me, well, I did go weak at the knees. I really fancied him and showed it by always offering to be the scribe in his meetings and helping to clear up the multitude of Post-it notes at the end, just to be in a room alone with him. I was surprised he came to my leaving do, to be honest. He said he never normally got invited since he was typically the reason for the event, so he'd been delighted when I'd shyly told him we were all meeting in the pub to send me on my way. He bought everyone a round of drinks, which was nice, then offered to walk me home. I wasn't quite so shy when I'd got him outside my front door in the dark and drunk on gin and bitter lemon. And the rest, as they say, is history.

So this was new. A man actually telling me they fancied me . . . sort of. A whole new experience. One I decided I should enjoy! I looked at Toby and wondered whether – if he knew I had grey pubic hair – he would have made any such suggestion at all.

'You're just not my type,' I said cheerily, giving him a peck on the cheek. 'Have a good weekend.'

To be honest, I was on a bit of a high after my discussion with Toby. It was amazing what a touch of flattery could do for your ego. I thought it might be a bit weird at The Mustard Factory after that, but he behaved as though it had never happened and that was fine by me.

Today was expenses day, though, which was always a bit tough with Toby as he was rubbish at keeping on top of them. He just threw receipts in a carrier bag and expected me to understand what they were for.

'This hotel receipt,' I said. 'I presume this is the one where you went to pitch for a client?'

'That's right.'

'Did you get the business?'

'No, not that time.'

'So the receipt says there was breakfast for two?'

'Yes, that's right. I met the client for breakfast the next morning after the pitch. He wanted to talk some points over. Not that it did me any good.'

'In your room?'

'Excuse me?'

'In your room? You met the client in your room. It says you had room-service breakfast?'

Toby stared back at me, saying nothing, totally looking a little uncomfortable.

'And it was a "he", you say? Eating Eggs Benedict? I don't think so. I've *never* known a man to order Eggs Benedict.'

He broke out into a grin. 'It was the assistant brand manager,' he admitted. 'She er . . . I asked her out for a drink afterwards. And she missed her last train home. I couldn't put her out on the streets, could I?'

WTF!

This man! This man with the wife and the toddler and the dog called Blizzard. I thought it was all bluster and show. I didn't think he was actually that kind of guy. I thought perhaps he just needed to know he could have whoever he wanted. Including me. Not actually *have* whoever he wanted.

'And you think we should put this through on expenses?' I asked him.

'Tell you what, I'll pay for the Eggs Benedict,' he offered. 'If that makes it all right?'

'But it doesn't make it all right, does it?' I said.

'In the eyes of the tax man?' he asked.

'In the eyes of your wife,' I pointed out.

His smile faded.

'Come on, Cathy,' he said, putting his hand on mine. 'It was only a bit of fun. I'll never see her again.'

'Course you won't. Clearly you're not that good in bed. You didn't get the business, did you?'

'Harsh,' he replied.

'Honest. How old was she, out of interest?'

'Early twenties, I guess.'

'I thought you were all talk. I didn't think you were actually a dick. You can tell me to butt out but please don't be a dick, hey?'

'Butt out,' he said, looking serious.

We stared at each other across the table in the Connections Room.

I had a right to give him my opinion, I thought. I was his work mum, after all.

'I thought you were better than this, Toby,' I said, instantly realizing I had never sounded more like a work mum.

He swallowed and looked away. 'Like I said, just a bit of fun.'

'Would Phoebe see it that way?'

'Butt out,' he repeated.

'Do you know what,' I said, gathering up my things and getting up. 'This is good. This is really good. You are a proper wake-up call, you are. You've reminded me that I have a husband who I trust to the end of the earth, *and* he thinks I am pretty. And do you know what, that makes me feel really, really good. It makes me happy. He's a good man, a total pain in the arse, but a good man.'

'Why are you telling me all this?' asked Toby.

'I'm not. I'm telling myself.'

25 September

It was my turn to host book group this month. Tania popped in during the day to say she couldn't face it but she had made a carrot cake for us all. I mean really. Her wife has cancer and she's making carrot cake for a book group she can't attend. She's unbelievable. While she was here she noticed the sign that Freddie had made for the fridge door.

DAD
TEENAGERS AND MENOPAUSAL WOMEN
CAN GET AWAY WITH MURDER IN THIS HOUSE
MUM SAYS SO

That made her smile. I also told her that Freddie had really listened when I'd done my announcement about the menopause and had gone away and done his own research. She looked impressed until I told her that I was having regular updates on menopausal acne which was something that I had been blissfully unaware of until he'd pointed it out.

We didn't speak for long. She seemed distant, no doubt too much weighing too heavily on her mind. She said Hazel was in bed asleep at home. I didn't ask how she was as I sensed Tania didn't want to tell me. There wasn't enough hope in her eyes. I just hoped I was reading her wrong.

It was a brief and slightly sombre book group, albeit Paula was there and so we had to try and provide some light relief somehow. We couldn't let down the depressed member of our group by being miserable, even though we were all pretty upset for Tania. After a long silent pause, I asked Louise how her work was, hoping that she would be able to lift us with her usual tales of office debauchery. Unfortunately, nothing had happened recently, except that her 4-year-old son had got stuck in a huge toy grabber machine in an arcade on holiday, and the fire brigade had had to be called. He'd been so desperate to get a toy that he had managed somehow to climb in through the exit hatch.

We laughed harder and longer over this than necessary, albeit it *was* very necessary. Even Paula laughed. Which was *really* necessary.

October

Have 'The Chat'
(The Really, Really Important One)

1 October

I was feeling a bit nervous. I thought this was probably the most important goal of my entire year and I really wanted to nail this one.

I had probably known that Mike and I needed to have 'the chat' since possibly before we were married. Certainly we should have had it after we moved in together, and I suspected it would have been a helpful discussion when he asked me to marry him. I was certain that if we'd had 'the chat' then we would have had maybe not a happier marriage but perhaps a more contented one. But that was in the past and this was now. The chat was most definitely needed and I reckoned, if successful, should see us through to our golden wedding anniversary with a bit of luck.

5 October

'Could we have a chat?' I asked him after dinner. I was sick with nerves but we were alone and I'd got Robbie to cook turkey lasagne, which I was hoping had put Mike in a good mood.

'What about?' he said, looking at me accusingly. My palms began to sweat.

'Have you had the chance to talk to any teachers yet?' I asked. I thought I'd better check on the current status with the teaching thing before I even began with 'the chat'.

'No, I haven't,' he grumbled. He didn't look away from the TV screen.

'But you are going to?'

'Yes!' he exclaimed. 'When I get the chance.'

'So you won't apply until you talk to some real teachers then?' I asked, trying hard not to sound desperate.

'I said so, didn't I?' he said, looking at me angrily. He picked up the remote and turned the sound up.

I decided now was not the time to advance to 'the chat'. I was all tongue-tied and nervous and I needed to get him in a good mood. This was not a conversation to have when he was grumpy.

'Did you get my email about the works do in Hampshire?' he suddenly said. 'Did you book our train?'

Bingo, I thought. Perfect. A night out with free alcohol. That should do the trick.

7 October

I thought MUM'S KNEE had been quiet for a while. I'd spoken plenty to my sisters since our trip to LA. More than normal, in fact. The glow from spending quality time together was still flowing and we regularly chatted on the phone about this and that. However, suddenly a notification popped up that I had been added to the group LOOKING AFTER MUM & DAD.

314

Lizzy: *Mum's run out of loo roll and it's already dark so she doesn't want to go out. Any chance someone can drop some off tonight?*

I thought I'd reply with some light-hearted banter. That proved to be a mistake.

Me: *Only if you agree to give me a bigger share of the Will.*

Nicola: *That's not fair. I need it more than you. You're not having any of my share.*

Me: *I was only joking! Can't you take a joke?*

Nicola: *You can't joke about Mum and Dad dying.*

Me: *I wasn't. I was joking about their Will!*

Lizzy: *Shall we not mention the Will any more?*

Me: *Sorry. My bad. Won't mention it again. I'll send Freddie down in the car. He's passed his test and he was on about asking his grandparents to buy him a car.*

Nicola: *What! No way! If they buy Freddie a car then they will have to buy Tilly and Jude one when they are 17.*

Me: *I was joking, Nicola!!! Of course Freddie hasn't passed his test! Are you insane?*

Nicola: *Oh right. But you're not going to let him ask Mum and Dad for a car when he does, are you? Because you know that's not fair, right?*

Me: *I suspect Mum and Dad will be long gone by the time Freddie passes his test, by which time he'll be able to buy one with his inheritance.*

Nicola: *Have they left the money to Freddie? They never said. Have they left some to Tilly and Jude too? Why wasn't I told about this?*

Me: *Calm down, Nic. You heard them. It's split between the three of us. I'm really sorry I mentioned anything to do with Wills now.*

Lizzy: *So can someone go take some loo roll to Mum and Dad then?*

I wait a full minute for Nicola to offer.

Me: *I'll go. Barbra Streisand needs a walk anyway.*

Lizzy: *Thanks, Cathy.*

Nicola: *Yeah, thanks. I'll do it next time.*

7 October

So tonight was the night for 'the chat'. Mike was in a very good mood as he loved the consultancy's annual Christmas party with other halves. They always had it in

October. They used to have it at Christmas but they had a consultation about it and decided they would get better value for money if they had a bash at a different time of year when venues were more willing to do a deal. Then they sat back and felt very pleased with themselves for being so smart, as is the way of consultants. In fact, I had to agree it was a great idea. We'd been to some amazing venues during the low-demand period of October when weddings had slowed down and it was too early for Christmas.

I had a few butterflies in my stomach that night, knowing we were finally going to have 'the chat'. I knew I would need to line my stomach with a few free cocktails just to pluck up the courage.

Nearly twenty years of marriage and we still required alcohol to reveal our true feelings.

I had to say, though, that I had some cracking memories of drunken nights out with my husband which ended tearfully in each other's arms.

'I really love you, you know,' would come the slobber in the ear in the back of the taxi sometime after midnight.

'You too,' I would slobber back, trying to hold back a late-night kebab belch.

Love liberated by lager.

How terribly British.

The night began in the usual way. Mike in his element, glad-handing all his colleagues, sharing tales of consultant mirth in the vein of, 'Do you remember that new client pitch when we made the MD get in the lift at their HQ and tell us between the ground floor and the fifteenth what his company actually did? Only one word per floor. Totally threw him. Utter genius. We need to do more pitches like that when we make the client do all the work.'

Guffaw, guffaw, guffaw. Self-congratulatory pats on the back all round.

I smiled sweetly and sipped my free Cosmopolitan. I could cope with anything accompanied by a free Cosmopolitan.

I started by asking polite questions of the partners. When I say partners I mean wives, of course, as sadly 80 per cent of the consultants were male. It always surprised me, actually, as can you imagine offering a woman a job which required many nights away in hotels where someone cooked your food and made your bed. Most women, I reckoned, would work for free for that.

We stood at the bar in a gathering of four couples, the men holding forth, making sure their opinions were heard on every subject from the hotel we were staying in to the state of British politics. The wives stood around grinning inanely, patiently waiting for their opportunity to enter the conversation, but the men had it covered. So eager were they to outdo each other with their insights on boring subjects that the wives couldn't get a word in edgeways. After my third Cosmopolitan I got bored of this so I interjected some general questions. You know, the tedious stuff, like if they had children, where they lived, had they been on holiday this year, in an attempt to involve the whole group. But the men kept butting in. So full of their desperate need to share, they totally overlooked the fact that their wives were perfectly capable of speaking for themselves. So I decided a new line of questioning was required. I asked one lady who looked to be in her late fifties and had a fabulous body as well as an incredible Eighties-style mahogany tan if she did yoga, and of course her answer was yes. Had to be, bound to be.

She didn't work.

Her husband was a consultant

She had a body to die for.

I complimented her on her physique then asked if she found yoga helped with the menopause. She looked slightly shocked and the group went very quiet but, given I had wrapped the question in such a compliment, she responded that yes, she felt it had. So then I asked if she had any other recommendations on how to deal with the midlife female affliction, given she clearly looked so fantastic. The men were suddenly quiet and awkward. They looked at their feet and shuffled, whereas the women were equally quiet but obviously all ears. Waiting, interested, fascinated by the conversation, which moments earlier, quite frankly, had been as dull as ditchwater.

The lady in question smiled at me. 'I had a really, really great therapist,' she admitted.

She looked nervously at her husband. He had been the most vocal moments earlier as he had talked us through the new bike he'd bought at the weekend for an exorbitant amount of money. He smiled sheepishly at his colleagues.

'You have to talk about it,' she continued. 'Or else you think you are going mad. Honestly.'

'So you talked to a therapist,' I said, nodding encouragingly. This was good. This was really good.

'She was amazing,' she replied. 'Totally got me through it.'

'A mate of mine recommended her,' added her husband, unable to *not* participate. 'Apparently she has some very famous clients, although they are not allowed to say who, of course. Patient confidentiality and all that. But she certainly has helped, hasn't she Patricia? And I should think so too. She's costing me a fortune!'

He laughed a big laugh. The other men had the decency to temper their chuckle. Patricia looked resigned.

It was one of those moments. I had the right response (for once) on the tip of my tongue but did I dare say it? Was this the right time to succeed in the constant life quest of saying the right thing at the right time? I *never* usually had the right response. Could I waste this one? I glanced at my husband. He was smiling sympathetically at Colin.

'Maybe if *you* would only listen for just five minutes then she might not need a therapist . . . Ladies, shall we go and order another round of Cosmos?'

Patricia looked momentarily startled, then grinned like a Cheshire cat. 'Good idea,' she said, leaving her husband's side and leading the middle-aged women's stampede to the free bar.

When we finally sat down to dinner, Mike introduced the man sitting next to me at the table as Louis, a recent graduate recruit whom Mike was mentoring. He was sitting next to his girlfriend Marnie, whose pert, wrinkle-free boobs were already spilling over the cutlery, making every man at the table desperate not to stare and every woman of a certain age stare with a mixture of envy and distaste.

'Your husband is a brilliant mentor,' Louis told me.

'You don't have to tell me that,' I told him. 'I'm married to him, he's not my son.'

'No seriously,' he said. 'He's the best. Everyone says so. Everyone wants him. All the old graduates tell you that you are as lucky as hell to get Mike Collins. Actually takes it seriously. Wants you to learn. He's not worried about you being better than him. He *wants* you to be better than him. Takes pride in it. That's a rare thing.'

'Right,' I said, looking curiously at Louis. He seemed genuine. And after all, there was no advantage to buttering me up.

'He does this great introductory speech to all the new graduates,' he continued. 'So funny, but so inspirational. Makes you proud to work there straight away.'

'Does he do a lot of work with the graduate programme then?' I asked.

'Not really. He's just a mentor. The chap who runs the programme, who does all the recruitment and training and what-have-you, well, he's not great, to be honest. Thankfully he's taking early retirement so hopefully they'll put someone better in.'

The Cosmopolitans had slowed down the whirring of my brain somewhat, but I was sure there was something in this conversation that was useful. Somewhere. I just couldn't quite fit the pieces together.

Then I didn't have to.

'Mike should do it,' said Louis casually. 'He'd be brilliant. Unfortunately, I don't think he would want to step away from full-time consultancy. Shame really, because he'd be great.'

I stared at Louis and thought about kissing him. Louis, this stranger with the girlfriend with the pert boobs had offered a solution to our dilemma on a plate. I literally could not believe my luck.

'You should suggest it to him,' I said urgently. 'You know, in passing. You never know. I think he might consider it, especially if you told him how good he would be at it. Tell him all the graduates think he should take over this job you are talking about. He might think about it if you said that.'

I knew if *I* mentioned it to Mike it was dead in the

water. If I mentioned it then it would be a tactic to get him off the idea of teaching. If I mentioned it then it would be my idea and not his and that would kill it immediately.

Louis shrugged. 'If you think so. Sure. I'll say something. As long as you don't think he'd think I was an idiot for suggesting it?'

'No, no,' I said. 'He'll be flattered, seriously. Promise me, later, you'll mention it. Then come and tell me what he says. Will you do that? Please?'

Time to back off as I was sounding like a maniac.

'Okay,' he shrugged. 'I'll mention it.'

I fought the impulse to ask him to give me an exact time when he would ask Mike. I picked up my glass and took a large slug of wine while I tried to calm down.

The meal was very pleasant. The wine flowed. Like, really flowed. I was actually struggling to hold it together. What with the excitement of a possible solution to Mike's career-shift plans hanging out there, and needing to be ready to finally have 'the chat', I was a nervous wreck.

After the meal, we danced. We danced like idiots when we were drunk, Mike and I. I liked it. I liked it a lot. We touched hands and twirled each other round like a proper couple. We needed more dancing in our lives. Dancing somehow made intimacy so natural. Touching natural. Dancing helped you stay in love. I was convinced of it. Especially when it was to the legend that is Lionel Richie.

Then, suddenly people were starting to drift off to bed and I couldn't find my husband.

'Fancy some fresh air?' he said when I finally found

him huddled in a corner with Louis. 'I need to talk to you about something?'

What are the chances?

Pretty high actually, given we normally only talked when inebriated or on a long car journey.

We stumbled out onto the back steps of the hotel into the fairly pleasant night.

'I've had a great idea,' he said, eyes shining.

'Oh yeah?'

'Bill, who runs recruitment and training and is the ambassador for the consultancy, is retiring next year. I'm going to go for his job.'

'What you mean like *teach*, but at your existing company?' I asked, my eyes wide in pseudo-surprise.

'Exactly!' said Mike. 'I don't know why I didn't think of it before. But one of the grads came up to me just now and asked me if I was up for it. Apparently all the grads want me to do it, which is nice, eh?'

'Wow, that's amazing. Just perfect. You can share your knowledge. You can teach people everything you've learnt. Just like you wanted to.'

'It would be perfect, Cathy. And I would get to spend most of my time in the Birmingham office, so no more hotel rooms. There would be a bit of travel, but not half as much as I do now. And I'd get to manage recruitment, and what have I always said?'

'Recruitment, recruitment, recruitment,' I sang back to him.

'Exactly. Recruitment is everything to a company.'

'Have you mentioned it to anyone else? Is there someone you should talk to tonight? You know, strike while the iron is hot and all that.'

'I said I'd meet Chaffer for breakfast, actually. I'll talk

to him then. But to be honest I've been through everyone else and I can't think of anyone better placed to do it than me. Not unless they recruit from outside, but it should go to someone who understands the company. Someone who knows the ins and outs. I tell you, I'm already buzzing with ideas. I think we should do a recruitment road show round the top universities. We should be at Freshers' Weeks. Stand out from all the others. Talk to people at the beginning of their studies. Give them something to aim for. Get on their radar right from the start. What do you think?'

'Like you say, I think you were made for it.'

Did I dare ask? No, leave it. I didn't need him to confirm that he'd dropped the teaching idea. His enthusiasm said it all.

I felt a flood of relief flow through me. This truly was a dream come true. It sounded like we had both found roles that we could be happy in for the next few years. I nearly asked if I could be the one to inform Helen that her services were no longer required, but I thought I had better not push my luck.

I felt so relieved I felt like crying. Perhaps now I would be okay to really settle into my funny little corner at The Mustard Factory with the fairy lights and the rickety chair and the sex mug.

But I couldn't let the emotion stop my initial intentions for the evening. I had to press on. This could be a double-whammy night if I played my cards right.

'Actually, I need to talk to you about something too,' I said. There, I'd said it now. It was out there. I'd have to verbalize my thoughts. No backing out. I needed to talk.

'Oh yeah, fire ahead.'

'Shall we walk?' I asked, indicating a well-lit path. Side by side is always easier than face to face.

I took a deep breath. The time had finally come to have 'the chat'.

My hands were clammy, my throat was dry. It felt as though I was about to ask for the earth, and I kind of was. I knew the answer to the thing I was about to request could make or break our marriage. Never had I said something so important that could affect my future happiness so much. It was something I should have said a long time ago but somehow there had never been the right moment. It seemed like too big an ask. Too big a deal. I convinced myself that I was being unreasonable. That he would take offence, or be angry and say I wasn't being fair. That he'd look at me differently.

I convinced myself that he actually might love me a little bit less if I dared have 'the chat' with him.

By now we were at the bottom of the glorious garden that scrolled down at the back of the hotel. The stars were looking down on us. I didn't think that I had ever been in a more romantic spot than this with Mike. It was a moment for poignant declarations of love rather than 'the chat'. But I knew it was now or never. Even if he did love me less after I'd said it, I had to do it or live with the consequences for the rest of our marriage.

'So,' I said, pausing by a stone-encircled pool with a fountain in the middle. 'As I said, I really need to have a chat with you about something.

'Of course,' he said. 'Go on.'

'Well, I've been thinking for a very long time and I wanted to ask you if can we . . . can, we can . . . possibly share all the housework . . . equally?'

I paused.

325

He furrowed his brow.

Oh God, he loved me a bit less already. But I needed to press on. This was important.

'I mean *properly* share it. Not just you promising you will do more and then forgetting or not really meaning it or just you taking the kitchen bin out on a Sunday if it happens to be full. Or even you thinking you are sharing it because you've finally learned what a loo brush is. I mean *properly* sharing it. I mean you actually picking things up if the place looks untidy and you putting the dishwasher on *and* emptying it. I mean you putting clothes in the washing machine when the laundry basket is full rather than waiting for the washing fairy to do it. I mean you sweeping the kitchen floor. Yes, actually sweeping it. And not just after a dinner party. I mean whenever it needs doing. I mean being familiar with the mop on a regular basis. I mean me coming home one day and finding you cleaning out the cupboard that has the salt and pepper in just because it needs cleaning. Oh my God, I cannot tell you how happy that would make me. In fact, how much more it would make me love you. If I found you cleaning a cupboard out so I didn't have to do it, my goodness, the single sexiest thing I can think of.'

'Seriously? Do I have to do it naked or something?'

'No. Just do it. That's all. All I'm asking for is for you to have a woman's attitude to housework. To do it because it needs doing. Not because you have been told to. Not because I'm in a bad mood so you are trying to avoid getting shouted at. Just because it needs doing and there is absolutely no reason why it should be left to me. Do it because you understand it's not *my* job. It's *our* job.'

I paused for breath. I was breathing really hard now

and feeling quite emotional. He was looking at me with concern. As though I was going slightly mad.

I tried again.

'Do it because you don't want me to spend what is hopefully the second half of our marriage feeling resentful of you every time I pick up your socks or clean the toilet that you have just used or clean out the cupboard with the salt and pepper pots in it. Because I will. Because I don't know how *not* to. Do it so we can spend the second half of our marriage enjoying each other free of Domestic Situation Resentment. Yes, that's it, DSR. I'm done with it, Mike. It taints most marriages I reckon. You ask most wives. We *all* suffer from DSR.

'Domestic Situation Resentment?' Mike repeated back to me.

'Yes! You're getting it,' I said. 'Domestic Situation Resentment is not something I want to live with for the rest of my life.'

'I didn't realize that's how you felt,' he said.

'So my near-constant low-level sulking didn't cut through?' I asked.

He shook his head.

'So you'll do it then?' I asked. 'It's a big commitment. A complete change of mindset. Every time you walk in the house you need to be immediately thinking about what needs to be done rather than thinking I need to sit down and stare at my phone for half an hour. It's really exhausting, I'll warn you now.'

'I'm sorry,' he said. 'I'm sorry that I assumed you would do all that stuff.'

'It just sort of happened,' I admitted. 'We were both complicit. I should have said something sooner. It's my fault really. No, I don't mean that, actually. That's what inflicted me with DSR in the first place. Thinking it was my fault. Let's just agree it happened and now it won't.'

He looked at me for a long while, thinking. Biting his bottom lip. Was he about to say no?

'Can I ask you something,' he eventually said.

I nodded.

'Can we sit down and you tell me what you want me to do *exactly* to get rid of the DSR? I'm not sure I can view it like a woman. I just don't see it. I don't *know* when the salt and pepper cupboard needs cleaning. It always looks fine to me. My first thought of the day isn't that the dishwasher needs emptying or that someone needs to sweep the crumbs up off the floor. You cannot rely on me to see it. In fact, I guarantee you I *won't* see it and then . . . and then . . . you'll be mad and you won't say anything and then—'

'The DSR will kick in again,' I said.

'Exactly,' he replied.

'You like the DSR thing, don't you?' I said with a grin.

'You know I love an acronym,' he smiled. 'But you will *have* to write me a list. You will have to tell me exactly what I need to do to keep the DSR at bay. Because I just won't be able to tell on my own.'

'Years of domestic ignorance,' I said.

'I'm afraid so,' he said.

'Okay. It's a deal,' I told him. 'When we get home tomorrow, let's write ourselves a list and divvy it up between us.'

'Good. And will you agree to tell me if you are suffering from DSR in the future,' he asked sincerely.

'I will,' I agreed, all misty-eyed. 'Perhaps we should renew our vows? I do solemnly swear to inform you of any bouts of DSR for as long as we both shall live.'

He took my hands in his. 'What a lovely idea,' he said. 'Let's do it.'

'Only if we can rewrite *all* the vows,' I replied. 'Actually make them useful, like promising not to laugh at me when I'm standing in just tights in the bedroom.'

'It's not a good look,' he said.

'It's not a good look on Claudia Schiffer, never mind me.'

'Okay, let's write our own vows,' he said.

'An updated midlife version,' I said.

'Good idea,' he nodded.

And then, dear diary, we kissed.

Under the stars, in the most romantic situation I have ever been in with my husband, having finally had 'the chat'. The really, really important one.

13 October

Well, we certainly took advantage of being on the pill last night, if you know what I mean! 'The chat' had a dramatic impact on my libido. A really dramatic one. The propect of a DSR-free marriage really got my pecker up. So to speak.

Mike had his breakfast with Chaffer (I'm sure that can't be his real name, but I cannot be bothered to hear the story of how Chaffer became Chaffer), who agreed that Mike would be a great candidate to run the graduate programme and indeed asked him if he would consider managing the ongoing training programme for all the consultants.

I saw Louis in the foyer while I waited for Mike to check us out and offered my thanks to him for putting the right word in.

'Is he up for it then?' he asked excitedly.

'Oh yes,' I told him. 'Stroke of genius. You have no idea how glad I am to have met you. You made last night a magical night in more ways than one.'

Unsurprisingly he ducked when I lunged forward to give him a peck on the cheek and said he had to dash, giving no reason as to why.

26 October

Well, that was a fun book group, not! It was so bad, I called Mike in Manchester when I got home. Needed a reassuring voice. Needed a friend. Needed my husband.

Tania wasn't there. How could she be? She had popped in earlier in the week and we'd sat and drunk brandy while she had to put into words the news that the doctors were now saying that Hazel probably wouldn't make it. I held her hand and rubbed her back as she spluttered and sniffed and practically dissolved in front of me before blowing her nose, gathering herself up and taking herself home to be the 'strong one' as her family went through hell.

'She just wants your thoughts and prayers,' I told the rest of the book group when they inevitably asked me what they could do to help.

'Shall we pray now?' said Louise, who had cried for the last half-hour in response to what could be the death knell as far as Tania's wife was concerned.

'Why not?' said Fiona with a shrug. 'Feels like we've got do something.'

'Shall we all hold hands and . . . and say our own prayer?' suggested Sonja.

And so we did. We sat in Fiona's lounge and linked hands. Then bowed our heads and screwed up our eyes. We all got lost in our own thoughts to the background noise of tears being snuffled away.

Then a voice cut through. It was Paula.

'Please God, can we have a miracle for Tania's Hazel and make her better because Tania loves her and wants to keep her?'

'Amen,' I said.

'Amen,' chorused the rest of the group.

29 October

Oh my goodness, it finally happened. I looked at the calendar and finally realized something.

I haven't had a period in a while!

This was the thing I'd wanted to achieve from the beginning of the year. A period-free life. Finally I could tick it off my list.

I was free . . . finally, after what must be thirty-four years, barring the pregnancy phase, of course, of the monthly torture.

But then I had a wobble.

I started to think. Always fatal.

Why had my periods stopped?

Was it the pill? Had my cunning plan worked?

Or actually was it the menopause starting? Had that kicked in? Was I entering the point of no return? Were my ovaries shrivelling up right now? Were the hot sweats and the possible anxiety and depression and the forgetfulness needling their way into my body?

I wasn't ready yet. I wanted period-free time without

the menopause. A little honeymoon 'period', shall we call it, before all the other symptoms of the menopause kicked in.

And then I had a terrible thought. A truly terrifying thought. A thought so horrific it made me sit down on the sofa with a 'plump' and put my head in my hands.

There was another reason why my periods might have stopped. Perhaps the most obvious reason.

What if I was pregnant?

We had been having rather a lot of sex recently, what with 'the chat' resulting in addressing the DSR issue and with actually being on the pill making it less of a faff. And I know the fact I'm on the pill should have meant that I shouldn't get pregnant but we'd all had it drummed into us that no contraceptive is 100 per cent effective and I might have missed taking the pill the odd day here and there because . . . well, you just do, don't you, so I might be pregnant.

I might be pregnant!

I couldn't be pregnant, not at 48. I just couldn't. I had to stop being so ridiculous and believe that either taking the pill had finally put an end to my periods or that the menopause had actually started.

Either way, I kind of wished I would have another period.

Just to be absolutely, 100 per cent, sure.

November

Fall in Love Again

1 November

Day three of realizing I haven't had a period. I was seriously considering buying a pregnancy test. It was really niggling at the back of my mind and I knew I was being stupid and the odds were really stacked against me, but still, I couldn't seem to stop worrying about it.

But I had been into the chemist and I just couldn't do it. Couldn't have the assistant look at me like I must be way too old to be having sex, or worse, that I'm getting it for my daughter!

3 November

Still no hint of bleeding! Seriously, I started this year desperate to never ever bleed again from my vagina and now I would do anything to see just the tiniest spot! I was starting to feel paranoid that I was pregnant and I was having all sorts of nightmares of me being the only mother to turn up at Freddie's graduation with a toddler in tow! Or Kirsty having to explain to her sixth-form tutor that her mum couldn't come to parents' evening because she was breastfeeding. Oh my God, breastfeeding?

Can you imagine breastfeeding at my age! I mean I probably couldn't even produce milk, could I? I'm like an old dried-out cow, surely?

I knew I just needed to take a test. It was simple, really. Take the test and then I would know, but I felt totally stupid. Jesus, I needed to get this out of my system and as Tania really didn't need to hear my paranoid problems about potential breastfeeding issues surrounding this baby I was not pregnant with, I figured I needed to discuss this with the next best thing.

MUM'S KNEE

Me: So you can't get pregnant at 48, right? Especially if you are on the pill?

Nicola: Are you having sex?!!!! You know you have to have sex to get pregnant, right? Pregnancy 101.

She actually used a shocked emojji face after the exclamation marks which I thought was harsh.

Me: Yes, I'm having sex.

Nicola: Me and Lizzy had money on you not getting any.

Me: Seriously? Why? I cannot believe you even discussed it.

Nicola: Well, you were kind of uptight in LA.

Me: And you weren't?!

336

Nicola: *Because I wasn't getting any . . . doh!*

Me: *Well, I'll have you know me and Mike are still . . . I can't believe we are having this conversation.*

Nicola: *You started it.*

Lizzy: *If you are pregnant, what does that have to do with mum's knee?*

Me: *Nothing?*

Lizzy: *You posted in the MUM'S KNEE group chat?*

Me: *Because it was the first one I found with all three of us in. I'm hardly likely to set up a group called AM I PREGNANT?*

Lizzy: *Are you? Are you out of your mind!*

Me: *I feel like I'm going out of my mind. You see I went on the pill to stop my periods, but it takes a while you know and I perhaps forgot the odd one and then Mike and I had sex.*

Nicola: *Aaaah – so it was a one-off.*

Me: *No! But, you know, it was a special occasion and . . .*

Nicola: *I feel so much better. I was starting to feel jealous of your sex life.*

337

Me: I am married and you are single! I'm supposed to be having more sex than you.

Nicola: You'd think, wouldn't you????

She added a winking emoji!

Lizzy: So you're on the pill but you've been a bit lax?

Me: Yes, so now I don't know if my periods have stopped because of being on the pill, the menopause, or I'm pregnant.

Nicola: Jeees – what a pickle! Are you old enough to be menopausal?

Me: Oh yes.

Nicola: Blimey, that means it might happen to me soon. And I'm single. I can't be single and menopausal! That is like being welded to the shelf. I am never going to get off the shelf!

Me: I'd like to point out this thread is about me and not you, Nicola.

Nicola: It's actually supposed to be about Mum's knee.

Me: Like I said, I'm not setting up a thread called AM I PREGNANT?

Lizzy: Why don't you just take a test?

Me: Because I feel ridiculous buying a test. Like I'm some pathetic teenager.

Nicola: I have one. I think I bought it when a condom burst with Laurence.

Lizzy: Too much information.

Me: Way too much information.

Nicola: I'm on my way out. I'll drop it in.

Me: I'm not home. I'm starting Christmas shopping.

Lizzy: If you dare tell me you have nearly finished I will have to kill you. BTW, what are we getting Mum and Dad this year?

Nicola: No clue.

Lizzy: Shall I set up a FAMILY CHRISTMAS PRESENTS thread.

Me: Oh, that would be great (sarcasm emoji if there was one!).

Nicola: I gotta go. I'll post the test through your letterbox, Cathy. Bye x

Me: *Don't do that. Barbra Streisand will eat it – or piss on it, so we'll only know if Barbra is pregnant and not me.*

No response for five minutes.

Lizzy: *I think she's gone.*

Me: *I'd better go before anyone in the household finds a pregnancy test on our doormat.*

So I abandoned the Christmas shopping to go and rescue the pregnancy test before some weird fate befell it. When I say abandoned, of course it was a blessed excuse as I cannot stand Christmas shopping. It makes me want to cry in confusion. How can the act of giving be so . . . awful. Anyway, something weird had happened. The test had disappeared. Nicola swore blind she'd posted it. I'd looked in all the likely places that Barbra might have carted it off to in my absence. Her bed, under our bed, buried in the garden, but to no avail. Absolutely no sign of it. Which was puzzling as that meant that somebody had it and was not saying anything which led me to a multitude of different conclusions that I could not even begin to contemplate. And I couldn't ask who had it as I would then have to explain why we had a pregnancy test posted through the letterbox in the first place.

So I started by asking some subtle questions to see if I could get to the bottom of this mystery.

To Kirsty my question was: 'So are you seeing anyone at the moment?'

'No.'

'Not even casually?'

'No.'

'Have you been seeing anyone since the summer.'

'*No*, Mum!'

She was in the clear. She had never been a great liar, ever since I called her bluff over 'borrowing' her best mate's tooth when she was eight to try and claim extra cash from the tooth fairy!

Next Freddie. I flung open the door to his room.

'So how's it going with you and Kim?' I asked.

'Great – really good.'

'Are you having sex?'

Freddie looked at me aghast. A rare occurrence from him. He was kind of hard to shock.

Then he went red and looked away.

'No,' he mumbled. 'We're taking it slowly.'

'Excellent news,' I announced and walked out of his room.

So that left Mike. Why the hell was he hiding a pregnancy testing kit? Before I began the descent downstairs to find him, he emerged from our bedroom and dragged me in, shutting the door behind him.

'The kids are in, you know,' I told him.

'I found this,' he hissed, pushing a white box at me. 'It's a pregnancy test,' he whispered in my ear.

'I know, I've seen one before.'

'It was on the doormat when I came home. Kirsty must have dropped it. What are we going to do?'

He was pale. Very pale.

I tried to calm him down.

'Nicola posted it through the letterbox earlier,' I said.

'Does she think Kirsty is pregnant?'

'No. This has nothing to do with Kirsty. She left it for me. I think I'm pregnant.'

341

He went even paler.

'You . . . you can't be. You went on the pill.'

'Yes, I know, but it's not a 100 per cent effective, is it, and we've been having sex—'

'Because you are on the pill.'

'No – if you remember the pill was about stopping my periods, not about having sex, but in actual fact the pill has stopped my periods but I don't know if it is the pill or I'm pregnant or it might even be the menopause, Mike.'

He went even more pale.

'You might be menopausal? God help us all. I thought we had a few months, maybe even a year or so?'

He looked slightly delirious. I thought I might need to slap him. In fact, I had always wanted to do that. It looked so much fun.

'Look,' I said. 'My periods have stopped and I'm not 100 per cent sure why and I can't rule out pregnancy so I think perhaps I should just take a test to put us out of our misery.'

'Okay, okay,' he said, shaking slightly. 'Let's do it then. We'll get through this,' he said, grabbing my hand. 'Together. Whatever the outcome. I'll get another job or something, I don't know, but we'll work it out.' He was still very, very pale.

I weed on a stick like I had done for the first time over seventeen years ago. And yes, I did feel ridiculous. Immature. Stupid.

We sat on the side of the bed, really close, waiting for the lines to appear, Mike rocking slightly like some madman.

And of course I wasn't pregnant. Of course I wasn't. I was 48! I was on the pill. We weren't having sex *that* much. We would have been extremely unlucky if we'd

342

happened to have sex at the same time as the pill not working and me ovulating. I mean what were the chances? I felt ridiculous, immature, stupid all over again.

Mike didn't speak for about five minutes. Clearly in shock at the rollercoaster of events this evening. He'd expected to come home to a stir-fry and his turn to clear away. Not the threat of further fatherhood.

When he finally did come out of his reverie, he said this.

'I feel a bit disappointed. I was thinking that maybe another one, now the other two are close to leaving home, would be nice.'

I slapped him.

It felt really good.

8 November

An ambulance turned up next door earlier, and I knew that had to be bad. Tania texted me later on to let me know that Hazel had gone into a hospice and they were all there by her bedside and could I go and feed the cat? I of course asked if there was anything else I could do and Tania just replied, 'No – nothing.'

I crept into their house, feeling like an intruder. A house that had been preparing to say goodbye. There were cards and flowers and chaos. Tidiness is irrelevant in a house about to say goodbye. Dirty pots littered the table and the sink as though they had just upped and left in a panic. I thought I'd at least clear the pots away and load the dishwasher. That had to be okay. Didn't it? I moved slowly and silently between the dining room and the kitchen, not daring to make a noise. Hushed tones were required now. I fed the cat and let it out, breathing in the fresh air outside. Somehow the air inside was stifling. Thick with anticipation of sorrow.

I caught sight of the hundreds of Post-it notes on the dining-room wall as I prepared to lock up. One stuck out, with wobbly handwriting, unlike the lucid flow of the others. It had to have been written recently by Hazel. Probably taking a supreme amount of effort. It was a simple message.

YOU = LOVE

10 November

No news from Tania yet. Mike and I were discussing whether we should call her to see if she needed anything, when Freddie appeared in the kitchen in his Zac Efron/ *High School Musical* fancy-dress outfit.

'Can I have a chat?' he asked.

Mike and I glanced at each other and sighed. I wasn't sure what this meant. He looked deadly serious. We'd informed him of his dad's new career plan and he was still seeing Kim, so his university application was still on course. Although, come to think of it, I wasn't sure if he'd actually physically applied yet.

He stood while Mike and I sat at the table.

'I just wanted to tell you what brilliant parents you have been,' he announced. I looked at Mike again. This was troubling. Compliments! This had to be followed by bad news.

'Mum,' he said turning to me. 'You've kicked my ass so many times I just wanted you to know that it has been worth it and I am striving to be the human being you wish me to be.' I swallowed. A tear was threatening the corner of my eye.

'And Dad,' he said. 'You are such an inspiration to me. You go out to work every single week just like you are supposed to, and do a job I don't understand but I know you do it well because we have cool holidays and can afford coffee at Starbucks and stuff.'

'Thank you, son,' said Mike gruffly. 'I'll take that as a compliment.'

'And I want you to know that I really appreciate you giving up your dream of becoming a poorly paid, under-valued teacher so that I could have a parent-free university education. I really, really appreciate that. And I realize that you have made a big sacrifice by agreeing to do this new job thing for your company where I understand you are in charge of recruiting new graduates and that you will be reading hundreds of applications and deciphering from what they write down exactly who is worthy to work for that fine company that you work for. Am I right?'

Mike nodded. 'That will be some of what I do, yes.'

'Well, bearing that in mind, will you help me with my university application? They want a personal statement and I'm screwed if I know what to write. I've tried three times and each time I sound like such a knob. So will you do it? Please, Dad? You're so much better at that sort of stuff than me and you really want me to get into university, don't you?'

Mike looked at his son and grimaced. I held my breath. Would he choose to be cruel to be kind or had Freddie succeeded in flattering him into submission?

Mike got up out of his chair.

'Tell you what,' he said. 'You show me what you've done so far and perhaps I can give you some pointers. Come on, let's do it now.'

'Thanks, Dad,' said Freddie with a grin. Then he winked at me behind his dad's back. Don't push it, I thought.

25 November

I'd been thinking a lot about my mission this month which was to fall in love with Mike again. Not that I had fallen out of love, just I wanted to do something to rekindle that early doors feeling. When they can do no wrong and everything about them is utterly fantastic. I wanted a reset that would set us up for many further years of happiness into old age. But I couldn't think of what to do. A date night seemed too unspectacular and I didn't trust us not to fall into talking about the kids or the fact there was a hole in the roof or about what Christmas presents we were going to buy for his family. I didn't think that was out of the ordinary enough to put the electrodes on the heart of our romance. It had to be something more special than that. I mused about going back to our old haunts; maybe we should have a little trip down memory lane. But shockingly many of them had been knocked down or were now frequented by spotty youths with fake IDs.

I even considered trying something new. Skydiving, perhaps. Something a little dangerous that would remind us that we are still young at heart and up for it.

But I was too scared. I wasn't young and up for it and so that wasn't going to work.

In the end I didn't need to think of anything. It just happened.

An occasion that never failed to jerk us all back into falling in love.

An occasion guaranteed to make us hug more closely and hold hands harder and feel more deeply.

A funeral.

Hazel died two weeks ago.

Watching Tania's grief has been both terrifying and awe-inspiring.

She is the strongest person I know and I witnessed her crippled by pain and then, out of nowhere, summoning an inner strength to be able to hold her daughters together and navigate their path through the shock and the absolute devastation.

She orchestrated the funeral to a level of passion and perfection worthy of a West End production. Thankfully I had been called upon to run errands, to find obscure items to pay tribute to Hazel, such as pussy-willow branches and pink tulips, which had served the purpose of making me feel better by helping and giving me and Tania something to talk about to deflect from the horror.

Then yesterday we baked. Tania's family came over from Jamaica and we baked, in her kitchen and mine, the food that would be served to the mourners after the service. Robbie very kindly offered to help, along with Kirsty and Freddie and, in the absence of any words that would bring comfort at this horrendous time, Tania's relatives taught us Jamaican songs as we all mixed and stirred and beat and whipped. We sang and we hummed and there may have even been some jiggling of hips, all of us seeking respite from the overhanging sorrow.

And then all too soon the moment arrived. I sat between Mike and Kirsty, clutching their hands for dear life as Tania entered the crematorium following her dead wife's coffin.

I fixed my eyes on the stained-glass window at the back of the church when Tania got up to say what she wanted to say about her dear departed wife. I listened to her words and let myself fall back in love with my husband.

Hazel joked before she died that she wanted a proper gay funeral, began Tania. *And by that she meant she wanted John Hannah reading 'Stop All the Clocks' just like he did in* Four Weddings and a Funeral. *John Hannah, mind, not me. She was very clear about that. She said John Hannah in that one speech had done a better job of encapsulating love than any other heterosexual who ever lived.*

I will not recite the W. H. Auden poem to you because I'm not John Hannah and Hazel would have been disappointed. So I will have to try and tell you about my love for Hazel in my own way, which I hope will do her justice.

It was like she wasn't human. She was a presence, an angel; whenever she was near me she made me glow. She was wise, she was funny, she was quiet, she was peaceful, she was content – she was so many things that I am not.

I walked into the junior common room and she had commandeered the tape deck and was swaying to Kate Bush whilst wearing one of those long hippy skirts with bits of mirror sewn into it. Her confidence irritated me and so I walked up to her and told her that I much preferred Madonna. I could tell she wasn't impressed by my musical choices but none the less she offered to buy me a drink and the opportunity to try and convince me of the virtues of her beloved Kate Bush. The argument as to whether 'Into The Groove' is by

*far the better song to 'Babooshka' began that
night and continued until the week before she
died, when I finally conceded so she could tick it
off her bucket list of things to correct me on
before she was gone.*

*She also wanted me to concede that it was me
who made the first move.*

It wasn't.

*The next day she put a mix tape of music in my
pigeon hole,*

I reckon that was the first move.

*I didn't see her for a whole week and then she
put another tape in my pigeon hole. Classical! I
thought she was trying to educate me and again her
confidence really irritated me.*

*I went round to her room and demanded an
apology.*

*She didn't apologise. She thought I was making
the first move.*

I left her room three days later.

We never looked back.

*She asked me to marry her on a trip to Jamaica
in 2010, before it was legal for us to get married.*

*We eventually married in 2014 in a glorious
explosion of Pacific food and music and dancing.
We've danced to the same tune ever since.*

*She saw the real me. She saw my defensiveness,
she saw my insecurity, she saw my wobbly bits
and, in the last ten years, a lot more wobbly bits.
She saw all of me. The imperfections and the good
parts too.*

*I'm here to tell you she wasn't perfect. She read
the iPad on the toilet, she put ketchup on curry*

– dear God, why she did that I have no idea! She couldn't straighten a duvet cover on a bed to save her life. Just couldn't do it, and she put chocolate in the fridge. I mean, what sane person does that?

But that is not how we remember the dead, is it? Because none of that matters. It's white noise when it comes to grief. To loss. The irritations melt away.

Now this is going to sound really weird, but bear with me. I was sort of grateful it ended this way because we got to love again.

With all our hearts.

Knowing our time was limited.

We got to love like it was the last thing we would do together on earth. We got to love like nothing else mattered. Especially not the ketchup on curry or the crooked duvet or the chocolate in the fridge.

We got to experience 100 per cent, full-throttle, knee-wobbling, heart-wrenching, tear-pouring utter love. We got to live in a way that we never have. Pure and utter devotion.

The last few weeks have been some of the happiest of my life.

We talked more, we laughed more, we cried more, we felt more, we were . . . more.

Most afternoons we held hands watching quiz shows. I have never felt more connected to someone in my entire life.

My regret now, of course, is that we didn't manage to live like that, 'in love', all the time. That 'in love' often got overtaken and gobbled up and faded away by ketchup on curries and

*crooked duvets and chocolate in fridges. That we
forgot to put all that aside and be 'in love' with
all the intensity of when we first fell for each
other and when we had the knowledge that it
would end.*

*To be mindful of this person who thought I
looked like Whitney Houston, who was the first
person I ever met who I didn't have to explain
myself to, or defend myself to. The first person I
ever met who made me feel like I belonged. Who
looked at me and said with her eyes and mouth
and words that I was just right. Right for her.
Perfect for her.*

*The day she picked me I won the lottery. I won
her heart. The heart of the kindest, warmest,
gentlest, most sincere person I have ever met.*

*We were in it together, and now I will carry on
with her as the wind beneath my wings, making
me fly on the memory of our love and devotion
and what being 'in love' with her felt like.*

Goodbye, Hazel – and thank you.

That night, after all the due respects had been made,
after solemn quiet words had been whispered, after many
long awkward moments had been endured and when all
who remained was Tania and her daughters along with
Tania's relatives and her closest friends, Tania begged
her relatives to sing again. And so they did, melancholy
tunes to begin with followed by soaring, wonderful,
joy-filled songs. Eventually Tania grabbed Keresi and
Mabel and got up to dance in some kind of glorious
tribute to Hazel's life. They smiled through the tears and
urged us all to join in.

So we all danced.

Me and Mike.

Me and the rest of the book group, who had come out in full support of Tania.

Me and Freddie.

Me and Kirsty.

Kirsty and Robbie.

He'd asked Tania if it was all right if he sat at the back of the funeral. He'd not been to a funeral since his mother's and he really couldn't remember any of it and he really wanted the chance to sit in a church and remember his mother.

Tania, being Tania, had welcomed him with open arms and told him she'd be honoured if he came to Hazel's funeral and remembered his mother.

Then he'd served food and kept everyone's glasses topped up until finally Kirsty persuaded him to dance and I watched as I saw the spark of something light up before my eyes. I swallowed. Here we go again, I thought. But this time I knew that Robbie was a good person. A man who knew how precious love was. He'd treat her well, and Kirsty had grown up so much this year that I knew she could handle herself. I was still going to worry, though. I was always going to worry.

Mike and I strolled home sometime after midnight and slumped down on the sofa.

Mike took my hand and held it. He lifted it to his lips and kissed it. Then held it in his lap until twenty seconds later he was fast asleep.

I couldn't remember the last time we had held hands on the sofa.

I had a feeling we would be doing it more often. No, I was going to make sure we did it more often.

I was really not sure any more why we were bothering to give books out at the book group. I mean, at the moment we were going through this ritual every month whereby not enough of us had read the book so it was not worth having a decent chat and then we would give another book out that we knew not many of us would read. But we made a pact this month that we would make the effort, because we all loved books and actually we acknowledged that we needed to read. We all needed some escape.

Tania didn't come. The funeral had only been last week, after all. It gave us all a chance to discuss it in a way we couldn't have done if Tania had been there.

We were all in agreement that it had been a very fitting funeral, albeit I have never in my life heard anyone criticize a funeral. We had all been very moved by the wake, too. The singing and the dancing at the end of the night had, we all thought, been unusual but somehow appropriate. It had allowed the joy of life to infiltrate the desperate sadness and reminded us all we have so much to live for. That we are lucky to be alive. Something we all knew that Hazel in her wisdom would have been desperate to leave as her legacy. In fact, I half wondered if Hazel had demanded that Tania sing and dance at her funeral, knowing how much it would help her. Perhaps there was a Post-it note up in their house, leaving such instructions.

'I can't remember the last time I danced like that,' admitted Sonja. 'Made me realise how much I missed it.'

'Perhaps dancing should be obligatory at funerals,' said Louise. 'It's so life-affirming. Why is it you get to a certain age and you stop dancing? I really miss it.'

We all agreed wholeheartedly.

Then we talked at length about Tania's bravery and her passionate speech about the love of her life. One or two more tears might have been shed.

Then Paula dropped the bombshell.

She announced, ever so quietly after just one glass of prosecco, that she had left her husband.

The gasps were audible. Mostly from Sonja, who wept and shouted at her really quite angrily that at no point had Paula confided in her what she had been planning.

'Is that what has come out of the counselling?' I asked. 'Did it make you realize that something was wrong?'

'It wasn't the counselling,' she admitted. 'Or, maybe that started me thinking, but it was the funeral. Listening to Tania talk about Hazel.'

And we all knew. She didn't have to say anymore. We all knew exactly what she meant. The indescribable way a funeral could set some things completely straight in your mind. When faced with your own mortality, it was amazing the decisions you could make.

'Do you feel better?' asked Louise eventually. 'I mean, do you feel better for leaving him?'

'Yes!' she gasped. 'I'm so sad that I couldn't make it work but we have both been unhappy for a long time. I feel relieved. The relief is enormous.'

Then the strangest thing happened. We all clapped and said well done.

Well done, Paula.

December

Dance with Hugh Jackman

1 December

'The chat' was still having dramatic results. My DSR levels were at an all-time low. The list drawn up by Mike and me the day after the consultancy party went up on the fridge, and by and large we had stuck to it. There were some minor issues at the beginning. Mainly in agreeing the standards to which the chores should be delivered. Mike's inability to wipe down a surface properly was really quite astounding. Took him a few practices to get it right but now he seemed to have got the hang of it. Of course there had to be some compromises as he was still away so much, but the improvement in my happiness was enormous. Quite frighteningly enormous. Who knew how much DSR I was holding on to?

Consequently we were still having more sex, especially since we got over the pregnancy scare. Mostly because I was not going to bed quietly seething about the washing-up. I was going to bed delighted with my husband for clearing the glasses and putting on the dishwasher without asking. A situation much more conducive to sex, I can tell you, and something men should seriously consider when they overlook the clearing up every single night.

Beer mixer tonight. The last one of the year! And partners were invited as it was Christmas! Yey!!

After some deliberation I invited Mike along, but of course I had to sit him down and give him some very strict guidelines.

'Tonight, Mike,' I said, 'you are my husband and not a consultant. Do you understand what that means?'

'That I should always stand a respectful twelve inches behind you and only speak when spoken to?' he asked.

'Pretty much,' I nodded. 'And if someone asks, say you work in recruitment and not management consultancy.'

'Why?'

'Because consultancy sounds, well, a bit obnoxious, and you might be tempted to offer them advice on their businesses which would be embarrassing to say the least.'

'But I have so much experience, I could offer some useful insight.'

'They're all young, Mike,' I told him. 'Young enough to think they know everything without really knowing anything, and you'll just come across as a dinosaur. And you'll mention some of the big companies you've worked with and they'll dismiss them as corporate monoliths that will ultimate bring about the end of the world and they will try and tell you that the future lies in small, local and sustainable, which it almost definitely does but you will feel the need to defend what your generation has done for the economy that the younger generation are totally taking for granted, and it will all end up in a big argument with someone and that will stop me from enjoying the Christmas beer mixer which I would really like to do. So please will you say you work in recruitment and please will you avoid telling them how to run their businesses? For my sake. I love working at The Mustard Factory. Don't ruin it.'

'I get it,' he said thoughtfully. 'I shall listen. Just listen. I will treat it as a research mission. Listen and learn, not, not—'

'Preach,' I said.

'Not preach,' he agreed. 'I will try not to preach.'

'Did you enjoy it?' I asked Mike after we left at the end of the evening. He'd behaved impeccably. Whenever I'd glanced over at him he'd been wearing his best interested face as he nodded earnestly at some whippersnapper.

'I actually did,' he said. 'I met some really interesting people with some really interesting ideas. It . . . it was surprising. Not what I was expecting. I learnt a lot. It made me really think about how we need to talk to the next generation of workers coming through. They see the world differently. I'm going to raise it at our next grad-uates' meeting. Get them to tell me what they are thinking. I really feel like I should know.'

I took his hand as we walked. For all my mickey-taking about the consultancy mentality, actually when he decided to listen, he listened. And he learned. And that was a very fine thing.

'Couldn't weigh up Toby, though,' continued Mike. 'He was the first guy to take you on, right?'

'That's right.'

'Bit awkward, I thought. Didn't really know what to say to me.'

Not surprising, I thought. 'I think that he's actually not great with grown-ups. He was a bit immature when I met him, to be honest, but he's getting there . . . He calls me his "work mum", and let's just say I've been trying hard to make him grow up.'

'Bit full of himself, was he?' asked Mike.

'Something like that,' I agreed.

My relationship with Toby had been slightly strained since I'd expressed my disapproval of his behaviour. But I was pleased to see that he'd brought Phoebe with him tonight and he had appeared attentive. Affectionate even. Perhaps some of what I had said had got through.

'Loved the collection by the way,' said Mike, nodding at my chest.

I was wearing the SUPPORT SEX WORKERS T-shirt. I'd sent an email round to the entire building at the end of November asking everyone to support my reduce carbs campaign by supporting sex workers. I'd ask if they would all refrain from sending Christmas cards this year and instead give the money they saved to a charity I have found that provides shelter to prostitutes trying to leave their profession. I thought I'd wear the T-shirt tonight and go round with my SUPPORT SEX WORKERS mug and make people cough up cash. It worked. I got nearly £300 and someone has suggested that I set up a team of employees at The Mustard Factory to look at reducing carbs for the entire building and possibly some other charity events.

I'm in. I belong. I belong at The Mustard Factory. How flipping cool am I?

20 December

Well, that went well. Like really well. Like off-the-scale well. Best book group of the year, I reckoned. Like, you know when you've planned something and you thought

360

it was so going to blow up in your face and everyone would think that you're such a weirdo but then you did it and it was all you'd dreamed of? That was how well it went. So many things could have gone wrong, but I went for it. It was an experience I wanted to have and fortunately it turned out that lots of other people really wanted that experience as well! There was a lesson there, wasn't there? Just do it. I really should think about writing slogans for a living next year.

So we started at 3 p.m. Prosecco laid on in spades. The book group had been somewhat surprised that I'd been very forceful in saying I would organize our Christmas gathering and very, very secretive. They'd peppered me with questions as to where we were going and when I announced a kick-off time of 3 p.m. on a Saturday afternoon, well, you would have thought I was asking them to travel to Venus.

'Three p.m.!' exclaimed Sonja. 'Oh, I get it now, are we going for afternoon tea?'

'No,' I said, 'nothing so staid. We shall meet in the Red Lion for prosecco at 3 p.m. Then we will take a ten-minute walk to a secret location, so wear flat shoes or trainers even, something you are comfortable in. Then we shall engage in a highly enjoyable activity from 4 p.m. until 7 p.m. when some mystery guests will arrive and we shall continue to party.'

'But we normally just have a takeaway,' moaned Fiona. 'Why can't we just have a takeaway? I really don't like not knowing what we are doing.'

'Trust me,' I said. 'You are going to love it.'

I had crossed my fingers behind my back.

*

I knew that the prosecco build-up was key. I'd said the 3 p.m. to 4 p.m. slot could also be used to discuss this month's book, knowing full well it wouldn't be. That come the flow of prosecco, gossip and chat would trump literary comment.

Today's hot topics included Fiona's 17-year-old son wanting to take his girlfriend away for the night to a hotel and Louise's mother-in-law saying she would not take a taxi home on Christmas Day and instead wanted someone in the house to drive her back at 5 p.m. We all tried very hard to keep it light for Paula and Tania's sake, of course. They had both been very brave and agreed to come, but insisted that both their circumstances were not to be discussed. That they wanted escape and lightness, even if it was just for a few hours.

At 3.50 p.m., having vigilantly topped up everyone's glasses the minute they were showing signs of being remotely half-full, and satisfied that everyone was comfortably merry, I clapped my hands and announced that we must now leave to start the next part of the secret Christmas party. There was a bit of huffing and puffing as glasses were drained and coats were shrugged on, but soon we were on our way through the fairy-lit streets to—

'The Methodist Hall!' exclaimed Louise. 'What are we doing here? Christ, I see enough of this place during the week bringing my two to dance classes, never mind being here at the weekend.'

'Have you hired a magician?' asked Paula, her eyes actually shining for once. 'I do love a magician.'

I looked at her, feeling a moment of doubt.

'Sort of,' I said. 'We are kind of going to perform a little magic here this afternoon.'

'A magician who teaches us how to do magic?' she asked. 'That would be great.'

'Not exactly,' I said, opening the door and guiding them in.

They all stood huddled at the back, their mouths open, as they took in the scene. The room was in darkness apart from a glitterball rotating gently and disco lights skipping across the floor and walls. In the centre stood a man dressed as a ringmaster, with his head bowed underneath a spotlight as the theme tune to *The Greatest Showman* boomed out of hidden speakers.

'You flew in Hugh Jackman!' breathed Fiona.

'No, sadly,' I replied. 'But the next best thing. This is Leo and he's going to teach us how to dance, *Greatest Showman* style.'

'You are kidding me!' exclaimed Sonja.

'Ladies, ladies, ladies. Roll up, roll up, roll up for the greatest show on earth,' announced Leo, striding towards us with a massive grin on his charming face.

Everyone's jaws gaped open.

He was perfect. Mind you, it had taken ages to find him. Literally hours online. I'd chanced upon the new trend in hen parties where you and your fellow hens get taught a dance routine from a famous show or film. *Grease* was very popular apparently, along with *Dirty Dancing* of course, and *Mamma Mia*. Then I'd spotted one company that offered to teach you a routine from *The Greatest Showman*. And I knew that I absolutely wanted to do that. Dance like that. Pretend I'm dancing with Hugh Jackman.

And I kind of knew the others would too. I mean they'd all said it at the last book club. They'd all said they wanted more dancing in their lives. I mean who wouldn't? Who wouldn't want to feel the joy of dancing a funky dance to 'This Is Me', with a bunch of like-minded mates?

I knew I couldn't tell them, however. I knew midlife anxiety would make us all bottle it. We were too old, would be the cry. We couldn't do it, they would say. It was ridiculous, they would tell me.

But they had all said they missed dancing. They all said dancing made them feel alive.

And I really wanted to learn this dance. I wanted to stamp my feet and twirl around and feel free and feel as one with my fellow dancers. I wanted to do it so badly I'd tricked my book group into joining me. It was good for them all. They would love it, I knew they would. Just had to get them started.

'So guys,' I said. 'Coats off and Leo has a load of shots lined up. How about we all have one and then we get started?'

Sonja. God, I love Sonja. Someone had to break. Someone had to endorse, so thank goodness for flipping Sonja.

'Wow,' she said. 'I have always wanted to dance like that. This . . . this is brilliant!' She took her coat off and threw it on a chair.

Then Tania took my breath away. She stepped forward and hugged me. Hugged me the hardest she ever had.

'Let's do this,' she whispered in my ear as I tried to fight back the tears.

Muttering, everyone else took off their coats and lined up in front of Leo to take a shot.

Game on.

*

Of course we were no Darcey Bussells, but the joy of concentrating, of focusing on the music, on the steps, of working together, of encouraging, of high-fiving – well, never had three hours flown past so quickly and so joyously!

We were all totally and utterly absorbed. So much so that I wondered why an alarm was going off on my phone at 6.50 p.m.

Then I remembered.

'So, one last run-through before our guests arrive,' I told them.

'What guests?' asked Paula.

'We have some mystery guests arriving and – er – we are going to perform our dance for them.'

'What? Are you *insane*?'

Leo put his hands in the air, silently asking for calm.

'You're ready,' he said. 'More than ready. And ladies, when you perform, really perform, you will feel an adrenaline rush like you've never felt before. Trust me. You don't want to *not* share this. You have *got* to share this. This is going to be *epic*.'

'But in front of who?' asked Fiona.

'I invited your families,' I said.

'You did what?' pretty much everyone said.

'Just a few of your nearest and dearest. Give them all a chance to see us having a really good time.'

'Give them all a chance to see us making total fools of ourselves, more like,' muttered Fiona.

'Bloody hell,' I said to them. 'Just listen to yourselves. Literally ten seconds ago you said you were having the best time, and now you're saying you're making total fools of yourselves. What's that all about?'

'Come on,' said Fiona. 'It's been a laugh and all that, but performing in front of other people – seriously? I'm a middle-aged mother of two teenagers. Nobody wants to see me act like one myself,' she declared.

'I do,' I said.

'But I'll get it wrong.'

'So what?'

'We'll all get it wrong.'

'So flipping what?'

'Come on – you can do it,' said Sonja, putting her arm round her.

Again – thank the lord for Sonja.

'I'm going,' Paula said suddenly, walking towards the back of the room to pick up her coat. 'I can't do this.'

'You can and you will,' I said, standing in her way. 'You want to. You know you want to. I saw your face earlier. You looked happy, Paula. Happy. Come on and do something that makes you happy. That's all this is.'

'It won't be the same if you don't do it too,' piped up Louise. 'Come on – in for a penny. Let's all do it and enjoy it,' she said.

'I can't,' said Paula, shaking her head.

'Do it with me?' asked Tania, holding her hand out to her. 'I want to dance with you, Paula. I think it will do us both good.'

The room went silent. Paula took Tania's hand.

'Right, that's settled then,' said Leo stepping forward. 'Time for one last rehearsal before everyone arrives. Places please, ladies. Places please.'

The music struck up, Leo raised his cane and off we went.

*

The adrenaline was unreal.

When I stood there under the spotlight in front of Mike, Freddie, Kirsty, Kim and Robbie, wow, I thought my heart was going to explode out of my chest. But we did it, we got through it. I bumped into Fiona twice and at one point Sonja was centre stage when she should have been stage left with the rest of us, but she improvised with a little tap dance until she could make her way back to us as her son and his girlfriend laughed and cheered. I'd managed to track him down and persuade him that he would make his mother's year if he turned up.

The best bit was at the end. The standing ovation. Mabel and Keresi leapt up and embraced their remaining mum, tears of joy perhaps mixed with the odd sad one flowing down their cheeks. Louise's 7-year-old daughter instantly demanded that Leo teach her the steps. I'd invited Paula's mum and dad, given that inviting her husband would have been inappropriate and, apart from looking slightly bewildered at the scene, I watched Paula's dad put his arms around his daughter and thought that perhaps that was a very good thing.

My family dashed over to me. Freddie got there first and announced I was a disgrace but he had never been more proud, and could we ask Leo to stay longer so he could learn some moves. Kirsty was beaming, holding hands with Robbie. 'You rock,' said Robbie, to which Kirsty agreed. He really was such a good influence on her. Kim looked bewildered but then that was typically how she looked at me.

Mike took me to one side. 'Impressive,' he said.

'I've wanted to dance like that since last Christmas,' I explained. 'I had to make it happen somehow.'

He nodded.

'And you did,' he said.

'So I did,' I replied. 'So I did.'

31 December

I've just reread my first entries in my diary from the beginning of the year. Quite the weirdest feeling when you look back and realize where you are now compared to where you were then. So many things didn't happen as I thought they would, but then again so many things did.

My periods stopped. Eventually and after considerable anxiety and a pregnancy scare!

I started the year being jealous of Tania's Christmas and ended the year in the middle of it as the Collins family tried desperately to help fill the gaping-sized hole left by Hazel. We had laughed and we had cried. Probably one of the best Christmases we have ever had, if I were honest, as death forced us to truly appreciate the mere fact of being together.

Mum's knee had got fixed – hurrah – and I was still talking to my sisters, which was a bonus. Albeit I wasn't best pleased when Nicola set up a WhatsApp thread titled – HAVE YOU WEED ON THE STICK YET?

I was working, with younger people, and it was great. I felt wise, I felt experienced and I got to go to beer mixers. That somehow made me especially happy.

Freddie had a nice girlfriend, which was not something I would have expected at all, and he'd applied to university. Albeit the same one as Kim. It would never last, but if she got him to university then aah, well. She was useful.

And Kirsty had survived her first love. Wow – big relief. One heck of a hurdle to get over, but thankfully it seemed

368

to have taught her to go for the good ones, and for that I was grateful to Carl. He had also been useful in a way this year. Her relationship with Robbie was slow and steady and gentle. More like a friendship flourishing. I didn't think that would last either, but for now they were doing each other good.

No sign of the menopause as yet. It was still lurking out there, ready to pounce, but I was ready. I felt ready. I felt robust. I felt as if I'd really faced up to it this year and when it came I was confident that I wouldn't have to suffer on my own.

The book group were doing well. I was still learning stuff. Taking it all in. We had an impromptu meeting round at Paula's on Christmas Eve so she wouldn't be on her own. We didn't discuss the book but we got very drunk and danced to 'This Is Me' again. She was going to be fine. Eventually.

And Mike and I had found each other's hands again. He is sitting next to me on the sofa, actually. Holding my hand as I write.

We hold hands all the time now.

I think it had really helped, both of us finding things away from each other that made us happy. The Mustard Factory for me and his new job for him. It took the pressure off, somehow. We had positive things to say to each other about our day rather than moans and groans. I felt interesting, which I hadn't done for a long time if I thought about it. I had stories to share with my husband that he hadn't heard. He looked interested in what I had to say.

And the absence of Domestic Situation Resentment as a result of 'the chat' – oh, my goodness, that was the single best thing ever to happen to my marriage. Seriously.

I realized we didn't need minibreaks, we just needed 'the chat'.

I thought I'd better call my sisters to wish them Happy New Year. Then I remembered Nicola was out and Tilly and Jude were staying over at Mum and Dad's, so I picked up the phone and called Lizzy.

'Happy New Year,' I shouted cheerily as soon as she picked up.

'It's only four in the afternoon here,' she said. 'I'm just overseeing the caterer's. We have guests arriving at eight p.m. for a pool party.'

'Me and Mike have just watched Jools Holland and Mike has been asleep for the last hour. I shared a kiss with Barbra Streisand at midnight.'

'Sounds lovely,' said Lizzy.

'I was ringing to thank you, actually. I've just been reading through my diary and well, I have to admit it made a real difference. I know I didn't exactly put in the type of motivational goals you would have done, but all I can say is that it did the trick. I *know* I'm happier than last year. I did stuff I never would have done, had you not sent it to me.'

'Wow, Cathy, that's just great. I'm so pleased.'

'So go on then,' I said, 'tell me how many marathons you have run this year and what other out-of-this-world things you have managed to achieve?'

There was an unexpected pause. 'I didn't actually get round to my marathon training, or in actual fact get round to running any marathons,' she admitted.

'What!' I exploded. 'But that was your motivational goal *last January*. You total, utter failure.'

'Somehow I never found the motivation,' she said, actually sounding a bit miserable about it.

370

For once I felt a bit sorry for her.

'Perhaps you couldn't find the motivation because you knew really it wasn't going to make you happy?' I said.

'Maybe you're right,' she replied. 'To be honest, the thing that made me the most happy last year was all of you coming over, and that wasn't even on my list of goals!'

'You see, I said that you had the wrong idea about all this,' I said. 'But I think you should give it another shot this year, and I know exactly what should be the very first thing you put on your list of motivational goals.'

'What's that?'

'Cleaning Mum and Dad's toilet.'

She went quiet for a minute.

Then she laughed.

Then she said, 'That would make me very happy indeed.'

ACKNOWLEDGEMENTS

I'd like to start by thanking all those people who make publishing books happen. Thank you to my agent Madeleine Milburn, for making me sound good in front of important people and looking after my interests. I also really appreciate the rest of her team who do a great job of feeding back on ideas, making sure I get paid, and talking to all sorts of people who might want do something with my novels.

Thanks to Kate Bradley who has made my first experience of publishing with HarperCollins a joy despite the fact it all happened in 2020! Thank you so much for your understanding and encouragement. I have loved our chats and I really look forward to actually meeting you one day! I would also like to thank the rest of the team at HarperCollins who package my words up and put them in the hands of other people. It's a complicated and difficult business, and I appreciate everything you do. And I mustn't forget those at the end of the chain including the booksellers, bloggers, and reviewers who do everything they can to promote. I can't thank you enough.

I am a wife, a mother, a sister, and a daughter – all roles in women's lives that feature heavily in *The Wife Who Got A Life*. I feel like I should make it very clear that none of the characters portrayed in this book are based on any of my relatives, or friends for that matter. I am lucky enough to be blessed with the most excellent people in those departments. So, I must thank my husband for being my biggest cheerleader and supporting me in whatever I do. We became colleagues in 2020 as he has largely worked from home, and I am very grateful that he has not once frowned at the bizarre life of an author that he has now witnessed. He has even happily accepted that watching *MasterChef* over lunch is essential research and part of my job! You are an absolute star, Bruce. My two children, Tom and Sally, have been at home more than usual during the writing of this book and have been very encouraging – and often pretty blunt – in their opinions on my ideas. I wonder where they get that from! Being your mum is my favourite thing in the whole world. You are both amazing. I could not be prouder to be sister to Andrew and Helen. Both key workers, they are thoroughly good people and do loads of good. You are the best. I must also thank my mum and dad, the greatest parents anyone could wish for. You have set an amazing example in so many ways. My mum is not just a wife, she's a farmer's wife, which is a whole different ball game. They have worked together their entire married life and my mum's support of my dad and the farm is truly awe-inspiring. What a wife!

And finally, friends and book group members. The other positions in life that feature heavily in this book. Thank you to all my friends who let me rant on about this and that and are happy to rant back at me about this and that as we try to work out how to navigate through this thing called life. I don't know what I would do without you. As for the 'Secret Book Group' (so called for reasons that I couldn't possibly divulge) you are all lovely, funny, and wise. I love that we enjoy reading books, then getting together and talking about them as well as all sorts of other things. It's great. Thank you to all of you. You know who you are!

Read on to find out more about the funny and fabulous Tracy Bloom

Is there anything you wish you'd known before you embarked on a writing career?

That it's terrible for your waistline, all that sitting around nervously eating biscuits. It should be compulsory for writers to join a gym. Also, that people you know often assume they are a character in one of your books, so you spend your life worrying that they think the fiction you have written reflects your real opinions of them. I wonder if people who write crime novels have the same problem!!!

You are known for being very funny, how hard do you have to work at that?

I've never been asked that before! In general, I try and see the lighter side of life so there is an element of instinct in there – I never intentionally try and write jokes. It seems to come easiest when I get the character right. If I manage to create someone who sees life in a certain way that is funny and entertaining, then somehow the humour just flows. It's magical when it happens.

Tell us about your heroines, why do you think they resonate with readers so much?

I hope that it is because they are honest. My heroines are not trying to be something that they are not. They are just women, winging it like we all are, but being quite open about it.

How do you balance writing and family life?

To be honest, writing is a dream job when you have a family because you work from home and your hours are flexible. I grew up on a farm and my parents were always around, so I love that I can be around for my children too. I cannot imagine how hard it must be for parents who go out to work full time and have to juggle so many things. I am so grateful to be in the position I am.

What's the best thing and worst thing about being a novelist?

That's easy. The absolute best thing is the feedback from readers. It makes it so worthwhile when someone tells me they really enjoy my writing. I absolutely love it if a reader says I made them laugh out loud – I find that amazing. The worst thing about it is that it's so solitary. I miss being around people. But I have met so many amazing people through my writing that it does kind of make up for it.

Any tips for stretched women trying to juggle it all?

Go easy on yourself. Never be afraid to have a good cry, it always seems to help in some small way. Talk about it. Speak up. Ask for help. You cannot do everything. You might be amazed at how much other people want to – and can – help you.

What are you writing next?

It's very much a work in progress at the time of writing! Broadly, it is about a multi-generational group of women (mother, daughter, grandmother, auntie, niece, best friend) who all go on a hen weekend and have quite an adventure!